THE
LIGHT
PIRATE

ALSO BY LILY BROOKS-DALTON

Good Morning, Midnight

Motorcycles I've Loved

THE
LIGHT
PIRATE

LILY BROOKS-DALTON

GRAND CENTRAL
PUBLISHING

NEW YORK   BOSTON

Copyright © 2022 by Lily Brooks-Dalton

Cover design by Sara Wood. Cover photo of woman and landscape by Milan Balog. Cover photo of water texture by Getty Images. Cover copyright © 2022 by Hachette Book Group, Inc.

Grand Central Publishing
Hachette Book Group
1290 Avenue of the Americas, New York, NY 10104
grandcentralpublishing.com
twitter.com/grandcentralpub

First edition: December 2022

Grand Central Publishing is a division of Hachette Book Group, Inc. The Grand Central Publishing name and logo is a trademark of Hachette Book Group, Inc.

The publisher is not responsible for websites (or their content) that are not owned by the publisher.

The Hachette Speakers Bureau provides a wide range of authors for speaking events. To find out more, go to www.hachettespeakersbureau.com or call (866) 376-6591.

Library of Congress Cataloging-in-Publication Data

Names: Brooks-Dalton, Lily, 1987- author.
Title: The light pirate / Lily Brooks-Dalton.
Description: First edition. | New York : Grand Central Publishing, 2022.
Identifiers: LCCN 2022004498 | ISBN 9781538708279 (hardcover) | ISBN 9781538708293 (ebook)
Subjects: LCGFT: Novels.
Classification: LCC PS3602.R64557 L54 2022 | DDC 813/.6—dc23
LC record available at https://lccn.loc.gov/2022004498

ISBNs: 9781538708279 (hardcover), 9781538708293 (ebook)

Printed in Canada

MRQ-T

10 9 8 7 6 5 4 3 2 1

for Ofurhe

CONTENTS

THE
LIGHT
PIRATE

POWER

Somewhere west of Africa, so far from land the sky is empty in all directions, a storm begins. The water is warm, the waves are high. The air is heavy with moisture. A breath of wind catches, then circles back, churning itself into something new: a closed circuit gathering power, tighter and tighter. In this way, the storm grows. It matures. Learns to hold a shape. The warm water feeds it, fattens it, then urges it westward. Electronic eyes watch as it skims across the Atlantic. Soon enough, it earns a name. Reports are written about its speed and size. Preparations are made. There are other storms in this ocean, other pockets of hot, moist wind and rain-heavy cloud. But this one—this one will outgrow them all.

FRIDA WATCHES KIRBY from the kitchen window while she washes Yukon Golds beneath a thin trickle of water. Scrubbing at the dim yellow skins, she decides not to peel them. Maybe the boys won't notice if she mashes them thoroughly enough—and if they do, she will cite nutritional value. Outside, beneath a bloated purple sky knifed with the sharp fronds of a coconut palm, Kirby stacks sandbags against the door to the tool shed. Even with the AC blasting, Frida can smell the rich stink of thunder in the air, something like ozone and gasoline and dirt all mixed together. The hurricane is close now. She can taste it.

The baby kicks so hard she holds on to the counter until it stops. It feels as if this tiny, unborn thing could topple her. She asked—no, begged—Kirby to take them north, beyond the cone of uncertainty, but this is the third hurricane of the season and the third time she's wanted to evacuate. The first one fizzled into a tropical storm before it even reached land. Heavy rain and a stiff wind and that was all. The second crawled up the opposite coast, wreaking havoc in Sarasota and Tampa, then swung back out into the Gulf. Before each one, he listened quietly to her pleas, calming her fears without succumbing to them, but then this morning something in her husband shifted. "Get yourself together," he snapped. "We're not leaving." She was stung, shocked by the hardness in his voice. A new sound. Or new to her. It was just over a year ago that they met. Only six months since they married. There's so much to learn about one another.

Even if he were not bound to these storms by his work as a lineman, he would still be bound by something else. She has always understood this about him. He would still insist that this house is the safest place for them. This house—fortified by his labor, shielded from ocean winds by the wild tangle of live oak and cypress that looms just beyond the yard, but mostly guarded by the strength of his will. And isn't this at least partly why she fell in love with him? This faith in the strength of his own preparations. This promise of protection. A stolid, immovable weight—the anchor secreted inside his rib cage, holding him to the earth, to Frida, to Florida. If he believes they are safe, then maybe she can, too.

Resting a hand on her huge belly, she drops the last potato into the colander and twists off the faucet. The panic that has been with her all morning sharpens. It wasn't always like this. She used to be brave. Didn't she? The woman she was feels impossibly far away now, like a dream she can't quite remember. A thump outside startles her, but it's only Kirby laying down another sandbag. This is who she is now. The anxiety has become part of her. There's something about the way the baby has been stirring today that is almost urgent enough to make her get in the truck and go north by herself. There are his keys on the table. She could just leave everything where it is: chicken already in the oven, greens on the cutting board, potatoes in the colander. Would she take her stepsons? They wouldn't come even if she wanted them to.

All morning, the roiling clouds have been wrapping tighter and tighter around the sky and now all the blue has been squeezed out of it. Out the window, she watches Kirby admire his pile of sandbags in front of the tool shed and move on to the house, so sure his preparations are impenetrable. So sure of victory against his old adversary. The big coconut palm hanging over the yard sways. Its roots are sunk deep beneath the wilderness lurking at the edge of the property, but its trunk swings out over the lawn as if the wild is reaching for the house with those big fingerlike fronds. As if it's trying to caress the family that lives here, or to crush them all. Or both. Frida knows all about beauty and violence arriving together. She's seen it up close; she knows what nature can do.

Kirby lifts a conciliatory hand when he sees her there in the window, and Frida, still holding her belly, trying to shrug away this sense of dread, turns away without acknowledging him—not because she is angry but because she is frightened. When they fought earlier, he took her frantic appeals to evacuate as an insult. "Why can't you just trust me?" he asked, bewildered. She didn't know how to tell him that this was the wrong question without knowing what the right one was. They still haven't made up.

Kirby's boys come tearing into the kitchen just then, all arms and legs and sounds too big for those little bodies. They are immune to the fear that curls up on Frida's shoulders, nestling softly against her neck, pressing up against her windpipe—a gentle, invisible stranglehold. They feel only excitement in the simmering electricity of the atmosphere, the barometric pressure plummeting as each hour passes. She can almost see the current running through them: Lucas skidding across the tile floor in his dirty white socks, Flip leaping after him, midair, falling, fallen, and upright again, all in the space of a breath.

"Boys," she chides, doing her best impression of a mother. She has so little to guide her in these matters—when she was growing up, her own mother's defining characteristic was her lack of mother-ness. Everyone said so. It isn't that Frida regrets the way Joy raised her. How could she? Her childhood was singular, spent sailing between islands, with salt in every crevice and a vision of the sun permanently etched into the backs of her eyelids. She grew up everywhere and nowhere. The Keys, Puerto Rico, the Bahamas, Haiti, Panama, Venezuela. The only constants during Frida's formative years were her mother and their decrepit sailboat and the ocean itself. There was no school outside of Joy's instruction, and the friends she did manage to make could last only until Joy announced a departure date. When they pulled anchor, Joy always said it was time to find a new pair of sea legs. *What's wrong with the old ones?* Frida would think. But she never complained. Of course she used to be brave. She had to be.

"Boys!" Frida says again, louder this time, but it still feels like a performance, something she's only seen on television. They can tell, and so can she. If Joy were here, she would do all of this differently. She would be running through the house alongside them, playing their games, learning their secrets. She would be so unrelenting in her mission to win them over that finally these boys would have no choice but to love her. Except Joy isn't here. This is the ache Frida is learning to live with.

She hears Flip and Lucas hurtling through the living room, the brisk creak of the screen door opening, and then a slap as it swings back against its frame. Out of sight, Kirby roars and the boys shriek, even Lucas, who recently decided that twelve was too old for games like this. All three of them round the edge of the house, back into view—the boys darting past the window, Kirby lumbering behind them with arms overhead, fingers wiggling. Frida instructs her nerves to settle and shoos away this circling, spinning unease. *See,* she tells herself, *it isn't real. No one else feels it. Everything is fine.* She holds this assurance. Examines it. Does she feel better? Maybe. But then the baby, turning again and again, thrusting its limbs up against the constraints of her womb, up into her intestines, dislodges the seed of calm. Everything is not fine. Frida props her stomach up against the edge of the counter, and the Formica presses against her, against them both. She lets the edge dig into her, trying to quiet this spark inside her, but there is no suppressing it. Maybe this feeling is just a symptom of the murky greenish-yellow glow outside, or the way the baby is churning inside her today, or these unbidden memories of her dead mother, or the fact that this season, more catastrophic storms have made landfall than any other...a record that will undoubtedly be broken next year, and then again the next. But most likely, she thinks, it is the cumulation of these things packed together in the dense, hot air. It is the multitude, the crush of it all, the claustrophobic humidity of the atmosphere flooding her body, swarming along the surface of her skin. Surely that's it. It's overwhelm. Hypervigilance. Anxiety masquerading as intuition. But isn't there at least a chance it's the opposite? A pulsing intuition that she is trying her best to disown. A voice telling her that staying here will cost a great deal.

Kirby stops chasing his boys and returns to the wheelbarrow. He starts slapping the bags down in front of the kitchen door, the sound almost indecent, half-moons of sweat under his arms, a slick of moisture forming at his hairline, where just a few threads of silver are creeping into the brown. His every gesture claims competency, an all-encompassing aura of stewardship—over the sandbags and the doorstep they will shelter, over the ground he's standing on, over the boys that flit back and forth in the yard behind him, over this house, this day, this moment. Wherever he goes, he is rooted. It's what drew Frida to him when she saw him that first time, among the wreckage of San Juan. Even there, he exuded belonging.

She had planned only to visit Joy for ten days or so. It was the tail end of the summer before her last year of Rice's architecture program, meant to be a quick vacation to her floating childhood home. The boat was docked in their favorite marina off the coast of Puerto Rico—just for the season. With Joy, it was always just for the season. Even after Frida left at seventeen, Joy went on sailing between her favorite islands alone, never more than a handful of months in one place. She could have chosen the Caymans just as easily. Or maybe that bay off of Taboga, the one they anchored in after Joy showed Frida the Bridge of the Americas for the first time and Frida decided that one day she wanted to build such marvels. But Joy didn't choose either of those places. She picked San Juan.

Frida was excited to take a brief reprieve from the metallic crush of her life in Houston—two jobs, an unpaid internship, and soon a full course load, all clamoring for a finite amount of energy. She ached for the unrelenting enthusiasm of her mother, the old comfort of falling asleep wrapped in waves, the way a shimmer of salt clung to everything. It was meant to be a balm after the endless hustle of Houston, where she could never seem to break even and always felt like an outsider. Then, just after she landed at Isla Verde, they named the hurricane—out there in the Atlantic, whirling all alone. Poppy, they called it. No one who had endured Hurricane Maria took its approach lightly. Everyone was as ready as they could be; it didn't matter.

What happened next is both vivid and incomplete. A therapist she saw a few times suggested that the missing pieces would return as the shock wore off, but Frida doesn't want them. She remembers plenty: wading through floodwater and debris, trying to convince overrun funeral parlors to cremate Joy's remains; the crowds in front of the airport, everyone waiting for the chance at a seat on a nonexistent flight to the mainland; sitting with a roomful of strangers in the FEMA shelter. And then there was Kirby, entering her field of vision like a beacon, like the first glimpse of land after so many days at sea. He was a man who knew what to do next when no one else did. She watched him and his crew survey the destruction and begin their work. Clearing debris, restringing electrical wires, planting new poles in the ground. Just one task at a time. The truth is, Kirby's happiest when he's fixing things. Sometimes she worries that this is the reason he married her.

Frida sets the potatoes on the stove to boil, the little diamond chips on her finger catching the witchy chartreuse light that is brewing beneath the bruised clouds—an unseen sunset illuminating the yard. Poppy was only a year ago, but time gulped Frida down whole. It feels as though she's lived decades since then, and now somehow, she is here, looking at a life she barely recognizes. She's loosely cognizant of the choices she made along the way: keeping the baby, saying yes when he offered this ring, breaking her lease and dropping out of grad school, moving to this little town on the east coast of Florida. But at the same time, she cannot shake the feeling that she's been washed ashore on a strange beach. Did she really choose or did she just succumb? Is it a decision to hold on to a life raft, or is it something else? Tears form in the corners of her eyes. It's the hormones, she chides herself. All of this is just hormones. She loves Kirby, she loves her unmet daughter, and in this house they will build the kind of family she has always coveted. There is even space for these two little boys who don't belong to her. She doesn't need sea legs anymore; this ground is firm. It can hold her. It can hold all of them. She checks the oven, where the chicken fat is spitting in the bottom of the pan but the bird is not yet done.

The boys wash their hands the third time she tells them to, and even though she can see them barely obeying—no scrubbing, no soap even—she says nothing, considering the battle won. She lays a stack of plates and a handful of silverware down on the table, and Flip, the youngest, begins to set them out without being asked. She tries not to let her surprise show at this small gesture. He's always been her favorite of the two, and she likes to think that he is beginning to come around to her presence here. Out of the corner of her eye, she watches him line up the plates so that the pattern at each setting is straight, his little brow wrinkling in concentration, measuring the width between the edge of the table and the dishes with his fingers so they're all evenly placed—something she learned to do working in fine dining back in Houston. She has not taught him this, and Kirby certainly hasn't. It must have been their mother, an exacting woman she finds fearsome and fascinating and has met only once. The divorce wasn't clean. She can feel the fissures it left behind even when she doesn't always understand them.

Her first summer with these boys that aren't hers was unexpectedly hard. She had no idea what she was walking into until her lease in Houston had already been broken and the ring was on her finger and the baby was the size of a grapefruit. Kirby worked long hours, and when he was gone, the boys behaved badly. Lucas in particular, with Flip always a step or two behind. No one was thrilled about how things went—not Frida; not Kirby; not their mother, Chloe; and certainly not the boys themselves—but summers and occasional weekends and every other holiday with Kirby were what the hard-won custody arrangement decreed. Frida's preferences had no place on the calendar. So she did her best. She is still just doing her best.

Behind her, Lucas opens the fridge and begins to root through the crisper. She watches him dump a thin plastic bag of apples out into the drawer and then move on to the shelf above it, the bag floating softly down to the tile floor like a silver jellyfish.

"We're about to eat dinner, buddy," she says. "Nothing for you in there."

"What is it, though? For dinner?" he asks, and she knows that this exchange is futile, that he has already decided not to like whatever she has made. A sense of defeat blooms inside her. The roast chicken is evident, steaming in its pan, stuffed with lemons and parsley, rubbed with butter. It looks good, mouthwatering even, but that doesn't matter to him.

"Chicken and mashed potatoes and greens."

"I don't want that."

"I thought it was your favorite."

"Not the way you make it." She tries so hard not to hate this kid, but he makes it difficult. Lucas lifts the lid on the potatoes and groans. "You didn't even peel them? Isn't there anything else?"

"The skins are nutritious."

From under his breath, "Yeah, right."

"Go tell your dad it's almost ready, please."

He opens the kitchen door and the sandbags come up to his waist. Scrambling over them, he goes in search of Kirby, who has moved on with his wheelbarrow. Frida drains the potatoes and begins to stamp the masher down into their soft yellow-white flesh. She is ferocious in this act of mashing, channeling all of her aggression and dread and determination into a dinner that she already knows will not be enjoyed. Again, she eyes the keys to Kirby's truck on the table, and again, she imagines leaving this kitchen without a word—potatoes half-mashed, table set, the smell of garlic still on her hands—and driving away. It would be so easy. At the same time, it is impossible.

WHEN LUCAS COMES around the corner to tell Kirby that dinner is ready and it looks disgusting, he's busy pulling out window coverings from beneath the porch. The plywood is labeled by room—NW KITCHEN, S HALL, SE BED—and crusted with a sheen of gray mildew. A hot, wet, fertile smell drenches the air, so rich with anticipation that the ferns clustered under the porch are almost quivering. In its own way, the earth is also preparing for what draws near. But Kirby does not spend his time considering such intangibles; he's focused on what is useful.

"'Disgusting' is a mean word," Kirby murmurs, still arranging the wood.

"Well, it's true."

Kirby steps back to count the pieces. He knows he should say something more to Lucas, but he can't think of the right thing. All this animosity between him and his ex-wife, Chloe, has splattered onto his sons, and now onto Frida, too. He knows it's his fault, but not seeing how to correct it, he goes on hoping it will be resolved without his intervention. These tactile preparations, however, are the kind of thing he does best, so instead of turning his attention to a conversation about feelings with a little boy who doesn't want to have it, he looks to his checklist. The sandbags have all been stacked. The lawn furniture has been taken in. Only the windows are left now. He knows he's overdone it with the sandbags. They're piled higher than is useful, but he wants Frida to see that he has been listening to her. It is his visible testament to how very seriously he's taking all of this, both the hurricane and his pledge to keep her safe. He hoped she would notice this gesture and soften, but it's clear she's still upset. It irks him, especially after he's tried so hard to be patient with her, to be understanding and gentle about what she's been through. He shouldn't have snapped earlier, but it frustrates him that she isn't getting better. If anything, she's getting worse. The nightmares, the crying jags—it's as if hurricane season has snatched away all the progress she's made since Poppy. They've made. And now, the boys are back for the weekend, clamoring for his attention, not to mention a baby coming next month, a mortgage to pay, a new work crew to navigate…and first, these windows to cover. There's a charge in the air; he can feel it pulsing. Whether it's the hurricane coming closer or the chemistry of his many responsibilities colliding, he isn't sure. The source hardly matters to him. All he knows is that he's exhausted.

When he met Frida, the divorce was still new enough to sting and his determination to do better was at its peak. With Chloe and the boys, he hadn't paid enough attention. He didn't see it then, but he sees it now. The constant traveling, the overtime, those fleeting weekends after sixteen-hour days of storm duty when all he could do was sleep—it added up. At home, he became a visitor. It shouldn't have surprised him when Chloe filed the paperwork, but it did. She became an enemy when he wasn't even looking. Probably because he wasn't even looking.

With Frida, he was determined that it would be different. He let the erratic contract work go and found a steady municipal job. Swallowed the pay cut. Bought a little house a few hours south from his boys with what was left after the divorce. Frida was still grieving the loss of her mother when they came here, but beginning to emerge from the shock of living through Poppy. She was getting better, and so was he. They were tender with each other. No one had ever been curious about his inner life the way she was. She wanted to know where he'd come from and how he felt about it and what he yearned for. It made him feel known, and that was new. Chloe had tolerated him—up until she didn't—but Frida savored him. They painted the house a crisp white before the boxes were even unpacked, just the two of them out here in the yard with rollers and a ladder, sweating in the midday heat, feeling the proximity of all that death they'd left behind in the floodwater and at the same time, preparing for new life. Creating a way forward.

It was a different kind of partnership for Kirby. She convinced him that knocking down the wall separating the kitchen from the dining room would make the house better, then she wielded her own sledgehammer, pregnant and nauseous but determined to share the labor. And she was right. She started sketching out an addition they could build someday—another bedroom for when the boys came to visit, with a big screened-in porch where they could sit and watch the egrets hunt for grasshoppers. That's the Frida he married: making things better at every turn. Making *him* better. He thought it was mutual, but lately it feels like they are both falling apart.

"Dad," Lucas says, sensing that his father's attention has wandered. He's eager to help, to be on Kirby's team, but Kirby is still thinking about his other team. He wants to reconcile the woman he remembers scrabbling across this roof as easily as if it were the deck of her mother's boat with the doom-obsessed stranger sullenly washing potatoes in the kitchen. He wants to understand her, but he's too tired, too irritated, to wrap his head around the transformation of these last few months. "Dad!" Lucas insists. "Can I?"

"Have at it." He lets Lucas climb under the porch for the last few window coverings, just to give him something to do. Watching his oldest sort through the plywood, lining the pieces up against the siding, he notices that Lucas is organizing them so that they're grouped by room. "That's good," Kirby says, "putting them in the right order. Efficient." Lucas beams.

Kirby knows that Frida is having a hard time with the boys, Lucas especially. If it were a matter of acting out, a kick, a punch, a tantrum, that would be something he could handle. But these nuances Frida seems so upset about…it's not his forte. He can admit that he got so carried away by the clean slate of this little white house that he neglected making the boys feel like it belonged to them, too. His life with Chloe and the boys and then his life with Frida felt separate. He didn't think about how to integrate them. But what's done is done, so he goes on hoping that patience is all they need. They'll go back to their mother's in a few days and he'll redouble his efforts with Frida then. One problem at a time. For now, it's just a matter of getting through the weekend.

When Lucas has retrieved the last of the plywood, he wipes his hands on his T-shirt and little gray mildew smudges appear. "That's good for tonight," Kirby says. "We'll bang 'em up in the morning." He'd like to put them up now, but letting Frida's dinner get cold will only make things worse. Heading in, he glimpses her standing there in the window, the curve of her hand resting on top of her belly as she frowns at him, framed by green curtains and her voluminous dark curls, as if she's been standing there for hours, perfecting her pose, waiting for him to come round the corner so he can see this icy vision of martyrdom.

"When's the storm getting here?" Lucas asks, clawing at his shirt. Always grabbing at some article of Kirby's clothing, these boys. Always asking for a little more of him.

"Tomorrow afternoon," Kirby says. "But probably won't be a direct hit. Forecast says it'll make land farther north."

"I saw the Robisons leaving this morning. Jimmy said they're 'vacuating. But we're not, are we?"

"Well," Kirby says, and fixes his eyes on his oldest. "That depends. Are you scared of a little wind?" Lucas shakes his head before the question is done being asked. "Are you scared of a little rain?" Another shake. "Then we're not evacuating." He says this last bit as Lucas clambers over the sandbags stacked in the open doorway. Kirby doesn't intend for Frida to hear him say all of this, but she does, and when he follows Lucas into the kitchen and catches the look on her face, puckered and tearful, he's instantly ashamed of himself. He only meant to make his son feel safe. But then his guilt swells too big and it changes into something bitter, something charred. He can feel it turn—the apology he knows he should offer, the *sorry* on the tip of his tongue, burns.

"Wash your hands, Lucas," Kirby says, his mouth full of ash.

"I already did."

"So do it again."

Lucas makes the sound of a child being forced to do hard labor and stumbles toward the sink, suddenly limp under the weight of this task. This time, he uses the soap.

DINNER IS EATEN quietly. The boys pick at their food. The chicken is dry. The mashed potatoes are lumpy. The greens—the greens are bright and well-seasoned, but these boys don't like greens unless they're cooked in molasses, the way their mother makes them, and even then they are dubious.

"Eat," Kirby commands, confused by their ravenous eyes and heaping plates. What he doesn't fully understand is that these boys aren't hungry for food. They're hungry for him. His attention. His affection. Even before the divorce they were hungry, fed on scraps when he had the time and energy to play. Now they are starving. At their other house, Chloe tells them that Kirby abandoned them all. They don't believe this, not yet, but they're scared that it might be true. "Frida cooked you dinner and you will eat it," Kirby adds, but this only gives them another reason not to. Over the summer, Flip and Lucas tormented Frida because she has what they want. What their mother never had. It's the only way they know how to be loyal to Chloe without sacrificing Kirby's attention. This weekend, as always, they can't stop thinking about how soon these precious hours with their father will end. They are such different boys, but in this yearning for more time they are united.

"They don't have to," Frida says. She can see that the harder Kirby pushes them to like her, the harder they will resist.

19

"They do, actually," Kirby replies, his tone sharp. So the boys eat the food they don't want, because their father tells them to. Lucas tears into his drumstick. Flip shovels mashed potatoes into his mouth. Still they're hungry. Frida is just an interloper, another heart for Kirby to feed, a reason the boys have less than they used to. She tries to win them over with kindness and pity, but this tastes wrong to them. Her smell is too mossy, her voice is too low, the food she cooks for them is wrong. She is an acquired taste that they don't want to acquire. Instead, they eye her round belly and see how little they are about to matter. The love in this house is finite. Tense. Transactional. There isn't enough for them, and soon there will be even less. They feel a storm coming, too.

THE RAIN STARTS as Frida scoops the cold, congealing mashed potatoes into Tupperware. There is too much food left over—Lucas and Flip were being fussy and she wasn't thinking about how long they might have to go without power when she decided to buy a whole chicken. She wonders if she should just throw the mashed potatoes away, but at that moment it seems like more work than to save them, so she clicks the lid into place and stacks the container in the fridge with all the other Tupperwares, little cloudy boxes with their rainbow of contents. It might be beautiful if she didn't know what was inside them all—fried plantains gone soggy; pink beans and rice; roasted carrots; overcooked chicken. But she does, and so all she sees is a constellation of food that no one wanted the first time. The recipes she knows by heart they hate, and the recipes she learns for them seem to go wrong. She always enjoyed cooking, but Kirby is useless in the kitchen and somehow the task of feeding them all has fallen to her. She likes cooking less now. She misses the grind of Houston—at least there she knew what she was working toward, and the only person she had to take care of was herself.

The boys are in bed and Kirby putters out in his tool shed. The quiet thrum of rain against the roof usually makes her feel peaceful, but tonight it sounds like a threat, soft and persistent—ready to intensify at any moment. Kirby comes in with his hand-crank radio, stepping over the sandbags in the doorway and spattering water across the floor. Rain pools at his feet. Frida doesn't want to fight with him, but he is so calm it feels like she must. If she doesn't remind him how vulnerable they all are, she worries he will forget. His comment to Lucas is still ringing in her ears. *A little rain. A little wind. Goddammit, Kirby,* she thinks.

"See?" she says, gesturing at the ceiling and the sky above it. On another day she might have held back. She might have seen the exhaustion on his face and remembered that he is also doing his best. But it's not another day. It's today, and today she is tired of feeling alone with the panic that lately seems like it is always whirling just beneath her skin. "It's starting and the windows aren't boarded up yet. Are you even listening?"

"For fuck's sake." Kirby slams his hands into the back of one of the chairs, pushed in neatly, and the entire table jumps forward a few inches. "I'm boarding them up first thing. I told you we'd be ready and we'll be ready. You think I haven't been tracking it? You think I don't know how hurricanes work? It'll hit farther north. And even if it doesn't, we'll be fine."

"Right, because you know everything, Kirb. You have all the information. I'm the one who doesn't know shit."

Except they both know, firsthand, how hurricane season goes. For years, Kirby made his living taking storm-duty contracts, traveling to wherever the aftermath was worst, and for her entire childhood, Frida and Joy were ruled by weather patterns. None of that helped her in San Juan. Is it any wonder she's so frightened now? The most significant moment of Frida's life is wrapped in the howl of a hurricane, the dark funnel of grief and a bright pinpoint of the eye shining above—the brightness that used to be Kirby. It used to be this house, and the life they were building inside it. Now, it's not that she doubts her husband's expertise in these storms, but rather that she doubts his expertise in her.

"Fri," he says, trying to de-escalate the fury he sees on her face, "we'll be okay. I promise. I've been prepping for hurricanes since I was a kid. I know how to do this."

He reaches for her. The baby kicks again, hard, and she suddenly doesn't have the energy to point out that they have this in common. That there is not one expert in this house but two. Soon, a third. Because what will this baby know but storm after storm?

Tears come, falling along with the rain outside—warm and steady, not yet thunderous. The prelude to something greater. Something torrential. She lets him hold her, both of them standing in the rainwater seeping from Kirby's boots.

"I'm scared," she whispers.

"Don't be," he says, and it makes everything so much worse.

THE POWER GOES out in the middle of the night. It's the kind of thing that most people sleep through, but Kirby is not most people. He is immediately awake, aware of the various degrees of silence where there was once a humming refrigerator, the tick of a wall clock, a purring fan, the quiet groan of the central air vent. The constant buzz of electricity waiting to be dispersed. It all clicks off in the same second, and Kirby hears it as if it were a sonic boom.

He rises quietly. In the bathroom, he notices the outline of a philodendron silhouetted against the bathroom window. It waves to him, a dark flutter of its enormous leaves. The winds are picking up. For a moment, he worries that he's left boarding up the windows too late. It could be the storm moved more quickly than folks realized. Could be that Frida was right. Is it already here? An uncharacteristic pang of doubt shatters any sleep that still clung to him.

He dresses quickly, his Carhartts in a heap on the bathroom floor where he left them, the same stinking T-shirt he wore the previous day, still damp with sweat. The house is beginning to warm without the AC. He goes outside and fishes his headlamp out of the glove box of his truck. Putting it on, he's glad the plywood is already sorted, relieved that the wind, stiff and uneven, is not yet dangerous. There's a lull in the rain and he hurries to make the most of it.

Frida thinks he isn't taking the forecast seriously, but he is too good at his job not to take it seriously. He's just not willing to indulge her panic. There's no lie in saying it will probably be nothing but a thunderstorm here in Rudder. This kind of reasoning used to soothe her, back when the trauma of Poppy was still fresh in her mind—but she doesn't want to hear him tell her not to worry anymore. So then what is he supposed to say? It's been a brutal season. Next year will be bad, too, but naming these realities changes nothing. He learned to close his mind to the carnage of other places a long time ago. In his line of work, he had to.

At the top of the ladder, with a piece of plywood under his arm and the drill in hand, he shines his headlamp on the window frame. It looks exactly as it did the last time he was up here. The plywood fits perfectly, as he knew it would. The holes have already been drilled and the screws zip into place. There is comfort in this. Comfort in physical tasks and their tools and the precision of a bit fitting into the head of a screw. If only the trouble with Frida could be so simple, so accessible. He imagines going into their bedroom with the drill, applying it to a secret compartment in the sole of her foot, the back of her neck, and resetting a mysterious switch while she sleeps. He imagines her undisturbed smile upon waking, the smile she used to give him, pure, as if seeing his face was all it took to make her happy. Is it unfair to wish she were…easier? Less work? It is. He knows it is. But he wishes it anyway. He wants to retrieve those days spent standing on this same ladder, paint roller in hand, making a weather-worn house feel new again.

Flip and Lucas come tumbling outside, awake and curious, and the feeling of that hot afternoon sun on his back fades. The smell of new paint leaves him. The rain begins again and the boys holler up at him, wanting to know what he's doing up out here in the dark. On the other side of this wall, the best friend he's ever had is curled around the child they'll share, two overlapping bodies busy with the work of creation. This is what he has now. As the warm rain wets the earth, he is reminded that it's enough. It's more than enough. He is luckier than most. Today, he will be whatever this besieged family needs from him.

Kirby sets the boys to work and they are excited to help. Together the three of them ready the house, closing its glossy eyes against the coming storm, shutting those plywood lids one at a time.

INSIDE, FRIDA HAS already been awake for hours. She builds a fortress of pillows around her naked body now that she is alone in this bed, one between her thighs, one at her back, one clutched against her breasts. Safely ensconced, she listens to Kirby and the boys boarding up the bedroom windows and lies very still. He is just outside, perched on his ladder, pressing the bit of his drill against the wall where their headboard stands, but it feels as if he is miles away. The bright light of his headlamp filters through the curtains, illuminating the pale pink nightgown she shed in the night, then the light is gone, four twirls of the drill, a thump, and the darkness is complete. She peels back the sheet; it's too hot for anything to be against her skin but the air itself. She instinctively looks for the glow of the alarm clock, but it isn't there.

He calls to the boys, "No, the big one," and then there's the whining motor of the drill again, the shriek of a screw, the thud of the board snapping up tight against the window frame. She knows it's early. Knows that Kirby woke to the outage, as he always does, and was unnerved, knows that he didn't expect to lose power until the afternoon at least. He'll likely be called in to fix the downed line as soon as dawn breaks—or does not break, depending on the sky. Again, she wishes that just this once he had listened to her and the four of them were waking up somewhere in the Panhandle, far from the hurricane's path. She wishes for a code she might speak that would convey this sense of emergency, this unhinged feeling she has that if he doesn't let her be frightened, doesn't let her exist in this fear completely and without apology, if he doesn't listen, she might never recover.

None of this feels like a symptom of pregnancy, but maybe it is. She has to at least consider that, doesn't she? Maybe this dread is part of making a life. She wishes her mother could be here to stroke her hair, to listen to her belly, to tell her little fibs about how much it will or won't hurt when it's time. Instead, she's surrounded by men and little boys. Is it true that she doesn't know a single woman here in Rudder? She tries to think, surely that isn't the case, but it is. There's a neighbor—an older woman who lives alone—but they've only exchanged pleasantries in the grocery store or met by chance, walking along the road.

Frida lived in Houston long enough to make a few good friends, but after Joy died, after Poppy, she couldn't imagine going back and resuming her studies as if nothing had happened. So she lingered in San Juan, even after flights resumed. Her friends called to check on her, asking when she would be back, but she didn't have an answer. She wanted to be close to people who understood what had just happened to her. Most of all she wanted to be close to Kirby. And he wanted her there, too. She'd never felt so wanted. She realized she was pregnant a few weeks before Kirby's contract ended, and when he asked her to come home with him, it seemed fated. Now, it just seems rash.

The bedroom, so dark already, grows darker still as Kirby seals off the windows in the hall. Frida keeps her eyes open, watching the shimmer of molecules forming and reforming in the blackness. Kirby and the boys move on to the living room. She can still hear the thump of the ladder and the whine of the drill, but either they have stopped speaking or the wind is sucking their voices up into the brewing atmosphere. Not long now.

KIRBY LIGHTS THE gas stove with a match and makes the boys eggs while he waits to be called in to work. It's possible they won't call—possible that they'll wait till after the storm passes. But every hour with the power back on is another hour to bill. He glances at the clock on his phone, 5:37. They'll call before six if they call at all.

He can tell that the boys are thrilled by this change in their routine: the early-morning quiet, the darkness, the urgent, rugged work of boarding up the windows as the wind starts to move faster and faster. They jab at each other with their elbows and drink orange juice straight from a slowly warming carton, condensation dripping down the sides. They are giddy in his presence, as if he is a girl they are trying to impress. Kirby almost laughs at the thought, at the idea that one day soon they will indeed be trying to impress girls, but his humor is short-lived. There is too much on his mind to enjoy the spare moments with them this morning. He is busy waiting for the crush of the day's responsibilities to bear down.

"Let your brother have some," he says as he sees Lucas take another chug, juice slipping down the corners of his mouth and onto his shirt while Flip waits his turn. His tone is harder than necessary, but his oldest has been difficult lately, pushing everyone a little too far. Lucas grins and burps, triumphantly unperturbed, then crushes the empty container and tosses it into the recycling bin. *This fucking kid*, he thinks, and resolves that he will talk to him after all. He should have done it last night when Lucas called Frida's dinner disgusting. He'll do it later today, when they are all stuck in this little house together and there is no escape.

Feeling good about this, Kirby lights a candle directly from the burner's flame and sets it next to the pan, then turns off his headlamp. Work will call soon. He checks the screen of his cell phone. Probably any minute. Most people don't realize how temperamental the flow of electricity is, but Kirby knows it better than anyone. Temperamental and deadly. He's spent the last fifteen years climbing poles, working on lines, cleaning up after blizzards and hurricanes and tornadoes. He knows what can happen in a single moment of negligence working with electricity—people die, or they lose limbs, or they lose skin. A lot of skin. He's seen it. When people ask what he does for a living, he just tells them he keeps the lights on, because no one seems to know what a lineman is, and they nod approvingly. They like how simple it sounds. No one wants to think too hard about how tenuous these staples really are, about the human cost of turning on a lamp or opening the refrigerator. It's the places that know true disaster where people understand the kind of work he does. The places that are used to going without power for weeks or months or lately—years.

When he took the Puerto Rico contract, it was just another storm duty assignment. Another way to escape the prefurnished studio where he'd been spending his rare days off, after Chloe kicked him out but before they'd figured out a joint custody arrangement. Except it wasn't just another assignment. Before his crew even arrived, they knew that the whole grid needed to be replaced. They knew that the parts being shipped over were inadequate. They knew that they didn't have enough hands to do what was needed. Everyone did. They'd known all this since Maria and yet in the years since, billions had been spent on inadequate patches. And after Poppy, they spent even more to do even less. He'd never worked a job to run out the clock before. They worked to keep the lights on, didn't they? But the lights weren't coming back on, not here. The government had left this place to drown and sent men like him to pretend they'd done all they could. Kirby had never felt so useless. He'd known for years how decrepit the U.S. electrical grid had become. Every lineman knew that. But he'd imagined, as they all had, that one day the work would get done. The lights, somehow, would stay on. Turns out that in a territory where no one could vote, they wouldn't. Somewhere in the back of his mind he knows that Puerto Rico was only the beginning, but he doesn't dwell on that. Those worries are above his pay grade.

The eggs start to smoke. He flips them out onto plates and passes them to the boys. Running their forks through singed egg white, they make faces but eat anyway. Kirby is unaware of just how special this moment is to them. He cannot see how anxious they are that this will end too soon. The rain has begun again, thudding sideways against the house now. The soil-rich smell of humidity and chlorophyll has crept in through the cracks without the AC to strip it from the air. Shrubs knock on the side of the house with their soft knuckles, requesting refuge from the rising wind. Even so, the house is quieter than it usually is; it still feels like the middle of the night. He jots down a list of last-minute things he planned to do this morning for Frida and pins it to the refrigerator with a plastic magnet that looks like the earth: verdant green and blue.

When the phone finally does ring, Lucas reaches for it and swipes across the screen before the first trill has finished. "Hello?" he says, eager to be part of Kirby's day. Kirby plucks it from his hands, trying not to be annoyed. It's his foreman, telling him what he already knows. He listens anyway, then steps back into his muddy boots.

"Let her sleep, men," he says to his boys, meaning Frida, and swings open the kitchen door, steps over the sandbags, and disappears into the predawn darkness. Just like that, the moment is gone. Later, he will wish he had said something more, had paused to hug them, to caress their soft, sleep-worn heads. He will wish he had done many things. But how could he have known?

A CLATTER OF dishes in the sink. Frida hears him telling the boys to let her sleep, and then his boots on the linoleum, his truck rumbling to life outside, the sound softening as it disappears down the length of the driveway. Is it possible he kissed her goodbye when she was sleeping? No. She's been awake since before he got up.

She rises eventually and finds the boys taking turns with a battery-operated video game in the darkened living room. Flip's face is three inches away from the glow of the screen; Lucas eats cereal dry from the box on the sofa.

"Morning, kiddos," she says. She doesn't expect them to acknowledge her, and they don't. In the kitchen, an unattended candle burns next to a dirty pan. It occurs to her to be sanctimonious about this, but she's too tired to care. All the anger she felt yesterday has seeped away during the night. Now there is only the fear she can't seem to shed. She puts the candle on a saucer and lights a few more.

The morning wears on and the house stays dark. Frida contemplates the blackened window over the sink, a blind eye that can no longer look out—only in. The sound of the rain flows and then ebbs and then flows. She returns to the sink to wash the boys' dishes, only to be reminded of the power outage when the faucet spits and runs dry. Instead, she makes herself oatmeal with bottled water, and while she stirs she wonders how to fill this day. The hurricane is too close to let the boys outside, and the thought of them cooped up with her all day, and tomorrow too, probably, almost knocks her over. Joy would know what to do with them, but Frida is at a loss. They would probably prefer she leave them alone.

Planning activities for little boys who hate her is not how this year was supposed to go. If she'd gone back to Houston, she would have her master's degree by now. She'd have a job, too. No more waitressing or making lattes—she'd be beginning her career as a proper architect, sitting in some open-plan office full of glass and crisp modern shapes. And a view—she imagines that today is clear and sunny in Houston, far from the turmoil lurking off the coast. In this fantasy, Joy is alive, sending postcards from Turks and Caicos. There is no pregnancy. Frida's body is her own and her potential is enormous. She designs buildings and bridges and parks. Her work is feted. Her future is bright.

But she can only imagine this for so long before the sound of the boys screaming at each other drags her back to Rudder. To this house, which feels tight and uninspired. She and Kirby agreed when they married that after the baby came, she would finish her degree somehow. There's a good program in Miami. He promised that they would make it work. But it suddenly hits her that this is just as much a fantasy as her elegant, sun-filled office. She rubs her belly and feels ashamed for imagining that it is flat and empty. *I didn't mean it*, she tells its resident. Except maybe she did.

She's found Kirby's list by now, knows that there are things she must attend to before he gets back, but she can't bring herself to do much more than stand in front of the stove and contemplate this breakfast she doesn't want. The baby kicks. Or is it a cramp? A pain grips her abdomen and then lets go. The oatmeal bubbles, slow and viscous. In the other room, one of the boys gives a shout of victory and she can't tell which kid it is and more importantly, she doesn't care.

KIRBY PARKS IN the yard and goes to meet his foreman, who leans against the town's bucket truck, already halfway down a thick cigar.

"A little early for that, isn't it?" Kirby says.

"Nah." Emilio flicks ash onto the ground. "I been awake for hours. Early don't mean much when you can't sleep." He rolls the smoke in his mouth, letting it escape in a long, slow line. His silvery hair is slicked straight back, gray stubble creeping down his neck. His head barely comes up to Kirby's shoulder and he must be nearing sixty, but he moves with a kind of efficient, understated power, like there's a reservoir of strength standing by: tightly coiled, always ready. Kirby likes him more and more the longer they work together.

"So what are we playing with?"

Emilio shrugs. "Probably just a short circuit. Didn't give details. Won't know till we get out there."

"Whatever it is, we'll get her done fast," Kirby says. Emilio nods his approval, puffing hard on his cigar. He's done talking, and Kirby lets the silence stand. No matter how well Emilio and Kirby get along, he's still the new guy. He doesn't want to overstep.

Wes arrives, and the three of them lean against the bucket truck while they wait for the last two. It's a crew of five—two on the ground, two in the air, and Emilio supervising. Thus far, Kirby has found the work of maintaining a single municipality's grid mild compared to storm-duty contracts, but he knows saying so won't win him any goodwill here. Wes is scraggly, tall and thin like an adolescent pine tree, with a mouth that never stops flapping. He's a squirrelly son of a bitch and Kirby doesn't like him, but he keeps it civil.

"Whose dumbass idea was it to call us in with a Cat Four comin' in for a landing?" Wes asks.

"Utility director assigned it. Like always," Emilio grumbles. He's not interested in Wes's bullshit, either.

"You mean Cat Three," Kirby says.

"Upgraded it on the way here. Headed straight for us, too," Wes says. "Just watch, this line'll be out again in a few hours. Wind changed overnight. Lookin' like a direct hit."

"That so?" Kirby tries not to show his surprise. He should know by now that hurricanes do whatever they want. A direct hit…he can feel his stomach twist as Wes chatters on about the forecast. It's nothing he hasn't seen before, but he wants to get home. He doesn't want Frida to hear all of this on the news.

The groundmen are late. When they do arrive, they are together. Brenda is at the wheel, a Black woman with a ball cap pulled down over her eyes who looks like she would rather be anywhere else, while Jerome, a scrawny white twenty-year-old, sits beside her, chattering away. Brenda pulls her truck alongside them and rolls down her window, hooking her arm over the side. "Sorry," she says, rolling her eyes toward Jerome by way of explanation. "We'll follow you." She smacks her hand against the door for emphasis, her T-shirt sleeve cuffed to hold a pack of cigarettes.

"Hey, lovebirds," Wes calls into the cab, and makes a wet kissing sound.

Brenda fixes him with a rigid stare and cuts the wheel with ferocious precision, backing up abruptly to make room, her eyes never leaving Wes. *That's the right way to deal with that*, Kirby thinks. He's never worked with a woman before, but he likes Brenda. She's quiet and strong and a hard worker. Jerome, on the other hand, is a liability.

He's been begging rides ever since Kirby started—something about a DUI. Kirby doesn't ask for details that aren't offered.

At the job site, they find a downed line and a few heavy branches in the road. Brenda can't get out of the truck fast enough; she's clapped a hard hat over her box braids and is setting out cones before anyone else has even turned off their engines. The line is slithering: a hot, sparking snake slapping against the pavement. Kirby knows that's 13,800 volts or so trying to find a home and he'd rather it wasn't him. Emilio's cigar has burned down to a nub, but he won't throw it away until it begins to singe the hair on his knuckles. Kirby gets the hot sticks from the truck as quickly as he can and tosses one to Wes.

"Careful, Kirb," Emilio says, eyeing the arc of the line. "It's spittin'."

Kirby reaches up to the cutout with his stick and knocks out the rod while Wes runs down to the cutout on the other side and does the same. The line bounces up a few times and then quiets.

"Get up there, already," Emilio says. "I wanna be home before this shit gets bad."

"You and me both," Kirby says.

Emilio saunters over to the groundmen. "You're the chain saws, kids, let's move it along." This is intended for Jerome.

In the air, Kirby rods out the line. The rain begins again, just a sprinkle at first, quickly thickening into something heavier. Wes is at the other end, ready to crimp the new line to the old one. Emilio gets back into his truck and fills out OSHA paperwork with the radio blasting so loud Kirby can hear the beat from up in his perch. Brenda finishes slicing up the branches while Jerome hauls it all into the woods. They operate separately but in unison, each with their own task, each with an eye on the mottled sky.

Chances are, the crew will be out again by tomorrow night—the only question is what kind of devastation they'll be cleaning up after. Kirby replaces the fuse, feeling the futility of this morning's work. The entire state of Florida is overrun with contract linemen, and probably more arriving at this very moment now that the category rating has been upgraded—speeding down empty highways, evacuation traffic in the other direction backed up for miles while the electricity workers head straight for the cone of uncertainty. The cities will repurpose airport runways and shopping center parking lots to hold them all, filling the empty pavement with trucks and equipment, just waiting to swoop in on the devastation. Motels will be jammed with contractors from out of state. Wherever this hurricane makes landfall, it will be an event. The utility company has been pouring money into preparation, and FEMA services are on red alert. No one expects the best anymore, not after the multitude of direct hits this year, and what happened to Puerto Rico last year, and the coast of Georgia the year before that. A sudden gust of wind knocks Kirby against the edge of his bucket. He mutters a few choice expletives, then slams the last fuse shut and flips the switch.

"We're hot," he shouts over to Wes, who is hanging from a pole down the road. Wes gives him a thumbs-up.

On the ground, Kirby starts strapping the equipment back onto the truck. The groundmen finish with the fallen branches. Emilio cracks a window and lights another cigar. "Took you long enough," he says. The cigar smoke curls upward in a steady ribbon for just a second before the wind comes and takes it; Kirby watches it go.

THE POWER FLASHES back on, and with it comes the hum of the refrigerator, the buzz of a lightbulb, the quiet thump of a clock. Most importantly, the whir of the AC. Frida hears the boys shriek with excitement and scramble for the television remote. This evidence of their delight has a strange dissonant quality to her—their easy joy is unrelatable. She recognizes it, but only vaguely, as if it is an emotion she dreamed once. In the dim cave of the house, she feels her dread widen and calcify. The empty spaces between furniture fill; the ceiling creeps downward. She goes to the bedroom, then back to the kitchen, to the bathroom, to the bedroom once more, turning on lights, then turning them off again. Nowhere seems right. Another wave of discomfort rolls through her. A different person might call it pain. A midwife might call it a contraction.

She remembers Kirby's note on the fridge, asking her to fill the water jugs and the tub when the power comes back, and so she makes herself do that and tries to focus on the gush of the faucet, the shine on the taps, the hum of the pump kicking on. She packs the jugs into the freezer and the fridge, as many as can fit around the food, and then lines up the rest in the hallway. She fills the bathtub with cool water and sits on the bath mat, letting her arm dip beneath the surface. It levitates there, her fingers just barely touching the bottom. Frida watches her sleeve drag in the water and lays her cheek against the cold porcelain edge of the tub. She feels diminished. Dim.

Losing light like nighttime coming on fast. Is it visible? Can they see her fading? It seems she is growing—her stomach, her ankles, her breasts—but surely it isn't right that there is more of her now than there was eight months ago. Surely she's shriveled since then.

Her stomach is propped up on her thigh, her temple leaned against the edge of the tub, waiting for the hurricane to sweep away this festering anticipation. This tightness in her abdomen. She can hear the philodendron tapping on the bathroom window, but she can't see it. All she sees is darkness where the light used to be.

After Poppy, she remembers walking for a long time through the torn streets of San Juan, stumbling over debris, the mud sucking at her sandals. Demolished homes on either side, their roofs peeled back like the thick skins of oranges, exposed rooms filled with trash and muck and water. An unbearably blue sky hanging over all that wreckage. There was almost nothing left whole in that city, only pieces. Pieces of road, pieces of buildings, pieces of vehicles. A strange puzzle. Stray dogs followed her as she walked, their ribs threatening to burst from their thin hides. She passed a crew of linemen, newly arrived. Frida could barely stand to look at them, set against that clear blue sky she felt so insulted by. But she made herself look. She made herself absorb the sunlight, the flutter of a gull passing overhead, the tap tap tap of a lone hammer, some ways off, the sound of someone beginning to rebuild. She saw one of the linemen hanging off a freshly raised wooden pole, saw his heavy work boots, saw the solidity of his broad frame, saw his sweating, sun-beaten face beneath the brim of his hard hat; at the same time, he looked down and took in her stained dress, her tangled hair, her burning gaze pointed right at him. It wasn't love at first sight. It was the feeling she got when she saw the Bridge of the Americas as a child, when she walked onto her first college campus, when she signed her first lease. The recognition of something that would later be important. A crux. A beginning. *This. Here. You.* Laying the foundation of a future she hadn't yet imagined. Love came later.

Another wave of pain rolls through her. She grits her teeth, still unwilling to name it. *It isn't time. We aren't ready.*

THE BOYS KICK at each other even as their eyes are fastened to the television, vying for couch space without committing to battle. By the time the commercial break comes on, Lucas has corralled Flip onto the third couch cushion, his own short body splayed across the other two. This is the way of things between them: the inevitable two-to-one ratio is a foregone conclusion. Flip hugs the arm of the sofa, curling himself into the corner that's left to him. Lucas wriggles down farther, stretching his feet to invade Flip's territory, always striving for more. Beating him away with a pillow and a curdled whine, Flip lashes backward only to realize that Frida is standing in the doorway, holding on to the frame. He isn't sure how long she's been there. Her gaze seems to settle on the television screen—crudely drawn creatures dashing across a ship deck, then plunging into the sea to look for buried treasure—but Flip can tell she isn't really watching, that none of this is registering beyond flashing colors and high-pitched sounds.

"Lucas is hogging the couch," he says, if only to bring her back into the room, to tug her attention away from whatever dimension it has drifted into. He won't admit it to Lucas, but he's beginning to like Frida. She's kind to him. He didn't even mind the potato skins. Lucas kicks him again and he bites back a squeal.

"Narc," Lucas whispers, not knowing exactly what this means but feeling reasonably sure it fits the occasion.

"Turn it down, please," she says, as if she's only just remembered why she came into the room at all. "I'm going to lie down for a bit. Just stay inside, okay, and when your father comes home, tell him I need to talk to him."

"Are you okay?" Flip asks.

"Fine," she says. "Just..." She struggles for an appropriate symptom, something that won't alarm them. "Nauseous. Lucas, be nice, please."

Lucas picks up the remote and begrudgingly turns down the volume so she can see him doing it, then throws it at Flip, who cries out at this fresh injustice and turns to protest, only to find that Frida is already gone.

The episode finishes and the programming blinks over to local storm coverage. They gag as if they've ingested poison and Lucas turns off the television. These are Florida boys, born and bred; the drama of anticipating extreme weather is not special. Without the glow of the screen, the room becomes dark. A sliver of dim light creeps in through a rectangular pane on the front door that Kirby didn't bother covering, but that's the only evidence of a day that is passing unseen. The door to Frida and Kirby's room is closed. The boys are alone, and there is something unusual charging the dust particles that swim in that lone splash of light. A silent voice that wants their attention.

"Let's go outside," Lucas proposes. "We could walk to the trailer park and play horseshoes." That summer, he made a friend who lives in the park, and although this friend has evacuated, it seems like a sensible destination to him. He swings open the front door, quietly, so as not to wake Frida. The coolness rushes out while the wet heat rushes in and that quality of strangeness thickens. There is an urgency here. There is information.

"I don't know," Flip says. "We're not supposed to." He can feel a kind of data wrapped up in the humidity, but he doesn't know what it means. He just knows it's there. A message he doesn't understand.

Lucas doesn't notice—he's too busy being the oldest, which means knowing everything. He rolls his eyes, hard, and leans out over the sandbags, gesturing at the sky. "It's not even raining and there's nothing to do here. Come on. We'll be back before what's-her-name wakes up."

"Don't call her that."

"You coming or not?"

Flip peers outside. The sky is fiercely lit from within the thunderheads, but there is no wind. There is no rain. The air is hot and eerie and still.

Flip hesitates. "Not raining *yet*," he allows. "Could come on any minute."

"We'll be back way before it starts." Lucas scurries over the sandbags heaped in front of the door and into the muddy driveway. Flip hangs back in the darkness of the house, still uncertain. A layer of intangible information settles on his skin, moving through his nose and mouth. But its message is quiet, and his brother is loud. "For chrissakes, Flip," Lucas says. It's the phrase that their father utters when his temper is about to unravel. It works exactly how Lucas wants it to. Flip climbs over the sandbags and pulls the door shut behind him, careful to latch it softly.

"Fine," he says, "but just real quick."

Lucas is already halfway down the driveway by the time Flip catches up. On the main road, there is no one. This is unusual, but not unheard of. The birds seem to hush as they walk. The crickets are silent. Skinny pines tower on either side of the road. When they get to the trailer park it is abandoned. The usual chatter of television sets and radios and kids is absent. No laundry hangs and no cars remain, except the broken-down ones. Lucas climbs the steps to his friend's red double-wide and tries the door. It's locked. He jiggles the handle anyway, just in case that's all it takes.

"Let's try some more," he suggests. "See if anybody left theirs open." Lucas is already on to the next trailer, locked, and the next, locked again. His little brother toes the sand and shakes his head. "Flip," Lucas snaps, "don't be like that, help me."

"I don't think we should," Flip says. "What if somebody's home?"

"Nobody's home, dipshit, they always 'vacuate the trailer parks first. Dad says 'cause they're so light, see, don't hold up if winds are bad."

Flip reluctantly tries the door of the trailer nearest to him and is relieved to find that it will not open. "They're all locked," he declares, but Lucas pays him no mind and keeps searching.

The trailers are laid out in a grid—four rows wide and eight deep. The roads in between are sand, packed down by big tires and heavy rigs. Some of the smaller RVs have just up and driven away, evident from the empty lots and dead grass left behind. The cheerful awnings that Flip remembers from past visits are rolled up tight. The iron set of horseshoes usually scattered near the fire pit is gone. A forgotten wind chime tinkles somewhere, but the lawn furniture, the little bikes with tasseled handlebars, the potted plants, the overflowing garbage cans, the flamingo lawn ornaments, the rooster-shaped weather vanes: all gone.

A few rows down, Lucas discovers an unlocked door. It swings out into his unprepared hand and he startles, taking a step back on the porch and releasing his grip in surprise. The rising wind smashes the door up against the siding, and the gloom within seems to leak out, to mingle with the murk of the clouds that are bearing down on them. He can just make out the shapes inside—a pair of La-Z-Boys angled toward a big TV, tidy piles of magazines and books on the floor, a galley kitchen, blinds half-drawn but with slivers of light slicing through and illuminating the dirty dishes in the sink—remnants of a simple breakfast for two. Lucas leans in, curious, stubborn, aware now that he is crossing a line but incapable of leaving a discovery of this magnitude unexplored.

Down the rows, Flip sees his brother disappear into one of the trailers. He abandons his own half-hearted search and runs along the sandy road, feeling suddenly unnerved by being so far away, as if Lucas has stepped into another world and not simply through the threshold of an abandoned trailer. Flip's sneakers slide on the sand as he jogs, his gangly arms and legs flailing, perhaps unsure of how long they are today, whether they have grown another centimeter in the night. He calls out to his brother as he climbs the steps.

Inside, Lucas is lounging in one of the La-Z-Boys, swiveling from side to side. He kicks over a stack of magazines by accident and laughs, then kicks another stack, on purpose this time.

"Look what I found," he says, gesturing all around to this palace he has claimed.

Flip hangs back in the doorway. "We should go," he says. There is a warning prickling against his skin. That's what it is—he can identify it now. But Lucas is stubborn. He isn't listening the way Flip is.

"Not yet."

ON HIS WAY home from the yard, Kirby leans against his steering wheel and looks up into the sky. Its colors have ripened since he left the job site. A severe wind sweeps in from the ocean, bending the trees toward the earth, blowing debris across the road. There is no rain just now, but the air is laden.

His determination to do better is still with him, especially now that the hurricane has adjusted its angle and increased its wind speed. When he gets home, Frida will need a part of him he has been withholding, he can see that now. She needs his patience. A measure of empathy. Even just his presence, the warm bulk of his towering frame notched beside her on the sofa as she worries. He's ashamed that he's been so careless with her fears these past few days. Kirby is not a subtle man, but he is willing.

Watching her struggle lately has required him to notice the dissolution that is occurring all around them. She is unable to look away, and by simple proximity to her horror, he is required to observe with fresh eyes. He would like to go on ignoring this overwhelming layer of doom. There is more than enough to occupy his mind and hands as it is—daily tasks, his work, the needs of his growing family. What good is it noticing all the problems he cannot fix? Ever since they met, the structures of civilization have been deteriorating more quickly than ever before, falling to unprecedented pieces month by month. Hurricane Poppy was neither the beginning nor the end. Dire environmental reports are coming to life, political coups, humanitarian crises in every corner of the globe. It's not just turning on the evening news that makes his heart fall anymore. It's the sound of his alarm clock in the morning. The passage of time and the erosion it brings. Everywhere he looks—despair and poverty, unkindness and unhappiness. All of this and also: a baby on the way. The sensation of a widespread ending, eclipsed by the imminence of one new life. Kirby feels a wash of overwhelmed tears coming on and swallows a sting in the back of his throat. He realizes that this is what she's been asking for all along. Just this. A shared understanding of everything that is askew.

The rain arrives, sprinkling his windshield at first, and then driving into it with unsettling force. Is this it, then? Has the storm finally made landfall, or is it just another rain band? He hopes that Frida got his note about the water jugs. The power lines swing, wild squiggles straining against their fastenings, and the palm trees bow down toward the road, deeper and deeper, until their fronds skim the asphalt. Wes wasn't wrong: The work they just did won't last the night. If that.

Pulling into the driveway, Kirby is relieved to find that all appears to be well, that nothing was accidentally left out this morning in the dark. He dashes for the kitchen door, the rain cutting his face and hands as he moves across the backyard. Inside, the rooms are dark. He calls out a hello, but the house stays quiet. It's unusual, this silence. It worries him. He wanders down the hallway, ducking his head inside each doorway he passes. In the bedroom he finds Frida, one leg emerging from underneath a pile of bedding. He sits down next to her and encircles her foot with his big hand, rubbing his thumb along her calluses.

"Frida," he says, a prick of worry entering his mind. She makes a sound but doesn't emerge, burrowing deeper into the mattress. "Where are the boys?"

"Living room," she says, still inside her cocoon. "Cartoons."

"No..." he says slowly, feeling the word take up space. "They're not. Frida, they're not in the house and it's starting out there. When's the last time you saw them?"

Now she emerges, sensing that the stakes have risen, that she has made an error, that something has gone wrong while she lay here. She sits up. Kirby forgets to hold her as he'd planned to, to tell her with his hands what he doesn't trust his words to convey—that she isn't alone, that he feels this impossible pressure of the world unraveling, too, that he's sorry he isn't brave enough to say it out loud. A new problem teases him away, the way they always do.

"Gone?" she asks. "But..." It's not her fault, he tries to remind himself, but the camaraderie he felt in the truck is slipping away. How does it dissolve so quickly? Kirby watches the tears forming in her eyes, watches her struggle for a sentence that might fill this space, and suddenly he cannot bear to see the gravity of the situation settling over her. It's too much—this breakability that she has encased herself in, a glass shell, permanently cracked, forever in the process of shattering before his eyes. He cannot be with her in this moment. Not when there is work to be done. He stands up.

"What can I do?" she asks.

"Nothing. Stay here," he says, and walks out of the room, knowing it sounded harsh, knowing that this is not how he wanted today to go, but unable to attend to both the task of protecting the tender bodies of his children and holding space for something so inconsequential as a feeling—Frida's or his own.

"Kirby, wait," she calls after him. But he doesn't. He can't.

FRIDA HEARS HIM stomp back through the house to the kitchen door. The engine of his truck rumbles and then it recedes into the distance. The silence returns, but now it has curdled. Pain rolls through her once more. She doesn't want to call them contractions; she can't face that word yet. They're probably just false labor pains. It's the stress, the anxiety, the low air pressure. Some old TV trope— a drama trick, an unearned climax. An old wives' tale. This pain isn't real; it can't be. Maybe if she stays very still it'll go away.

But how can she stay still when those little boys are missing and it's her fault? She sits up and gathers the sheet around her shoulders. Her mind leaps out ahead of this moment to touch on all of the most horrifying possibilities this hurricane could bring: Kirby losing control of the truck; the boys getting sucked into the river; all the debris that could connect with these delicate humans who are so precious to her. All three, she realizes now, even Lucas. He's only a child underneath that show of brattiness, and it was her job to watch them, to keep them safe. She realizes now that she has not appreciated this family as she should have, spending this whole summer not wanting the boys, not wanting Kirby, not wanting the baby even. Outside, the wind is eager for destruction. She can hear the windowpanes rattle against their frames, can hear the moans and the howls and the screams of air and water gusting, twisting, pressing into this small town just so.

Is she being punished for this not-wanting? And if so, is the fear her penance, or is it only the precursor of something worse?

She unravels herself from the sheets and paces the house, checking the boys' room, the living room, the kitchen, as if they are only hiding and Kirby has simply not looked hard enough. But they are in none of those places, and if Frida allows herself to truly examine the remnants of the past few hours in her mind, she will find a dreamlike auditory memory of the front door opening and closing, the sound of voices outside in the yard, the absence of the television's chatter, and a house that is too deliciously quiet to possibly contain her two stepsons. She cannot allow herself to examine this just now. She can barely remember to breathe.

Frida tries Kirby's cell but it goes to voice mail. She immediately calls again, unable to stop herself.

"Unless you know where I should be looking for them, I can't talk about this right now," he snaps at her. The sound of the rain beating against his truck dilutes the volume of his voice, but it cannot disguise his tone.

"I'm sorry," she whispers into the receiver.

"It's fine, Frida. Just let me handle this and we can talk later." He hangs up. While he looks out there, she resolves to look here. She paces the house once more, searching for clues, and thinks suddenly of the tool shed. Perhaps the boys went out to play some game and then lost track of time. Maybe they didn't hear Kirby's truck pulling into the driveway in this thunderous rain. Maybe they've been telling ghost stories in there this whole time and she will go out and find them and Kirby will come home and they will all weather the hurricane together and none of this will be very bad. It will just be this singular burst of panic triggered by the clot of disquiet that she has carried with her ever since Poppy. The dread she has felt circling all day will dissipate. The storm will wait. The baby will wait. The worst has already happened; how could it possibly visit her again?

She steps into a pair of tall rain boots by the door and throws on one of Kirby's jackets, eager to manifest this happy resolution, her night-gown streaming out from under the waxed brown canvas, pink silk tail feathers whipping around her legs. She pulls the door open and the wind knocks it back on its hinges. Immediately the storm sweeps into the kitchen. All at once—a mason jar full of coupons skitters across the counter then smashes to the floor; the oranges she picked yesterday roll after it, thudding among the broken glass; the curtains snap and twist. The storm has not waited. It's already here.

Frida ignores these things crashing to the floor and manages to climb over the sandbags in the doorway, her skirts flying up around her waist, a tutu now, the rain driving into her exposed skin, the enormous jacket wrapped around her belly. Stumbling into the yard, she protects her face with her hands and pushes forward, lurching toward the shed as pieces of debris, swept in from who knows where, roll through her little garden beds. She shouts the boys' names as she goes, but there's no answer.

At the shed, she wrestles with the door, knowing even as she yanks the handle that they won't be here, that this is wishful thinking at best. But she's come this far and so she gets it open and looks inside, where there are only half-full buckets of paint and toolboxes and a band saw and the ladder Kirby climbed just that morning to install the plywood on the windows. She is gasping for air, the baby constricting her lungs, crushing her organs with its mere presence. Her pelvis clenches in pain again when she takes in the emptiness of the shed, a pain that is radiating through her entire body now. She lays both hands over her belly, trying to funnel whatever is left of her well-being into her own womb, to mitigate the damage that is surely being caused by this agony. A bright, fully charged crackle of panic rips through her. She has so much to lose.

The hazy edge of the hurricane looms just beyond the breakers. Within, the eye is cloudless and calm, a kernel of stillness held in the arms of ferocious winds. They've named her Wanda, but this vortex goes by many names, given over the course of many lifetimes. A she is a he is an it. The ocean is whipped to a froth. The sky seethes. Wanda hurtles forward.

FLIP TAKES A step inside the trailer. "Lucas," he whines, "I think we should go back." Lucas stops swiveling in the La-Z-Boy and gives his brother a cold stare. He isn't opposed to this idea. Not exactly. He can see the sky darkening over Flip's shoulder, can hear the rain thickening against the roof, can smell the strange scorch of the hurricane in the air. He knows that it is unwise to be here. But he also knows that the only person waiting for them at home is Frida, practically catatonic in her bedroom, while Kirby works until the eleventh hour, as he always does. Here, in this empty trailer with his little brother, what he says goes. Lucas is in charge, and he will not cede that power so easily.

"Don't be a chickenshit," he says. Flip is wounded by this accusation and submits instantly, which is the point. He takes another step into the trailer and lets the flimsy door swing shut. His silence is his acquiescence.

"Come here," Lucas commands, and Flip obeys. He slumps into the other La-Z-Boy and the two boys swivel in unison for a moment, wondering what to do now. Lucas turns on the television and they watch. Flip fidgets, balancing his rear on the edge of the seat as if to leap out of it at any moment, while Lucas lounges, an extravagant splay of his limbs thrown across the sticky leather upholstery. His apparent ease is a lie, a fib for Flip's benefit, or perhaps for his own. Lucas can feel the sway of the trailer as the wind gusts. But he is not ready to go back. Going back is giving up—and that he will not do. There is more than a little of Kirby in his stubbornness.

"Let's see what else is here," Lucas declares when the episode ends. He hops out of the easy chair and heads to the bedroom, where the shades are drawn and a bed made up with pale wrinkled sheets looms ghostlike in the dark. Flip follows, reluctant but complicit. They inspect the bureau one drawer at a time, rifling through clothes and socks, then turn to the nightstand. There isn't much—a tube of hand lotion, crumpled receipts, a bottle of Tylenol, pens with chewed caps. But then in the back of a drawer Lucas finds something more interesting—a thin fold of twenties, maybe a hundred dollars, fastened with a paper clip. He holds it up, triumphant.

"Check it out," Lucas says.

Flip looks stricken. "You should put it back," he whispers.

Lucas did not intend to take it until Flip said this, but now he must. Something has come over him this afternoon, some primal urge to assert dominance, to insist upon the corruption of his younger brother, to make decisions for them both that are questionable. This indescribable feeling in the air that has touched them all, whether they know it or not. Whether they understand it or not. The elements may be speaking, but listening is a skill that Lucas has never been good at.

He makes a show of putting the money in his pocket. "What are you gonna do about it?" he says, and puffs out his chest like a bird trying to look bigger than it is. Flip shrinks away and turns toward the door. He does not understand any of this. He only wants to go home, for his brother to stop being a bully.

"Well," Lucas demands. "I said, what are you gonna do about it?"

"Nothing," he replies.

"That's right," Lucas says. "Nothing."

THE STORM WILL make landfall at any moment now. The wind and rain whipping around Kirby's truck is vicious, smacking against the body of the vehicle with the force of metal chains. It will get much worse, but even now, it takes all of his concentration to keep the truck on the road. Driving through town, he sees that it's mostly abandoned. He skims through the local AM radio stations for the emergency services updates, trying to keep his mind fastened to the question of where the boys might have gone as he wrestles with the steering wheel.

He goes to the high school auditorium first, where they've taped off dozens of eight-by-eight squares on the floor, a grid of displacement. There are the people who have done this before, with their tents and folding chairs and sleeping bags, and then there are those who didn't know what to expect, who have arrived with nothing but handbags and protein bars in the pockets of their raincoats. Kirby scans the crowd, trying to be quick and thorough at the same time. A woman with a clipboard approaches and greets him with infuriating calm.

"Glad you made it!" she proclaims, as if his arrival warrants congratulations. "We still have plenty of space left, don't worry. Over here you'll see—"

He cuts her short. "I'm not here for that," he says. "My boys are missing, twelve and eight. You got any strays around here?"

She scans the auditorium as if they might appear. "Oh no! I don't think so..." she says, then looks to the clipboard. "Names?"

"Lucas and Phillip Lowe."

They aren't on the roster. Every second that passes in which he still doesn't know where they are makes his heart beat faster. By now, there is a hummingbird inside his chest. She brings him to the ham radio operator who is set up at a little desk in one of the classrooms, an older man with a line of pens clipped into his breast pocket, intensely focused on the pile of equipment in front of him.

"Maybe George can help. He's our contact from the Emergency Operations Center." She quickly recounts the details of Kirby's search. "Lucas and Phillip. Twelve and eight," she says. "Wearing..." She looks at Kirby. "What did you say they were wearing?"

"I don't, um. A red T-shirt on the youngest, maybe. And...I'm sorry, I wasn't paying attention." How could he not have been paying attention? How could he not know?

"That's okay." She pats his arm, but he barely feels it. He's too busy staring at George, trying to disguise the panic on his face. The man isn't looking at him anyway. He's tuning his dials, speaking in half code into his mic, some of which Kirby understands, some of which he doesn't. George listens for a few moments and then turns back to Kirby.

"Not accounted for," he says. "But we're sending out the alert to everyone. You got a phone number?" Kirby gives it to him. "Anybody's guess how long these cell towers'll last," George says. "We'll call you if we can. You got a CB?"

"Yeah, got one in the truck."

"All right, good, well, stay on channel nine, then. We'll find 'em eventually. You raise 'em right and they know how to take cover. Twelve and eight's old enough to know." Did he raise them right? Did he raise them at all? Kirby can't bring himself to acknowledge such hollow optimism. He's incredulous that this man could be so calm, so certain that it will all be okay, and yet it occurs to him that he's been saying these things to Frida all along. Telling her not to worry. Telling her everything will be fine, even when it won't be. Even when it's all coming apart at the seams.

As he crosses the parking lot, the rain slices through his shirt. He throws up an arm to shield his face. It feels like the storm is ripping his clothes off—the fabric tearing apart and flying away into the wind, and then the flesh beneath it, too. Peeled back in bloody curls. If the old man is right and his boys are safe, this hurricane can do anything it wants to him. Kirby gets to his truck and beats his hands against the driver's-side window until he feels foolish. The sounds he makes as he does this are feral, but no one hears them over the yowl of the wind. Inside the cab he gets a hold of himself and tries to think, to *strategize*, as if such a thing were possible when his insides are exposed, his bones bare, his nerves snapping against the air like live wires. Still, he tries: Where else could they be?

FRIDA PROPS HERSELF against the doorway of the tool shed for a long, long time. The rain pounds into her aching back, and the wall of trapped heat presses against her belly. She is caught here, struggling to understand the emptiness of this place where she allowed herself to believe she would find the boys. She is unwilling to go back to the house, to sit alone, useless, waiting, while Flip and Lucas are lost, and she is unable to be in the open outdoors, to subject her body and the child within to the whiplash fury of the wind. So she occupies this in-between space and waits. She waits to be forced to choose—one or the other—but the moment doesn't come. She surveys the tool shed and its contents, a domain unfamiliar to her. This is Kirby's kingdom, not hers. All of this is Kirby's kingdom, she realizes. The house, the yard, the shed, the town. Florida. She's used to not belonging anywhere; she just thought that Rudder might be different.

She can feel the hurricane now, not so much against her body as inside it—the frantic swirl of elements crashing into and apart, into and apart. The path to and beyond this moment stretches and shrinks and stacks and for a brief second, or perhaps a very long while, she can see her life's entire shape as a blueprint, not unlike the renderings she used to study at Rice. There is the ground floor of everything she came from, watery and expansive: watching the sail catch the wind; cooking with Joy back-to-back in the tiny galley; carefully considering every option in their box of flags, gathered from all over, even though all Frida ever wanted to fly was the Jolly Roger. And then there is everything she built by herself, with sharp corners and high ceilings: the transition to life on solid ground, entering the world instead of skimming its edges like Joy, every scholarship she earned, every A, every opportunity she held on to with both hands. But she's looking down on all this from the third floor now— a cramped, unfamiliar warren of rooms in a style she didn't choose. A man she doesn't always recognize. Little boys who hate her. A daughter she hasn't met. Everything seems jumbled and ill-planned. Nothing fits together. What if it all collapses? What if a part of her wants it to?

She commands herself to pull the shed door shut and turns back toward the yard. The kitchen looks very far away now. The rain drills into her face, her legs, slamming down into the tops of her boots and rising to her ankles. A piece of debris—a neighbor's kiddie pool, maybe—flies across the yard and smashes into the jungle at the edge of the property. She can see the house moving ever so slightly, can see the plywood on the windows shaking against the screws.

For a moment, she thinks Poppy has whirled through time to come and collect her. Maybe it has. Frida has met this chaos before. In San Juan, she and Joy anchored the boat and sought refuge in a motel, like always. They weren't foolish enough to be caught out on the water, they just didn't know that land wasn't safe, either. She remembers the shriek of timber straining against its nails. Water rushing down from the sky and up from the rivers and in from the bay. Windows shatter-ing. The roof yawning back to reveal the sky. One minute Poppy was outside; the next, she was right next to them.

Another wave rolls through Frida's body—inarguable, indefensible vise-grip pain. How could her body allow such a thing? Her conscious mind ceases to remember, to think anything at all. There is only the rawness of the wind on her bare skin and the slice of the rain. The lights inside the house go out. The only thing she's aware of is a pain so intense her fear is not just part of her—it is all of her.

Another wave, and another, and another, until she is barely standing, her back sliding down the shed's doorjamb. Even now, she struggles to understand the thing she's both known and not-known all day. She isn't ready, but her daughter is.

FLIP HAS BEEN unsettled by the way this afternoon progressed, but the theft is too much for him. He turns away from Lucas, from the lump of someone else's money in his brother's pocket, and walks out of the bedroom, down the hall, past the twin La-Z-Boys. When he opens the front door, the wind snaps it out of his hand. He sees that something has happened while they trespassed here. The whole world has changed—the texture of the sky, the quality of the air. Even the ground, which was damp when they arrived and is now choked with water. The clip-clop of the rain has turned into a stampede. He was listening to it thundering against the roof, was loosely aware that the weather was worsening, but it isn't until he is face-to-face with that wind, that wild, clawing grip, that he is aware of just how much trouble they are in.

Lucas comes up behind him and together they face the storm. It is a strange and brutal kind of justice for these sins they have just committed. They recognize that this is their punishment. "We gotta go," Flip says, but really he shouts, because the wind is so loud he must raise his voice if he wants to be heard. And he does want to be heard. Very much. He wants to go home.

Lucas shouts something back but it's lost, the wind darting inside his open mouth and blowing up his cheeks, his eyes already watering as they stumble down the steps. They hurry forward, along the sandy path between the trailers. When a tire rolls in front of them and slams into the side of a tree, they begin to run. Flip is a few paces behind Lucas, every muscle tensed in anticipation of a rusty appliance hurtling out of the sky. His body feels as frail as a featherless baby bird's, as if the slightest thing could kill him. As if he is too small for this world, too new.

He isn't wrong. Flip thinks of the nest he found at the tail end of summer, built in an eave of the sunporch. Inside it were chicks so bare it was as if their organs might pop through that delicate, translucent skin. He felt an overwhelming tenderness for those birds. Lucas lost interest almost immediately, but Flip checked on them every day. Frida helped: one of their first moments of amity. When he showed her, she stepped down from the chair he'd put beneath the nest, and her face was rapturous. Alight. "They're beautiful," she said. It is those birds that Flip thinks of now as he runs. He remembers watching them stretch their wings and open their mouths and squawk their little hearts out every time he climbed up to see them. In the end, a possum came and did what a possum does. They never even flew.

WHEN KIRBY LEAVES the shelter, he heads for the beach. His boys would do almost anything for a beach day, and he's been promising them one since summer. They wouldn't be so bold—would they? He doesn't have any other ideas. The breakers are huge, crashing against the sand like the fists of gods, and he can feel the wind trying to separate his tires from the road. This is no time to be driving. He takes the shore road for a few miles, going slow, squinting through the deluge in both directions for any sign of them. There is none. The beachfront properties are dark and shuttered, the boardwalk utterly abandoned. The sky is stained a vivid purple and he can actually see the eyewall of the hurricane as it arrives, gray as stone. It's so close he could swim out to touch it.

By the pier, he sees two figures clutching at each other. They are too big to be Lucas and Flip, but he stops anyway and rolls down his window because no one should be out here like this. It's a teenage couple, the boy cradling a bottle of Jack Daniel's, presumably seeing how far they dare to venture from the sanctuary of their hotel's lobby.

"Are you fucking kidding me?" Kirby shouts. "Go the fuck inside before a tree falls on you."

"You go inside!" the boy replies. The girl sways into him, laughing and squinting at Kirby through the rain. He can see the rivers of mascara on her cheeks, pooling beneath her eyes. The kid next to her is just a stupid, drunk frat boy who missed his flight home when the airports shut down. Kirby has seen so many of these idiots that they're no longer individuals to him, just a category he could do without. But this girl—there is something about her that makes him look twice. Something that reminds him of Frida when they met. Her curls, her jagged edges, her bravery, the messy persistence of her.

Kirby rolls up his window and keeps driving, muttering to himself and looking back at the couple in his rearview. At the end of the board-walk, he turns west, up one of the little unpaved lanes. The palms that line it lean at unnatural angles, practically bent at the waist. He knows that the time to be outdoors is long past, that he should be driving like hell for home, but the idea of returning without his boys is impossible, and so he keeps searching.

Wanda has been at sea for long enough. She comes ashore, and when she does, the wind is no longer only wind. The wind is brimming, carrying a hundred million grains of sand, pieces of shell, dead jellyfish, strips of seaweed, drift-wood. Moving inland, carrying these spoils, she reaches down to gather more. Bigger things, heavier things: dinghies and signposts and trash cans and tree branches. She grinds against the earth, swallowing the town whole. Rudder is part of her for as long as she wants it. And everything in it is hers.

THE BOYS RUN like their lives depend on it, and by now, their lives do. Lucas is faster, but he turns to make sure that Flip is behind him every few minutes. It occurs to him that this is all his fault. The size of his mistake is suddenly clear. If only they had stayed home, like Flip wanted. He slows his pace so that Flip is running alongside him. They are vulnerable as they dart down the sandy trailer park lane and back out onto the road, going so fast they are skimming the ground, their little bodies moving toward home as if they might lift off at any moment, as if the furious churning of their legs could amount to the relative thrust of a bird's wings.

This startling momentum has in large part to do with the wind—which is stronger than anything they have ever experienced and is assisting their flight home, sailing up the backs of their shirts as they run and shoving them firmly west. But the wind on this stretch of road carries more than just two small boys; there is also: a broken microwave, a folding chair, a few flowerpots, some pruning shears, an empty bin, a lemon tree ripped up by its roots. The air is bristling with weapons, the rain cutting down into their tender scalps and the backs of their furiously pumping calves, the wind slamming into them at a speed that will quite literally carry them away should it increase any more. A small boy does not weigh so much more than a lemon tree.

As he runs, Lucas's thoughts cease; his guilt is on hold to accommodate this burst of adrenaline his veins require. He is only a body now, moving as quickly as it can, driven by a repository of energy that lies in wait for moments like this one. For a time, his legs move in exact unison, brief perfection, but it doesn't last nearly long enough.

One great sideways gust knocks Lucas's feet out from under him and he topples face-first into the asphalt. Flip pulls him up and pushes him forward. Lucas's nose is broken, a warm iron gush down his upper lip, skin raw where it met the road. He cradles his bloody face and tries to keep going, but the wind sends him back down to his knees. Flip is a few paces ahead by then; he turns and shouts *Come on*, but there is no sound. The sky seems to ripple above them, darker now, pulsing with movement. Lucas begins to cry, tears and rain and blood swirling into watery pink tracks on his cheeks, but he orders his legs to keep going and eventually he is running once more.

An empty recycling bin smashes into a tree trunk a few yards ahead of him on the road's shoulder. He runs faster. The red of Flip's T-shirt flickers in front of him—he is probably just a few yards ahead, but Lucas catches only glimpses of his brother.

Almost there, almost there, almost there, he thinks.

Faster, faster, faster, he thinks.

He knows he's almost home—but "almost" doesn't mean anything now.

FRIDA STILL HAS not moved from the doorway of the tool shed. Whether she cannot or will not is hard to say. The backyard—its patchy lawn flattened and full of migrating trash, its ailing citrus trees stripped of fruit—has become a wind-ravaged battleground. The stretch of earth between the tool shed and the house seems to sway before Frida, to ripple as if the ground is made of water. Perhaps it is? She is having trouble understanding what she is looking at. The pain that passes through her body again and again is debilitating; all of her energy is being funneled into simply bearing it.

At the edge of the tangled jungle that borders the yard, the trunk of one of the live oaks cracks and splinters. The sound is cacophonous, even in the midst of everything else. It seems to fall slowly, like a feather making its way down, but when it finally smashes into the ground, Frida feels it in the soles of her feet. As the other trees tip their branches to touch the earth and debris rushes past and rain drills down, the pain leaves her for a moment and she seizes her chance. Stumbling from the sheltered doorway of the shed, she wades into the rising water—so it is water after all. It's nearly to her ankles, pocked by the rain that is driving down so hard the drops hit the surface and then bounce back up again. The hurricane's voice is all around her and maybe also inside her, filling her head with a howling, mourning, bloodthirsty cry that seems to shake the ground. Frida battles forward and the mud sucks at her boots. The house grows nearer. The debris whizzes past. And the pain hits her again. It has a voice, too. Or is it her voice? Or is it theirs?

In the middle of the yard she has to stop. The violence happening inside her is so intense she can do nothing but bear it. She begins to keel over, her belly in her hands, filling her arms, pressing down on her legs, unable to stand up straight anymore. The house and the trees provide her some semblance of shelter from winds that will very soon be gusting fast enough to snatch a little boy clean off the ground and carry him into the clouds, but she cannot stay here. The pain will only get worse and walking will only get harder. She tries to make her legs move, but the mud grips the soles of her boots too tightly and then she is off balance and then she is falling, falling, on the ground, in the water and the mud, the grass beneath her palms, between her fingers, or is it seaweed, or is it whorls of soft baby hair, or are these her hands at all? How could these sensations possibly belong to her? How long until this ends?

FLIP SQUINTS TO see the road as he runs, trying to blink away the rain that is coming down so hard he feels like he might drown in it. It's not even coming down so much as it's coming from everywhere, pelting him from all directions.

If he were relying on his senses alone he would be hopelessly lost—he can barely see a few feet in front of him. But he and Lucas explored every inch of this road this summer. His memory shows him what is ahead. He knows there is a shabby blue house on his left, set back from the road, obscured by overgrown date palms; he knows an older woman with a kind face lives there; he knows that the road will curve to the right a few yards past this house, that then there will be a yellow mailbox, and then a little meadow where deer sometimes graze, where white egrets pose on their tall skinny legs, and then his own house. He knows that in good weather their home is maybe eight minutes away on foot. But now, in this chaos, he isn't sure that they will make it that far. If he is sure of anything, it's that they won't.

He hears a powerful whoosh behind him, and an entire felled cypress tree, roots and all, slides across the pavement. It shoots past him and careens into the ditch. Flip knows they have to get inside as quickly as they can; he knows that is what Kirby would tell them to do. He makes a beeline for the blue house on his left—he cannot see it yet, but he knows it's there. The woman who lives there is what

71

Kirby calls "neighborly." When she passes Kirby on the road they both lift a hand from the steering wheel in recognition. She will help. It doesn't even occur to him that she might have evacuated. He turns to make sure Lucas is behind him and screams *Hurry*. He notes the blood gushing down Lucas's face, the sluggishness in his gait. Yes, the house. They can make it to this house at least.

He lets himself imagine this refuge as he veers wildly about in the deluge, blindly searching for her porch. He will bang on the door with both fists and she will open it right away. Inside, everything will be fine. Lucas will be sorry that he was such a jerk this afternoon. The brothers will hug each other. The neighbor will hug them both. He will be wrapped in four arms and this shaking will stop, his eyes will stop smarting, a grown-up will be in charge once more. Inside, he will be safe.

Flip's body gives him another burst of adrenaline and he uses it as best he can, uprooted chunks of shrubbery rushing past him, little pieces of foliage driving into him. He can see the house now, just barely. It is exactly where he thought it was.

Almost there. But this wind—

The hurricane takes what yields. Nothing more; nothing less.

INSIDE THE BLUE house, Phyllis goes about her day, surrounded by squat candles and a battery-powered radio. She is prepared for this sort of thing. She is always, always prepared. The terms "prepper" and "survivalist" do not resonate for her, though she is certainly willing to cede that she is both of those things. The message boards have been lively since this hurricane was named, but there's nothing online that she doesn't already know. These perpetual questions—of whether to bug in or bug out, of what types of SHTF situations one needs to be preparing for, of whether to join forces with a local group or go solo—do not interest her. Her home is as fortified as it can be. Her provisions are fully stocked. She has enough guns and ammo to defend her property, but nothing extravagant like some of these yahoos, just an old handgun and a hunting rifle. She keeps an eye on the latest survivalist chatter and pipes in on the occasional canned goods or gardening thread. For the most part she observes but does not engage.

In her offline life, she downplays her own preparations if she discusses them at all—not because she is concerned about people knowing of her supplies and coming to rob her when the Shit Hits the Fan, as some preppers are, but because no one wants to hear about it. In the beginning, she was more concerned with spreading the word. She tried to convince her sister and her close friends that these preparations were necessary. That the world as they knew it was ending—maybe not today or tomorrow, but sooner than the powers that be would have them believe. Her sister recommended she see a therapist and eventually stopped returning her calls altogether. And her friends—well. They drifted away. So she learned to keep quiet about her work on the house, her investment in a second generator, her solar panel research, the stockpile of heirloom seeds in her pantry. She isn't bitter. They just couldn't see it the way she could. They weren't willing to look.

Now, with the hurricane beating at her shutters, she is not smug so much as confident. Comfortable. She is 90 percent certain that this house will withstand 175 mph winds—the 10 percent accounting for flukes, which are always a possibility. Every window has been replaced with hurricane glass. The roof was replaced a few years ago, with gale-force materials. Even in the event of a flood, she is fairly certain that the slight crest her home is built on, combined with its three-foot solid concrete foundation, will keep her above most moderate swells. But just in case, she has perched all of her furniture on top of cinder blocks and moved her most precious possessions to the second floor. She doesn't take chances on these sorts of things. She prepares for the worst.

The salary she earns teaching biology at the community college isn't enough to cover some of the more in-depth preparations she wanted to do, but when her father passed away a few years ago she was able to put her inheritance straight into the house. The investment was her version of a retirement plan—she had no use for stocks or bonds or annuities, so she spent the money on solar panels and an irrigation system. Her sister couldn't wrap her head around it. The last time they spoke there was no screaming, no horrible insults. Just a quiet chasm between them, becoming wider and wider until finally it had grown too wide. They'd never been close. The loss was more acute in theory than it was in practice. After a while, Phyllis realized she doesn't even miss their calls. She has no regrets. Her money is much better spent on supplies and modifications than sitting in some IRS account, only to disappear when the banks go belly-up. The generators, the garden beds, the fruit trees, the ground well, the weapons and the skills to use them—all of it. This is her future. She is done trying to convince anyone else that the sky is falling when all they need to do is look out the window.

Phyllis fixes herself a snack of sardines and crackers in the kitchen, then opens a fresh gallon of water and pours herself a glass. Outside, the hurricane wreaks havoc. In here, it is almost peaceful. Loud, but peaceful. She has a stack of tests to grade from her Intro to Biology course. Or maybe she'll begin that romance novel she picked up from the Goodwill instead. She adds some garlicky pickles she canned herself to the plate and licks her fingers. Not her best batch, but not her worst.

A repetitive thudding sound registers as she makes her way back down the hall to her living room—she assumed it was the trees knocking against one another, or a piece of debris battering against the siding. But no, it almost sounds as if it is coming from the front door. Is it…"knocking" is not the right word. It is an erratic, desperate pounding. She steps out into the hall, listens. Yes, it's coming from the front porch. She is hesitant to check. After all of this work to keep the outdoors out, why would she open the door and let it in? But there is something about it…something impossible to ignore. She undoes the dead bolts—there are three—and prepares to brace herself should the wind try to overpower her. She turns the knob.

There, on her front step, is a drenched little boy, his mouth open, his cries snatched away by the wind and tossed up into the sky. Quick as a flash, she reaches out, grabs a fistful of his shirt, pulls him inside, and slams the door.

KIRBY TUNES AND retunes the CB to channel 9. He checks the single reception bar on his cell phone, which flickers in and out. No news is hardly good news. He's driving at a crawl, barely able to discern road from ditch. At this rate, the eyewall is going to catch up to him and slam his entire vehicle into someone's house. He catches sight of an apartment building's sign on his right—THE PELICAN PERCH. It's a newer building, the kind with beach views and a door-man and probably a rooftop swimming pool. Kirby knows the type. A roost for wealthy snowbirds who will spend only a few weekends per year taking in the salt air before they tire of Florida and fly away to one of their other nests. There is an underground parking garage beneath, he recalls, and without pausing to consider he swings the steering wheel, jumps the curb, and manages to find the in ramp. There's a thin iron gate—there's always a gate with these people and their fucking beachfront properties. He drives straight through it.

Below, the garage is beginning to flood. Kirby idles there, surveying the half-empty lot—SUVs; a few sports cars in storage, wrapped up in tarps like enormous presents; an old painter's van, undoubtedly the maintenance vehicle, too dented to belong to anyone who might live here. The water does not trouble him in a truck this high and this heavy, not yet. He turns around to face the entrance of the garage and leans up against the steering wheel, straining to see what's happening on the street outside. Visibility is sparse. The radio crackles.

> Eye has made landfall in the township of Rudder   heavy
> rain potential flooding   a few blocks south of
>   Marriott, approximately half a mile wide
> speed measured 155 mph   repeat eye landfall

The eye. Of course. Could he…? He will. He can't just sit here and wait; he has to try. Kirby accelerates toward the ramp. Any minute now. He watches as a small fishing boat crashes into the storefront across the street from the mouth of the garage. So this is the eyewall, where the storm does its worst. He thinks about what these winds could do to a human body. Pictures it.

And then the quiet arrives. That eerie, inexplicable pause in the destruction. The rain ceases. The fishing boat falls to the earth, along with an accompanying shower of splintered siding and glass. Kirby guns it.

FRIDA TRIES TO hold on to the singleness of her purpose: making it back to the house. But there is so much happening, inside her and all around her. Her mind feels slippery, weak. She crawls across the flooding grass, dragging her limbs through the water that is continuing to rise. All she can do now is move in increments, and so she does. The wind rages above her head, but she stays close to the ground, on her hands and knees, making slow progress through the muck. There is a pause between contractions and she uses it to drag herself the rest of the way to the kitchen door, hauling herself to her feet with the sandbags as support. She loses a boot to the mud, sucked off her foot, and she goes on without it, hauling herself over the sandbags and falling through the door in one fluid motion.

Then the pain returns and she is overcome once more, on her back, on the floor, gripped with it. She watches the storm rage through the doorway, still open, and knows that she should seize the next moment of relief to separate herself from this violence. But she can't just now. The door slams against the side of the house, flailing in the wind. She is back to existing, to simply abiding what is happening within.

Frida has never seen a birth before, but she's read the books. She knows what the speed and intensity of her contractions means. It means she will have this baby soon and there will be no one here to help. Trying to remember any shred of information or advice that might get her through this and failing to think of a single thing, she sees the scattered oranges that were swept from the table and onto the floor when she first opened the door, the shards of the bowl they occupied surrounding them. The nearest piece of fruit is beside her head, a luminous globe not unlike a small sun, rocking back and forth in a dip in the tile as the wind comes inside. She tries to focus on this orange, inhales its ripeness, imagines that its skin, that rich flame of color, is emitting the energy she needs. She begins to push, almost involuntarily, and it is as though her pelvis cracks open. An agony not of this world floods through her. The door, she keeps thinking—*The door, I have to close it.* As if that matters now. It's still open. It stays open. She pushes again. Doesn't want to, isn't ready, but she can barely stop herself. Is this right? Is she doing it right? Nothing about this is right. From the floor she can see the dark sky spinning, can hear the storm screaming, or maybe it's her, or maybe it's both of them.

INSIDE THE EYE, the storm is quieter. The rain ceases to fall. The wind is almost gentle. Kirby drives as fast as he can without breaching its border. The roar of the eyewall, of its edges, seems to come from a great distance, though it isn't far away at all.

Where there was a cacophony a moment ago there is calm. The palms on either side of the road sway back into their upright shape. The sun shines through above him. Ahead, the wall of the hurricane is enormous—a churning mass of cloud that is somehow dark and luminous at the same time. The storm moves quickly, its eye roaming over the road he needs to get home. He is grateful for this miracle. But every mile that he drives has already seen the wrath of the eyewall, and the devastation makes him physically ill. He skirts the debris in the road when he can and drives over it when he can't. This is only the halfway mark—the other edge of the eyewall will come to bear soon enough and the destruction he's passing through now will double. Later, the surge will destroy what's left. There are moments when he can see the other side of the wall in his rearview mirror. He can only imagine what the destruction behind him must look like. Suddenly, improbably, the phone on the bench seat rings. He snatches it up, answers it without looking at the screen, his eyes fastened to the treacherous road in front of him.

"Yes," he barks.

"This is Phyllis Donner, from down the street? The blue house…" The connection is bad, of course; he strains to fill in the gaps of what she's saying to him.

Kirby is confused. "Okay…" he says, and almost drops the phone as he swerves around a tree limb in the road. "Can I…Are you all right?"

"I'm fine. I have your son here. I—he's not saying much, but he put in your number. I just want you to know he's okay. I'll keep him here until it's over."

Kirby is at a loss for words. Relief floods his nervous system. He scrambles, reaching; something is wrong with this, this tidal wave of relief has come too soon, and then he finds it.

"Where's the other one?"

"The other…" she says slowly, not understanding.

"The other boy. Which kid do you have?"

PHYLLIS HANGS UP and looks at the boy sitting on her sofa, dripping, a pink towel wrapped around his narrow shoulders. He's still shaking, so wet she can't tell if these are tears streaming down his face or rain. She sits down next to him.

Of course, she thinks. *Where is the other one?* There are always two, always together, these boys. She saw them everywhere this summer— riding their little matching bicycles, clambering down the edge of the ditch opposite her house to look for crayfish in the stream that trickles by.

She puts her arm around this tiny creature who seems to fancy himself so large but in reality is small at the best of times and smaller still in this moment.

"Where's your brother?" she asks, as gently as she can. He stares straight ahead, either unable or unwilling to speak to her. She wraps him against her, feeling his sharp little bones against her chest. "You have to tell me, hon." She holds his head against the drape of her breast, trying to still the severity of his shaking with her own solid- ness. He begins to sob. She holds him tighter.

"Gone," the boy says, but the word is choked from him as if there is an invisible fist tightening around his throat.

"Gone where?" she asks, and lifts his chin to make him look at her. Blood drips from his nose, cut with water. She can almost taste the iron, the salt, accumulating on the valley of his upper lip and then spilling over into his half-open mouth. He is panting, unable to catch his breath. She carefully wipes his nose with the towel, observing that it's broken. *We'll have to set that*, she thinks. But for now: "Try to breathe slow, honey," she says, and shows him. "Breathe like this. Where's he gone?"

He draws a ragged inhale through his nostrils; a bubble of bloody snot blooms and then pops as he exhales. "Just…gone."

"Did you see? What did you see?"

"I saw," he says, and will not say another word until long after all of this is over.

"OH GOD," KIRBY says, falling to his knees. "Oh my god. Are you okay? Where's your brother?" And then he crushes Lucas against his chest and wraps his arms around him before he even has a chance to answer. Kirby can't help it, he must fold himself around this child at all costs.

He finally lets the boy pull away from his broad, soaking-wet chest. He cups the back of his son's head in his big hand, presses their foreheads together.

"Tell me now. Where is he?"

Lucas begins to cry. Kirby looks to Phyllis, who turns out her hands to show him that she has no answers. "All I could get out of him is that his brother is gone. He won't say anything else."

Kirby holds his boy for another second and then tries to call Frida, but that slim, flickering bar of service is gone entirely now. He stares at the dark void of his phone's screen and keeps trying anyway. Lucas sobs against his father's chest, teeth chattering, unable to form words, just wails. Kirby is lost now, unsure of what he needs to do next. In this moment he feels exactly like his son looks, like he is a small boy who for a brief time pretended to be a man, only to realize that he doesn't know how to protect the people he loves. The worst has arrived, even after Kirby assured them all it wouldn't. He holds Lucas tighter, too tight, but also not nearly tight enough.

AFTER AN IMPOSSIBLY long time but also a relatively short while, after an overwhelming amount of screaming and agony and effort, there is somehow a baby girl in the room with Frida. She's wet, fragile, and upset about being evacuated from her home, though she is technically still attached to it. Frida wraps her in a dish towel within reach and wipes away the goop on the baby's face with her fingers.

The door is gone by now, ripped from its hinges, and the hurricane still rages just outside. The kitchen is in shambles: cabinet doors hanging askew, dirty dishes smashed against the wall. Somehow, nothing has touched Frida where she lies. Somehow, she has willed this small sliver of space she occupies into safety.

Frida looks down at the baby and something like electricity passes between them—a brief spark, a small jolt. Frida feels it enter her skin and skim along her veins, up into her thundering heart. At this moment, the wind outside pauses. If she didn't know better, she'd think it was over. Frida does know better, but she's still too exhausted to think about what waits on the other side of the eye. She just curls her body in the quiet center of the circling storm, sinking into the solace of her own kitchen floor, allowing the pause in all of this fury to wash over her. There is a *shhh* in her ears, a gentle rush like the faraway sound of a conch shell. The baby wails in her arms, but it's as if they are both underwater.

"Storm baby," she whispers, "Wanda baby." She hears her own voice from inside her head, as if spoken by someone else, and lays her screaming daughter on the floor, nestled on her back in the blue-checkered dish towel, stained with spaghetti sauce or blood or both. Her body is a crescent moon around her daughter—a meager barrier, but the best she can offer—and now that she has managed this much, whatever power of will has sustained her this long leaves her. She closes her eyes, knowing she should keep them open, knowing that her work here has only just begun, and yet all of that knowing is not nearly enough. Something has gone wrong. She can feel it. There's too much blood on the floor, too little left for her veins. She should try to stanch the flow somehow, but the distance between thinking this and acting on it is vast. The baby cries. The eye passes. The storm returns. In fact, it never left.

BEFORE KIRBY HAS time to search for his youngest, the other side of the storm comes to bear. Wind batters the blue house as he keeps trying to call Frida, unwilling to accept the futility of this action, allowing himself to imagine that she will answer and tell him Flip is safely in her arms, all the while knowing by the look on Lucas's face that Flip is not safe. He goes on dialing and redialing as if he doesn't know better than anyone the kind of labor it will take to resurrect this invisible thread of connection.

The three of them wait, not speaking. What is there to say? Phyllis busies herself, setting Lucas's nose and cleaning his face, drying his hair, insisting he drink a few sips of water. Kirby begins to pace. Every once in a while he goes to the door as if to leave and Phyllis has to remind him that there is nothing he can do out there. She guides him back to the sofa, to Lucas. But even beside one another, living through the same hell, they are alone.

When the wind allows it, they go home. It's so close but even that short distance is fraught. The road is strewn with wreckage: branches and trash and rainwater so thick and fast he can feel the current pulling at his tires. And rising. At home, the water is almost up to his knees. There's a storm surge coming—he's worked too many disaster zones not to expect it. He lifts Lucas down from the cab like he is a toddler again and carries him inside. He isn't thinking about Frida yet. He's still focused on the absence of his youngest and now, the weight of his oldest.

It's only when he sees her—on the floor, in the space between being and not being, curled around a screaming newborn as she comes loose, like a smooth silk ribbon slipping out of its bow—that he realizes how completely he has failed. He doesn't know what to do. Has he ever not known what to do? The sea of red she's floating in is too deep and the baby is crying so loud he can't think. He sets Lucas down. Call 911, of course, of course—but there's still no signal and even if he uses his CB…emergency services won't be coming out for another hour at least. Drive her himself? But the roads, the inevitable storm surge—Lucas—Flip—the hospital is miles away. He sets Lucas down, wanting to shield him from this moment but not knowing how. It is upon them. They are inside it. He would hurry to the other side, but the only thing more impossible than the moment they're in is the one that follows. Then the one after that.

He sees his daughter cry, her tiny limbs pedaling through this strange new element. He sees the blood, impossibly bright, mixing with the amniotic fluid on the tiles, shimmering. Beside him, Lucas is silent and small. Kirby gets down on his knees and bows his head close to Frida's. Her eyes are open, but she is looking at him from very far away. "Didn't I do good?" she asks him. "Kirb. Look at her."

"You did real good," he says. "You and her both." He takes his utility knife from his belt and cuts the cord. Time is moving strangely now. The tug of his blade against this otherworldly matter, curled like the cord of a telephone receiver, a silent conversation between mother and daughter. The thrust of the baby's feet as she kicks. The quiet smile Frida gives him when he fits his huge hand around his daughter's head and brings her to his chest.

"Her name…" Frida says. "I like Wanda."

"Fri, no."

She shakes her head, ever so slightly. "Wanda. Sounds right. I'm sure." Whether she realizes what she's asking of him or not, he can't know for certain. There's no time to discuss it. She drifts, and all he can do is watch her go. He hears the storm surge arriving outside, rushing against the sandbags he stacked so carefully, trickling into the house wherever it can.

"Hold your sister," Kirby says, and places his daughter in Lucas's arms. Kirby takes off his shirt, trying to stanch the bleeding between Frida's legs, knowing he can't help her anymore but needing to try anyway, feeling the blood soak through the knees of his pants and listening to the siren of his own wailing infant. This is how Wanda arrives. This is the world she belongs to.

WATER

If the ocean is a body, then the waves are its tongue, long and blue-gray, licking at the beach until there's nothing left. This body is wide and full and deep. It rises, wrapping itself around the world, squeezing the land tight between its thighs. Ten years mean nothing to a body like this. It's been here since the beginning.

EVERY TIME HE speaks her name he remembers. "Wanda." Her head snaps up, a guilty look on her face, though she's done nothing wrong. That he knows of. Kirby tries not to see Frida in the way she flicks her gold-brown eyes toward him, but that's impossible. All these years later, Frida is still everywhere he looks. "What did you get up to today?" She pushes her macaroni around on the plate with her fork, spearing it one cheesy tube at a time.

"Nothing," she says, in a way that means she got up to a great many things she doesn't want him to know about. Lucas gives a short, one-note laugh and serves himself more of the pulled pork. His son, his only son, twenty-two now, has grown into a quiet, careful man. After the hurricane, Chloe took Lucas away from him, raging that he had allowed such a thing to happen. She was right to punish him. Right to take his boy. The search for Flip's body lasted days, and by the time they found him—well. It is, has always been, unspeakable. Kirby knew the blame was his. He didn't fight Chloe on any of it, didn't object to threats of a lawsuit or the midnight phone calls when all she did was scream at him. He took it as barely a fraction of his due. If he could have died, too, he would have. But he couldn't. He was needed.

That first year alone with an infant was harder than anything he could have imagined. Every time Wanda cried, he woke up and remembered anew what he'd lost. It felt like drowning again and again and again, gasping for air alone in his bed as everything came rushing back to him. But there was Wanda, reaching for him. For her, he found his breath. He got up, made the formula, changed the diaper, and anchored himself to what he had left. To who he had left.

"Nothing, huh," Lucas says.

"Nothing fun, anyway," Wanda replies.

They eat off of paper plates in the twilit kitchen, the flame of a citronella candle quivering among the plastic deli containers that crowd the table. A half-empty bottle of cola sits, open, losing its fizz. It's been more than a week since they had power. Almost two. Kirby's crew, which now includes Lucas, work the lines as fast as they can, but it's becoming harder to get the lights back on after the hurricanes pound the coast, year after year, storm after storm. There is so much equipment they don't have, only so much daylight, and never enough line workers. This time, Miami took the brunt of the damage from Hurricane Valerie, and although the fringes that Rudder got were still enough to bring down the grid, it could have been so much worse. Even so, they've been working round the clock ever since the wind died down. The crew is smaller now. The work is bigger. Kirby watches Lucas from across the table and feels proud that his son has chosen to follow him into this battle against the elements.

When Wanda was three, Lucas returned to Rudder. Chloe moved to Minneapolis with her new husband, and Lucas chose to stay with Kirby. Insisted on it. He still has no idea what the kid went through to convince her, but he got his way in the end. Two became three. At fifteen, he was a different boy than Kirby had known in the Before years. The mean streak Kirby used to worry about, that cocky bravado, was replaced with something else. Vigilance. A tremor in his hands. A wary furrow on his forehead. Wanda, just beginning to become aware, to remember, fastened her soft brown eyes on Lucas and claimed him, just as she had claimed Kirby the day she was born. The rule of this household is that Wanda occupies its center. She is their sun, and in return for their venerations she gifts them with a levity they would have otherwise forgotten is possible.

The mosquitoes whine around the open door. Nights like these, it's either fling open the house and bear the mosquitoes, or swelter. The breeze ruffles their paper plates. "You're behaving yourself while we're gone?" Kirby presses.

In response, she looks at him and chews with her mouth wide open, smacking her lips.

"Don't worry," he says, "school's starting up again soon. Won't be long now."

"I never want to go back to school," she says, suddenly serious, mouth closed.

"Oh?" Kirby takes another scoop of potato salad.

"Or daycare neither. I'm too old for daycare."

"We'll see about that," Kirby says.

"I'm ten," she insists.

"Almost ten." *How did that happen?* he wonders.

After Wanda is in bed and the leftovers have been tucked away in the cooler on a bed of melting ice, Kirby and Lucas sit on the porch in the dark and listen to the buzz of mosquitoes, the singing frogs, the fluttering bats.

"You hear about Miami-Dade?" Lucas asks.

"What about?"

"Governor's pulling the plug on the whole county."

"Where'd you hear that?"

"Guy I know from high school lives down there now. Works at the power plant. He says they're winding down city services. Offering relocation packages to folks."

"That so." Kirby doesn't want to believe that this is true. And yet—watching the brisk disintegration of the developed world this past decade has instilled in him a mounting expectation that things will get worse. Always worse and never better. This is a collective experience, surely, a despair sewn into the fabric of his generation, but for Kirby it's more than that. He knows doom's true face. It's more mundane than he thought it would be: the strange glimmer in a swirl of blood mixed with amniotic fluid on tile. An empty bed. An unused bicycle. Frida felt it all coming. But now he's the one who has to live with it.

"They're trying to keep it quiet. Election year and whatever. But it's only a matter of time."

"Time before what?"

"Before everyone knows."

"Mm. Not sure what difference that'll make."

"People will…they'll protest. They won't go. There would be news coverage and, and…I don't know, it's not like people just won't notice a city like Miami disappear. They'll do something."

In the dark, Kirby nods. "I'm sure you're right," he says. But he isn't sure at all. All sorts of things have disappeared over the years. He knew Valerie hit Miami hard, but he didn't realize it was this hard. He didn't realize it was give-up-and-go hard. He remembers how it was in Puerto Rico. There were protests, sure, and there was news coverage—but none of it made a difference. The government didn't even bother with relocation packages. It just abandoned over three million people to their ruined infrastructure, their crumbling homes, the ravenous ocean. Politics, economics, racism, and geography coalesced to mark the first domino. But where there is one domino, there are more. "I'm gonna turn in," he announces, draining what's left of his beer.

"Leave the door. I'll sit awhile," Lucas replies. Kirby would like to say something reassuring to his son. Even more, he'd like to say something true. But the convergence of these qualities is rare when it comes to the future of certain parts of the world. The pause stretches, then deepens as he tries to think of something he can offer. It's no good. He hears Lucas's thoughts because they are also his own: *If Miami isn't worth saving, then Rudder has no chance at all.*

IN THE MORNING, through the haze of a dream she can't remember, Wanda hears them in the kitchen. There is the clink of a thermos, the clump of work boots. Low voices murmuring. It's too early for the sun, too early for most people. But not for her people.

She cracks her eyelids, and between the soft fur of lashes she sees Lucas pass by the open door of their bedroom. He's trying to be quiet, but his footsteps are heavy. It's already hot. More accurately, it never stopped being hot. She kicks the sheet off of her feet and shout-whispers his name. He comes in, puts his face next to hers where she is sprawled on the top bunk. "Morning, Wan," he says, and rests his chin on her mattress.

"You leaving already?"

"Yeah, in a minute." Her pillow is in the process of sliding off the bed and he lifts her head to slip it back where it belongs. She lets him. "I made you a lunch," he says. "It's in the cooler. But remember, open and shut real quick, okay?"

"I know," she says. He turns to go just as Kirby appears in the doorway.

"Ready?" their father asks, and Lucas nods. Kirby squints at Wanda to see if she's awake. "Don't get into any trouble. And when you open that cooler—"

"I *know*," Wanda says. She's heard all this before.

"Ah. Well. Have a fun day. Be good." Kirby and Lucas leave. She can hear the front door slam, then the truck doors, one, two, then the engine, then quiet. *Be good.* She is mostly good. But being good and having a fun day are not the same thing. There's a particular rule she'd like to break, one she's been toying with ever since her time became her own—but it's a big one. She's not sure she'll get away with it. To be good or not to be: This has been the week's soliloquy. Each night, she resolves that tomorrow is the day she'll ride her bike to the Edge. And each morning, she talks herself out of it. Except— today might be her last chance. The return to school looms. She dozes, thrashing around until the sheets feel sticky.

When the sun is up she stalls some more, lying on the grass to read her novel, in which a boy detective hunts a killer in a blustery ski resort. The book makes her unbearably curious about snow, a phenomenon she has never seen in person. In this heat, even imag- ining the cold seems impossible. And again, her mind drifts to the Edge. It would be cooler there, at least. Around eleven, she retrieves the peanut butter and jelly sandwich that Lucas made her, defiantly leaving the cooler open while she takes her time digging beneath last night's leftovers for the right kind of soda to go with it (grape), and then wanders through the stifling house as she eats. All the secrets that are here for her to find have already been found, but she likes to visit them when she's alone. She checks on the milk crate in the back of Kirby's closet, full of relics from her mother. She isn't supposed to know that it exists, but she discovered it a few years ago. Wiping her jellied fingers on her shirt, she sorts through its contents—a few books about architecture, a neatly folded bedspread someone sewed by hand, a wedding ring that doesn't fit any of her fingers. At the bottom, a nylon flag, so sun-worn the black is turning brown, a jaunty skull and crossbones smiling back at her. A photograph of Kirby and Frida in front of the house, and another of Frida with her own mother, the two of them young and happy on the deck of a sailboat. There is a spiral-bound notebook here, too. Handwritten, barely legible. Wanda has already scanned its pages for passages she might be able to decipher, but there isn't much she can make out besides a few sketches of something that looks like a tree house. This is how her mother's presence feels—near, but unknowable.

Frida's dresses still hang, pressed back against the wall, smelling of a woman Wanda never knew but likes to imagine. In her mind, Frida is so beautiful it's impossible to look at her head-on. She's just a warm feeling that surrounds Wanda with a pair of strong, pillowy arms. This is all Frida will ever be to her, but the absence is too ubiquitous to be acute. Wanda sits on the floor of the closet and finishes her sandwich, then presses her face against the soft hems of Frida's clothes, imagining what she might have been like. Kirby and Lucas both look sad when Wanda asks about her mother outright, so she's learned to acquire information sideways, in fragments: the name of the boat Frida grew up on, the university she went to, her skills in the kitchen, a bridge she designed but never built. In this fashion, she learns bits and pieces about Flip, too, but she doesn't ache for the idea of a brother in the same way. She has Lucas.

She tires of these fantasies about her mother and goes back outside to ponder whether today is the day she breaks her father's biggest rule. She started by breaking smaller rules this week, just to see what would happen. A few days ago, she climbed a tree she is not allowed to climb and sat up there reading until she heard Kirby's engine on the road. Yesterday, she sat in the forbidden mustiness of the shed and carved her initials into the floorboards under the workbench, then pawed through every drawer, every bucket, opened every toolbox. Afterward, she anxiously awaited her punishment for these trespasses. All during dinner last night, she anticipated discovery—but nothing happened. Kirby and Lucas sat at the table and exchanged condiments and shoveled food onto their plates and into their mouths, but nothing was said about Wanda's vandalism in the tool shed, or her adventure skyward. She isn't sure what she'd expected. Maybe an unseen camera, or a supernatural sixth sense. But apparently

Kirby has neither. Unchastened, she contemplates a new pinnacle of disobedience.

She's not often allowed to stay home by herself, but the woman who runs the daycare evacuated before the storm and still hasn't returned. Wanda hopes she won't come back at all, and the truth is, she might not. That's not unusual these days. The population thins with each passing year. Every time the schools close, a few more students are missing when they reopen. The inhabitants of Rudder are slowly catching on that the time to cut their losses has arrived. But Wanda doesn't think of it in these terms. She has been watching the town empty, the water rise, the storms pummel, as far back as she can remember. This is the rhythm she was born to. Kirby is old enough to remember arguments about whether climate change was real. Lucas is old enough to remember when tourists still came. But to Wanda, these things are only stories, so distant they might as well be fiction.

She would have preferred to be on storm duty this week, playing in the cab of the bucket truck while Kirby and Lucas work on the downed lines, but Kirby got in trouble after a surprise visit from the city manager the last time he brought her along. So here she is, home alone, forced to be either bored or bad. She squints up at the sky, trying to determine the time. Lucas told her you can tell by the position of the sun. One o'clock? Two? She can't remember which position is which. Clouds are piled high against the flat land, billowing layers of whipped cream that taste like warm, wet earth. She decides that today is the day after all.

The Edge is the place where the ocean meets the boardwalk. It's four or five miles away, over the causeway that spans the Intracoastal and down through the sandy blocks filled with Beachside bungalows, but Wanda has been there only a few times. Kirby doesn't like crossing the causeway, and she isn't allowed to ride her bicycle on the street by herself. When she asks if he'll take her, he always says, *No joy in visiting the scene of nature's crimes.* She doesn't know what this means, just that the Edge is one more thing Kirby doesn't allow. There is so much he doesn't allow.

Wanda doesn't remember things like the serenity of pale sand separating the most expensive houses from the water; sun umbrellas planted in the dunes like jewels; gulls descending en masse on picnickers who should know better; the scattered glimmers of jelly-fish abandoned by the tide. All this is gone now. All she'll ever know is the encroaching Edge. The place where the ocean eats away at the streets.

She goes over the route one more time in her mind. It's difficult to picture—she doesn't know the roads very well. The Beachside neighborhood might as well be in another state. It's out the driveway and to the left, that much is easy. And then it's a long while on that road, and then another left, sort of near the house with the pink shut-ters, and...here it becomes fuzzy. But, she reasons, this destination is hard to miss. Her bicycle is ready. There's nothing to bring. It's just a matter of figuring it out as she goes. So she goes.

When her tires leave the mud of the driveway and hiss against the damp asphalt, there's no point doubting her plan anymore. Leaning into the wind as it flies down the neck of her ratty, too-big T-shirt, she pedals faster. There is more excitement in this singular rush of speed than there was in all the days since Valerie hit. She pumps her legs, stands up on the pedals. She'd like to let out a whoop but reminds herself that this is a covert operation. Best not to draw attention. Crossing the causeway, she looks over the railing into the river, which froths against the bridge and reaches toward the ruined houses perched on either side of its banks. She's heard Kirby say that the causeway won't last much longer, and now, looking down at the hungry water, she understands why. The bridge feels tenuous and impermanent as she crosses it, like a swaying rope bridge across a yawning abyss.

The closer she gets to the waterfront, the more wreckage there is—

much of it old, some of it fresh. Houses lie in deconstructed piles by the side of the road: slabs of Sheetrock, strips of wall-to-wall carpet, scattered shingles covered in moss and mold. Many of the structures still standing are abandoned. Ahead, a stranded buoy perches on the embankment, nestled among green waves of soggy grass, but that's been there for years. In certain places, the road itself is just gone— eaten away in big, jagged bites by an invisible mouth. Here and there, the hum of a generator, but for the most part, quiet: After Valerie, the power is back only in the municipal buildings and the homes nearest to them. That means the emergency clinic, the post office, the fire station—and finally, as of a few days ago, the school and city hall. She dreads returning to her classroom tomorrow, although the promise of air-conditioning is a small consolation. Most of the residential streets, including hers, are still waiting for their electricity, for Kirby's crew to do a job they barely have enough hands for. Sweltering and waiting.

A station wagon loaded down with an entire life passes Wanda, and a little boy in the back seat gives her the finger as she turns to look in the window. She wonders if they're coming or going. Returning to see how their home has fared, or heading north for good? She tries to return the gesture, but she's too slow and by the time she is able to free a hand from the handlebars, the car is gone. She's in a part of town that she doesn't recognize. Everything here is battered and salt-stained. The smell of the ocean is strong, rushing into her like a physical thing as she rides—a shove, an embrace. She's close; that much she knows.

She begins to wonder whether she's gotten turned around and becomes too busy peering down side streets to notice the ocean looming up out of the sky right in front of her. Her arrival is sudden: One moment there's pavement, a sand-dusted street lined with rotting bungalows, and then, suddenly, the street ends and the murky water begins. The Edge of everything. In some places, the asphalt is jagged and broken; in others, it slopes right down into the sea. Wanda flips out the kickstand on her bike and approaches the water with caution. She has heard all kinds of stories about what the ocean can do to unsuspecting children, but it doesn't look so scary here. A wave sweeps up the street a few feet and then slips back out. She finds a rock to sit on and fastens her eyes on the enormous expanse before her. There is a boat out there. A shrimper maybe, trawling out past a mostly sunk marina. To the left, a crumbling high-rise grows up out of the water, a strange sea creature rearing its head. Wanda has heard the stories: These ruins used to be where the rich people lived, but they're all gone now. Their properties went from beachfront to waterfront to among-the-waves in just a decade. Twenty years ago, this would have been hard to imagine. Now, it just is.

Wanda is loosely aware of the Before. She knows that every year on her birthday the town mourns Hurricane Wanda and the havoc it wrought on their homes, and she knows that this is also the anniversary of her mother's death. Flip's, too. These are facts with which she is familiar. But none of it has depth for her. Like the surface of the ever-encroaching waves, it just is, and always has been. All that's left are artifacts: the ruined high-rises, the milk crate in Kirby's closet, the child-size bicycle stowed under the porch that she must never touch.

She understands that she isn't liked at school; that much is obvious. There are smaller reasons for that—her clothes, men's T-shirts full of holes, or her questions in class, one after another—but none of these things is the whole story. What she doesn't quite understand is that the town of Rudder is dying, and its inhabitants need a reason. Here is Wanda: born at exactly the wrong time, under exactly the wrong circumstances, given exactly the wrong name. The blame settles on her shoulders easily, small as they are. It's Rudder's own mythology, passed from parent to child, gossip that became stories that became beliefs—as thoughtfully constructed as the crumbling homes they live in.

Wanda did have one friend, Jules, and one was enough. But Jules's family moved at the end of the last school year and now Wanda has zero friends. Which is not enough. She sits here at the Edge for a long time, missing Jules, whose face grows fuzzy in her memory, and watching the gulls who perch on the high-rise as they chatter to one another. There is so much to observe, so many things to skim her gaze across, so many smells, so many textures. Even in its monotony, the ocean can't help but be mesmerizing. Wanda has never gotten to sit like this and just look for as long as she likes. This is her first real adventure, her first foray into the world beyond her house all alone. Without Kirby or Lucas she feels free, but also exposed. As it happens, she is both.

She doesn't notice the other kids arrive. There are four of them, two boys and two girls, out wandering these nearly deserted streets in search of something to do, not unlike Wanda herself. There is a brief moment—Wanda's back is still turned and the others are too far away to mark the distinct froth of her dark hair and the particular rattan basket attached to her bicycle—when these five children could be anyone to each other. They could be friends or they could be strangers. But then this moment passes. The newcomers recognize her and something shifts. They are not strangers. But they're not friends, either.

"What are you doing here?" one of the boys calls. It's more accusation than question.

"Yeah, this spot is private," the other boy says. "No freaks allowed."

Wanda turns. She recognizes this quartet as sixth graders, the grade just above hers. Older kids. They are often together, these four: a set of fraternal twins, Corey and Brie, and their respective best friends, Mick and Amanda. She isn't sure how to respond at first. She's naive enough to hope that what she says next matters, but old enough to know it probably won't.

"I'm not a freak," she says, and instantly knows it was the wrong thing. She plucks nervously at her T-shirt and hopes they move on. But they don't. They approach, hemming her in against the ocean.

"Aren't you?" Mick lunges forward and shoves her. It happens so fast she topples easily into the water. Her head goes under and as she plunges down to the bottom her arm scrapes up against the jagged pavement. It isn't so deep; her feet touch and she kicks off to get back to the surface, but she had no time to prepare herself. Water gushes up into her nose. Her eyes smart. She comes to the surface, gasping, spitting, her arms flailing in the dull gray water. Above her, the sixth graders are a blur. The other boy, Corey, steps in front of her. He crouches, blocking her exit, his face closer than she'd like it to be. A wave thuds into the back of Wanda's head and washes over his tennis shoes, but he doesn't seem to mind.

"What's the water like?" Corey asks. His voice is soft, almost gentle, but there is something hard underneath, something cruel. Calculating. Wanda paddles with her hands, her toes a few inches from the bottom.

"It's cold," she finally says. This is true; the water is cold, in a good way. The air is wet with humidity, like breathing steam, and the Atlantic, though warmer than it often is, feels chilly in comparison. She understands that this is not what he's asking, but the answer to that other question, the one beneath the words, eludes her. She ventures closer to the pavement, planting her hands to hoist herself out of the water, but Corey pushes her backward, his palm up against her forehead. His hand is hot and sticky on her skin as he shoves her. He would like to hurt her. She knows that now. They all know. Mick smirks, intrigued. The girls look uncertain. They don't want this. Wanda fastens her hopes on them. They are the audience, and the audience decides, don't they? To admonish or to join; to boo or to clap. Wanda looks at them through stinging, watery eyes, a white haze of salt caught in her lashes, silently beseeching them to protect her. But they say nothing. Corey puts his hand on the top of Wanda's head, his fingers digging into her wet hair, gripping it by the roots. "Why don't you stay awhile?"

And then she is underwater in a much more forceful way. She thrashes up toward the surface but he holds her down. She can feel his fingernails scraping against her scalp, pinching the skin. Everything is dark; she can't look up toward the sky, can't see through the murk. She doesn't fully understand what has just happened, why she is underwater, why she can't get to the surface.

Above, a few eerily quiet seconds pass. The sound of splashing, the call of gulls, the slap of little waves kissing the Edge. Corey holds Wanda down easily. All it takes is one hand, leaning his body weight into her struggle.

"Corey," Brie says, her voice sharp. "Enough." She knows that if she doesn't do something, no one will.

"Just playing." He grins back at his twin, wanting to see how far he can push this.

"Yeah, we're just messing," Mick says.

"Stop, seriously." Brie steps forward, as if to stop him herself, but then—the sixth graders are unable to explain what happens next. Below the ocean's gray surface, something unusual is occurring. The struggling shadow that is Wanda's flailing, submerged body brightens. It isn't the sun, which is hidden behind a thick pile of cloud. It is…something else. In the moment that it takes the sixth graders to witness this change, to examine each of the possible explanations and discard them, the light spreads, consuming the waves in streaks, until it looks like the entire ocean is shining in a way these four children have never seen. It's as though the water has swallowed a swirling, living galaxy: a trillion stars, burning cool blue or pale yellow or a hot, flickering violet. It's hard to say what color it is because it's every color and none at all.

Underwater, Wanda can't see any of this. She can't see anything— but she can feel something strange occurring in her body, a sensation she can't name rising to the surface of her skin. Corey releases Wanda's head in his surprise and she claws her way back up, spitting water, sucking air, grasping for the Edge so desperately it looks like she has four arms instead of two. He backs away from her and the light goes out. The water is the same gray it was before. It was only seconds, there and then gone. The older kids glance at each other, sheepish, unsure.

"Did you..." Mick begins.

"Yeah." Amanda nods. "That was—"

"Freaky." Corey's shorts are wet where Wanda splashed them, but he doesn't notice. "She's a freak. I told you."

Brie just stares: at Wanda, at the water. Trying to make sense of the two.

"Let's go," Amanda says, and the others nod, an unspoken consensus that they have crept too close to something they don't understand. Brie pauses as they hurry away from the Edge. For a second Wanda thinks the older girl might ask if she's all right, might help her up, but in the end she just looks at the ground, mutters, "Sorry," and runs to catch up with the others. Wanda is left alone, clinging to the broken edge of Beachside Drive, coughing up water and mucus. Eventually, she hauls herself back onto the pavement and sprawls there on her stomach. Her chest heaves against the road and she contemplates the particles of sea salt that have been caught by the fine hair on her forearms, stars trapped in a sun-bleached, gossamer net. She lies there for longer than she intends. The water slips up over her legs like a blanket, then back down, again and again. She's aware that something strange has happened, but doesn't know what. All she knows is that she feels different, like something inside her that used to be closed is now open.

LUCAS WATCHES HIS father pace, the veins pulsing in Kirby's forehead like a subterranean river system. Wanda wasn't here when they got home and neither was her bike. The quiet panic of these two men continues to mount with every second she does not appear: Kirby's face reddening, shade by shade; Lucas's fingernails floating up to his mouth, his teeth gnawing closer and closer to the quick.

"I'll go," Kirby says. "You wait here. Maybe she's…" Neither one of them wants him to finish his sentence.

"Try the creek first. She always wants to go looking for crawdads."

"Right, right." Kirby palms his keys. "The creek." Lucas watches as all kinds of horrors flicker behind Kirby's eyes. These two are skilled at imagining the worst. It's muscle memory. There is no comfort found in the usual reservoirs of hope: *what are the odds, it's probably nothing, pray for the best.* None at all.

"Are you sure I shouldn't look, too?" Lucas asks. "On the road. Or on the other side of the nature reserve." Confronted with the idea of waiting here in the empty house, he can feel his intestines twist.

"No," Kirby says. "Stay here. She could come back. I need you to call me if she comes back." Lucas nods and resigns himself to following Kirby's instructions. He's been following Kirby's instructions faithfully for many years now. Whatever part of him wanted to rebel died with his little brother. Now he does what is asked of him.

But in the end, Kirby's instructions are moot because at that moment Wanda rides into the driveway. Lucas sees her first, through the kitchen window, over Kirby's shoulder. Water drips from her clothes and her hair is matted, its volume diminished. He runs outside and Kirby follows. "Are you okay?" they both shout at the same time. She climbs off her bike and lets it fall on the ground, kickstand forgotten.

"Where have you been?" Kirby demands. Lucas watches her face carefully, trying to figure out an expression lingering there that he doesn't recognize. She looks different somehow. Older. "Why are you wet?" Kirby continues, not quite yelling, not quite speaking. A crack in his voice forms, then deepens, a chasm of helplessness revealed. "Was I not clear that you *do not* leave this property?" Wanda hesitates. "Where were you?" Kirby is almost begging now. Lucas tries to catch her eye, but she's staring at the ground, toeing the still-spinning wheel of her fallen bicycle.

"The Edge," she finally says. "I'm sorry, I rode my bike to the Edge."

"To the Edge." Kirby is aghast. He says it again, as if he can't quite believe it. "To the Edge."

"We're just glad you're safe," Lucas says, and opens his arms to her, but no one is listening to him and she doesn't come to him like she usually would. He doesn't share Kirby's shock—of course she would venture out. She's curious. Restless. Lucas remembers feeling all of that. What surprises him is this extra layer she's brought home with her, clinging to her. Another skin. Invisible but tangible. He can't describe it, but it's there. Something new.

"The Edge." Kirby is still wrapping his head around it. "And you…what, went swimming?" All three of them contemplate the pool of seawater at her feet. Her T-shirt is just beginning to dry, stiff waves of pale crusted salt against the dark blue cotton, but her ratty slip-ons still excrete water as she shifts her weight from one leg to the other.

"I…"

"Spit it out, Wanda."

"I...yeah, I went swimming. It was hot." She finally looks up, and in her gaze Lucas sees the lie as clearly as if she's admitted it out loud. The truth it hides is harder to discern.

Lucas watches Kirby unpack grinders from a paper bag for dinner. They've sent Wanda to wash herself off with wet wipes in the bathroom—this is no time to be wasting bottled water. The kitchen door is open again and that same citronella candle flickers. The same mosquitoes buzz. But tonight, Lucas has plans; he's almost forgotten about them. He remembers when Kirby sets only two sandwiches on paper plates and then crumples up the bag they came in. He should go, he realizes, if he wants to be on time.

"She can't stay here by herself anymore," Kirby says. He notices Lucas searching his pockets. "Car keys?" he says. Lucas nods. "Take the pickup."

"Thanks." Kirby throws him his keys, overhand, and Lucas catches them neatly. He looks at them, a mess of silver and bronze. So many. Unlabeled. He doesn't have the slightest idea what most of them open. The weight of his father's responsibilities tangled together in his hand. "Don't you think...that's a little punitive, though?"

"Punitive?"

"It means—"

"I know what it fucking means. Shouldn't it be? You saw her. The Edge, Lucas. She could have drowned. Or, or, I don't know. Anything could have happened."

"I guess, yeah."

"Swimming. Jesus. Maybe Phyllis would do it. Would watch her, I mean, in the afternoons. She's retired now, I think. And it looks like that daycare isn't opening up again anytime soon. Doesn't hurt to ask, I guess. Might as well." Kirby abruptly gets up and goes into his bedroom to make the call.

It does hurt to ask, Lucas knows. Asking doesn't come easily to his father. And Phyllis in particular—her presence down the road is fraught for so many reasons. He stands there, feeling the heaviness of Kirby's keys in his palm, running his thumb over the jagged edges of them, and listens to the low murmur of Kirby's voice. He knows why his father is afraid. Isn't he afraid, too? It's an all-the-time kind of fear, a rushing wind that's been inside his eardrums for years. They focus their fears on Wanda, on the safety of her tiny body, on the formation of her budding personhood, but it's so much bigger than that. How to quantify fear of the sky? Of the ocean? Of the ground they walk on? Sometimes he thinks this is what loving Florida means—being afraid of it.

He looks at his watch: already late. He says goodbye to Wanda through the bathroom door. "I'm heading out, okay?"

"To see Gillian?"

"Yup."

"Okay." Something about her voice makes him pause, but without seeing her face, he isn't sure. He puts his palm flat against the door, as if that might tell him something.

"You're all right, though?"

"I'm fine," she says. Lucas accepts this, for now.

Getting into Kirby's truck, he wonders again what it is she won't say. There's something. But as he pulls out of the driveway, his mind moves on. Someone waits for him nearby, and the thought of a certain girl, a woman really, just sitting, checking her watch, drinking her drink, has consumed him by the time he passes their mailbox.

Driving through Rudder, Lucas notices the toll that time has taken. It has become so familiar, so commonplace, that most days he doesn't even see the vacant storefronts and the abandoned homes. Cracked pavement. Craters so big he drives into the oncoming lane to avoid them; traffic so sparse the swerving doesn't matter. But tonight he sees it all, imagining it through Gillian's eyes. And he remembers how it used to be. Kirby bought that house with Frida when Lucas was eleven, and back then Rudder was a mystery to him. Now he knows all its secrets. Or most.

There is pride in staying. A certain sturdiness in his commitment to this place. To endure is to do right. His father taught him this, without intending to. But it's more than pride, more than keeping an unspoken promise he's outgrown. It's the land that kept him here. The kudzu that hangs from the live oaks. The egrets that stand by the side of the road. The rich chaos of the jungle, overtaking empty lots and broken-down cars. It's the struggle. There is comfort in staying close to the pain. When he was fifteen, his mother took him to Minneapolis to look at houses. It was his first time away from Florida. He hadn't seen Kirby in three years and he'd only held his half sister once. Stepping out of the airport, he felt that frigid Minnesotan air sucking the heat, the wet, the swamp from his lungs, and he knew where he belonged. He knew he would fight to get back. And he did. But now?

Gillian is waiting for him at the bar. It's a dive at the best of times, but without power, it feels almost romantic. The tables have all been dragged outside, where tiki torches sputter around the edges of the parking lot and tea lights flicker inside jam jars. A generator hums somewhere, supplying electricity to the important things: the ice machine, the beer coolers, the neon Budweiser sign that sizzles in the window. This isn't the first time the Dog and Bone has had to make do without power—its bartenders know their way around in the dark.

He finds his high school sweetheart at a picnic table outside, smoking a vape pen and peeling the wrapper off a bottle of IPA in little strips. She gets up when she sees him appearing out of the gloomy parking lot, and they hug. It's familiar and awkward all at once. He hasn't seen her in a long time, three years to be exact, and the last time he held her like this they were in love. It's hard to tell if that's still the case—how to act if it is, how to act if it isn't. He sits down.

"So. You're back."

"Hell no," she says before she can stop herself. "Well, just for a minute."

He cringes at the idea that returning for anything longer than a minute is so unthinkable to her, but Rudder was never something they could agree on. She couldn't wait to leave. "What for?"

"My parents. They're—" She stops and looks up at him, the candlelight flickering underneath her chin. He's always found her beautiful, but she's grown into her face in a way that he doesn't remember and didn't expect. She's even more lovely to him now. He already knows why she's here.

"They're leaving?" he offers. "I figured. Why else would you come back?" She's quiet, playing with the label on her bottle again. "To be honest, I'm surprised they've stayed this long."

"Well, they're already gone, actually. They haven't lived here for a while now. It's just the house…They didn't…well, they didn't want to deal with it. So that's why I came."

"To deal with it?"

"That's right."

"And so they're in, what, Denver? Must be nice having a spare house lying around." She stiffens. Money has always been the thing that separates them. Her among the Beachside bungalows, him tucked away in the swamp. The Intracoastal cutting a line between them. Now Beachside is mostly empty. A few stragglers, a few squatters. Beach houses don't have the same charm without the beach.

"It is nice," she finally says. "They're very privileged, Lucas. Happy?" He isn't happy, though. A waitress comes over and sets a cold bottle of Miller Lite in front of him. He looks up and recognizes her as an older woman who sometimes brings his crew water and sandwiches when they work on her street.

"On me," the woman says. "I know you all are working hard to get the power back on. Just to say—we appreciate you." He thanks her and looks over at Gillian, who doesn't seem to understand this transaction. She raises her eyebrows after the waitress disappears back into the shadowy bar.

"Your new girlfriend?"

This quip bothers him. "She means the crew," he says. "The line workers."

"I *know*." She always says it like this when she actually doesn't know, but Lucas lets it pass.

"Most people…they think we're not working hard enough. Or, I don't know. That it's our fault somehow. Everyone wants to blame someone." He hooks his finger around the cold neck of the bottle. Is this really what he wants to be talking about? He tries to think of something else. "Anyway, why now? This isn't the most convenient time to pack up a house, is it?"

Gillian laughs. "No, it's really fucking inconvenient, actually. But they wanted to get it done and I have a long weekend, so." She shrugs. "Here I am."

"A long weekend from?"

"Grad school. I guess it's been a while since we've caught up, huh. I'm just starting a grad program for psychology now. In Chicago."

"That's great. You always loved to psychoanalyze me, perfect choice."

"Right, so now when I tell you you're too good for this place, it's a certified opinion." She pauses. "Sorry, that didn't come out right. I just meant—it was supposed to be a compliment. I always thought you'd leave eventually."

"How do you like your program?" he asks her, not wanting to argue, feeling the heat rise in his chest. Because the fact is, as hard as he fought to stay, as ashamed as he is to admit it, the idea of leaving has taken root in him. But to demean this place in the process, to judge it as unworthy of himself, of anyone really, is to belittle its land, its inhabitants, its struggle, its history. He doesn't need Rudder to be not good enough in order to go somewhere else. It occurs to him suddenly that this might be the last time he ever sees her. The thought feels tragic and correct at the same time. She was everything to him once, but now she feels like a stranger.

"I like the program. Mostly." She goes on, telling him about

Chicago, about her summer travels in Europe, about the people from Rudder she's kept in touch with and the people she's lost track of. He listens, is politely attentive, but none of this matters. Not really. She's telling him stories about a world that doesn't know it's ending. This world is worried, of course, about climbing temperatures and vengeful wildfires and rising tides. The headlines are absolutely terrible, she says. Incessant. Exhausting. But they're just that. Headlines. Things that happen to other people, elsewhere. The Middle East, Indonesia, Northern California, the Bahamas: those poor people. Southern Florida and the Keys, Louisiana, Puerto Rico: those poor people. The safe zones have shrunk, will go on shrinking, but the people still firmly attached to the idea that there will continue to be such lines—between safe and not safe, between us and those poor people—are determined to go on as they always have. And here is one of them. He used to think these people were lucky. Now he isn't so sure. Lucas watches Gillian wave her hands around as she talks about her cohort. "They're all idiots," she says, then smiles sweetly, a little abashedly. "That sounds mean. But it's true."

They have another beer and then she asks him to follow her back to her parents' abandoned house, where she lights a few candles in the musty master bedroom and he undresses her on sheets that smell of mildew and potpourri. She's more experienced than the last time they were together, when they were both nineteen and eager and clumsy. It's evident in the way she moves, the sure paths of her hands. She knows what she wants and that excites him. They are both aware that this probably won't happen again, so they take their time. They remember how it was and let how it is now unfold. He knows for certain that they no longer love each other. Maybe it was strange to think that after all this time they still would.

She braces her hands against the headboard while he presses himself into her from behind, his arms wrapped around her torso, his face buried in the sweat-slick swoop of her neck, and they are not at all concerned about how much noise they make. There is no one to hear them, not in this house and not in the house next door, or the next, or the next.

It's two in the morning when he slips into the room he still shares with Wanda, but she's awake. He should have known. She's under a sheet, her flashlight glowing, flickering as she turns the page. She peeks out from the sheet when she hears him opening the dresser.

"Lucas," she whispers, fastening her big, liquid gold eyes on him.

"Wanda."

"What's she like now?" She was fascinated by Gillian when they were together in high school, in awe of her silky black hair and her shimmery eye makeup and her expensive clothes. Wanda was always staring when Gillian came over. At the time it embarrassed him, but thinking back on it now he's reminded of Flip and the way his little brother used to look at beautiful birds. They're both students of beauty.

"She's mostly the same." He's self-conscious about the smell of sex that surely must be all over him. He should've slept on the couch.

"Mmm." Wanda stares at the ceiling, probably imagining the Gillian she used to know. The girl who sometimes brought her sweet treats, which she loved, and secondhand Barbie dolls, which she didn't love. He braces himself for an interrogation. But then she's flipping through her book again, seeing how many pages she has left. Lucas watches her count, marveling at how quickly she's moved on. How easily she lets go. It's a necessity of living in Rudder. But even so, it's easier for some than for others. "Let me just finish this chapter, okay?" she asks.

"Okay," he replies, and Wanda pulls the sheet back over her head. He suddenly remembers her disappearing act that afternoon. The state of her when she returned. "How..." He pauses, not sure what he's asking. "How'd it go with Dad?"

"Fine," she says from under the sheet. He hears a page turn.

"And you're okay?"

"I'm *reading*."

Sharing the room used to bother him in high school, but he doesn't mind anymore. Finding an apartment nearby crosses Lucas's mind every once in a while, but he never does anything about it. He feels needed here and he's trying to save his paychecks, small as they are. Getting a place of his own at this point would mean he plans on staying. He leaves Wanda to her book and peels off his T-shirt in the diffused glow of her flashlight, then slips into bed wearing just a pair of shorts, already sweating.

He didn't mention to Gillian the college applications he's already printed out, tucked away in the bottom of his shirt drawer in a neat white stack, or the bank account he's earmarked for tuition. He hasn't mentioned them to anyone. Not yet. Not until he knows if they'll even take him, because they probably won't. He didn't mention it because he knew she'd misunderstand. It isn't that he wants to leave Rudder behind. It's that he wants to learn how to save it.

KIRBY WAKES WANDA at the crack of dawn the following morning to inform her that she'll be expected at the blue house at 3:15 and not a minute later. It's her first day back at school and also the first day of his hastily arranged agreement with Phyllis.

"Which house?" she asks, sleep crusted at the corners of her eyes.

"The blue one. Phyllis's. Across the road."

"Dad, no, I don't want to. I don't need a babysitter."

"You do, Wanda. Obviously you do, if you think that riding your bike down to the Edge by yourself is okay." She gets up and sulks around the kitchen while Kirby and Lucas empty the coffeepot into their thermoses. Lucas goes out to start the truck and Kirby turns to Wanda. "Straight to school, then straight to Phyllis's after." He leaves her sullen and silent at the kitchen table, not at all confident that she'll do as she's told. But what else can he say?

He goes out to the idling truck and Lucas slides over to the passenger seat. Kirby drives—Kirby always drives—and they discuss the job sites they have yet to service. There are so many. But it will get done. Somehow, it will. Kirby and his crew yank the town back from the brink of chaos, again and again and again. They clear the roads, they restring the wires, they turn the lights back on. The air conditioners, the refrigerators, the phone chargers, the televisions, the microwaves, the electric toothbrushes, the water pumps. But the thing is, even with every appliance running on high, power zipping along the local lines, into the transformers, the breakers, the wires, down into the sockets, into the homes, into the gadgets and gizmos, it can never go back to the way it was. Not all the way. They can't fix everything. They get to what they can before the next storm arrives and usually it's enough, but it's never everything. Whatever they replace might be gone in a week. A month. At best, the lifetime of a wire here is down to two years. Rudder crumbles before his eyes: roads eaten away by floods, trees felled by the winds, houses knocked off their foundations. Each year, more people leave. Each year, the town's budget for repairs and maintenance shrinks. What would it take to save it? The easy answer is money. The other answer is more complicated. Feats of engineering to protect them from the sea, higher roads, more durable utilities, global climate control, international policy decisions that should have been made decades ago. Time travel and politics. But in the end, it's always been money.

Kirby and Lucas pull into the yard and Brenda is waiting. She leans against the bucket truck, smoking a Winston with one hand and shading her eyes with the other. This is what's left of his crew. The others slipped away over the years: Emilio retired and Kirby took over, Wes accepted a job with a contractor based out of the Panhandle, and Jerome got his license back and then promptly drove his car into a utility pole. A pitch-black joke. The pole survived; Jerome didn't. The municipality used to promise Kirby they'd give him salaries for more linemen, but they don't even mention it anymore.

The three of them load a new pole onto the trailer and hitch it to the bucket truck, then they drive out, Kirby and Brenda in the bucket truck, Lucas in the pickup. At the site, they get to digging out the pole that broke off in the storm. It's already hot; they're drenched with sweat as soon as they start. By lunchtime, they've pulled out the old stump and they sit in their trucks, the air-conditioning blasting, eating their warmed-over cold cuts. Kirby calls the congressman for their district three times in a row, but there's no answer and the voice mail is full. He tries the offices of both senators, two times apiece. Nothing goes through. He's not a political man by nature; Lucas is the one who put this idea of petitioning the government for help in his head.

"Why bother with that shit?" Brenda asks, mouth full of turkey and pickles on rye. Kirby gives up on the calls and tears into his own sandwich.

"Because those sons of bitches on the city council are full of garbage. Municipality's going under, inch by inch. County don't give a shit. Mayor don't even live here anymore. Someone has to do something."

Brenda just laughs, but the sound is dismal. Joyless. "Do they?"

"They do," Kirby replies, not sure he believes it, either, hoping it's true.

Back in his dingy office that evening, surrounded by paperwork that predates him and equipment that doesn't work, Kirby does get through. It's a senator's office, the Republican, he thinks, but possibly the Democrat. Their names sound the same and neither has done much for him. He's so startled when a human being answers that he is speechless for a little too long. "Hi," he finally says. "I'm one of your constituents. I live in Rudder and I'm the foreman of our electrical maintenance crew."

"All right," the voice says. A woman. Young. Tired. "And what can the senator's office do for you?"

"Well, look, I've tried to address this locally, but we need help and the local government isn't up to it. The municipality's about to go bankrupt, but the county doesn't give us any money because of the municipality, you know how it is, everyone chasing their own tail. I can't do my job without personnel and equipment. My job is keeping the lights on, ma'am. Without my crew, this town is in the dark. I'm just trying to do my job."

"I'm sorry to hear that." He waits for her to offer some kind of solution, but the line just buzzes quietly; she has nothing to add.

"We need support. Financial support. New hires. Equipment. Every year we need more and every year we get less."

"I will be happy to log your comment."

"And?"

"That's all I can really do at the moment, sir."

"I mean, and then what?"

"Sorry?"

"So you log my comment and then what?"

"Well." She heaves a sigh, long and deep. "You want the truth?"

He does and he doesn't. "Yes."

"Nothing. We're working around the clock to organize relocation packages for Miamians, which…well, we're doing our best. We're trying to save cities, not towns. We just don't have the resources. You want my personal opinion, I'd say it's time to move." Kirby stares at his office wall. There's a calendar hanging from two years ago that he keeps forgetting to throw away. Through the slit of his blinds he can see Lucas and Brenda unloading gear from the bucket truck and hauling it into the open garage bay. "Thank you for calling Senator Joel Farrow's office, and have a good day." She hangs up. He wishes this exchange surprised him, but it doesn't. Even knowing that all he's doing is prolonging the inevitable, Kirby cannot bring himself to give up on Rudder. It isn't self-important to believe that if he leaves, this town is done for. It's just the way things are.

If the ocean is a body, then the Intracoastal Waterway is a body, too: skinny and twisty and tall. It tickles the ocean with its currents—freshwater greets salt in the bays, the sloughs, the deltas. It reaches: from the top of North America to the bottom, cupping the tip of Florida with its curving channels, wrapping around the Gulf and flowing west to Texas. But all bodies change. Even these.

ON HER FIRST day back since Hurricane Valerie, Wanda counts twelve kids, including herself. The fifth grade class grows ever smaller. A few more students disappear after every storm, taken north by parents who decided to make their evacuation permanent. The classroom is half-full. Other kids spread out, claiming two desks instead of one, littering the room with their backpacks and lunchboxes and binders, trying to make it seem less empty than it is. Wanda keeps her backpack between her knees, like always, and doesn't unpack more than the book she's using so that if she needs to, she can grab everything and go. She has never felt relaxed in this room—in any of the classrooms she's occupied. The older she gets, the better she is at keeping her questions to herself. It's hard for her not to raise her hand; there is so much she wants to know, but it's better for her this way. If the other children forget she's there, that's a good thing.

At lunch, the sixth graders who accosted her by the Edge stare and whisper but do not talk to her. This is uncomfortable but better than the alternative. Even the possibility that they might approach, the fact that Corey's pale blue eyes have found her at all among this thinning crowd of children, is enough to frighten her. She remembers his hand on her head, the salt water rushing up into her nostrils, down into her lungs. And the other thing—the thing she can't describe. She still doesn't know what that was.

After the final bell, Wanda gets on her bicycle and allows her jaw to unclench as soon as her tires hit the asphalt, feeling more and more herself the farther away from the school she gets. She isn't looking forward to spending the rest of the afternoon at the blue house—Phyllis is old and boring, as far as Wanda can tell—but anything is better than school. She pedals slowly, trying to prolong her freedom.

When she reluctantly knocks, Phyllis answers the door with a pair of waders slung over her shoulder and a large tackle box in her hand. It isn't at all what Wanda was expecting. Wanda stares at the waders— tall rubber boots that ascend and become trousers, knocking together where they dangle against Phyllis's torso. She wears a green shirt with bleach stains all over it, and her mostly white hair is piled into a bun on top of her head that has gone lopsided. "I thought we could check on some things," Phyllis says, and lets the screen door slam behind her.

"What kind of things?" Wanda asks, suspicious but also curious. It occurs to her now that, upon closer examination, she has no idea who this woman is. All she knows is that when her father encounters Phyllis in the grocery store, he gives her a solemn nod, and when they pass her on the road he lifts his hand from the steering wheel. This is Kirby's way of saying hello without saying anything.

"Plants, mostly."

"Check on…plants?"

"Dirt. Water. Sediment. Trees. That kind of thing."

Wanda stares at the tackle box. She points. "What's that, then?"

"For collecting specimens."

"Of…"

"Plants and dirt and water." Halfway down the porch steps, Phyllis stops and turns to Wanda. "We can do something else if you want," she says.

"No," Wanda replies quickly. "This is okay." As it happens, checking on trees and dirt and water sounds like exactly the kind of thing she'd like to do. Her reticence forgotten, she accepts the piece of jerky Phyllis hands her as they walk to the salt-splattered Toyota, once dark blue, now a pale and uneven gray, parked in the shade of a cypress. "What kind?" Wanda asks, the jerky already in her mouth.

"Alligator," Phyllis says.

"That's the good kind."

"I know." Phyllis puts the waders and the tackle box in the back seat, and as they drive along the bank of the Intracoastal, toward the causeway, Wanda stares out the window at the flickering river. "Did you know," Phyllis says, "that the Intracoastal is three thousand miles long?" Wanda did not know this. "It has lots of different names, depending where you are, but it's all the same water body."

Getting closer to Beachside, Wanda becomes tense. There is that tang of salt coming in through the open windows. She thinks again of Corey's hand on her head, of the sensation of water occupying spaces it wasn't supposed to: inside her, trickling into her eardrums, her nose, her throat. The burning in her chest, the sting in her sinuses, but another sensation, too—a different kind of pain, like bones growing in the middle of the night, a body expanding a little too quickly for its own comfort. She'd rather not think about any of this. She isn't sure how to categorize it, whether it is a big deal or a small one, a secret she must keep or a thing she should tell. It's easier to pretend it never happened, but even that is hard.

When they get to the embankment of the Intracoastal, Wanda knows roughly where they are but doesn't recognize the pullout as a place she's been before. In the distance, she can see the causeway stretching over the river, connecting Beachside to the mainland. She can glimpse it through the wilderness that grows along its edge. Water levels have ebbed somewhat since yesterday, but not much. The river is still choppy and high. Phyllis pulls on her waders, snapping the suspenders over her shoulders, and takes her tackle box from the back seat. Wanda watches as she navigates the underbrush, moving easily among the mangrove roots and across the marshy shore. This fluidity surprises her. Adults never seem to know how to walk in the wild. Even Lucas is clumsy. Kirby especially. But Phyllis moves like she belongs here.

"You come here lots?" Wanda asks when they reach the water at the same time. Phyllis kneels among the underbrush and sets her tackle box down, notched in between two roots, then slips seamlessly into the rushing water. A few steps and she's already waist-deep. She takes a little notepad out of the bib pocket.

"Sure do," Phyllis says, writing something down. Wanda studies her. "How old are you?"

"Old."

"How old?"

"Old enough," Phyllis says. "How old are you?"

"Ten." Phyllis slips the notebook back into her pocket and wades back over to where Wanda sits, fiddling with the latch on the tackle box. It suddenly occurs to her that if she's in the company of a scientist, she'd better be exact. "Almost. My birthday is in nine days."

"Hard to believe it's been that long," Phyllis says, absently running her fingers through the water.

"What do you mean?"

Phyllis just frowns and gestures at the tackle box. "Open that for me, would you?" Wanda is quickly distracted by the jumble inside the tackle box. There are petri dishes, vials, pH sticks, different-colored Sharpies, a little net. She resists the urge to paw through it. If this is a test, she wants to pass.

"What's all that for?"

"It's my field kit."

"What's a field kit?"

"It's for collecting samples. In the field."

"This isn't a field."

"No, that's true. It's *the* field." Wanda sits with this for a moment while Phyllis selects a vial and scoops up a sample of water from the river, then rolls up her sleeves and, in a separate container, collects some sediment from where it's shallow. "'Field' can mean different things. It's one of those words with different lives. It could be an open grassy area. Or someone's area of expertise. It can be a verb, too—to handle, take the lead on. Or, you know, to field a ball. But in ecology, the field is the place where I gather data. In nature. See?" Phyllis looks up at Wanda where she's still crouched among the mangrove roots. "Some of my work I can do in my study. But the other part of what I do is in the field. Like now." This is a lot of information about fields for Wanda to process.

"So I'm at work with you."

"Yes." Phyllis hands her the samples she's collected and Wanda takes them, aware she's holding regular things—dirt, water—that have somehow stopped being regular and become important. "Well, technically I'm retired from teaching, but I still like to work for myself on occasion. Curiosity never retires. Those go back into the kit, please. Carefully." Wanda handles the containers with reverence, eager to prove that she is a good assistant. Kirby and Lucas have taken her to work before, but they never let her touch anything. And anyway, she's not allowed to go with them anymore. Phyllis gives her an approving nod.

"What are they for?" Wanda asks when the samples are back in the tackle box.

"For measuring change. Like how much salt is in the water, or what kinds of creatures live in it, or what the sediment is made of, or…this is an important one, hand me that measuring tape." Wanda is pleased that she can identify the measuring tape, even though this one looks strange to her. She hands it to Phyllis. "Measuring the water levels." Phyllis takes it and finds a thick pole spiking out of the water, a little downstream. She measures the water against lines etched into it, writes something down, then wades back over to Wanda.

"Why?"

"Because everything is changing. And the way it's changing…well, I'm curious about it. We all should be curious about it, because the way we live has to change, too. Some creatures can't live in this water anymore. Others can. Someday, new ones might evolve."

"Like what kinds of creatures?"

"All kinds. Mammals, fish, amphibians. Insects. But even smaller ones, too. Infinitesimal creatures."

"Infini..." Wanda stumbles over the syllables.

"Infinitesimal. It just means very, very small. So small you can't even see them unless you have a microscope."

"And they live in the water?"

"They live everywhere. In the water. Inside our bodies. In our colons and stomachs and noses. Humans tend to think the bigger the creature, the more advanced. But tiny creatures have been around for much, much longer. Maybe they know more than we think they do."

It goes on like this: Phyllis supplying Wanda with a never-ending trail of information, leapfrogging from one question to another. Wanda is not used to her questions being taken so seriously or answered with such patience. She doesn't have to be afraid of the attention she's drawing to herself out here by the river. The anxiety of learning indoors is gone—there are no bullies to snicker when she raises her hand. So she asks until there's nothing left to ask. Until she is full of answers that need ruminating on.

Wanda insists on carrying the field kit on the way back. Phyllis moves a little more slowly now, favoring her right knee, while Wanda darts ahead. There is so much new information spinning through her mind, but she keeps coming back to what Phyllis said about "the way we live." She isn't sure what to make of that. Is there another way to live? It had never occurred to her. In the little parking lot, she waits for Phyllis to catch up. Watching her wind between the dying live oaks and the thriving mangroves, the rubber waders still glistening from the river, her hair glowing white beneath the dimness of the tree canopy, Wanda realizes she doesn't want to go home yet. The excitement of the afternoon is a taste that lingers. Except it's more than flavor; it's nourishment. Phyllis reaches her, breathing heavily, a slick of sweat shining on her cheeks.

"Shall we?" Phyllis unlocks the car and Wanda climbs in. Already, she would follow this woman anywhere.

KIRBY DREADS WANDA'S birthday parties. It was easier when she was a baby. There were no parties. No need to celebrate a day that felt like a foot on his windpipe. But then she started talking and walking and demanding to know whether there would be cake. To which he could only say, "Of course there will be." And now there is. The power is back on, so he hangs fairy lights from the trees the morning of the party and hooks them up to the house with an extension cord. This is perhaps the only thing on his to-do list that feels familiar. Lights. Yes, he can turn on the lights, at least.

The cake comes from the grocery store, like always. This year, an ice cream cake was requested and procured. The guest list is small. Wanda doesn't have any friends her own age to invite. There was one, he recalls, but she's gone now; he doesn't remember her name. This lack upsets Kirby: the stoic set of Wanda's little shoulders when they pass a kid she recognizes on the street, or, back when the daycare was open, the afternoons he would pick her up and see the remnants of someone's cruelty on her face. She never talks to him about it. Frida would be good at this, he thinks. She would know how to make their daughter feel better. She might even know how to win the other kids over. And at the very least, she would know how to keep their meanness at bay. If Frida were here, she would be in charge of the party: ordering him around, telling him where to hang the streamers,

135

the lights, where to set up the folding tables and chairs. The cake would be homemade, and the lemonade, and the snacks. The guest list would be longer. The music would be better. She was good at these things. Now that she's gone, he allows himself to believe she was good at everything. That they would be unconditionally happy if only she were still here. When she died, he was beginning to think he barely knew her. Now that he's lived with her ghost for ten years, he is an expert.

He's arranged the party for Sunday, the day before Wanda's actual birthday. He bought her a toy bucket truck, with a boom that lifts and lowers and little doors that open, and wrapped it in the only wrapping paper he could find in the house, a roll with green Christmas trees stamped all over it. He looked for ribbon, but there wasn't any. Brenda is invited, and Phyllis, and Lucas of course, and Emilio and his wife, who still live nearby, and the fire chief, Arjun, who is the closest thing Kirby has to a friend. In past years, he and Arjun hosted a softball game and then a cookout for all the emergency response crews, but it's been a while since they had time to put together something like that.

It doesn't seem like a good guest list, but it's the best he can do. Usually he can convince one or two of the mothers from the daycare to bring their kids, but when the whole place shut down he realized he didn't have anyone's phone number. He tries not to keep thinking about the people who aren't here, but it's impossible not to. Flip would be eighteen. A senior. What kind of man would he be? It's useless to imagine. He was eight ten years ago, and he'll go on being eight forever.

The party begins and everyone he invited arrives. Wanda seems happy. Lucas regresses to his most childish self to make up for the fact that there are no other children here, which Kirby appreciates. His remaining son chases Wanda around the yard in a game of one-on-one tag, and something about the way he wiggles his fingers and pretends to be an ogre scratches at Kirby's memories, but he senses danger in this recollection and turns away. After a little while, when Wanda has been caught and the adults have sipped their lemonade and eaten their Ritz crackers with cubes of cheese on top, they all gather around a card table set under the bedraggled citrus trees. Kirby brings out the ice cream cake, which, despite the heat, steadfastly refuses to melt. All the adults sing and use their bodies as a shield so that Wanda has time to make a wish and extinguish the flames with her own breath before the wind does it for her. She just beams at the cake, not blowing. They finish the song. Still the candles burn, flickering in the breeze that slips through the cracks of this imperfect fortress, and still Wanda watches the shivering flames, not blowing.

"Make a wish," he says.

"I'm thinking," she chides him.

"Oh, sorry," he says, and the guests laugh good-naturedly as they wait, clustered together, for Wanda to complete the ritual. Finally, she squeezes her eyes shut for a second, then blows. Everyone claps. Wanda insists on cutting the cake herself and makes sure that there is an icing rosette on every piece.

There are presents. A mini field kit from Phyllis. A set of glitter pens from Brenda. A dolly from Emilio and his wife, Claire. A plastic fireman's helmet from Arjun. Three new paperbacks from Lucas. When she opens Kirby's bucket truck last, she gasps and he feels proud, proud that she loves what he loves, proud that even if this party could have been so much better, it didn't turn out half-bad in the end. Golden hour peaks and then fades, the yellow sunlight slipping down behind the treetops. The sky dwindles to a dusky blue. The fairy lights Kirby hung earlier finally make their mark, casting a glow over the lawn. He goes around and pours a little gin into everyone's lemonade. Arjun and Kirby talk about their dwindling crews, while Emilio and Brenda throw darts, half listening. Claire dozes on a lawn chair. Lucas gets another slice of cake. The partygoers linger, sipping from their paper cups, making observations about the fruit trees, and a sense of quiet contentment settles. No one wants to leave just yet. They can all sense the finitude of these days in Rudder. They watch Wanda sitting cross-legged in the grass while Phyllis identifies each item in the field kit and explains how to use it, and each of them longs for this little girl's oblivion. Her naivete. But Wanda knows more than they could imagine. They forget how much children understand. She doesn't have words for what she knows, but she feels the quickening of change as strongly as the adults do. Perhaps more so. Kirby finishes his drink and watches his daughter play in the scrubby grass, caressing each item in her new field kit. He isn't used to seeing her this happy. It reminds him of when she was a baby, just beginning to smile. It occurs to him that she is the future of this place—if only it didn't seem like such a curse.

ON MONDAY, THE school assembly is solemn. The principal, a balding man the students call Mr. Gorgich, makes announcements about things that have changed since Valerie: PE is canceled for the foreseeable future, due to the live oak that fell through the gymnasium's roof. Outdoor sports are canceled, obviously, given the flooded fields. And the sixth grade teacher has "decided not to return," which means that the fifth and sixth grade classes will merge. Mr. Gorgich has more to say, but by then the room is awash with murmurs about the missing teacher. He soldiers through a brief list of remaining after-school programs. No one listens. Finally, he bangs his fist on the podium to regain their attention and asks for a moment of silence to commemorate the anniversary of Rudder's most devastating disaster on record. The most lives lost in a single day. He doesn't say Hurricane Wanda outright, but he doesn't need to. Wanda can feel the eyes burning into her. She can hear the scattered whispers. It's like this every year.

Afterward, her classroom is full of newcomers. The sixth graders crowd in and the fifth graders shrink to accommodate them. Ms. Landers, the young teacher with pink gums and a wide smile that is often genuine but today is fake, looks overwhelmed. "I wasn't expecting to…um, merge the grades, so you'll have to bear with me. I think we'll do two curriculums still, and just try and…share. Somehow. We'll figure it out." Her students, new and old, are all thinking the same thing: It's only a matter of time before she leaves them, too. Ms. Landers instructs the fifth graders to quietly read a chapter in their history books about the Seminole Wars while she holds whisper-conferences with the sixth graders, trying to figure out where they left off before Valerie.

Initially, Wanda is relieved by this assignment—she likes it when they all read quietly at their desks—but today she is having a hard time concentrating and this chapter confuses her. Phyllis has already started teaching her about the Seminoles, and tribes who might have lived in Rudder even farther back. The Jeaga, or possibly the Tequesta. Or maybe, with Gulf Coast territories ranging all the way to the Atlantic in some places, the Calusa people. And even farther back than that—so many thousands of years ago no one remembers what they called themselves.

Wanda turns a page to find a painting of white men in crisp blue uniforms valiantly fighting and tragically dying, while a menacing horde of Seminoles bears down on them in the distance. Examining it, she has questions, but she'll save them for Phyllis. Over the top of her book, she watches Amanda and Brie and Corey wait their turn to talk to Ms. Landers. Mick is absent—he's been gone for a few days now. Hopefully for good. This is how her peers slip away to new lives; they just disappear. When her lone friend, Jules, left last year, the two of them had a few days to say goodbye, but that was all. When people decide to go, they go. The homes here are so worthless the banks don't even bother foreclosing. Once the decision is made, all that's left is to pack up their cars and drive away. There is a contagious panic running through the town lately, a fear that if they don't get out now, they never will. Wanda feels it—how could she not—but she also knows she's not going anywhere.

From this vantage point, her three remaining tormentors from the Edge look smaller than she remembers. They seem almost vulnerable up there at the front of the room. Corey's hair is uneven, as if he cut it himself, and he can't stop fidgeting, putting his hands in his pockets and then taking them out, again and again. Amanda wears an old pair of pink jelly shoes with glitter sprinkled in the plastic and she keeps bending down to scratch bug bites between the straps. Her shorts are frayed and too big in the waist, a hand-me-down. They look anxious, exposed up there at the front of the room. Brie, at the end of the line, is…different somehow. She has the same underfed, overtired shadow on her face, like many of the children here, but she wears it with some kind of grace. She is liquid, poured into her body, her clothes, this room. None of the ill-fitting awkwardness applies to her. Everything fits her perfectly, even her tangled ponytail and the deep red of her sunburned shoulders and her raggedy cutoffs and her once-white sneakers, now brownish-gray. She catches Wanda looking and Wanda's eyes dart away, back to her textbook. She has never been comfortable in this room, but when the sixth graders arrive, whatever ease she has managed to eke out through the passage of time leaves and does not return.

As the weeks go by, biking to Phyllis's house after school becomes a celebrated part of Wanda's routine. It gives her something to look forward to, a way to shake off the anxiety that permeates her school days even more now that the sixth graders are a permanent fixture in her classroom. It is pure terror to be so close to Corey every day. She can still feel his hand on her scalp, holding her under the waves. She tends to her fear in small ways: sitting in the back of the room so there is no one behind her; keeping her questions to herself; eating her lunch alone in the mildewing library, where the windows smashed during Valerie are covered in plastic and all the books are beginning to rot.

Being so close to his twin sister, Brie, is a different feeling, one she can't quite place—not terror exactly, but…not safety, either. The rest of her peers blur together, a mass of familiar faces: bullies at worst and complicit at best. She keeps her head down and gets through it as quietly as she can. But after the last bell rings, when she hops on her bicycle and glides out of the parking lot, her day begins in earnest.

Sometimes they go to one of Phyllis's plots and gather data. Other days, they stay at the blue house and work in the garden, or cook, or do various projects around the property: building a new ramp for the henhouse, fixing a broken window box filled with herbs, climbing up on the roof to check the solar panels. Phyllis teaches her to use tools, to measure wood, to plant seeds, to purify water. When it rains, they read together. And Wanda loves every second of it. Survivalism—a term she doesn't even know yet—comes naturally to her.

Today, they walk through the tangled wilderness behind Phyllis's house. One of the chickens has gone missing. Phyllis lets them range free in the woods during the day and for the most part they don't wander too far, but occasionally some of the more intrepid souls lose their way. Blue-bell is one of these wanderers, a snow-white hen, just a few brownish-red speckles across her back and wings. She has been Wanda's favorite since she started helping Phyllis gather eggs. By now, tracking Bluebell to whatever grub-studded log she's pecking at is a frequent pastime.

The two of them walk softly, careful to leave the undergrowth the same as they found it. Above, the foliage is thick; only the smallest slivers of sky shine through to dapple the ground. The soil is wet but firm. They gather mushrooms as they go, and Phyllis instructs Wanda on the different varieties they find. "What's the mushroom rule again?"

"If you aren't sure, go home poor," Wanda recites.

"That's right." Phyllis smiles at her.

The sunlight that slips in through the treetops sends sloping rays of yellow through the shadow. It will start getting dark soon. They go slowly, their eyes sharp on the tangle of growth all around them, and occasionally Phyllis shakes a baggie of sunflower seeds she's brought, calling "Here, *chick chick chick*," in case Bluebell is near. When Phyllis sees something notable that Wanda does not, they play I Spy until Wanda finds it, too.

"I spy, with my little eye…something that begins with 'F,'" Phyllis says.

"A fern?" Phyllis shakes her head no. "Is it a plant?" Phyllis shakes her head again. "Animal?"

"It is."

"Is it…oh, it's the frog!" Wanda finally finds it, resting on a fallen log, almost invisible against the dull mosses.

"Do you know what kind?"

"Um…tree frog."

"Not quite."

"Oh wait, we were just looking at it, weren't we." She racks her brain. Phyllis quizzed her on the amphibian section of a field guide days before. Reading with Phyllis is so pleasant that she's not yet aware that this, too, is learning. "Southern chorus frog?"

"A-plus."

They keep walking, playing I Spy and calling out for the lost chicken, until gradually it begins to seem like maybe there is no chicken here for them to find. That maybe Bluebell has left them for good. Wanda doesn't want it to be true, so they keep looking.

They do find her, eventually. Wanda sees the puff of feathers first. "There!" she squeals, darting forward. "Chick chick chick!" Phyllis reaches out and catches her by the collar of her T-shirt before she can get too far.

"Easy does it," she says. "I don't think our girl is—I don't think she's still with us." Phyllis's eye has already caught the pink stains, the eerie motionlessness beneath the fluttering feathers. Wanda understands and begins to cry, unable to stop herself. She would like to take this brutality in stride, to show Phyllis that she isn't afraid of blood, but she can't. This chicken has a name. Wanda has eaten her eggs, chased her through the woods, held her. There is a necessary tension between knowing how nature works in theory and witnessing it. Phyllis pulls her close, not wanting her to see more than she already has. "It's okay, she had a good life."

"How do you know?" Wanda presses her snotty face into Phyllis's chest, unbothered by the wet spots she'll leave behind.

"I guess I don't. But I like to think she did. She was free to roam and she had a safe place to sleep. That's all most of us can ask for." They walk back, arms bound together. There is no more I Spy, no more mushroom gathering. By the time they get to the house, Wanda has worked through her tears. When Kirby comes to collect her, he asks what they did today and Wanda's face is grave. "We lost a chicken," she says. "But she had a good life."

LUCAS WAITS UNTIL everyone else has gone to bed to work on his college applications in the living room. It's late and he's having a hard time keeping his eyes open. The sofa cushions sink to accommodate him and he has to keep reminding his body that there is still more to do today. The TV is on low, but he isn't watching it. The ambient sound is soothing—it's a rerun of an old half-hour comedy show that aired when he was little. The studio audience's laughter swells and recedes, washing over him like a benevolent tide.

He tells himself these applications aren't a secret, but they are. The idea of being accepted seems far-fetched, and this way, when the rejection letters start arriving in the mailbox, he won't have to admit it to anyone. So he keeps his efforts to himself. Still, there are things he needs—supplementary materials—and the task of hunting those down, *asking* for them, is excruciating. When he asked Brenda for a letter of recommendation she just stared at him.

"A what?" she said.

"Look, I can't ask my dad. I'm lucky if I can find even one high school teacher who remembers me. And I need two letters."

"I'd help, except I don't write letters. You're better off asking someone else."

She agreed in the end. He wore her down. That's the trick with Brenda—perseverance. Next, Lucas tracked down his old guidance counselor and he agreed to write one as well, without nearly as much wheedling. Asking people to write letters seemed like the hard part until he sat down to write the essay. His first sentence stares back at him.

You might not know what a lineman is, but you'd be lost without them.

It's all he has. He wanted to write about storm duty, about climbing poles and digging ditches and clearing roads and replacing insulators. About trees snapped in half like twigs and houses with their roofs torn off and blacktop roads peeled back to dirt. But now—it feels wrong and he can't figure out why. He intends to study civil engineering, so it makes sense to write about the job he has now. It's a practical topic choice, but it has the right amount of emotion, too. When he was little, all he ever wanted was to be a lineman on Kirby's crew. Isn't this the kind of thing admission boards want to hear? Unsure, he chews on his already-shredded fingernails and stares into the blue light of his laptop.

The idea of college seemed ridiculous to him when he was in high school and everyone else was filling out their applications. College was what people with too much time and too much money did. A rite of passage for a different kind of person. But the longer he stays in Rudder, the more he understands that it is the people with college degrees, the ones who work at city hall, who run for public office, who look at blueprints and make decisions about how much money to spend and where—these are the people that are killing his town. Other towns, too. Entire counties. Sprawling cities. States. Countries.

Maybe that's what he's trying to write about. The ideas that underlie the physicality of his labor. The plans that went awry. The ways in which these people have failed him and everyone else who lives here with their shortsightedness. He thinks of Gillian, of her exhaustion with the news. He's exhausted also, but he can't look away. It's here, unfolding in front of him. On his doorstep. Every day, he and Kirby and Brenda drive out and they fix one problem at a time. It used to make him feel useful. But lately—the rate of destruction is too brisk. The problems too large. Yes, this is why he's applying. This is the point he's trying to make. He deletes his first sentence and starts again.

> *I live in a dying town called Rudder, in a dying state called Florida. Most of the people who leave this place want to escape it. I want to save it.*

That's not bad, he thinks, rereading it. Maybe it's too dramatic, but then again—what is the mood of this place if not that of a sodden drama? The storms that batter them are pure exhibitionism. The fleeing populations. The Intracoastal Waterway swelling to meet the ever-advancing ocean on that skinny spit of land they still call Beachside, even though the name refers to a rind of pure white sand that is gone. Two water bodies rushing to touch in the middle. Sometimes melodrama is just the truth. He keeps going.

A few paragraphs later, there is a rustling in the doorway. Lucas looks up and sees Wanda, sleepy, holding a stuffed penguin coming apart at the seams by its flipper, her hair standing up in thick snarls. He tries not to be annoyed. Fails.

"What are you doing?" she asks.

"I'm… What are *you* doing? You should be asleep. I'm just writing emails."

"To who?"

"To none of your business. Go to bed."

Wanda lingers, looking at him with those brown eyes that are too old for her face. The penguin grazes the floor. She's wearing one of Kirby's old T-shirts, the neck so big on her tiny frame it's slipping off one shoulder, the sleeves drooping down past her elbows. Lucas looks at the blinking cursor, and back to Wanda, who hasn't moved.

"Did you have a bad dream?"

She nods.

"Do you wanna tell me about it?"

She nods again. He closes the laptop with a sigh and pats the cushion next to him; she comes and sits. "I was drowning," she whispers.

"That sounds scary."

"It was."

In the end, Lucas carries Wanda back to the room they share. He hoists her up onto the top bunk easily, but groans to make it clear that she is heavier than the last time he did this, to suggest that one day soon he won't be able to do these things for her anymore. He's spent ten years trying to atone. He desperately wants to be the kind of big brother that Flip should have had. It's part of why he's still here: in this room, a grown man sharing a bunk bed with a child. Is it enough? Will it ever be? He tucks her in and turns to go back to the living room, thinking maybe he can write another page tonight.

"You're not staying?" she says. "I won't be able to sleep unless you stay."

He grumbles, but he stays. For now.

At the job site, Kirby works from the bucket, cutting down branches that have fallen into the lines, while Lucas and Brenda work on the ground, gathering it all up and feeding it to the woodchipper.

"This letter you want me to write…" Brenda begins. Lucas quickly looks up toward his airborne father, but Kirby is too busy wrestling with foliage to hear. "I'm not sure what I'm supposed to say."

"Just say I'm reliable. And a hard worker. And…I don't know. Congenial."

"I guess." She hoists a branch into the chipper, which chews it up and spits the wood chips out into the underbrush. He studies her face, but it's a vault. She picks up another branch, this one bigger than her entire body. He steps forward to help but she says, "I got it," and it's clear that she does. The muscles up and down her arms come into focus underneath her skin as she heaves it into the mouth of the woodchipper. She wipes the sweat away from underneath the band of her hard hat. "You hear about Braylen?" she asks.

"Braylen who?"

"Tropical storm. Down by Cuba."

"Oh, right," Lucas replies. "Braylen—they ran out of alphabet again, huh."

"Running out every year. Got that overflow list now. They were saying it'll probably be a Category One by tonight. Maybe Two, even. Growing fast. Could be another big one."

Lucas isn't convinced. "Nah, I reckon it's too late for another real big one." Brenda just laughs and laughs. She laughs so loud Kirby stops what he's doing and looks down at them. "What?" Lucas says. "What's so funny?"

"You think the weather gives a fuck about the calendar? This is what it is now, kiddo. You and your dad." She shakes her head. "Thinking the rules still matter."

He's quiet then, because he knows she's right.

THAT NIGHT, KIRBY considers their barren fridge and proposes ordering pizza for dinner. His kids' response to his suggestion is lackluster, so he says it again, louder, to remind them that it is their duty to be delighted.

"I'll call it in," Lucas volunteers. They don't need to discuss the order; everyone knows it's two large pies so that they'll have a slice each left over for breakfast: the first with half plain cheese, half pepperoni, and then the second with absolutely everything. Kirby tosses Lucas his wallet and migrates to the living room, where he turns on the TV. A weatherwoman is announcing Hurricane Braylen's progress through the Bahamas: *A Category Two as of this evening... We expect to see northwestern movement and an increased wind speed overnight.*

In the kitchen, Kirby hears Lucas hang up and mutter, "Weird."

"What's weird?" he shouts.

"It just makes that error tone."

"You try it again?"

An exasperated sigh. "Yeah, Pop. I tried it again."

"I'll drive down," Kirby says, heaving himself out of his chair. "Order in person." The truth is, he's happy to go. Lately, the only time he has to himself is when he's sleeping, showering, or shitting. Actually, it's not just lately, he realizes. It's been years. The truck's engine is still warm from the drive home from the job site. As he pulls out of the driveway, he clicks off the radio station Lucas likes. Kirby prefers the silence. It's dark by the time he gets to the little strip where the pizza place is, and when he pulls in, there are no other cars. A CLOSED sign hangs inside the door, and a big piece of poster board is taped in the picture window.

GONE NORTH

GOD BLESS

Kirby gets out of his truck even though he can read it fine from the front seat. Peering in through the darkened glass, he tries to remember the last time they ordered from here. It couldn't have been more than a few weeks ago. The tables are still there, lurking in the darkened dining room, laid with red-and-white checkerboard vinyl as if the restaurant might open at any moment, the shakers full of red pepper flakes and Parmesan cheese still crowded around the napkin dispensers.

The loneliness that washes over him when he sees this, the ghost of the pizzeria where he's taken his kids for a decade, is so intense he puts a hand on the window to steady himself. When he turns back to his truck, he notices a figure sleeping on a pile of cardboard in the corner of the strip mall and can't help but approach. He's overcome with a peculiar need: to wake them, speak with them. They are the only ones here. The road is empty. The parking lot is empty. For a moment, it seems like he and this sleeping figure are the only two humans left in Rudder. "Hey," he calls. "You know what happened to the pizza place?" Even before the words are out of his mouth, he realizes the futility in the question. But he just wants to say something. He wants to see the color of this person's eyes, to hear their voice, to know that something as simple as asking a stranger a question and receiving an answer is still possible. The figure twitches and turns over, eyeing Kirby. His forehead is smudged with dirt and a beard has taken hold of his face, sprouting along his cheeks and neck in uneven snarls. His eyes are a crisp, lucid green. Something at his feet moves and Kirby realizes it's a dog. A dirty gray pit bull with a long, sloppy pink tongue.

"Says right there in the window," the man grumbles. "Can't you read?"

"I can," Kirby says. "I just…I was just curious. If you knew anything else." He feels bad now for waking him. It must be hard to get any sleep like this: outside, on cardboard and concrete. He slides a five-dollar bill out of his wallet. "Here," he says, thrusting it down at the man, who takes it.

"What's this for?" he asks. His dog whines softly, licking its human's hand.

"I don't know, man. For whatever you need. Storm's coming."

"I know."

"Could be bad."

The man stares at him. "Already is," he says.

Kirby buys a rotisserie chicken and some sides at the grocery store, then drives home. When he tells the kids the pizza place is closed for good, they don't seem surprised. Neither of them asks why. They all sit at the table and eat chicken straight from the plastic tray it came in, pulling the meat off the bone with their fingers while sounds of the local hurricane watch slip in from the TV in the living room to hover above their heads like dark clouds.

"Why'd they name it Braylen?" Wanda asks.

"Because that was the next name on that spillover list," Kirby replies. "Already went through the alphabet once this season."

"No, I mean…why's Braylen on the list at all?"

"Well. Someone picked it. Who knows why they pick the names they do. It's, um…random, I guess."

Kirby watches her sit with this, chewing, staring down at her plate. He waits for it, feels it coming, but even so, he's unprepared. It isn't as though he didn't know this conversation would happen someday. He just never figured out how he would meet it. "So then—" She struggles to find the right question. "My name. Is because of the list, right?"

"Yeah, in a way," Kirby says. "It's because of the hurricane you were born during. Hurricane Wanda. It was the next name on the list, and then your mother liked it, I guess."

"Why?" Wanda frowns, and Kirby realizes that she's angry. And why wouldn't she be? Frida named her after the storm that mutilated a hundred miles of Florida coast, and then she died before she could understand what a name like that might do to a baby. But it isn't Frida's fault. Kirby is the one who could have decided to name her something else. He should have, knowing everything Frida didn't. The thing was, when it came time to put something down on paper, he couldn't think of anything better. He couldn't think at all.

"Because she knew right away that you were a powerful girl and she wanted you to have a powerful name," Lucas says suddenly. "And Wanda is the *most* powerful name." Kirby's gratitude is immediate and enormous.

"Oh." She absorbs this, painting grease circles with her sticky chicken fingers on the surface of the table. No one chides her about the mess. "I never thought of it that way."

Kirby feels he should add something. "She wanted you to know where you come from. And you come from storms, which can be hard, and people don't always like them, but storms are important. They're nature. You come from, um..." He looks at Lucas, floundering. "From..." He's lost.

"You come from the elements," Lucas finishes. "From the wild." The three of them sit in silence, listening to the weatherwoman drone on about the cone of uncertainty.

"That's sort of cool, I guess," Wanda finally says.

"It is," Kirby replies quickly, relieved. "It's very cool."

If the ocean is a body and the river is a body, then the groundwater is a body, too. The body no one sees. It lies in wait beneath the surface, rising through the cracks and crevices, filtering up and up and up until the limestone above is full and wet. This body sprawls, buried. Sleeping but not. Hidden but not. So deep beneath the earth that it stretches under the ocean floor, so close to the surface that it can tickle the sky when it rains.

HURRICANE BRAYLEN TEARS through central Florida with sharp teeth and a full-throated shriek—a Category 3 by the time it makes land in Homestead—then pushes out toward the Gulf. On the east coast, people breathe a sigh of relief, but Wanda is less occupied with the news than the adults in her life are. None of this fazes her. She doesn't listen to the reports about the damage done to Lake Okeechobee's earthen dam as Braylen passed over, or the concerns about where funding for reinforcing the Hoover Dike might come from. The flood of 1928 doesn't mean anything to her. Lake Okeechobee is fifty miles away. To Wanda, this distance is enormous.

These days, she is primarily concerned with that which is very small. The organisms she cannot see, or rather, the organisms she cannot see without help. Phyllis has shared the magic of looking down the tube of a microscope and glimpsing the squirming throb of tiny lives pressed between two rectangles of glass. A droplet of water expands beneath Wanda's gaze and becomes—a world. She can't get enough. Wandering through each day, she is overcome by her recent understanding that these tiny things are living absolutely everywhere. Inside her, even.

There are other things that interest her, but lately, everything comes back to Phyllis. The activities of her brother and father, the dreaded bustle of her school days, the ever-dire news—all of this pales in comparison to the enchanted expanse of Phyllis's house. Wanda is enthralled by the things she discovers here. Today, Phyllis shows her the pantry. With a mixture of pride and bashfulness, neither of which Wanda is paying the slightest attention to, Phyllis brings Wanda to a room she wasn't previously aware existed. Inside, she is astounded. Shelves as high as the ceiling are built into the walls, and there are more shelves, freestanding, in the center. Lining them are hundreds of canning jars labeled with Phyllis's cramped cursive scrawl, Ziploc bags of dehydrated fruits and meats, gallons of fresh water, jugs of kerosene, big plastic bottles of cooking oil shining buttery yellow like lanterns.

Light from a single window filters in through jars of strawberry preserves, casting a pink glow on the wood floor. Wanda wanders among the shelves; the aisles are narrow, so she moves slowly. With reverence. "It's like a food library," she whispers. "You have everything." Wanda picks up a jar labeled PICKLED RED ONIONS, then another that says TOMATOES. She shakes them gently, as if they are snow globes. The slivered onions spin in their rose-colored vinegary cylinder, dancing.

"Here we go." Phyllis selects a jar of dilly beans and gets the lid off with some difficulty. "These are the green beans from last year." She offers the jar to her young friend. Sprigs of dill float among the beans and a whole clove of garlic twirls at the bottom. Wanda selects a green bean from the middle of the jar and pulls it out. Vinegar drips on the floor. "Go ahead," Phyllis says. "Try it." The flavor is so strong Wanda's tongue puckers around it, garlicky and dilly and a little spicy all at once. She has to fold the bean in half to fit the whole thing in her mouth.

"It's good," she says, crunching. "Sour."

"Better than boiling them, don't you think?" Wanda nods and takes another. This one she nibbles, taking her time with it. Phyllis eats one, too, then screws the lid back on. "We'll put this in the fridge now that it's open." She turns to go, but Wanda doesn't want to leave just yet. She's still mesmerized by everything this room holds.

"What's it all for?" she asks, running her hands along the plywood shelves.

"It's for…" Phyllis pauses. "Emergencies."

Wanda accepts this. She knows all about emergencies.

The next time they visit one of Phyllis's research plots, it's tucked away in a part of town Wanda's never been to. Each plot is new to her still. "Eventually," Phyllis tells her, "you'll know them all." They take the car, and after Phyllis parks on the shoulder of a sandy road, she pulls on her waders and checks to make sure she doesn't need to add anything to her tackle box from the trunk. Wanda waits, fidgeting, sliding her feet in and out of her muck boots, eager to begin.

Finally, Phyllis slams the hatchback shut and they set out, trudging through the forest without speaking, swatting at mosquitoes, carefully brushing aside plants to avoid bruising their tender leaves. Phyllis taught her this—they call it "walking gently." It makes Wanda feel good to be this quiet, to listen to the birds and the frogs and the wet slurp of her boots in the soggy mosses. Wanda's boots are tall enough to keep her feet dry if she's careful about where she steps, but Phyllis can walk practically anywhere with her waders on.

"Don't you think I should have some waders, too?" Wanda asks, speaking quietly in this delicate place. She is eyeing all the routes across the swamp she cannot take.

"Maybe," Phyllis says. "We'll see if we can find some small enough."

Little metal tags begin to appear on the trees, and this is how Wanda knows they've entered the sanctum of the plot. Their progress slows. Phyllis starts taking measurements, checking in on each of her specimens. She keeps meticulous data because she always has. This project of local observation began in earnest when she retired from her teaching role at the community college; it is the work of her remaining years. She loved her students, but she has always been more comfortable out here, in the field. Sometimes she thinks about publishing some of her findings, but that has never been the point. The time for marking ecological change and acting on it has passed, and if she's honest, there is a relief in releasing those fervent, unfulfilled desires for solutions. Now all that's left is to behold these environments as they transition. The great rewilding, as she likes to call it. Humans have spoiled so much, but nature is resourceful. It dies and is reborn as something new. Her work now is to watch this occur.

She lets Wanda hold the clipboard and write down the numbers while she calls them out. They go on like this, sweat and condensation rolling down Wanda's skin in thick streams, and eventually they come to a little lagoon, where the soft ground gives way to cloudy water and a blue heron eyes them from a young mangrove island. The heron watches them for a long minute and then lifts off, beating its wings against the thick air. Wanda turns to Phyllis.

"Can I do this one?" she asks.

"All right." Phyllis passes her a vial and Wanda selects what she hopes is the most solid path toward the edge of the water. It looks promising. Except, it isn't. The mossy surface disintegrates under her foot almost immediately and her entire body pitches forward, cutting through the silty murk. The swifts that have been fluttering among the mangroves depart, rising in a cloud, while Wanda plummets headfirst into the brackish pond scum.

She is stunned by the force of the water rising up to meet her. It's a full-body slap, a surprise that nearly knocks the wind out of her. She is above, and then suddenly she is below, panicking, clawing through the lily pad stems and the seagrass and the silt, trying to scratch her way back to the surface, eyes squeezed shut, water slipping through her grasping fingers. And then, something else—

It spreads through her, an internal wave, rolling over every part of her at once. Not warmth exactly, but something else, bright and cool. She recognizes it from that day at the Edge, and her intrigue outgrows her panic. She stops struggling. Opens her eyes. And even through the swirl of mud and flora she can make out sparks. Little lights, popping into existence in great swaths, spreading until it is as though she is floating through a wet sky. This time, she can feel their consciousness, a sensation of curiosity surrounding her, inspecting her. They want to tell her something, but Wanda doesn't know this language.

Wishing she could stay but needing to breathe, she kicks upward, breaking the surface and immediately registering the blur that is Phyllis, a few yards away, moving toward her. Wanda finds some solid ground, heaves herself onto it, and takes in all the air she can get. Over her shoulder, she sees that the dark, impenetrable lagoon she fell into is something else now.

A smoldering, shivering spray of lights burns beneath the surface, bright and translucent. Bats are just beginning to swoop, cutting across this opening in the trees, coming down low for the mosquitoes. The blue heron calls out, hidden but not far. The frogs chirrup and chirrup and chirrup. Wanda isn't sure what just happened. She looks to Phyllis for an explanation, but even Phyllis is baffled. They sit, staring at the luminous water in silence until it begins to fade, the water returning to its dull muddy swirl. It all happens quickly, but it feels like hours.

"I've never seen bioluminescence here," Phyllis says slowly, reaching for an explanation, latching onto the only thing that makes sense to her. "Dinoflagellates, maybe. They respond to agitation, to movement. I guess you surprised them."

"Dino..."

"Dinoflagellates. Maybe. Or something else. Bioluminescence pops up all over the place. Different habitats, different times." She sifts through her memory for everything she's ever learned about bioluminescence, but this is not her area of expertise. There is something here that doesn't fit. She pushes it away and focuses on what she knows to be true. "Fireflies, glow worms, comb jellies. Krill, I think.

Some do it all on their own; others are just hosts for bioluminescent bacteria or algae." Phyllis stares, uncertain about her own hypothesis. What she doesn't say is that she has never seen or heard of bioluminescence that looks like this—that is every color at once, that she knows for a fact was not here two months ago. The water has gone dark now; the sky is darkening also.

"What's it for?"

"Oh, different things. But I suppose the main categories are to distract predators, to find mates, and to communicate. Adaptation always comes back to survival, remember—survival of the individual, survival of the species."

Wanda finds a stretch of solid ground where she can sit and empty her boots. The water that gushes out still glows softly, but as she pours it into the lagoon, the light dissipates, blends, becomes opaque and muddy like the rest. She can still feel that sensation of a voice without words speaking to her, but she doesn't know how to explain this to Phyllis. Beside her, Phyllis flicks her hand through the water and waits. Nothing happens. The water stays dark. "It's strange how..." Phyllis says, but then doesn't finish. Wanda leans over and imitates Phyllis, skimming the edge of her hand across the surface. A swipe of light, there and then gone.

"Like this," she says, and does it once more, as if showing Phyllis a trick she's learned that can be replicated with the right technique. Phyllis tries again, but there is nothing where her fingers meet the water except dull ripples. Her mind is working overtime, trying to process this new data, searching for a plausible explanation, but still—nothing quite lines up. Wanda puts her boots back on and they sit, quietly contemplating the lagoon.

"It's all changing," Phyllis says after a long silence. "It's changing so fast, Wanda, it's hard to keep up."

"But we'll be ready," Wanda replies. "Won't we?"

"Maybe," Phyllis says, suddenly doubting all of her preparations, all of her years of careful study. In the end, it's all guesswork. Sitting here, she is reminded of just how much she doesn't understand. "That's the plan."

They drive home in the dusky silence, lost in two different streams of thought: Phyllis ticking through hypotheses and experiments and variables, while Wanda wonders if she only imagined those lights whispering to her. And if it was real, what were they trying to say?

Kirby is already parked in the driveway when they get back. Wanda's clothes are still soaked. He raises an eyebrow at Phyllis when he sees Wanda.

"What happened here?"

"Oh." Phyllis had forgotten that part. She looks at Wanda, dripping onto the gravel. "She...fell in."

"Ah," Kirby says. "Get in the back, Wan. I love you, but you smell like something that's been dead for days." He opens the tailgate for her and gives her a boost, then nods at Phyllis, who watches them, still standing motionless beside the car. Kirby shuts the tailgate and Wanda sits down on the wheel well with a squelching sound. "If you'd ever accept any money—" Kirby begins.

"I wouldn't," Phyllis says quickly. She doesn't want his money. Not for Wanda. Not for anything, really. She has no use for it anymore. Just one of many things that are changing.

After the truck has rumbled off, Phyllis takes her field kit inside and goes straight to her study with the water sample from the lagoon. She positions the slide under the microscope and looks and sees something she's never seen before—organisms that are awake and shimmering and moving in the kind of intricate pattern such simple creatures should not be capable of. Yet here they are.

AFTER LUCAS SENDS in his applications, he tries to forget about college. Unfortunately, this is impossible. He thinks about it constantly. It's a tic, a reflexive rut he can't seem to escape. He goes back over his applications in the middle of the night, searching each piece for a fatal mistake. But there aren't any. Brenda wrote a nice recommendation. The guidance counselor came through. His essay turned out all right. And most importantly, no one else knows—there's no one to ask him if he's heard anything or to watch him while he checks the mailbox, turning each envelope over in his hands like it might be the one. He is safe from everyone's expectations except his own.

Christmas approaches. The Lowes aren't very good at celebrating things, Kirby and Lucas in particular, but for Wanda's sake they make an effort. There is a tree—a raggedy artificial thing Kirby keeps in the attic. And lights. The Lowe men do know how to put up nice lights. They let Wanda plug them in when they've all been strung, as they do every year, and their shabby living room comes alive. When she was little, Wanda would clap and say *Ooh* as if magic had occurred. This year, when they come on she admires them quietly, a faraway look on her face. As if she's staring at something no one else can see. She's been different lately, he notes, not for the first time. He chalked it up to her obsession with Phyllis before, but now he realizes that's not quite it. Maybe it's just that she's getting older.

New Year's is nothing much. Someone sets off a few firecrackers nearby at midnight, but that's all. Lucas is already in bed when he hears them pop. The next day is a Wednesday; Lucas and Kirby go to work the same as always. Hurricane season lasted longer than usual, so there's still plenty to repair. It lasts longer every year. No direct hits this season, so that's something. There are murmurs coming out of central Florida: concerns that the Hoover Dike won't last another year with no plans to reinforce it. Fears that Lake Okeechobee will burst free. But it's only one of so many murmurs about so many things.

One day in February, Lucas drives to buy groceries and then keeps going. He doesn't plan it, but somehow he ends up on Beachside, and then he's in front of Gillian's parents' house. There is a line of artless graffiti scrawled on the siding: *Miami Vice will live forever.* He sits for a while before he gets out, trying to understand what he's doing here. The door is ajar. Inside, stepping over the leftovers of a squatter, long gone by the looks of it, he remembers the first time he came to this house. He was sixteen. Gillian wanted to introduce him to her parents, and it wasn't until he was on the porch, ringing the bell, that he understood how different they were from his family. The house is modern and luxurious—or it was. Now it reeks of mildew and urine. Some of the windows have been blown out, probably by gale winds, maybe by humans. A white shag carpet in the living room that he used to worry about spilling something on is now a grayish yellow. They left most of their furniture behind: ornately carved cabinets, beds with four posters and tall headboards, a pale pink sectional so soft you could disappear into it. So much has been abandoned that he wonders what Gillian actually packed up.

He roams the floor plan, thinking of Gillian in her graduate program, sitting in classrooms, in libraries, in boys' dorm rooms. He doesn't realize that she probably doesn't live in a dorm anymore. Why would he? Her life is a cipher to him. There have been no letters about his applications—nothing either way. He sits down on the sectional and a puff of sourness rises from the upholstery. Here, in this place where he first learned about money, about all the things he didn't have and all the paths he couldn't take, he allows himself to imagine that the letters he's waiting for aren't rejections after all. He imagines that they are invitations. And then, just a few seconds into the warm rush of a daydream, he plummets back to this sinking spit of land with the certainty that he can't possibly leave. He can't leave his crew, his father, his sister. He can't leave this town—not the way Gillian did. Not the way her parents and all the other Beachsiders did. In the end, it won't matter what the envelopes hold. He'll stay. His daydreams melt into a hot shame in having applied at all. This is where he belongs. It's what he deserves.

In March, the afternoon thunderstorms begin. It's too early for it. The rainy season is meant to start in May, but the sky doesn't follow anyone's rules but its own anymore. At work, they do what they can in the rain, but when the thunder rolls through and the bright zippers of lightning appear on the horizon, Kirby tells them to cab up and they either wait it out in their trucks or head back to the yard to call it a day.

On a particularly stormy afternoon, they abandon the work site. Brenda goes home and Kirby stays behind at the yard to make calls from his office. He sends Lucas to pick up Wanda by himself, forgetting what he's asking of his son. Lucas says, "No problem," and leaves before Kirby has time to remember. His father has enough to worry about. The rain on the windshield is heavy as Lucas drives, pounding against the glass and transforming his view of the road into watery smudges. He has the radio turned up loud to drown out the thrumming against the body of the truck. When he was younger, this kind of weather got the best of him. Every time it stormed, he could feel his nerves sizzle, like live wires slapping against the road: useless, frantic energy.

It took years for Lucas to stop holding his breath when he passed the blue house. What happened there—he doesn't remember it completely. Just fragments. But some pieces are impossible to forget. He slows and turns into the driveway. There: the gravel he tripped on as he ran, his short twelve-year-old legs tangling beneath him. And over there: the tree that caught his little brother's body after the wind picked him up and threw him. He saw it happen. Saw the jolt of impact. Heard it. He used to torture himself by trying to determine when it was that Flip died—the exact moment when his brother became meat. Was he somehow still alive while Lucas was pounding on Phyllis's door? If Lucas had been braver, could he have saved him? By the time they found his body, it was so traumatized no one could tell which blow was fatal. He knows this from eavesdropping; neither of his parents ever discussed it with him.

The jungle is thick around Phyllis's house, even thicker now than it was back then, like all this time it's been trying to swallow her home whole. One day, he thinks, it will succeed, and this house will disappear completely. He honks and waits in the truck, hoping he won't have to go to the door to collect Wanda. He doesn't want to climb those steps, or to use his fist on the thick door, or to stand on the long wraparound porch. Just imagining it is already too much.

Sweat soaks through his shirt. The flow of air in his throat shortens, tightens. *No, no, no,* he thinks, *not now. Not again.* He thought he was past all this, but his body tells him otherwise. His lungs seem to shrink. He forces them to open and close, to fill and deflate, like working a stiff, unwieldy bellows. He sees Phyllis opening the door—it isn't today, but it's so suddenly vivid it might as well be. He's on the porch and it's ten years ago. He's feeling her drape a bath towel, pink and worn, around his shoulders, hearing her tell him to breathe deep, to hold each breath carefully, like a fragile butterfly: Imagine the gentleness of its wings inside his lungs, she says, the feathery tips of its antennae, the tiny curl of its proboscis. He does this now, leaning his head against the cool cradle of the window. Wings with indigo diamonds painted on velvety black, the dim shimmer of a compound eye, legs as thin and delicate as an eyelash—

The tightness in his chest slowly subsides as the butterfly takes form in his mind. The rain keeps pounding. The door stays shut. Finally, after what seems like hours but surely isn't, surely couldn't be, except who can tell when the sun has left them so completely, he gets out of the truck and climbs the steps. He knocks. Is this really the first time he's been on this porch since that day? Before he can think too hard about it, the door swings open, and there's Phyllis, the bright spatter of her white hair appearing like a lighthouse on this gloomy afternoon, a warm glow spilling out behind her.

"Lucas!" she says. "You're early. Come in." What can he say? He hesitates, then steps inside. The house is the same, but just different enough to soothe his sparking nerves. The couch he sat on with the pink towel wrapped around his shoulders is in a different place, with a different slipcover. The living room seems more open, less cluttered. Phyllis calls Wanda down from upstairs. "She's in my study," Phyllis explains. She looks toward him, but not at him—staring absentmindedly past his shoulder. "Wanda is a special girl, you know," she says.

"I know," he replies.

"But—maybe even more than we thought."

Lucas tries to make sense of this, but his adrenal system is too heightened to absorb it. He's about to ask what Phyllis means by that when Wanda gallops down the stairs, coming down so fast it's like she's falling. He forgets his question. Leaving this house is the only thing he can think about now. "Put your shoes on, Wan," he says. "Time to go."

These days, Wanda is always bringing something home from Phyllis's. Vegetables from the garden, still covered in dirt; a fistful of wild-flowers; a dozen shit-stained eggs; glass jars packed with jam; a loaf of bread, even. Things she's gathered or harvested or made from scratch under Phyllis's careful tutelage. Somewhere along the way, Phyllis taught her what to do with all of these spoils. As if overnight, Lucas notices that Wanda has learned to cook. She makes salads with the fresh, gritty lettuces; she boils pasta and stirs in Sungold tomatoes and olive oil and cheese. She makes stir-fries and soups and even, on occasion, a chocolate cake, which is a recipe he begins to suspect she knows by heart. He watches her make it one Sunday afternoon to be sure, and it's true. It is a poem she's memorized.

Lucas sits at the table and pretends to read something while Wanda leaves behind a glorious mess, skipping around the kitchen, climbing up on her little step stool and then hopping off it, measuring flour, shaking salt into the palm of her hand and then brushing it into the mixture. He wasn't even aware they owned cake pans. It makes him think of Frida—the way she moved so easily in this kitchen. The meals he should have appreciated but didn't. Half an hour later, Wanda's cake emerges from the oven in two layers, and after it cools he watches her fill the middle with cream she's whipped herself and jam she brought home from Phyllis's.

She'll be okay without him, he realizes with a little jolt. Not just that; she will thrive. Slowly, steadily, the idea of an envelope carrying an acceptance—an invitation that he might possibly receive but also, *also*, one that he might actually accept—solidifies. She spreads another layer of whipped cream on top and for the first time, he allows that his penance—for Frida, for Flip—might one day come to an end.

He looks at Wanda placing a ring of huckleberries around the edge of her cake. Everything he and Kirby told her about where her name comes from, it's all true. He didn't know that when he said it, but he knows now.

ALL WINTER, PHYLLIS and Wanda have been experimenting with different bodies of water. They've discovered the organisms Phyllis found in the lagoon's water sample everywhere they look— the Intracoastal Waterway, the swamps, the creek, even the ocean it- self. Wanda knows this is strange because of Phyllis's incredulity, but she is too young to be truly surprised. What's more, the organisms come out only when Wanda is near. They flock to her, glow for her, and then they dissipate. Perhaps it explains why Phyllis has never found them before, but it hardly satisfies her desire for a scientific explanation. These mysteries have consumed them both for months, lending a certain vitality to their time together. Wanda is thrilled by the hunt for an explanation, but she doesn't require one. To her, these organisms are a magic she doesn't need to name. To Phyllis, they are science that requires categorization. And who is to say they cannot be both?

The more Wanda interacts with these bodies of water, and by extension, the creatures living within, the stronger her sense grows that they are trying to communicate with her. She describes them to Phyllis as whispers, but it isn't something she hears. Not exactly. Maybe it is more accurate to say that she feels them, but even that is not quite right. Phyllis encourages all of Wanda's observations, no matter how strange or unscientific. Privately, she is skeptical. The human mind inevitably reaches for personification to soothe the shock of forces or creatures it doesn't understand. This is all well and good for a child. But Phyllis is a scientist. She relies on the data.

That spring, Wanda and Phyllis stop at a tag sale on the way home from surveying a forest plot. Wanda's never been to a tag sale before. Kirby calls them junk stores whenever they pass one and refuses to stop. On either side of the driveway, knickknacks are laid out on top of big blue tarps, the corners held down with rocks or chipped furniture. A middle-aged woman with inky dyed hair and skin too pale for Florida inspects a pile of china, picking up each plate and turning it over in her hands before she decides whether to buy. A man in a lawn chair smokes and reads a magazine, holding reign over the yard with a cash box at his feet, a baseball cap tipped back on his head.

"If you see something, just make an offer," he calls out without looking up. Phyllis nods and begins perusing. Wanda slyly watches the man, sure she knows him. It's Arjun—he came to her birthday party last year. The red plastic fireman's hat he gave her is still on her dresser. She has faint memories of the softball tournaments he and Kirby used to put on every year, for the firemen, the linemen, the cops, and the EMTs. Arjun was the master of ceremonies at these gatherings, the center of everything, as if the games and the grilling and even the placement of the picnic tables radiated out from him in a burst of activity inspired by his presence. There hasn't been one for years. Now—she looks at the array of broken treasures carefully arranged on the ground. This is a moving sale, an everything-must-go sort of affair. He is not an epicenter of people anymore, but of things. She hovers, picking up an old lamp with no shade, then putting it back down. Arjun finally raises his eyes and recognizes her, too. She remembers how much he used to smile; now he just looks tired, emptied of the charisma that used to overflow.

"You're Kirby's kid," he says. "How's your dad?"

"He's okay." The fire chief nods and lights a fresh cigarette with the one he's still smoking. Takes a deep, sharp drag. "You're going?" Wanda asks.

"I'm going," he says.

"Where?"

He shrugs. "My sister lives in Montana. It's supposed to be better up there. Anyway, have a look around. Whatever you want, just go on and grab it, okay? Call it a birthday present. I won't be here for your next one."

"Okay." Wanda feels sad that Arjun is leaving. He has always been kind to her. She sees Phyllis inspecting old books in the garage and she moves to join in, but something stops her. A glimpse of movement out of the corner of her eye, except there's nothing there. Arjun has lost interest in her. Phyllis is preoccupied. But there it is again, another flicker—whether it's a thing she sees or hears or feels is hard to determine. It wants her to follow—she understands this much at least—and so she does. Past a card table laid out with empty picture frames and old bedsheets and a milk crate full of records, past a bicycle with a worn seat, past a little wagon piled with stuffed animals, to the narrow space between the house and the garage. For a moment, she thinks she's mistaken. There's nothing here but weeds and rusty garden tools and—*ah*. She immediately knows it's meant for her.

It's only an old canoe, tucked back behind the lawnmower—an algae-crusted, mud-smeared vessel with two bench seats and what looks like gator teeth marks on the hull. A torn life preserver lies in the bottom, its orange reflective tape shining, and one long, double-ended paddle is stashed under the seats. There's nothing special about it. Only this feeling, this whisper, that she will need it.

WHEN THREE WEEKS have gone by since he started calling his supervisor to file the crew's overtime requests and he still hasn't been able to get anyone at city hall on the phone, Kirby resolves to go in person. He leaves Lucas and Brenda at the job site after lunch and heads over. Pulling into the parking lot, he can already feel that something is wrong. It's nearly empty. The flagpole is bare. The lawn is overgrown, sprouting wildflowers. The windows are dark. The fears that he told himself were premature are beginning to seem entirely plausible. Inside, the hallways are dim shadowy stretches and the offices are all empty. When he gets to the city planning bullpen and finds a lone employee flicking through a box of files, he feels as though he's come upon a ghost. Kirby pauses in the open doorway, reassuring himself that this is just an ordinary man, in a regular building, doing his job. He raps his knuckles against the pane of frosted glass.

The man yelps and puts a hand on his chest. "You scared the shit out of me."

"Sorry," Kirby says, but he isn't. He's relieved there's someone else to confirm how eerie this building has become. They look at each other. The man is middle-aged, with a hairline creeping back toward the tops of his ears. A deep pink flush of rosacea spreads across his cheeks. Kirby tries to remember if he's ever met this man before, but nothing about him seems familiar. "Are you…Do you work with Declan?"

"Well, I did," the man replies. "But he's gone now."

"Gone?"

"Yeah, gone," the man says. "Look around, buddy. Everyone's gone."

"Well, yeah. I see that. Look, I'm the foreman." Kirby receives a blank look. "The electrical foreman?"

"Oh sure, sure." The man waits to see what he wants, his hands still resting on the edge of the cardboard bank box. Kirby looks closer— the man isn't filing at all. He's cleaning out his desk.

"I haven't been able to get my crew's overtime approved," Kirby finally says. "For a while now. I've been calling. Is there someone I can speak to?"

"You don't know? Look, it's really not my job, to deliver news like this, but…someone should have told you. Didn't you get an email or something? The whole municipality is shutting down. Is shut down. We're…well, we're bankrupt, is the thing." Kirby just stares at him. It's not that he's surprised, just that he can't imagine what to say or do now that this news is being delivered as a fact, rather than a possibility. The man is uncomfortable with Kirby's silence. "So, no overtime," he adds, dumping a mug full of pens into the box and waiting for Kirby to leave. But Kirby doesn't want to leave.

"Don't you know what I do?" Kirby asks. The man just keeps at it with his packing: a stress ball, a few pairs of reading glasses, a framed picture of a little boy holding a fishing rod that's too big for him. He doesn't want to look Kirby in the eye. This reaction, when people find out that their job has ceased to exist, that there are no more city services, no more Rudder—he's seen enough of it. Everyone's reaction is different, but no one's is good. Kirby barrels forward anyway, feeling that he must explain how vital his job is. "I keep the electricity on. The water pumps. AC. All of it."

"I don't know what to tell you." The man sighs, wondering why he chose this day of all days to come gather his things.

"So I'm just supposed to stop? With no plan? Are the county's linemen taking over? A contractor?"

The man shakes his head slowly. "I couldn't tell you, really. But. County's not far behind," he says.

"So then…what, the entire town falls off the grid? The whole county? No more power? No more air-conditioning? No more…fuck, no more gas? How will people live?"

"Look, guy," the man says, and then takes a deep breath. "Believe me when I say that the repercussions of the fiscal situation we find ourselves in have not escaped me, or anyone else. But the fact is, the population is migrating. The entire coastline is eroding, the sea level's rising—I mean, it's not like it's news to you. The cost of infrastructure is too high to sustain. And getting higher every year. Fewer taxpayers, bigger problems, less money. Et cetera."

"Well, what about relocation packages, then? Didn't they…didn't they do that in Miami? Federal relocation allowances?"

The man struggles not to laugh. It's despair, not humor, but he's learned from experience that it's never a good idea to name the absurdity of it all in these situations. "Yes, Miami did receive some federal money for relocations. But we're not Miami."

"So we…"

"Got nothing."

Kirby shakes his head, as though he doesn't understand. But he does. He understands perfectly. "You've known for how long? About the bankruptcy?"

"Understand that I'm just the messenger. My salary is forty K a year, you know? Was. I'm as pissed as you. We've known for a little over two weeks. And before that…we were still trying. But yeah. Two weeks or so. Look, someone should have sent you an email, obviously, I'm sorry about that, but I don't know what else I can say."

Kirby slowly turns to go, still in shock.

"Good luck out there," the man calls.

By the time Kirby reaches the parking lot, he realizes that he's known for weeks. Months, even. It was the same with the beaches. The same with the floods, the hurricanes, the sea level. Didn't he know all of this was coming? Didn't everyone? They've known for years. Decades. It didn't make any difference. None at all. Because now it's here and despite all that knowing, he's lost. Everyone is. They had all hung their hats on the question of proximity. Yes, it will be bad, they'd said to one another, but we have years. We have time. Somehow we'll solve this along the way. He doesn't even have the energy to be angry.

Kirby gets in his truck and lays his cheek against the steering wheel. He wants to cry, but he's forgotten how. His eyes water and he waits for it; nothing comes. He just sits, unsure what to do next. The smooth plastic on his cheek is hot without the AC, burning really, but he can't manage to reach over and turn the truck on. The only thing surprising about any of this is that he's alive to see it. That's the real bet they all made, isn't it? It will come. But not until we're gone.

Kirby drives to the Edge. He never crosses the causeway anymore unless it's for work, but today he wants to look the ocean in the face. When he gets there, though, he can't bring himself to get out of the truck. He feels set apart behind his windshield; not safe exactly, just—other. The saltiness of the air slips in through the vents, even though the windows are closed. The tide creeps forward. Soon it will lap at his tires. Just because there is glass between him and the Edge doesn't mean it won't swallow him whole. He realizes now that this idea of being separate isn't real.

All these years, he's known, but now he knows in a different way. He thought he was prepared, standing knee-deep in the surf, watching the wave approach, watching it get closer and closer, seeing the white of its crest, legs braced, leaning in, and then it knocked him off his feet anyway. Just like when Frida and Flip died: the sudden smack of it hitting him and then the long, deep, dark churn of being inside it. He finally gets out of his truck and lets the water touch his boots. This is the truth.

When he gets home, Lucas and Wanda are waiting for him. He's exhausted. His body, so accustomed to physical labor, doesn't know what to do with this churn of emotion. His heart aches as if it's a muscle he's worked too hard. His children sit at the kitchen table, smiling at him. Greeting him. He wonders how to tell them, or when. But he sees now that his children have something they want to tell *him*. Something that delights them. He cannot rob them of whatever this is. Not yet.

Lucas offers a few sheets of creased paper to Kirby with a sort of yearning he hasn't seen on his son's face in a long time. It reminds him of when he felt like he could protect his children from all this…a morning he hasn't allowed himself to think about for many years. Putting up the hurricane plywood on the windows with his boys. On the ladder. In the rain. He remembers how excited they were to help. How eager. How grateful to be near their father, to have his attention in that dark, damp hour before dawn.

He takes the papers.

"Dad," Lucas says.

Kirby looks down at what Lucas has given him, and it takes him a few minutes to realize they are acceptance letters. To colleges. *We are delighted to inform you.* Three of them: Georgia Tech, Michigan, UC Berkeley. Lucas waits for him to say something, but Kirby doesn't have the words he needs for this moment. He looks at his son, his mouth empty of sound, still searching for the right shapes. Words never did come easy.

The letters fall from his hands and he pulls Lucas toward him, cupping the back of his head, holding him as he did all those years ago when he was small. His son is too big to be held in this way—there's too much of him—but he stretches his arms as wide as they'll go anyway, hugging with his whole body.

"So proud," Kirby whispers eventually, just loud enough so Lucas can hear. "You did real good."

Is the rain a body, too? Or is it many? All of these water bodies—the oceans and the rivers and the groundwater and the rain—they all give and they all take. This is the nature of being a body.

WHEN GOING TO college was just an idea, it had no shape to it. Lucas would lie in bed imagining huge amphitheater classrooms, majestic chalkboards, library carousels, each with its own little light, but he didn't spend time thinking about the other parts. Bureaucracy, for example. Class enrollment, health insurance, registrar paperwork, financial aid requirements. This sort of thing occupies him a great deal now—form upon form upon form. If going to college has a shape, he thinks, that shape is a sheet of A4 paper.

There are also the logistics of moving. This he feels more equipped to address. There are tangible items on this list, actions and objects: tuning up his car, packing his belongings, buying the textbooks he will need. And finally, there are the feelings that accompany moving: wisps of heartache hiding underneath the mundanity of his to-do list, bursts of pleasure to be shedding a life that doesn't fit. It feels as bad as he was afraid it might, and it feels as good as he hoped it could.

When he calls to tell his mother the news, she says, "Finally," and rants on and on about Kirby, about Rudder, about Lucas's lost potential. He doesn't talk to her often anymore, but after this, he knows he will talk to her even less. Things have been frayed between them since she remarried and moved to Minneapolis. No, longer—they've been frayed since Flip died. They love each other because they have to, not because they want to.

He's more protective of Rudder than usual because he worries he's betraying everything he comes from by leaving. Thinking of all the Gillians, the people who gave up on Rudder too soon, the people without whom Rudder couldn't survive, he tries to assure himself that he isn't one of them—but he is. Kirby sits him down and tells him about the municipality going bankrupt, then insists it changes nothing for Lucas. Though it does change some things. In some ways, it makes it easier. Lucas might have given up on Rudder first, but now Rudder has given up on itself.

Kirby promises to find work near whichever school he chooses, and in this sense at least, the future feels hopeful for his family—an experienced lineman can always find work. Lucas picks UC Berkeley, which offered him a generous scholarship, and applies for a loan to cover the rest. California has its own problems—fires, drought, earthquakes—but it's still functioning with some semblance of how things used to be. That's how the world is divided now: the places that still function, and the places that don't. Florida doesn't. Their local governments are dissolving, their infrastructure crumbling. Louisiana is fading, too. The Outer Banks of North Carolina are gone entirely. The Bahamas. Indonesia. More will follow.

The way he imagined leaving is hard to let go of. He wanted to leave Rudder in order to return with the missing pieces: the prodigal son, coming home with exactly the right tools at exactly the right time. It won't be like he wanted. He sees that now. The dream dies gradually. It hurts to let it go, but this is part of what he wants to learn, why he applied in the first place—how to see what is. And then, what to do about it.

The summer months set in. Mornings are hot and damp, hung with clear skies and a baking sun. It takes only a few hours before the ground begins to sizzle. The clouds roll in around lunchtime and shortly after, thunderstorms rip open the sky. Every day, the warm rain pummels them. Soon, the ground is full and wet, like unwrung laundry. This is how summers always are, but the rainfall has been extraordinary for months. The earth can accept only so much before there is nowhere left for the water to go.

A strange pause settles over the Lowe household. Kirby, for all his capable certainty, is unmoored. Lucas has never seen him like this. Those years just after Frida and Flip died, when he was living with his mother, he was consumed by his own haze, being shuttled from one therapist to another, trying this medication and that. Back then, Chloe was furious with him for not getting better. It's part of why he chose Kirby when he had the chance—he didn't want to get better, and neither did Kirby. They could at least be broken together.

Now, watching his father roam the house, pacing from room to room, he isn't sure he'll be able to leave him like this. Kirby assures him that the necessary things have been set in motion: job applications have been sent, new places to live are being considered. But without the tether of work, of going to the yard every morning, of each new job site, Kirby seems adrift. Confused by the hours he is expected to fill, almost childlike in his uncertainty of how to fill them. Lucas knows it's only a matter of time before the job offers start coming; people need linemen everywhere. During this in-between time, he sometimes notices his father taking the bucket truck out to work alone, unpaid, unasked, maybe just to feel some sense of normalcy. He wonders if he should ride along, but he hasn't been invited and it seems wrong to insert himself.

One afternoon, when the thunderheads have begun rumbling but the rain has yet to break, Brenda comes to say goodbye. It's July by then, the heat creeping above one hundred during the day and dropping only slightly at night. She pulls up in her little Nissan pickup, sky blue with a silver stripe down the side, a black tonneau cover over everything she could fit in the bed, and honks to let them know she's here. The Lowes spill out the kitchen door, all three of them.

"I wanted to come by before I leave," she says.

"When will you go?" Lucas asks.

"Tomorrow. Early." She leans against the Nissan. Sweat darkens the edges of her tank top and she's taken her braids out, letting her hair float in a black cloud beneath her ball cap. She looks different to Lucas, like the weight of Rudder has begun to slough off her shoulders. "Gonna get a real early start, before the sun comes up," she says. They stand, awkward, shifting from one foot to the other as they discuss routes and traffic and how many days it'll take to get to Wyoming. The thunder comes closer. Brenda congratulates Lucas again on UC Berkeley.

"You deserve it," she says. Lucas isn't sure this is true, but he tries to accept the compliment gracefully. She slaps Kirby on the back. "These two," she says, gesturing at Lucas and Wanda, "you did good, old man, with these two. Real special kids."

"They are, aren't they," Kirby replies, and he sounds far away, as if he is someplace else, in the future maybe, watching them make their way in a world that extends beyond this town. Lucas asks Brenda about her new job, something near Laramie. It's transmission only, she tells him, no more residential bullshit, just middle-of-nowhere type jobs. Lucas wonders if she and Kirby will realize how good they would have been together after it's too late. Or maybe they'll never figure it out. Maybe this is part of what makes them perfect for each other.

After a while, there's nothing left to talk about. When they start to say their goodbyes, Brenda gives them each an unprecedented hug. Kirby kisses her on the cheek. Lucas thanks her for the recommendation letter and she pretends it was nothing, even though he knows she worked hard on it. Wanda won't let go when it's her turn. "Will I ever see you again?" she whispers into Brenda's neck. Lucas's heart breaks for all of them. Wanda especially.

"Of course you will," Brenda says quickly and nuzzles the side of her head, awkward and tender.

But she won't.

WANDA'S TIME IS her own now that school is out. Kirby doesn't make her go to Phyllis's anymore; she goes because she wants to. Sometimes she stays home if it seems like Lucas will pay attention to her, but this happens less and less—by now, he is occupied with preparations for his new life in California. It's become clear that they have all arrived at an ending of sorts. That things will never again be as they were. There's talk she doesn't completely understand—about the municipality, about taxes, about federal money and county money—but she understands enough to know that everything is changing. The house, usually so empty during the day, is full of men behaving strangely.

On a particular afternoon, while Lucas is busy packing in their room and Kirby is pacing, looking for a project, Wanda rides her bike to Phyllis's in the downpour. When she gets there, soaked, Phyllis dries her off and then they go out again, in the car this time, to a Target in the next town over. Driving through the rain, which smears the landscape across the windows in a rich green blur, they go slowly. The roads are almost empty. The air-conditioning is a little too cold against Wanda's damp clothes, but it's nice being too cold. It's rare. When they get there, the parking lot is scattered with only a few cars.

Inside, they drip on the linoleum just after the automatic doors and look out over the empty aisles. It feels like the store is all theirs. Phyllis takes a cart and they begin to roam, rolling past shelves picked clean. The store has been so combed over it takes real work to find the things they're looking for. Wanda stands on the end of the cart while Phyllis steers, her arms bent back to grip the edge like the figurehead of a ship braced across the bow.

They're plundering what remains of the Bic lighters—Phyllis sweeps all six five-packs into the cart—when a man and two children appear at the end of the aisle. Wanda looks up and sees two sets of identical blue eyes, pale as stovetop flames. The twins. Corey leers at her. But what can he do here under the fluorescent lights, Phyllis barely two feet away? He can't hurt her, surely he can't, but she's scared anyway. "Hurry up," their father barks, already in the next aisle. It sounds like an order. Brie pulls Corey on, averting her eyes from Wanda. "Come on," she mutters to him. He resists for just a second, then follows. Wanda steps down off the cart. Being here no longer feels fun.

"Can we go?" she asks. Phyllis hasn't gotten everything on her list yet, but she reads Wanda's face and leads her to the checkout line without asking why.

Driving home, Phyllis asks, "Do you wanna tell me what that was about?"

"Those kids," she mumbles, before there's time to pretend. It feels good to tell Phyllis the truth. Corey isn't quite so terrifying here in the car.

"Kids can be cruel," Phyllis says after a moment. She looks at Wanda out of the corner of her eye. "What did they do to you?"

Wanda tells her. She's never said any of it out loud before. She tells her everything, about breaking Kirby's rules, riding to the Edge, about the four of them finding her, what they did, what they said, and finally, she tells Phyllis about that strange feeling that came over her when she was underwater, so vivid she'll never forget it. "I was so scared," she finishes. "And then after, I didn't know how to tell it."

She isn't sure what's happening when Phyllis pulls the car over onto the shoulder and puts it in park. Turning to Wanda, she brushes a frizz of damp hair away from her eyes and lets her hand linger on the side of Wanda's face.

"Thank you for telling me," she says. "I bet that was hard to talk about." She doesn't say anything else, just goes on looking at Wanda, stroking her cheek with her thumb, waiting, as if she knows something Wanda doesn't. And she does. Wanda begins to sob into the space that Phyllis has made for her, inside the cool cocoon of the car, the humid jungle beating down on them, comforting in its tenacity. She sobs so hard it feels like her ribs are cracking. Phyllis gathers her up, as if she's known all along that something needed to come out, and she squeezes her tight and she says, "That's good. That's a good cry."

After Wanda is done, they start driving again, the rain still coming down as hard as ever, sluicing across the windshield in waves. "I'm gonna miss you," Phyllis says. "You're my favorite, you know."

When she gets home, she tells Kirby she doesn't want to go. He sits down with her at the kitchen table and explains that without any work, he can't stay in Rudder. He says he thought she understood. And she did. She does. She just...doesn't want to leave Phyllis all alone here. She doesn't want to leave this house. She doesn't want to leave the land Phyllis has taught her to see and love and tend.

"Phyllis will be all right," Kirby says.

"I don't want to go," she insists again.

"Me neither," Kirby replies with a sigh. "But we can't stay. We just can't."

"Why? Phyllis isn't going."

"That's true. But Phyllis is...well, a survivalist." Wanda wants to know what that means exactly. Why can't they be survivalists, too? "It means she's been getting ready for years, prepping," Kirby tells her. "Preparing."

"We're not ready?"

Kirby shakes his head. "We are not." He looks so sad that Wanda, even in her fury at being forced to leave, reaches out to hug him. "I'm sorry," he says, his voice catching. "I should have done it different."

LATE AT NIGHT, when the rain has stopped and both his children are sleeping, Kirby looks at the emails on his phone that have trickled in these past few weeks: a half dozen job offers stare back at him, in a half dozen places. Unanswered. They'll keep. He puts down his phone and goes out onto the porch to be in the dark for a while.

The water drips off the gutters and makes soft kissing noises against the wet earth. He will choose a new job, find a new home for himself and Wanda, a place Lucas can visit. He will pack up this life and move to another—just not yet. It's hard leaving this place, and Wanda isn't making it any easier. He never imagined that he'd move. Flip is here, running through the yard, playing board games in the living room, standing on a chair to peek into a bird's nest under the porch's eaves. And Frida is here, reaching for Kirby in their bed after an argument, standing barefoot in the kitchen, asking him what he thinks the baby will be like. Who she'll become. They're all still here. Even a younger Lucas, still twelve, bratty and hardworking and eager for love. How can he leave them behind? How can he leave the memory of that morning, covering the windows in the dark, the boys handing up the wood, Frida sleeping naked in the heat, just a few inches away on the other side of the wall? Is it possible he can take these ghosts with him? That morning is something he must keep, however sharp or bitter it feels to carry. He must keep it at all costs.

He allows himself fantasies of staying—a rogue lineman, keeping the lights on with no pay, no help. Raising Wanda to be his assistant. They could manage it for a little while. He's certain they could. But why? For whom? Soon, the power plants that serve these lines will shutter. It's only a matter of time. And what then? Nursing a dying creature isn't always the kind thing to do. It's the end of Rudder for the Lowe family. He understands it, he just doesn't quite know it.

He could've learned something from Phyllis, with her solar panels and her hand-pump well; the chickens strutting around in the jungle behind her house; the garden, always yielding something. The willingness to see and plan for everything that most people ignored. But it's too late now. He learned all of this the hard way. He put his trust in electricity, in a kind of civilization that requires politics and oversight and dollars. The house isn't worth anything. And once the power goes and the supermarket folds and the gas stations sell their last gallon, money won't be worth anything, either. Not here.

They'll be gone by the time all that happens. They'll go and he'll work and he'll earn: doubling down on this doomed infrastructure elsewhere. Someplace where he probably won't be alive to see it collapse. Is the idea that he probably won't be there to see it fall apart a comfort to him? It isn't, not anymore. The strange thing is it used to be.

After breakfast, Kirby drives. Kirby is always the one to drive. But now, there's no job site, no Lucas in the passenger seat, no Brenda following close behind. The only thing that remains of his routine is the driving. He goes to the yard out of habit. And once he's there, he gets out and walks around the building, checking that all the equipment is strapped down or moved inside. He already knows it is. But checking feels good. It feels useful. The dirt has all turned to mud, inches deep, squelching over the toes of his work boots with every step. It's been a wet year. The wettest he can remember. There was a time when the implications of this would register, but there is so much more than rainfall to worry about now. He flicks up the bill of his cap to see the gulls overhead, screaming at each other.

"You lost?" he says under his breath. "Ocean's that way." Gradually, he becomes aware of another sound underneath the squawking. Something delicate. A young sound. It's close, near the chain-link fence, maybe? He paces, listening. Getting down on his knees, he parts the tall grass and sees, lying on its back, its tiny legs helplessly pedaling the air, a kitten. Black, like a smudge of soot. He scoops it up without thinking and on the enormous bed of his palms it mews with everything it's got—not much—then tries to take the edge of his thumb in its mouth, teeth needling his calloused skin with futile desperation.

"Where's your mother?" he whispers. He listens for the rest of the litter nearby, but there's nothing, only the cawing gulls moving back toward the sea. He realizes he shouldn't have touched it, that maybe now its mother, if she is here somewhere, won't take it back. Is that true? He isn't sure. The round, dirty belly heaves, the kitten so young its eyes are still shut tight. He touches that perfect mound of stomach at the peak of its roundness, and the kitten curls around his pointer finger, claws scrabbling against the knuckle, already sharp but too soft to pierce his weathered skin. He puts it back and hopes that it'll be okay. As he walks toward the truck the mewing begins again. A thin, quivering wail.

He gets in the truck and shuts the door. The wail can't penetrate the windows. He watches the tall grass and waits—waits for a long time, hours—but no mother comes. The afternoon thunder rolls in and the rain begins. Soft at first, then hard. He watches the force with which it hits his windshield. There is a meanness about the rain today. This whole season has been vicious, lashing Rudder with more than the ground can absorb. He can't stand it. Eventually, he realizes he doesn't have to.

The kitten is still there when he goes back, hidden in the grass, and when he picks it up, its body is so cold and damp and limp he worries he's too late, that it's already dead. But then it moves, and he can feel the shudder of a heartbeat, or maybe the heave of a breath, against his hand. He tucks the kitten inside his breast pocket, where it fits neatly. It's the safest place he can think to put it. Back in the truck, it begins to knead his chest through the thick cotton of his shirt: weak pushes, delicate pinpricks. Without thinking, he tucks his chin down and exhales on the kitten, slowly, as if this air, warm from his lungs, might be a spell that will keep it alive. For a brief moment he imagines putting the entire creature in his mouth and holding it there, warm and safe, protected by his teeth, pillowed by his tongue, breathing his air. Is this strange? He doesn't know anymore.

He drives to Phyllis's and extracts the kitten from his pocket after knocking. He offers it to them both when Phyllis opens the door, Wanda just behind her, the warm light in the hallway spilling out onto the porch. Standing there with his hands full of fur, he feels that they are both helpless creatures: wet and lost.

"Oh, Kirby," Phyllis says when she sees him, and he can't tell whether this is admonishment or approval or something else.

"I found it," he mumbles, as if to say, *An event occurred and I succumbed to it*, which is not incorrect. Wanda squirms past Phyllis to see what all this fuss is about and when she glimpses the living thing in her father's hands, she gasps. She examines it carefully, so close her nose almost brushes against his fingertips.

"Where did it come from?" she demands. "Where's its mother?"

"I'm not sure. It was in the grass." All three of them gaze down at the kitten, which has begun to squirm, nuzzling its tiny nose into Kirby's wrinkled palm, searching for a nipple.

"It's hungry," Phyllis says.

"We should feed it," Wanda says. "Bring it inside."

And this, an immediate understanding of what the kitten needs— nourishment, of course—but also the implementation of the action itself, the swiftness of it, nudges something deep and impossibly tender in Kirby. How is it that his daughter is the first one to know what to do? Isn't this his job? He follows them back into Phyllis's house, into the living room, where he has not set foot in many years, and here they care for this creature too small to care for itself. They lay it in a cardboard box lined with dish towels while Phyllis fetches an eyedropper and a cup of milk, and together all three of them sit on the floor while Wanda drips milk into the kitten's wide pink mouth, its claws grasping at the glass stem of the dropper and sliding off and reaching up to try to grasp it once more. He is reminded of what it felt like to hold Wanda for the first time, to hear her wail, to have nothing to feed her and no one to help, worried that if he looked away from her, even for a second, she might die.

It falls to Phyllis to explain that the kitten might not make it. "It's too small," she tells Wanda, "and its mother may have left it because she knew it wouldn't survive. Mama cats do that sometimes."

But Wanda isn't willing to entertain this possibility. "It will live. I'll feed it," she insists. "I'll keep it safe." Phyllis catches Kirby's eye, anxious for Wanda's heart, and he feels ashamed at his shortsightedness. He should have known this would happen.

"All right," Phyllis says, "but it'll need kitten formula. Cow milk isn't good for it."

Kirby nods. "We'll get some, then."

"And you'll have to feed it every few hours."

"I will," Wanda says.

They drive to the grocery store to search for formula, he and Wanda, the kitten in its box on Wanda's lap. In the parking lot, he realizes it's been a little while since he shopped here. That became Lucas's chore at some point over the past few years, a thing his son seemed to enjoy. He'd take off and be gone for hours, then come home with a few bags of groceries. Kirby never asked where the extra time went.

"I'll be right back," he says to Wanda, who never takes her eyes off the kitten. Abandoned shopping carts shimmy around the parking lot, rolling back and forth in the wind. There aren't many cars for them to bump up against; he watches as one sails from one side of the lot to the other, crashing into a bedraggled hedge when it can go no farther. The sliding glass doors at the front of the store are boarded up with plywood. One manual door is left unblocked, a piece of printer paper with a new set of hours duct-taped to it.

Inside, the registers are all closed but one. Its light flickers above the conveyor belt, a bored woman swiping through gallon after gallon of spring water. The store is gloomy with the front boarded up; some of the long fluorescent bulbs overhead have burned out, casting strange oblong shadows on the floor. Going deeper, he sees that many of the shelves are bare. There are wooden pallets full of bottled water and nonperishables that no one has bothered to shelve. A few customers rip into the plastic shipping wrappers themselves, loading up their carts feverishly, as if the grocery store might vanish at any moment. And actually, it might. It will.

He wanders down the bakery aisle, thinking to get a treat for Wanda while he's here, but the baked goods are all rotting in their plastic clamshells. Mold sprouts on the Danish; icing has slipped off the cakes, slumping into melted pools at the bottoms of the containers. The pet aisle looks more like how he expects it to: kitty litter and dog food still on the shelves. Kirby scans the various cat foods. It seems improbable that a small Floridian grocery store would carry a thing so strange and exotic as kitten milk formula, but it does. It occurs to him that while he's here he should buy other things. Practical things. But he isn't sure what to get, so he goes to the register with just this.

The woman at the checkout watches him approach, snapping her gum. She swipes the purchase through without comment, and although he had initially felt a certain tug of self-consciousness about this item, now he is disappointed that she hasn't asked him any questions.

"I found a stray kitten," he explains. "My daughter is over the moon about it."

"Good for you," she says. "Bag?"

"No bag."

Coming back to the truck through the empty parking lot, he can see Wanda through the window, still staring into the box on her lap. She's talking to it; he can see her lips moving and wishes he knew what she was saying.

At home, Wanda shows Lucas. The two of them lie on the floor of the living room and watch the kitten assess its surroundings, still unsure on its feet. Eventually it falls asleep on Lucas's chest, so comfortable it pees, without even waking. Wanda shrieks with laughter and Lucas is good-natured. Kirby sits in the kitchen, watching them. He'll miss this. In a strange way, he already does.

That night, he hears the kitten mewing and he's on his feet before he can identify the sound. He just hears the urgency and goes to it. Standing in the doorway of his children's room, a film of sleep clouding his eyes, he sees the dim outlines of them both breathing deeply in their bunks, and then he sees the kitten, standing on shaky legs, its erect tail quivering. He sits on the floor next to the box and scoops up the kitten, holding it against his bare chest. It quiets, then presses against him, then begins to sputter, a sound that might one day become a purr. He casts around for the formula and whispers, "Please don't die," as he feeds this tiny creature, kitten milk going everywhere, claws flying as it grapples with his hand. Eventually it quiets, tired or full or both, and it falls asleep in his hands, and he falls asleep, too.

LUCAS IS READY to leave by the beginning of August. Wanda mopes in the background as he packs his car, flitting around the yard with the black kitten fastened to her shoulder, pretending not to care. He can feel her gaze every time he comes outside with another load, staring down from the live oaks that edge the yard or peeking through the slats of the porch. By now, the kitten's eyes are open and they track his movements as well. Two pairs of eyes, asking him not to go.

Their pleas are impossible to ignore. Even as he's filling his car and emptying his room, he wonders if he should stay. A few more days. A week. Another month. Until Kirby finds a new job. Until Wanda's eleventh birthday. The bargaining goes on. Eventually, Kirby makes it easy: he tells his son he accepted a job offer with a contractor based in Northern California, and all the tightly wound uncertainty about when he might see them again unspools. They'll be close. He finishes packing up the car. It's done. It's decided. He's ready.

He leaves the next morning. He hugs Kirby, then Wanda. Steam rises from the wet earth as the sun warms last night's rain. The driveway, a mud pit now, sucks at their shoes when they're still and spatters on their ankles when they move. The kitten, clawing up and down Wanda's torso like it's the trunk of a tree, stops moving long enough for Lucas to rub its tiny forehead with one finger. "Bye, little guy," he says, and it hisses at him.

"It's a she," Wanda says. "Her name is Blackbeard."

"Blackbeard," Lucas repeats. He tries for another pat and the kitten swipes at him, needlelike claws extended. He snatches his hand away, a little too slow. "Bloodthirsty, huh."

"No," Wanda says, exasperated. "She's a wild animal."

He examines the scratch—a thin red line, about the depth of a paper cut—and shrugs. He's willing to cede the point. Kirby tells him to drive safe, and all three of them assure one another that they'll be together again soon. Looking back at them in his rearview mirror just before he turns onto the road, Lucas believes that it's true.

"WHERE WILL YOU go?" Phyllis asks. The porch light glows between them, a cloud of gnats clustering around it. Kirby waits while Wanda gathers her things inside. Conversation has never come easily between him and Phyllis, but he'll miss her. And Wanda will be bereft without her. He tries not to think about that now.

"Mendocino," he replies. "Next week."

"That soon," she says, and Kirby understands this to mean that she'll miss them also.

"It's time."

"I know." She pats his arm and gives him a smile. "It's good. You'll be happy there. The redwoods. They'll suit you."

Driving home in the dark, Wanda and Blackbeard beside him, he can hear the swish of water against his tires. In the driveway, it crests his boots. Wanda splashes up the steps in front of him, the kitten clinging to her shirt, her feet wet and wrinkled and bare. "The whole yard is a puddle," she announces from the top step, fiddling with the door. It sticks to the frame when it's particularly humid, which is to say, always. He reaches over her to give it a thump with his fist on the top left corner. It gives, and she stumbles inside.

"One big puddle," he agrees. Kirby looks out at the yard from the top step and watches the water glisten, the stars reflecting off the surface like a second sky, then Wanda flicks the kitchen light on and he goes in without noticing that the sky is in fact dark and overcast, that the water does not reflect light but rather is the source of it.

The next day, when Wanda asks if she can go to Phyllis's again, he knows he should say yes. There's plenty for him to do here. It's time to pack, time to choose what stays and what goes. He's even beginning to look forward to it. He imagines them arriving on the doorstep of a house that means nothing, surrounded by trees so tall he has to lean back to see the tops. A house that is fresh, scraped clean of memories. It feels good to imagine them in a house like that. Hard, but good. It's time to set all of that in motion.

Instead, he says no. It's selfish, but he can't bear to be alone today, the rain already slapping against the windows. He wants her near. Searching for a reason, a thing for them to do together, he says, "We could go to the movies. A matinee." He can't recall the last time he took her to the movie theater. She looks at him, dubious.

"A movie?"

"Yeah, a movie. Popcorn, candy. It'll be fun."

"I don't think those are open anymore," she says.

"Of course they are."

In fact, many are closed. But Kirby is too attached to the idea to give up, and so he keeps calling and calling until he finds one an hour west that is playing one matinee today. It's rated R, but he's too delighted to care much about whether it's appropriate for Wanda. "You'll cover your eyes during the grown-up parts," he tells her.

At the theater, the same man sells them their tickets and their snacks. He raises an eyebrow at Wanda but doesn't say anything. Inside, they are the only ones. As it happens, the film is full of sex and gore and it's well over two hours long. During a tense moment, Wanda drops half a box of Skittles on the floor, a cascade that rattles down the aisles, but there is no one to be bothered. She falls asleep somewhere close to the end. Afterward, they play the claw game in the empty lobby. Kirby supplies quarter after quarter as she fails to grasp hold of the plush pink elephant tucked among the plastic eggs filled with action figures.

"One more?" she pleads.

"One more," he says, until he truly doesn't have any more change. They leave empty-handed, but Wanda doesn't mind. Outside, they run for the truck, the rain pelting them with its warm, sharp drops, and on the way home they discuss special effects.

"So they didn't really die, right?"

"Right, no one died. It's just tricks and makeup."

"Hm." The rain sluices across the windshield, so thick he can barely see. He lifts his foot off the gas and squints to make out the lines on the road. "I liked it," she announces finally. "I thought it was a good movie. I'm glad we went. I really liked the game at the end, also, with the claw. Do you think Blackbeard is missing me?"

"For sure she is."

"And she'll come with us to California, won't she?"

"Of course she will."

The rain has become so torrential that Kirby slows the truck to a crawl. There's no one else on the road, no hot glow of taillights to follow. If he weren't so familiar with these curves he might pull over, put his hazards on, and wait for the rain to slow. But he knows this stretch by heart, so he keeps going, slow and deliberate. During the rainy season, the road floods quickly here where it's low, but Kirby isn't worried; his truck is high and they're not so far from home.

He forges on until something stops him—there's a thump and then a groan and when he gently lays on the gas, the truck's wheels spin and go nowhere. He gives it some more. Still nothing. Reverse gets him nowhere, either.

"Well, that's no good." He looks over at Wanda, who isn't scared. "I guess we're all caught up."

"On what?" she asks.

"Oh, who knows. I'm sure this rain's been knocking all kinds of things down. It's all right, I've got the chain saw in the back. I'm going to go see if I can drag it out first. Hand me the headlamp in the glove box."

He clicks on the light and gets out, crouching down to see what's gotten caught in the truck's undercarriage: just a sturdy branch. He shuts the door to keep the cab dry and goes around to the front to get a better look, shining his headlamp on it. If he can get Wanda to reverse while he pushes, that'll probably do it. No need for the chain saw.

As he calculates this, some miles away, Lake Okeechobee breaks free of its banks. It's been brimming all day. All week, actually. The water pushes past the earthen dam, still weakened from Braylen. The rain has been too much this year, but it seemed like such a small problem compared to everything else. What is a very rainy season next to a Cat 5 hurricane? Next to the end of Miami? It isn't the problem of a single storm—it is the pattern set by many. The people that used to watch the dam, that tended to it, have all been laid off. They kept the dam strong since 1928, but now, there's no one left to open the gates when the water is too high. No one to reinforce the walls when they begin to weaken. Everyone worried that this would happen one day. No one knew it would be today.

A few inches of floodwater sloshes around Kirby's ankles. He doesn't realize there is about to be so much more. He stands up, clicking his headlamp off and thinking about how delighted Wanda will be to step on the gas while he pushes, to sit in the driver's seat and hold the steering wheel. A fine ending to this very good adventure they've shared. She'll have to stretch those short legs of hers to reach the pedal, but he knows she'll manage somehow because she is resourceful. She is capable. This, his last thought, makes his heart ache and swell at the same time.

When the wave sweeps him off his feet he is still imagining her working the pedals, still feeling a tender admiration for his daughter. He has only a few seconds to panic before he is underwater and his temple connects with something hard, maybe a piece of debris, maybe the ground itself. He doesn't have time to understand what has happened, or what it means, or who it will affect. There is only a cold burst of adrenaline and then there is nothing. Just a deep, dark current: a soft blackness that delivers him back to wherever it is he began.

The waves slam against the doors and sweep over the hood, the windshield, the windows, swallowing the truck whole. Wanda calls out, but there is no answer except for the murmur she used to think was trying to help her. She can see its familiar glow in the floodwater, shimmering outside the window. The lights whisper to her, loud and urgent, but the only voice she wants right now is her father's.

It's a sound she'll never stop wanting. The flood moves on, holding what remains of Kirby tight and rushing away to claim new territory. The murmurs fade and the lights dissipate—for now. The water recedes, a new tide rushing out toward the coast—for now. There is no more room in the seabed, no more room in the limestone, no more room in the soil. The water bodies expand upward, outward, inward, and the rain keeps beating down. This is the way things will be from now on. The levels will rise and fall and rise, but the water will never leave this place again.

LIGHT

The light flows in every direction. It is composed of many minds, many eyes. It is one creature, and it is many. An awareness that grows and deepens. An intelligence that is made to join and join and join. This is how life began; this is how it goes on living.

SO MUCH HAS changed. The passage of several decades meant little to this peninsula, but it has meant a great deal to the creatures who live here. Wanda pilots her canoe between two sunken houses, slick with algae, veiled by Spanish moss. Her paddle slices the warm, sludgy water, sweeping aside garbage and leaves as she shoots forward, through the gap and out onto what was once Beachside Drive. A traffic light hangs ten feet or so above the water, dim and unlit. A relic. The sun has set, its fire fading from the sky. There's another vessel, maybe half a mile down the way, heading toward the open water. The people who have stayed wait until dusk to move about; daytime temperatures are fatal. Wanda slips behind a ruined storefront and waits for the boat to pass. Sightings like this have become increasingly rare, which is a good thing. She breathes easier when she's sure it's gone.

An orange tomcat sits in the bow of her canoe, looking out over the water with a feral intensity that is reflected in Wanda's posture as well, although they are intent on different goals. Wanda is paddling for home, while the cat eyes a squirrel scampering through a tangle of mangroves. He sinks low on his haunches, tail flicking, biding his time. The tom waits until the canoe is a few feet away from the trees, then leaps. He slips between the gnarled trunks and disappears. The squirrel pauses, alert, then vanishes also, into the bramble. Wanda paddles on. He'll find his own way back to her—or he won't. She can't afford to be sentimental about animals any longer. Keeping herself alive is all she can manage. The human body is so delicate, so vulnerable. In this place, there are many, many ways to die.

After spending twelve feverishly hot daylight hours hunkered down on the second floor of an abandoned colonial, she's anxious to get home. She was out fishing just before dawn and didn't have time to return before the sun rose. It's possible she could have made it, but being on the open water during daylight hours is a deadly thing. She's seen too many lost causes to take the risk—boats that roam aimlessly with the tide, their occupants either gone overboard, thinking the water might cool them (it won't), or worse, still there, their flesh decomposing so quickly not much remains by the time Wanda comes upon them. It's the heatstroke that does it. Bodies boiled from within. No, it's best to find shade before the first rays of sunlight glimmer and to wait until the very last rays disappear to leave it. Wanda doesn't take chances on such things; Phyllis taught her better than that.

Even now, with the glare of the sun ducked down behind the waves, sweat drips from her face. She remembers a book she read once as a girl—there was snow in that book, coming down so fast and hard it was—what do they call it? A blizzard. She's never seen such a thing. Her catch, fat and heavy, hangs off the edge of her boat in a cheesecloth sack, trailing low in the water as she rows. This was worth the discomfort of fitfully dozing on a moldy oriental rug all day. The fish grow more and more elusive every year—living deeper down and farther out, rising to the surface only when they must. To find a school of them flitting about in the bay as she did in the early hours of yesterday was rare. A moment to be taken advantage of.

Now, heading inland, she debates whether it still makes sense to venture out to the freshwater spring tonight. It's a long way by boat, which is the only way. A whole night's journey there and back, leaving her no time for her other tasks. She needs to prepare the fish for drying as soon as possible. They've already sat too long. Gutting and cleaning and filleting and salting and setting them out—all this takes time. If Phyllis were still here, it wouldn't be a problem. They would divide and conquer, tending to the necessities of the human body as a team. But Wanda is alone now. Just one person, surviving on instinct and maybe a sense of duty. Phyllis taught her how to live, so now she must go on living. Tomorrow night will have to do for replenishing her water supply, Wanda decides. If these fish aren't ready to cure during the daylight hours they'll spoil for certain. Wanda cuts long, deep strokes with her paddle, on one side, then the other, shooting through the water now that she's on a straightaway. The sky becomes translucent above her, the universe on the other side bleeding through as the blue deepens and the stars prick the atmosphere.

By the time she arrives, it's dark and the temperature has cooled a few pivotal degrees. Her home hangs above, scattered among the canopies, a patchwork of salvaged siding and shingles and fence posts and shutters, connected by ladders and ropes. They built it equidistant between food and fresh water, as high as the trees would allow. It's a rudimentary structure—made to be rebuilt after the hurricanes pass through if need be. An open invitation to the winds. "Better to bend than to break," Phyllis always said. They called it "the nest" back when they were hauling materials into the swamp. They joked that they were a pair of birds, too heavy for their own good. It's hard having no one to joke with anymore. This life was always hard, but it's been so much harder these past few years.

She knows her dock is close before she sees it and then there it is, a black outline against the soft shimmer of ripples, illuminated ever so slightly by a dim reflection of the Milky Way on the surface of the lagoon. Wanda cuts the water with the broad side of her paddle to slow her momentum, then coasts in. She reaches out and snags the mooring post with a loop of rope, pulls it taut, ties it off. Hauling the cheesecloth bag up out of the water, she slings it across her shoulder and climbs, the ripe smell of the fish wafting over her. On a platform she's designated as her kitchen, she guts and heads the fish, fillets them as thin as she can, salts them. There are so many things she doesn't have enough of, things she yearns for but will never have again, things she hasn't had for so long she's forgotten they ever existed—but salt is not one of them. The water takes, and it gives, too. She lays the fish out on her drying rack in neat rows and throws the entrails in the water. A quiet splash, the sound of an alligator snacking. When the flood came it killed a great many creatures, but some did manage to thrive.

Wanda brings the drying racks up to the top level of her home, closest to the sun. Here, she has her screen boxes set out, to keep the flies and the scavengers away so that while she sleeps through the hottest part of the day, down below, the food stays safe as it dries. From time to time a crafty predator will break into her screen boxes and steal what she's laid out, but every time it happens, she makes a better box. It's been a while since anything managed to steal from her.

Her nightly work done, there are still a few more hours of darkness before the sun crests the tops of the mangroves and living things must either take cover or go crisp in the daylight. She allows herself to rest. The work has heated her; it's important to notice such things. She lies down, taking advantage of this time with the stars before she must move down below the foliage. Phyllis taught her the names of constellations, but she can't remember which is which anymore. She could never see their supposed shapes: a bear, a lion, an archer. Such a human sort of order imposed on an unplanned spray of light across infinite darkness. But that was Phyllis's way—naming things, categorizing them. When Phyllis was still with her, they would spend these moments of rest talking about the things they'd noticed that day. They reminded one another of the beauty here. An ibis, with a flash of silver dangling from its beak. Young mangroves rooting down into the water, an island in the process of becoming. An orchid blooming on the side of a decaying house, its thick, bare roots clinging to the rotting wood. A school of fish jumping headfirst into the waves.

It's much harder to do this alone, but she tries. She pictures it in her head. There is no point using her voice anymore. *Iridescence on mackerel scales. Wet, pulsing fish guts. The sky reflected on the water. The sound of one night bird courting another.*

Overhead, a brightness darts across the sky, and then another, and another. A meteor shower, she realizes. Phyllis used to plan for these. The year after Wanda's father died, Phyllis would wake her in the middle of the night, carrying blankets to lie on and a thermos of honeyed tea to sip from. They'd go to the roof and look up and Wanda would feel slightly better just being beside Phyllis: this woman who knew when to look and where to look and how long the whole thing might last. Phyllis knew, even then, that Wanda needed help finding beauty amid the violence. She still needs it. But there is no one to show her now. And this, this spectacle unfolding above her—it doesn't comfort her the way it should. All she sees is a reminder of how much she's lost.

The grizzled tom that departed her boat earlier scratches his way up one of the tree trunks and comes toward her, rubbing his body against hers. There is a small but tenacious population of feral cats wandering the swamps. This one is bolder than most. He reminds her of a kitten she had once, but that creature left her, too. Like everyone else. Or, more likely, it was taken from her. A gator, a coyote, a sinkhole. It doesn't matter which. Another lost love.

The tom ignores the fragrant fish fillets, laid out in the screen boxes to await the sun, which is a relief to her because she can't spare any. Instead, he pushes his face into her limp hand, insisting that she scratch him first on one side of his head and then on the other. This is a different sort of hunger, one that she understands all too well. She obliges and he purrs and then when the sun begins to rise they retreat to the shade below; down, down, down to the darkest place they can find. She sleeps in stops and starts, sweating, dreaming of canned peaches, thick and soft and sugary on her tongue. She half wakes and thinks how cruel it is to remember them now that there are none left.

When the heat sinks and the dark rises, Wanda rises, too. She packs away the dried fish and gets the canoe ready. With the empty jugs strapped down, she climbs in and heads for the spring. This swamp is her home; she knows its twists and turns as well as any person could. But even so, the swamp is ever-changing. A maze without an exit. Things die; new things grow. The storms are always moving the landscape in unexpected ways. If she traveled in the daylight, she could observe these events, take notes, keep abreast of the shifts. But the daylight is no longer her domain. She travels in the dark, when the only way to navigate is ramming the bow of her canoe into a newly fallen tree or getting lost because her landmark has been swept to sea.

It's easiest to save these kinds of errands for nights when the moon is fat and yellow, but seeking freshwater on the brightest nights of the month is its own risk. If it's easy for her, it's easy for everyone—and the idea of the remnants of Rudder out in force, rowing their boats and their rafts, pushing their skiffs, flocking to the spring as if it is their lifeblood (it is), frightens her. It's hard to say how many are left. The number, like the landscape, changes all the time. In the dark, everyone is a stranger.

Some chose to stay. Others had nowhere to go. And now, a new generation is being born: children who have never known anything but this. Still, for every one that stayed, hundreds left. Thousands? Possibly millions. It's hard to say; numbers like this don't feel real anymore. If they ever did. Most of the refugees crushed north into the cities and the plains and the mountains, where there are undoubtedly many problems but not seeing another human being for months on end probably isn't one of them. Or maybe it is. Wanda would not know.

Tonight, there's no moon at all. And without the moon, she hopes that there are no foragers to disturb her. The hull of her canoe slips through the water, the darkness whispering all around, the warmth rising from her paddle as she cuts down through the hot, wet air, into the water, and up again. She prefers it this way, threading her way through the swamp with only her ears and her memory and the ambiguous shapes that loom up out of the blackness to guide her. Creatures chatter and call and scamper. Nocturnal eyes glow, staring as she passes. The sounds the water makes all around her are as full and varied as an orchestra: water slapping against the hull; the sharp dip and soft sweep of her paddle's edge; the seamless whisper of an alligator's back breaching the surface; dew falling from a palm frond, ringing the water like a bell; a brisk allegro measure of splashes as frogs jump, one after another.

Wanda paddles for hours. Her arms are strong and sinewy. She will tire eventually, but she likes to think she could persevere forever. She imagines that her muscles could go on without her, cutting the paddle down on one side and then the other, over and over, until she reaches the Gulf. It's her mind that quits first. A sort of cinching around her neck when she strays too far from home. She rests, the grip pulled into her chest, her breath a little ragged. She should wait for her body to cool after this much exertion, but she's so close. Just a little farther. She rotates her crackling wrists and takes hold of the paddle once more: a soft splash as one blade slips beneath the water, and then the other. She can just barely discern the mangrove islands from the open water, and just barely is enough. Roots and fallen trees scratch at her hull, but she is agile in the water. The shades of darkness speak volumes to her practiced eye. She finds the opening through the cypress trees, guided by the sound of the chimes hung in the branches. She didn't hang them there; whoever did is either very kind or very foolish. Marking this place for oneself is also marking it for others. A risky thing. She leaves the chimes alone, even though they make her uneasy. The sound of them tinkling here in the darkness reminds her: This place does not belong to her.

With a practiced flick of her paddle, Wanda glides down the swampy corridor, sawgrass whispering as she passes. The sound of the chimes grows faint behind her. She enters the lagoon, and there, in the center—movement. Wanda feels for the knife she carries on her hip and flicks the blade open. Dangerous creatures lurk in these swamps; she is one of them.

AFTER KIRBY DIED, Phyllis cleared out her study and told Wanda it was her room for as long as she wanted it. They never did find his body. The water washed a great many things away that day. Lucas, already in California by then, came straight home when he heard. He arrived in the middle of the night while Wanda slept upstairs, delirious from driving straight through. Phyllis was waiting for him. She took his arm, steered him inside, and held him on the couch while he bawled into her shoulder. She could feel him dissolving into that twelve-year-old boy she'd found on her doorstep, gasping for air, pressing his face hard into her.

"Forewing…hindwing…" he whispered into her blouse. A lepidopterist's prayer.

"What's that now?"

"Butterfly parts. Like you said."

The last time she held him like this came rushing back to her. She hadn't known what to say to him then, the hurricane raging just outside, but she'd been worried that that aching boy would seize and convulse in her arms if she didn't manage to distract him a little, so she taught him butterfly anatomy. How devastating that he held on to it all these years. How perfect. "That's good," she told him, rubbing slow circles on his back with her palm. "Real good."

When he managed to gather himself, they talked about what

would happen to Wanda. Lucas hurried to sacrifice—to move back home, to drop out of school before he'd even begun and give up his scholarship—but there were holes in this plan. Phyllis pointed them out. Kirby wouldn't want that. Wanda wouldn't want it. And besides, how would he earn? He said he could go to college and make a home for her at the same time, a fresh start for them both in California. Phyllis nodded. "Could do," she said. "Let's sleep on it." She made up the couch for him as soft and deep as she could, but the effort was lost on him. He was asleep before she could turn out the light.

In the morning, she gathered these two tearstained children that weren't hers at the table. Lucas, not really a child, but not quite a man, either. And Wanda, her little protégé. "I've been thinking," she told them, "that if Wanda wanted to, and you agreed, she could live here. With me."

Lucas shook his head. "No, we're family. We're going to California like Pop wanted us to."

"I don't wanna leave," Wanda said, a whine creeping in. "I never even wanted to go to California. Why can't I stay with Phyllis?"

"I could move back—" he said.

"Just think it over," Phyllis said. "There's time."

The three of them sat and filled their mouths with Phyllis's biscuits, smeared with butter and jam, so that they had an excuse not to talk for a little while. True, there was time—but not much.

The question of what to do about Wanda went on in murmurs and late-night conferences between Phyllis and Lucas. They had the same conversation, again and again, but there was no easy solution. Lucas had only a week before the beginning of his first semester. Just a few days to decide. He and Wanda spent their time splashing through the inches of water that still rippled across the low roads, wandering this town that would never be the same again. Phyllis watched them venture out each morning: solemn, hand in hand. She could see Lucas trying to be older than he was, braver than he was. *It's unfair for one family to lose so much*, she thought, standing on the front porch as they disappeared behind the cypress trees. In the end, Lucas relented to Wanda's impassioned plea to stay with Phyllis. Of the three of them, she was the only one who seemed certain. They agreed that they'd try it for a year.

On Lucas's last evening in the blue house, they made a feast. A crawfish boil, with Phyllis's own sweet corn and potatoes, and crawdads that Lucas and Wanda caught themselves. They spread it out on the newspaper-covered picnic table in the backyard, next to the garden, but it was impossible to forget the deep sadness lurking on either side of this perfect hour—the absence of Kirby, Lucas's impending departure. They studiously spoke of neither while Blackbeard whined at their feet and Wanda fed her pieces of claw meat dipped in butter.

In the morning, Wanda had to gently but firmly put Lucas in his car and insist he go. They all agreed again that Lucas would get settled in California and when it was right, maybe in a year, maybe two, Wanda would join him. At the time, they believed it. Phyllis and Wanda stood in the driveway and watched his car disappear while Blackbeard mewed at their feet, throwing herself against their legs, begging for their hands in her fur. Wanda bent down and obliged her, carefully attending to her nose, then ears, then chin, then belly. Phyllis watched, brushing tears from her eyes, suddenly struck by the newfound gravity of her own choices. The stakes were so much higher now.

Just like that, Wanda became hers. Her burden and also her joy. The blue house seemed to expand. It breathed. With Wanda inside it, the house lived. And so did Phyllis. She hadn't been unhappy before Wanda came into her life. Not in the slightest. Phyllis had always found great fulfillment in her own self-determined research projects, and before that, when she taught, in her students, and before that, in her own schooling. Her life pre-Wanda had been a full one. Forestry work, academia, her research, a few lovers here and there, but most of all, caretaking the land she lived on. Her garden, her chickens, the slow, satisfying task of removing herself and her home from the grid entirely. Of becoming utterly independent from a failing system. She'd had everything she wanted out of her years on this earth. And then Wanda came and she got something she had never even known to yearn for—a companion.

Phyllis had tried living with a man twice and neither time suited her. There was Gabriel, when she was young, who taught her about guns and prepping and eventually left with another woman, and then there was Julian, who wanted her to put research aside to raise a family with him. She said no and he left, too. She liked the sex well enough—it was the rest of it that she was ill-suited for. The demands on her time, her attention, her space. She'd always been this way. Even as a child, she'd reveled in being left alone. Her parents didn't understand her, and neither did her sister. Eventually they gave up on convincing her to join in, and let her be. She'd always been a satellite, orbiting out beyond the gravitational pull of family and community and togetherness. It was a peaceful way to exist. A good vantage point from which to learn. She'd never dreamed that she would find so much joy in the very thing she'd always been certain she did not want: a child. Then again, Wanda was not just any child.

Florida's infrastructure limped along through the tail end of that summer after Kirby died. Rudder was bankrupt and Miami was under mandatory evacuation orders by then, but other pockets of the state continued to function. It was an in-between time. The flooding of Lake Okeechobee had hastened certain changes that might have taken decades otherwise. But here it was: happening more quickly than anyone had anticipated. Florida, returning to herself. Swamps that had been dredged and drained and developed reappeared, bubbling back up to the surface in parking lots and on highways and in gated neighborhoods. Sinkholes opened up and swallowed entire blocks whole. Houses and roads and crops disappeared into the edges of the ever-encroaching wild. Power was unreliable but it still flowed in some places. Cell and radio towers still stood. The question was, and always had been: For how much longer? Hurricane season had a slow start, but its peak was brewing. At sea, pockets of hot, moist wind formed, whirled, fed. They grew, waiting to be named. It wouldn't take much to push the places that still functioned past their brink. And after—well, after was what Phyllis had spent her life preparing for.

In the blue house, Wanda's presence began to take root. The study became hers in a much more permanent way. A twin bed frame with wooden pineapples carved into the headboard was assembled, hauled home in pieces from an abandoned house. A lamp shaped like the moon appeared on the desk, plucked from a garage sale. Little spiky sky plants were hung from nails on pieces of purple thread and dry driftwood. Rocks and fossils and shell fragments gathered from the permanent plots lined both windowsills. A wallpaper of botanical drawings accumulated, tacked one by one to the wall, each more detailed than the last. And the milk crate that had been Kirby's, the remnants of a mother she'd never known—these artifacts of Frida finally were hers.

Together, they settled into a new routine while society disintegrated all around them. The school did not reopen in September, so Phyllis devised a sixth grade syllabus of sorts and for the first time, Wanda delighted in her studies. Data collection and biology became the focal point of her education. Drawing, fishing, canning, gardening, and first aid were also core subjects. Irrelevancies like cursive and gym and a version of U.S. history Phyllis referred to as "garbage" fell by the wayside. She taught Wanda another kind of history, an older one. Before the country had states. Before it was a country at all.

She taught Wanda how to use hand tools, how to make soap, how to shoot a rifle. Literature became a leisure activity that Wanda pursued on her own, no assignments required. It was a good syllabus. Each module was carefully designed for the world that was coming to bear rather than the one that was quickly receding. Without peers, Wanda relaxed into learning in a way she never had before. She asked as many questions as she wanted without rebuke and Phyllis answered them all to the best of her ability.

At the end of September, Hurricane Salina approached. They listened to its progress on a little hand-crank radio and when it was close, they stripped the garden of its produce, herded the chickens into the house, set the furniture up on bricks, and moved the valuables to the second floor. They latched the storm shutters and brought the solar panels in just as the sky began to darken, and by the time the winds arrived, they'd tucked themselves away, too. The blue house was as indestructible as an old house could be. Phyllis had spent years making sure of it. As Salina raged, the humans waited. The chickens fluttered and clucked in the bathroom, exploring the tub while Blackbeard listened, pawing at their shadows beneath the door. Outside, debris hurtled through the sky and wind clawed at the trees. The ocean waves swelled to the height of four-story buildings. The Intracoastal rose and then overflowed. The streets became rivers, the swamps became lakes. Rain fell in sheets, not drops. And then, after many hours of waiting and enduring, the storm moved on.

Under clear skies, Phyllis and Wanda took stock. The water did indeed trickle into the house, but only just. Being farther inland and on high ground kept them drier than some, but nothing here was fully dry anymore. The ground was sodden. The air, too. Water coursed down the road set just below the house in a thick, sludgy brown river. Sewage and seawater, trash and mud. The garden would not yield again that year—its greenery was flattened, its soil swollen. One of the old lemon trees had broken off at the waist, a bow it would never rise from. All told, they were lucky. They were ready. This was how it would be now.

In other parts of the state, counties began to announce closures. Through that winter and into spring, whole communities slipped away, one by one. Piecemeal evacuation orders were issued and military vehicles began to patrol, ready to take refugees if they wanted to go. Many left. Some held on. Eventually the federal government announced the widespread closure of Florida as a whole, as if it were a rundown theme park with a roller coaster that was no longer safe to ride. And in some ways, it was. Hadn't Florida always been the end of the line? The butt of the joke? Alligators that stalked Disney World's children. The Florida Man. Headline after headline, rejoicing in absurdity, in poverty, in addiction and mental illness, in aimless violence. In one year, they said, Florida would be released back into the wild. Released, they said, like a creature the country had tried to tame but ultimately couldn't. They made it sound like there was a plan. An orderly transition that would unfold. A whole year to wind things down, to strategize. But it didn't happen like that. Once the announcement was made, the changes came even faster. That summer, panic spread. Supermarkets stopped restocking. Gas stations sold their last gallons. Hospitals and clinics closed their doors. And finally, well ahead of schedule, the post office stopped delivering with little to no fanfare.

Phyllis observed all of these developments and was unsurprised. She watched the military's trucks splash through the sodden streets of Rudder, collecting refugees, reminding holdouts that they would be alone if they stayed. A melancholy twist of excitement gripped her. She had been right. About everything. The only thing she hadn't planned for was the little girl who chased her chickens through the swamp, who drew orchids at her dining room table, who begged to explore the sunken lowlands of their town by canoe. Phyllis had never had to worry about anyone but herself until now. Should she do it differently? Unsure, she carried on.

Lucas called in a panic when he heard about the statewide closure. He'd been calling every weekend since he left, but the phone calls had gotten shorter. His life in California fuller. He told Phyllis he was uneasy with the idea of them staying, and she didn't blame him. But she had spent decades preparing to stay. It was more than stubbornness or ego that made her determined to press on. She couldn't turn away from the principles she'd arrived at as a young woman, fresh off her undergraduate degree, working as a park ranger in the Everglades and understanding for the first time that the very idea of civilization was irreparably broken. "It will get bad out there, too," she told him. "At least here we're ready."

Lucas wanted to trust this, but there was doubt in his voice as he once again cycled through the options for Wanda, each option its own sacrifice. He asked her outright: "Do you think I should bring her here? I could move out of the dorms. Find a place. Take out another loan."

Phyllis answered him as best she could, knowing full well that it wasn't her decision, and also that she was desperate for Wanda to stay. "She's old enough. She can decide." Was this dishonest, knowing that Wanda would not want to go? Was it wrong to want to keep her so badly? If she were a parent, maybe she would have chosen differently. Maybe she would have moved, just as Kirby had planned to, anything to get Wanda a few more years of normalcy. But nothing was normal anywhere and she wasn't a parent. In fact, this was why she'd never wanted to be. She did the best she could. Phyllis knew she would live with these questions for many years, but a decision was made. For now, Wanda would stay.

The dissolution of society was a peaceful thing to watch in many ways. In others, violent. Time took on a dreamlike quality. Days of the week ceased to matter. Months bled together. At the height of that summer, Phyllis and Wanda encountered a middle-aged man throwing rocks through the post office's windows. They were riding their bicycles, tires whizzing through the water in the street, shallow but enduring, when they heard the breaking glass. Phyllis's hands jerked on the handlebars at the sound.

"Why's he doing that?" Wanda asked as the man threw another

rock, shattering another pane. Phyllis tried not to stare, but he looked familiar. It was difficult to place him. His face was dirty, his clothes stained.

"I'm not sure," Phyllis replied.

"Does he want to steal the stamps?"

"That could be."

"But probably not?"

"No, probably not."

Phyllis craned her neck as they passed and the man stared back at them: cold, angry, the bottoms of his pants sodden, sticking to his legs. And then his face clicked into place. She hadn't recognized him without his uniform; it was the postman.

"Sometimes people feel so angry it eats them up inside," Phyllis told her, glad that they weren't on foot. She held her breath, waiting to see if the man would approach them. He didn't, but that didn't make her feel safe.

"Why's he angry?"

"Most of the time when people are angry, they're also sad."

They pedaled on in silence and Phyllis thought the conversation was over, but then Wanda said, "I can understand that."

"I know you do, sweet pea."

The realization of just how much she needed to impart to Wanda had been on her mind for months—that was what the syllabus was for—but now, confronted with the rage of a man left behind by civilization, it occurred to her that while teaching Wanda how to sterilize canning jars and purify water and identify the many varieties of epiphytes was useful, there was a subject she had neglected. Maybe the most important instruction she could offer: on the people who stayed and how to survive them. In this respect, she was a student herself.

WANDA HOLDS THE blade down. She doesn't want to use it, but she will. It wouldn't be the first time. The movement in the center of the lagoon is just shadows, but she can hear the water parting and rippling, slapping against the tree trunks and their roots. It's too late to slip away unseen, so she coasts into the lagoon as quietly as she can, trying to discern the source of the water's disturbance as her canoe glides closer. But the night is too dark, even for her. A clouded curtain has slipped over the stars, and whatever dim glow they offered is gone. The shroud of foliage around the lagoon is pitch black. Impenetrable. If she wants to see what or who is here with her, there's only one option left. But using it has its own consequences.

The thing that will happen if Wanda touches this water is familiar to her now. A light will spread in all directions: a quiet, brilliant sunburst with her at its center. It will move of its own accord. A living thing, awakening. More accurately, a million living things. A billion. Another impossible number. When she was small, turning on these lights was an accident. They saved her, surprised her, warned her, and then they failed her. She could feel them nearby when her father got out of the truck on a watery night and never came back. Why didn't they help her then? Why didn't they save him?

Over the years, Phyllis taught her to think of the light as a tool. She taught her to use it sparingly. Carefully. But what Phyllis struggled to comprehend—what Wanda has always just *known*—is that the light is more than a collection of single-celled organisms. It is more complex than she has words for. Phyllis needed it to be science, and so for her it was. But for Wanda, the light has always defied categorization. Now, with the knife in her hand and the water at her fingertips, she prefers the knife. The knife is a tool she has mastered. The water...is not.

There is another flicker of movement in the center of the lagoon. She can feel the ripples rolling through the hull of her boat. Whoever is here with her is large and unafraid. It could be a gator, which is manageable—or it could be a human. A human would be much worse. Either way, she realizes that she has to see what she's dealing with. There's no way around it. The knife is useless until she knows what she's using it for. Reaching down toward the water, knowing as she does that the cost of summoning these creatures is never straightforward, she rakes her fingers through the wet and tightens her grip on the weapon. She will see and be seen. This is the bargain.

The light begins at her fingertips and spreads, quickly, smoothly, across the face of the water. It radiates in all directions, pulsing through the lagoon, darting along its surface. Wanda sees the source of the movement then—and it's neither alligator nor human. It's a pair of manatees, playing. She folds back the blade of her knife and the tension goes out of her shoulders. The manatees roll through the water, under and over, caressing each other with their bulk, flitting away and then circling back. The lights please them, and it seems that the feeling is mutual: the glow burns brighter where the manatees play, a luminous ribbon entwining their smooth curves.

"Hello," she whispers.

She fills her water bottles with the fresh water that flows into the lagoon from the spring below, and when she's finished, she sheds her clothes and slips into the clean, clear water. The lights spin all around her, shimmering and rippling, as if they are trying to speak to her with their patterns. It's been a long time since she woke these creatures; she's missed them.

When she was young, Wanda couldn't get enough of being surrounded by this cool, shimmering intelligence. It felt like being held by a friend so old she didn't remember meeting them. Like coming home to swim in her own primordial fluid. She didn't question them back then, she just accepted their presence. But acceptance was not Phyllis's way. She busied herself trying to define the light, poring over everything she could find about bioluminescence and single-celled organisms—about their evolution and chemistry, about their ability to regulate the color, intensity, and regularity of the glow according to specific needs. And in the end, Phyllis became convinced that they had discovered a new species.

She remembers the progression of Phyllis's shock, then her curiosity, then her excitement. She remembers how special she felt, knowing that the lights only came out for her and no one else. In the beginning, it never occurred to Wanda to doubt their whispers, their brightness. But that was before Kirby died. She'd like to trust them now, to feel that same easy faith she did when she was young, except that nothing is easy anymore.

She swims toward the manatees and they surface for her, rolling their bellies up toward the night sky so that she'll scratch them, taking turns, circling. She usually washes with a bucket in her tree house, or just waits for rain. It's been a long while since she allowed herself this luxury of submersion, but the presence of the manatees makes her feel safe. The water is cooler here, where it bubbles up from a crevice in the earth. She can feel the salt on her skin dissolving. The lights whisper, an indecipherable hush. On either side, the manatees nudge up against her, gently butting her with their round heads, rubbing their slippery gray skin against hers. One of them swims beneath her feet, tickling her toes. She looks down, and through the glimmer of the lights, she can see into the underwater caves, where the spring is hidden. A submerged staircase is visible—a remnant from the days when tourists came and swam in the spring or went scuba diving in the caves. There are reminders everywhere, but this rippling vision of the staircase touches something she'd forgotten. The last time she saw these stairs she was standing on them, descending into the caves with one hand on the decaying railing, the other lost in Lucas's palm, their father a few steps behind.

She doesn't think of them as much anymore. For many years after her dad died and her brother left for college, she could think of nothing else. But since then, she's lived an entire life. Their faces ripple in her memory, as blurry as the softly lit caves beneath her feet. She couldn't have been more than six or seven that day, wearing an old pair of boys' swimming trunks, her chest bare, yellow plastic floaties Velcroed to her arms. She remembers being scared as they descended into the cave, huddling so close to Lucas that he eventually picked her up and carried her the rest of the way down. Looking over his shoulder, her arms wrapped around her brother's neck, her eyes found Kirby. He winked at her. And she wasn't afraid anymore.

The manatees dive deep and leave her alone on the surface. The water is so clear here that she can still see them, playing in the caves below, the lights swirling around their thick, graceful bodies. She dives, too. Down, past the staircase she walked with her brother and father; down, past the platform where scuba divers sat to pull on their flippers and oxygen masks; down, into the caves where the manatees are playing. The pressure in her lungs feels good, the same way her arms feel good after paddling for hours—like her body is wide awake. She holds her breath for a long time, dragging it out to the very edge of her capacity. Here, deep down, surrounded by dark and light in equal measure, her brain is quiet. She isn't scared. She isn't hungry or thirsty. She isn't too hot. She's just floating, holding on to one of the manatees to resist her body's insistence on rising to the surface. There is no qualifier, she just is.

But the manatee understands better than she does that she's been down here too long. That this isn't where she belongs. It brings her up gradually, nudging her toward the world she'd rather not rejoin. Her ears pop as she rises and the moment of gentle nothingness ends.

There is pain again. In her eardrums, in her lungs, behind her eyes. Her head breaks the surface and she gasps, heaving, lying across the manatee's sedentary bulk while its partner circles them both, rubbing its bristly snout against Wanda's legs. Water trickles out of her ears and sound returns. Her breath evens out. The manatees leave her here and dive deep once more. She feels exposed suddenly, floating on her back, spent. The safety of the caves has left her. The gentle company of the manatees is far away. The memory of her father's face and her brother's arms recedes. The lights shiver, agitated. They whisper to her, a frequency she couldn't possibly explain, not sound, not even light, just an inexplicable knowing, passing seamlessly from one consciousness to another. And what they tell her is this—*Someone is coming.*

A YEAR AFTER Kirby's death, after his own departure, Lucas announced that he was coming back for a visit, and Phyllis didn't know what to feel. It was after the government had given up on Florida, but before the official deadline to evacuate had passed—a deadline she had no intention of meeting. She worried that he was coming to take Wanda back to California with him. It would make sense. They'd had their year together. The arrangement had always been temporary. And despite her apprehension, it would be good for Wanda to see her brother again. It would be good for Phyllis, too. She wanted them to be together, to be happy. She just wished it didn't mean losing them both.

Lucas texted photos as he drove across the country—roadside attractions, national parks, selfies from the driver's seat of his car— and Wanda's excitement increased with every message. When he got to the border, though, he was turned away by the National Guard. They were getting people out, not letting them in, they told him. He called Phyllis from the edge of Alabama and told her not to worry. He said he'd find another way.

A week later, he arrived aboard a fishing boat coming down the Intracoastal. He told Phyllis that it was easy enough to park his car in Georgia and then find a boat that would take him south, but they both understood that "easy" was a relative term. It was a great deal harder to come to Rudder than it had been a year ago. How difficult would it be to visit in another year? In two? The tethers between this part of the world and the rest were coming loose, and that meant certain things that neither of them was ready to reckon with. He slept on the couch and spent his days letting Wanda show him the things she'd learned and everything that had changed. So much had changed. Phyllis cooked for them and cleaned up after them and it felt almost like being in a play, saying the lines a mother might as convincingly as she could. But she enjoyed it. She liked the chatter while they ate, the nearness of them while she worked in the kitchen or the garden, how still Wanda sat when Lucas braided her hair into intricate patterns. Where had he learned such things?

Lucas and Phyllis studiously avoided the question of when he would leave and whether he would take Wanda with him. But they had to speak of it eventually. One night, he waited until Wanda was asleep, and caught Phyllis before she went upstairs.

"I have to start thinking about getting back," he told her.

"So soon," she said.

She already knew he had a job waiting for him, and then the fall semester after that. He'd found summer work on a firefighting crew. It was easy work to find—out west, the fires were bigger, the droughts longer, the temperatures so hot pavement melted and power grids failed. None of it was new, but a place can only take so much. Rural towns were beginning to disappear, blinking off like dead bulbs on a strand of Christmas lights, while the cities soldiered on. Soon, even the epicenters would falter. Phyllis didn't need to say any of this. She could see it on his face—they both knew.

"I'd stay longer if I could, but the crew is shorthanded as it is."

"I understand."

"Wanda..." he began, then stopped. They stared at one another and Phyllis waited for him to claim his sister. "I asked her what she wanted to do," he continued. "Where she wanted to live. And...she doesn't want to come to California with me." His voice fell ever so slightly as he said this.

"Oh." Phyllis waited.

"I know what it feels like to be snatched away when you don't want to leave. And I don't want to do that to her. But I also...I don't know when I'll be able to come back. It'll be a while. And I—well, let's be honest, Florida cell towers are running on borrowed time. Either they fall apart on their own or they shut down. What happens when they go? This place just disappears, Phyllis. I'm not sure I can spend two weeks just getting here every summer. If I can even count on the fishing boats next year. And how the hell do I get back? How long will that take? I don't know what to do. She's my responsibility, I can't just leave her. And I can't drag her off, neither. But I can't be in two places at once. It's either California or...this." He swung his hands around, as if he were holding all of Rudder in his arms for just a second, then he let them fall into his lap. "And I don't...I don't want this."

"It's okay. I do," Phyllis said, patting his arm. "We do. Want this."

"I see what you mean now, about it getting worse out there. I really do. It's just going to be Florida all over again. Slower, maybe. Or faster, who knows. It's not like one is better than the other when it's all headed down the same road."

There was no satisfaction in knowing she'd been right.

Wanda stayed. She wanted to. Phyllis wanted her to. And Lucas had finally seen that the rest of the world couldn't offer her anything better. *He* couldn't offer her anything better. They both impressed upon Wanda what staying could mean, and Phyllis was pretty sure she understood. As much as any of them understood. They found a military passenger truck heading north on Phyllis's CB radio. It was already filled with refugees, but they were happy to add another. These trucks were a fixture now; Phyllis saw them driving around, week after week, announcing their presence on bullhorns. Rounding up as many people as they could convince to go.

The three of them met the truck at the old school. The auditorium had caved in since the last time they'd been here. When Phyllis told the driver it was just Lucas leaving, he frowned and gave her next week's schedule of passenger vehicles passing through this part of the state. Wanda started to say that they didn't need it, but Phyllis shushed her. Let him assume they'd follow. It was easier that way.

"How much longer will you be making trips?" Lucas asked, climbing up into the back of the canvas-covered truck. The driver slammed the tailgate behind him and gave it a stern pat.

"Till the end of the year. January first and we're outta here. Hear that? Don't wait too long, ladies." He trudged around to the front of the truck. Inside, Phyllis could see more than half a dozen people huddled on the bench seats. They looked tired. Worn. Bereft, like the world had just ended. Which, for them, she realized, it had. Lucas looked down from his perch in the truck, his rucksack between his knees, all the hesitation and fear he'd confided in her evident on his face.

"We'll be fine," Phyllis called up to him. Lucas gripped the edge of the tailgate, and for a moment he looked like the little boy she remembered so vividly.

"Are you sure?"

"Positive," she lied. A scientist knows nothing is ever certain. Phyllis and Wanda watched Lucas disappear, waving until the truck turned the corner, and then they trudged home through the ankle-deep floodwater, the sheen of oil slicks swirling around their muck boots.

Phyllis's feelings regarding Wanda's light had spanned a broad spectrum since that day in the swamp when she first saw it. She'd begun this exploration with utter disbelief, moved into cautious experimentation, then swung over to obsessive curiosity and a constant, feverish excitement. The world was crawling with undiscovered species, but she'd never imagined that she might find one herself. Ever since that first glimpse, she'd been reading and thinking and hypothesizing. She'd gathered all the books in the house that touched on bioluminescence, either directly or circuitously, and methodically reread each of them late at night. It was an extraordinary discovery, but what to do with it—she wasn't entirely sure. There was so much she didn't know. So many resources she didn't have.

In the evenings, after Wanda went to bed, Phyllis began to tinker with a scholarly paper. It felt almost unethical not to share this with a wider audience, but at the same time, without the kind of rigid, supervised experimentation she no longer had access to, her findings would be a laughingstock—if they were even published. Still. She could not ignore the data, and the data showed that the organisms glowed only in response to Wanda's presence. They clustered around her, sensing her in the water, sensing her even when she was *near* the water. It was unmistakable. Phyllis had tried every variable she could think of to disrupt this pattern, but the creatures were steadfast in their attraction.

Was it an oil on her skin? The pitch of her voice? Phyllis couldn't make sense of it. It was beyond the scientific tools at her disposal. Her most educated guess was that somewhere along the way, Wanda had acquired an intestinal bacterium that was either related to or the same as the organisms they found in the water and this was how they recognized her as one of their own. Maybe she was the origin, spreading new specimens to each suitable body of water she interacted with. Maybe it was a supernatural gift, an infection, a genetic mutation. Maybe, maybe, maybe.

A guess is not the same as knowing. Phyllis had spent her entire career seeking knowledge in one form or another, but the pursuit itself taught her infinitely more about the absence of knowledge than its presence. What is magic but science that is not yet understood? What is science but magic with an explanation? In the matter of Wanda and the local water bodies, she continued to collect data but acclimated to the idea that there were many, many more questions than answers. In this matter, and in every other. When she had been young, this truth had unsettled her. The older she got, the more she allowed it to soothe her.

Whatever secret aspirations she might have harbored to publish one more paper, to share one last thing with the outside world, laughingstock or no, they fell by the wayside as the following spring approached. The nearby cell towers were finally decommissioned after the refugee trucks ceased their evacuation efforts, and Rudder's separation from the rest of the country became complete. She was ready for the logistics of all of this, but she wasn't ready for the grief that slammed into her when she picked up her cell phone one morning and saw that the signal was gone. The final tether: cut. This was it. The beginning of the end. How quickly it all unraveled.

WANDA LETS THE water slip over her head like a seamless veil without waiting to see who is coming. She doesn't trust these whispers, but she trusts the swamp's human remnants even less. Beneath the surface, the bulk of the manatees glimmer deep in the caves. She looks around for the curve of her boat's hull, finds it, swims to it. On the way, she takes stock of a new vessel coming into view. A raft, by the look of its underside, a flat square sliding out into the openness of the lagoon through the channel. *They've only just arrived*, she thinks, *that's good*. They're still getting their bearings, probably transfixed by the glow of the water. There's a chance they haven't even seen her canoe yet. She surfaces as quietly as she can, on the opposite side of the canoe, and pulls herself aboard. This maneuver is impossible to do silently—but she does it quickly, and that's what matters.

"Ahoy there," the newcomer calls out. It's as if they're teasing her; that word, "ahoy," that isn't a serious word, is it? She hasn't spoken to another person in a long time. Certain nuances have begun to drift away from her. "Don't be scared," they say, "I'm just here for the fresh water."

She isn't reassured by this, but what choice does she have? There is no way out of the lagoon but past the raft, and scrabbling up into the tangled mangroves that enclose it will only make her an easy target. Besides—the canoe. Without this vessel, she wouldn't survive. She cannot just leave it behind.

"Hello," Wanda ventures, still catching her breath on the bottom of her canoe. Her voice comes out crackling, a plastic bag caught in the weeds. She's drenched; the pools of water she's brought aboard with her are still glimmering, but faint. By the time she sits up, the lagoon has darkened. Just a strange sheen on the surface lingers.

"Did you swim?" Their voice is low and smooth. A woman, she thinks, but she's not sure. Nuances again.

"Yeah."

"I never seen the water do that here. It's pretty."

"It's probably just the bacteria," Wanda says, surprised she can find that word after all this time. One of Phyllis's old theories. It occurs to her that this is almost a conversation now. The stranger asks her name, and without thinking, she answers: "Wanda."

Even this, an exchange of greetings, of observations, the offering of her name, this is the closest she's come to another person in a long time. A living person. Bodies gone crisp in their boats do not count. She's missed it. She knows what loneliness is—how could she not?—but the absence of loneliness has become less familiar. The sensation of closeness frightens and thrills her at the same time.

"Wanda," the woman repeats softly. "Like the hurricane." Wanda forgot how much her name means, how clearly it marks her. It's never been just any name. The thrill curdles to fear. It would have been so easy to swim into the swamp grasses and hide until the stranger left—but again, no, she couldn't risk someone taking the canoe. She did what she had to. And she will do more, if she must. She feels again for the knife on her hip.

"I'm Bird Dog," the woman says. The strangeness of this name is eclipsed by everything else that makes this moment strange. None of the fear coursing through Wanda is present in this person's voice. The opposite. She is calm, nonchalant. As if this—a meeting of drifters—is not notable. Wanda can hear that she's already started filling her bottles. She lets go of the knife. The water has returned to its customary blackness. "I was going to eat something before I turn back," Bird Dog continues. "There's enough, if you wanted. It's just papaya. I could cut you a piece."

Wanda squints through the dark, but there is nothing more her eyes can tell her.

Even though she knows she should leave, she stays. She does want something to eat, actually. But more importantly, she wants to keep talking. She wants to not feel afraid. She wants this feeling to last a little longer: of speaking aloud and being spoken to. Phyllis would not approve. She always taught Wanda that if you see another person on the water, you hide. And if you can't hide, you run. But Phyllis isn't here anymore; she couldn't have known how much it would hurt to be so alone.

"All right. Thanks." Wanda paddles toward her and after a minute, she hears the stranger finishing with the water bottles, then cutting into the fruit. Wanda can smell it. The juice drips onto the deck, sticky. She already knows it's perfectly ripe.

"Here it is," she says. Wanda collects the offering by touch, trailing her fingers along the raft, following the trail of fruit juice to the flesh that sits, waiting for her in a sweet, mild crescent on the edge of the stranger's deck. She tries to eat it quietly, but she's hungry, and the silence is not thick enough to mask her urgency. Bird Dog eats, too, the smack of their mouths against the fruit filling the lagoon. Bird Dog cuts another slice. Wanda can hear her blade sawing into the skin, then slipping through the fruit flesh.

"There's more," Bird Dog says when she hears the wet plop of Wanda's rind, sucked clean and dropped into the water. A treat for the manatees. A second later, there's a break in the water's surface as the two manatees rise in unison, chuffing out through their nostrils, inhaling deeply. A leisurely crunching as one of them snacks on the rind. Wanda can almost smell its breath, warm and earthy and a little sour. She feels Bird Dog go tense on her raft.

"Only manatees," Wanda says.

Bird Dog relaxes and Wanda takes the second piece of fruit. They listen to the manatees splashing around near the musk grass and the water lettuces that grow at the edges of the lagoon. "They're hungry, too," Bird Dog says, and laughs. It's a good laugh. Belly-deep and slow. The kind of laugh that starts low down and bubbles up—pure, like spring water. "You remember what folks used to call them?"

Wanda thinks, but her memory of the Before time is cloudy. "Sea…something."

"Sea cows." Bird Dog laughs again, because it's just another saying, nickname, object, idea that is obsolete. Cows don't exist here anymore. Or pastures, or grain, or milk. A shorthand that is now too long. "Someday we'll call cows land manatees, don't you think?"

"That sounds right," Wanda says. "Or unicorns." Bird Dog laughs even harder. Wanda allows a smile that no one can see, pleased with herself for making a joke.

"You been out here a long time?" Bird Dog asks.

"Since the start of it."

"Alone?"

"Not…" Wanda pauses. Admitting solitude is admitting weakness. "Not always."

"I'm fishing tomorrow, near the old marina." Bird Dog rinses her knife. "If you wanted, you could come." Her invitation is spoken softly, as if to speak it any louder would be to reveal how much she wants Wanda to say yes. But Wanda can hear it anyway. The wanting. As if Bird Dog shouted it. She can hear everything in this lagoon: the scamper of tiny feet in the branches of the mangroves. Manatees snacking among the grasses. The lapping of the water against the hull of her canoe. Mangrove leaves rubbing up against each other. Frogs, singing in the backs of their throats. And the faint, fast thrum of Bird Dog's pulse. *If you wanted, you could come.* She does want. But wanting and surviving do not always go hand in hand.

"I could, I think," Wanda replies. She isn't ready to leave, but there's nothing left to do here. Her water jugs are full. The papaya has been eaten. Even the manatees seem to have departed. Everything Phyllis ever taught her about how to survive, how to stay safe, swirls, sinks. And overlaying it, this new feeling, warm and soft and expansive. The spaciousness of wanting something she doesn't need. It feels good, but she is afraid that when she finally dips her paddle back into the water and propels herself toward home, away from Bird Dog, it will fade.

"After the sun goes down," Bird Dog says. "The flagpole?"

"The flagpole," Wanda agrees.

They leave the lagoon together, through the channel, foliage drooping down over their heads, roots reaching up to grab at their boats. Bird Dog goes first and Wanda is impressed with how she handles her vessel; the shape of a raft is hard to manage in these narrow spaces, but what little Wanda can see looks effortless. They say goodbye near the wind chimes. Wanda waits to make sure Bird Dog is gone and there's no one else lingering in the shadows to follow her home before she departs. Phyllis taught her to suspect such tricks. Remembering this, she also remembers how dangerous humans can be.

Heading back to her nest, she tries to convince herself not to go tomorrow, firmly assuring the Phyllis that lives on in her mind that she would never take such a risk. But even as she promises her dear dead friend she won't, a part of her knows she will. Something is awake now, some part of her that will not, cannot, go back to sleep.

Dawn is creeping close by the time Wanda returns home. A growing light sizzles against the horizon. Heat rises from the water. She leans into the last stretch, pushing herself harder, paddling faster, driving the blades down like she is trying to punish the water, or herself, or both. The fullness of the night follows her no matter how quickly she goes—the forgotten sensation of a human being's company, of using words, sharing food, making plans; the manatees' skin on hers, moving so slowly, so gently, touching her like she was one of their own; and being surrounded by the glow that has been chasing her since childhood, cool and kaleidoscopic and fearless. She has been empty for so long. It's strange to feel this full.

The tom waits for her on the dock, cleaning his face with an orange paw as she has watched him do a thousand times, but now, in this barely broken morning light, it is a wonder. She lets the canoe coast the last few meters, watching him. It's both sensual and necessary, this methodical application of one part of his body to another part of his body, the tender, firm motion of his paw and the long, lithe lick of pink tongue skimming across pink toe pads. A gust of hot wind drives her hull into the dock with a sharp crack, and the tom, startled, disappears into the trees. Wanda hauls her water supply up the ladder in as few trips as she can, hurrying to unload the canoe before the sun clears the rim of the encroaching ocean and the wind blows from hot to scorched. She's exhausted and energized at the same time, unspent adrenaline still buzzing in her veins. Sleep will fight her, but she must rest.

Hidden beneath the canopy, Wanda dreams in restless fragments. A feeling of having forgotten something flits in and out of her consciousness. She dreams of Bird Dog, a faceless presence, just out of sight, urging her on as she dives into the lagoon. The manatees are waiting for her somewhere in the depths. She cannot see them, can only feel them, but they're down there, gigantic and slow, floating deep in the caves. The lights surround her, urge her on. She dives and dives, deeper and deeper, swimming for so long that she forgets which way is up and which is down, realizing it doesn't matter—what matters is that she keep swimming. She's getting closer. But it's not the manatees she's looking for; it's something else, something she can't explain. The lights whisper—*A little farther, a little deeper, almost there.* The exertion is beginning to take its toll; she can't go on swimming much longer. Her muscles burn. Her heart races. The temperature has risen while she slept. Her body reaches its limit in both places.

When she wakes, she hasn't yet found the thing she was looking for, but there is a new problem. She discovers that she is burning, her skin dry and pulsing. It's the beginning of the end when a body ceases to excrete sweat. Phyllis taught her that. She lies still, taking stock of her own organs, aware of how easy it would be to die of heat-stroke right here, in her sleep, to dive so deep into a dream that she'd find a sweltering, stifling blackness and never manage to resurface. She stays very still while she waits for the afternoon to cool, for the sun to set.

Even just a few degrees can bridge the gap between life and death, but that's nothing new. She has been living on this brink for many years. The idea of drenching herself in the drinking water she's just rowed so far to collect is difficult, but she must lower her body temperature now, before it rises any higher. It can't wait. She can feel the urgency in her pores, in her veins. Then, unexpectedly—a dot of coolness on her face. Another on her arm. Rain. A breeze comes, dislodging the scorched air that has settled over her. And there it is: a reprieve. For now.

The clock of her lifetime is round and bright. There is so much they want her to know, more than she can possibly understand. There are eons to share, in both directions—past and future make no difference to them; both matter, both are needed. But now is always the center.

OVER THE NEXT few years, Phyllis heard little from the outside world. She occasionally cranked her radio and listened to the broadcasts that managed to carry, but the signals were faint, her interest even fainter. Eventually, she stopped listening entirely. There was a lightness in not knowing. A clarity. There was no need to follow the goings on of a world she and Wanda were no longer part of. In the years before the border closed, she had been consumed by a constant undercurrent of anxiety: lists that were never finished, home improvements that were never good enough, plans full of holes. What if, what if, what if. But then all that ended and something else took its place. Something quiet and rich and straightforward. The life she'd been planning for arrived and she gradually settled into it.

Phyllis and Wanda began to let the wild determine their days. It was strange at first, to allow such simplicity. Days of the week ceased to hold meaning. The time stopped being a number and became a question of light and tides. Months lost their shape. The water level went on rising, past their ankles, to their knees, to tickle their thighs. Storms came and went. Some creatures died out completely and some thrived. Plants and trees, too. And wasn't that the point of all her years of preparation—to count herself among those who thrived? She'd planned well. Phyllis and Wanda grew their own food and tended to their own hens and hunted in the swamps and fished in the overflowing water bodies. Life was hard and it was good. They had everything they needed.

Which is not to say there weren't things they missed. The loss of Lucas's phone calls hung heavy on Wanda. Phyllis could see it in those months after the cell towers quit. She felt it herself. But Wanda was resilient and Phyllis was old enough to succumb to her grief in the way that only many decades and many losses can teach. The murkiness of years passing eventually allowed them to pretend that he'd left just a moment ago and was bound to return any day. Gradually, her brother became a myth. They told each other stories of what he was doing in California—saving entire forests from the flames, building brand-new cities, rescuing little towns from the brink of collapse. As the years passed, his accomplishments grew bigger and bigger. It soothed Wanda to imagine it all. Privately, Phyllis didn't believe such things. Not that Lucas wasn't capable, or special, or talented—she just didn't believe that the world was salvageable. The last she'd heard was that things were disintegrating faster than ever. The more land that became uninhabitable, the more the crush of refugees overwhelmed kinder climates. It wasn't sustainable. Everything would have to collapse in order for a new kind of society to be built; or, more likely, for some other epoch to have its day. Humanity was an ecological disaster, as far as Phyllis was concerned. A misstep made by an otherwise magnificently intelligent system of life and death. Evolution could do so much better. Someday, it would.

Wanda was sixteen the day a visitor came. The two of them were working behind the house; they heard him before they saw him. Phyllis could see Wanda's head snap up from the garden bed she was weeding and took heed. Wanda had grown another six inches by then; she had sharp eyes and sharp ears and a wiry, coiled look to her. She looked more like Frida with each passing season, but harder. Stronger. They both tightened their grips around the gardening tools at hand— a spade for Phyllis, a shovel for Wanda—and waited to see who or what would appear from the rustling tangle of weeds that grew alongside the house. Phyllis had just enough time to admire Wanda's steady grip on the shovel and the calm, shrewd narrowing of her eyes as she waited to launch her attack at the right moment. Tendons stood out on the backs of her hands. Phyllis had taught her what she could, drilling moments like these again and again, but there are some things that cannot be taught. Some things that a body innately knows—or doesn't. They both waited to see which it would be.

When a man with broad shoulders and a filthy, scruffy beard came around the corner, Phyllis gritted her teeth. His clothes were wet and muddy, his gait was slow, but he was enormous. He froze as he spotted them, then slowly let his heavy pack drop to the ground. This had become her deepest fear, the thing she realized, a little late, she hadn't prepared nearly enough for—intruders. She thought of the two guns she kept in the linen cupboard upstairs, the knives in the kitchen, the ax in the shed. The gardening spade in her hand was a poor excuse for a weapon, but it was too late to grab anything else. She stepped in front of Wanda as seamlessly as she could, her mind whirling with everything she should have done to be better prepared for this moment. None of it could help them now. He smiled at them, a glimmer of pale teeth among all that mud, and suddenly Wanda was rushing past her. Phyllis tried to snatch her back, but she was too fast. She flung the shovel aside and in a few steps she was face-to-face with the intruder, flinging her arms around his neck. Only then did Phyllis realize that this wasn't an intruder after all. It was Lucas. Older, hairier, worse for wear, but it was him.

Over Wanda's shoulder, Lucas caught Phyllis's eye. She let the hand holding the garden spade fall to her side as she considered what it must mean for him to come back, after all this time. He'd been gone so long, she'd let herself imagine that Wanda was hers to keep. But watching Wanda hang from his neck, her toes brushing the ground, her face buried in his chest, Phyllis understood that this dream had never been real. She tried to let it go as gracefully as she could.

"You're back," she said, willing warmth into her voice. Wanda finally let go of him and Phyllis took stock: He looked tired, as big as ever but malnourished, as if holding up the mass of his own body was too much for him. Mud caked his face and neck. Water dripped from his pant legs, pattering softly against the grass. Phyllis stepped forward and took her turn. It felt strange to hold a man in her arms. He smelled of swamp water and body odor, the moisture in his clothes steaming ever so slightly in the heat. He leaned into her, heavy enough that she had to brace her feet.

"Easy now," she whispered in his ear.

"A little off the beaten path, yeah?" He laid his head on her shoulder for a moment, then pulled himself back up to his full height and released her. Glancing at the smear of damp and dirt across her shirt, he added, "Sorry about that."

"It's nothing," Phyllis said. "We've missed you."

He nodded and turned his attention back to Wanda, who was practically vibrating with excitement. She almost looked like a child again. "I can't believe you're here," Wanda said.

"I'm here," he replied, picking his pack up off the ground with a groan.

"For good?" Wanda asked, taking the pack from him and easily swinging it across her back. Phyllis watched Lucas's face as he followed his sister around to the back door.

"I—" He glanced at Phyllis. His eyes pleaded with her, but for what?

"Let him get settled, Wan," she said. "He's come a long way."

The three of them went inside and Phyllis turned on the air conditioner in the kitchen. They didn't use it often—it overpowered the solar panels' capacity if they weren't careful—but this was a special occasion. Wanda had so many questions, she couldn't manage to allow him the space to answer any of them before she asked the next one. She wanted to know how long it took to get here and where he came from and did he find a boat to bring him down and did he have to swim and if so did he come across any gators and what was college like and what was California like and did he still live there and if not where and if so did he like it and on and on. Phyllis left the two of them together while she went looking for something dry for him to wear. Upstairs, she leaned against the wall in her bedroom and listened to the soft murmur of their voices. Wanda's high and constant, Lucas's intermittent and deep. She found an old pair of too-big shorts with an elastic waist and an oversize T-shirt and went back down.

In the kitchen, Lucas had his face right up next to the air con-ditioner while Wanda still hadn't reached the end of her questions. "Wanda, honey," Phyllis said, putting the clothes on the table. Wanda understood and stopped talking long enough for a few beats of silence to fill the room. Lucas turned away from the cold blast of the AC unit and saw the clothes.

"Thanks," he said, and held up the shorts, raising his eyebrows at Phyllis as he tested the elastic.

"Best I could do."

"I appreciate it. I'll change. Everything in my bag is wet, I think. I had to swim a stretch at the end there."

"It's fine, we'll give them a wash."

He nodded. "The water…it's so high."

"Higher every year," Wanda chimed in.

"Wanda, show him where the towels are." They trooped upstairs, Wanda chattering, Lucas *mm-hm*ing, and left her there to contemplate the puddle that was slowly forming around his bag. She wondered how long he might stay and how much of her heart he would take with him when he left.

It was strange to have another body around the house, but Phyllis was surprised by how quickly they adapted to his presence. Days passed. He silently trailed behind as they went about their chores, and eventually she started giving him things to do. He seemed grateful for the work, so she gave him more. Phyllis sent him up onto the roof to do solar panel maintenance. That took a few days. Then she asked him to muck the henhouse, to set rat traps in the attic, to clean the pantry, to build a new raised garden bed. There was a great deal to do during the daylight hours, but in the evenings, when the work was done, Wanda brought forth her stockpile of questions and Phyllis watched as Lucas slowly succumbed to her persistence.

The picture he painted of the world outside what was formerly known as Florida was dire. He told them he moved around a lot, taking contracts on linemen crews where the need was greatest. He'd gone back to electricity after all. Phyllis didn't ask what had become of his college degree. All those big dreams for making big changes. The answer was right there on his face. His eyes seemed to float across the room without seeing anything when the conversation turned to the years he'd been away. Phyllis stayed quiet during these inquisitions, witnessing Lucas's reticence and Wanda's eagerness, a delicate balance between the two siblings rediscovering one another that she didn't wish to upset.

When they weren't working or resting, Wanda took Lucas out in the canoe and showed him what Rudder had become. Phyllis saw them off on these adventures, Blackbeard twining between her legs, mewing as Wanda got farther and farther away. The blue house was built on some of the highest ground Rudder had to offer, but beneath it, the water had claimed almost everything. It was a difficult, in-between phase for navigation—in some places, it was too shallow for the canoe; in others, too deep to wade. Phyllis didn't like Wanda going out on her own. She imagined her getting stranded, the canoe stuck among the weeds and debris, Wanda forced to swim through polluted water with who knew what lurking behind every ruin, but with Lucas joining her, she didn't worry quite so much. She was glad for them to have the time together. Waving them off, she reminded herself that it was practice for the day they would leave her for good. She braced herself for this eventuality. But it didn't come. And it didn't come. And still, it didn't come.

Finally, it came. But not how she expected. Wanda was off hunting for eggs in the swamp where the chickens liked to lay sometimes when Lucas told Phyllis he was leaving. She sterilized canning jars at the stove while Lucas sliced beets into thick half-moons, a deep purple-red stain creeping across the knife, the cutting board, his broad sunburned hands. She stopped what she was doing.

"I've overstayed as it is," he said.

"I like having you here," she replied slowly, as if speaking to an animal prone to startling. "I like having both of you here. I hope you know that. That it's been—" A tremor crept into her voice. She swallowed it and continued, "It's been a great honor to be Wanda's guardian. And to have you here, too. But I of course understand if it's time to move on."

"That's good to hear," he said, scooping up a handful of beets and dropping them in the bowl. The vivid juices soaked into the weather-beaten crevices that crisscrossed his hands, illuminating the lines on his palms in bright, bloody slashes. She wished she were a palm reader. That his heart, head, fate lines were revealed to her in this moment. But Phyllis had no such skill for divination. Lucas continued, "Because I think that Wanda is better off staying. I'm not sure that there's anything for her out there. Certainly not with me. She seems so…well, she seems happy here. And I'll be honest, Phyllis, what's out there is not good. It's changing fast, and not for the better."

For all her time spent dreading Wanda's departure, now that Lucas was offering a future in which she stayed, she felt a catch but couldn't yet identify it. "She's happy because you're here, Lucas. You're both so welcome. I don't pretend to know what it's like out there, but here—"

"I'll tell you what it's like. It's falling apart. I never even finished my degree. You know why? The university went belly-up. The whole University of California system. Done. It's nothing but fires year-round there. And the East Coast isn't any better. Floods, refugee camps, heat waves, droughts. It's always too much of something or not enough. Even the places where the land is still good—there are too many people who need it. There's something wrong every place you go, Phyllis. At least here you saw it coming. You figured out how to make it work. I thought as much, but I needed to be sure. Check that she was okay. Out there, it's just things falling apart, piece by piece. No one knows what to do."

Phyllis stared into the boiling water, tongs still in her hand, canning jars lined up beside her. She wasn't surprised, but it was different to hear him say it. "Well, then…you'll stay. You'll both stay."

He shook his head. "I can't. You two fit, you make sense. I…I don't."

"I disagree." The water was boiling so high it began to froth along the edges of the pot, climbing up and up.

"I got a crew now, Phyllis. We look out for each other. And we—well, we can't fix it, but we can make it last a little longer, you know? It's not like I wanted it to be, it's not like I got my degree and a big job, but I got a chance to make a little difference. I got skills that are needed, Phyllis. Really *needed*. She's better off here and I'm better off there. I don't know how else to explain it. I can't leave my crew, not for good. Told 'em I needed some time. Had to come make sure my kid sister was okay. But I don't think I could sleep at night if I stayed, knowing I coulda helped."

"I think I see," Phyllis said slowly. She didn't, but told herself there was still time to bring him around. Let him get it all off his chest. "So UC Berkeley is…"

"It's done. Gone. UC Davis, UCLA, Irvine, all of it. The whole thing. Most schools are. A few of the fancy ones hanging on, I guess, but there's no point in it anymore."

Phyllis tried to absorb this. There were so many things Lucas might have said about what was happening north of Florida that wouldn't have surprised her. But this—this hit her like a sucker punch. "What will you tell Wanda?" she asked finally.

"I'll tell her the truth."

In the end, he was with them for a month altogether. Phyllis tried to convince him to stay; she tried so hard that maybe in the end she begged a little, but he had his mind made up. Wanda wailed like a child, but even that didn't change anything. It turned out he'd arranged it before he'd even arrived—the fishing boat that brought him would return to scoop him up by the old causeway on its way back north. It was done. Understanding that this had been his intention all along didn't make it easier, but Phyllis was finally able to stop imagining that she could have changed his mind.

The day before he'd arranged for the pickup, he used Phyllis's CB to coordinate with the fishermen. Then Wanda and Phyllis rowed him out to the causeway, the little canoe crowded with all three of them in it, the tide high. They waited for a long time, buffeted by choppy water, the sun beating down on them. Phyllis allowed herself to hope that something had happened and the fishermen wouldn't come. That he'd be stuck here, forced to reconsider. But they came eventually, appearing in the south as a tiny speck on the horizon. They were briefly confused by the presence of Phyllis and Wanda and then again by the understanding that they were staying behind, but these were men who knew how to mind their own business. They took their passenger and continued on upriver.

Lucas waved as they motored away. Wanda only stared, hands at her sides and tears running down her face, bereft at being left yet again. He'd told her he'd be back as soon as he could, but Wanda was too old for a lie like that. Phyllis busied her hands by bundling her young charge against her chest, even though Wanda wasn't so young anymore. She could feel her shuddering there, tears blooming on her shirt and a ragged, hot breath warming her old skin through the fabric. Still, Lucas went on waving. To Phyllis, maybe, whose arms were full, or to Wanda, who couldn't see him, or to Rudder, which didn't care whether he stayed or went. The old canoe heaved up and down in the wake of the fishing boat, until finally the trawler disappeared, Lucas with it. It was just the two of them now. And hadn't she wanted some version of this? It was shameful to realize it. She'd never imagined it would feel so hollow.

THE RAIN COMES down hard, beating the foliage into submission, washing away anything not secured in Wanda's little treetop nest. The weight of the water pounds against the cookware in her kitchen, the chipped china she has collected, the glass water bottles she filled last night. It's cacophonous, this torrent, crashing into everything. She lets it. There is nothing to do but let it. The rain is warm and sharp, and it feels good on her skin. It cools her. Clouds block out the sun and just like that, the fry of the afternoon has ended. She isn't sure how late it is. The harbingers of dusk are hidden behind the storm front. She sheds her clothes and showers where the water comes down heaviest, in thick, thudding sheets, working her fingers through her hair. It's difficult; there are some tangles that cannot be undone. Still, she tries. The dream stays with her as she washes herself. The whispers. That feeling of searching. For what? Her mind reaches back into her subconscious, but there's nothing to grasp on to there, just shimmering depths and the rush of water.

During weather like this, there isn't much she can do. The fish are driven down to the depths and the land creatures stow themselves away. She must follow suit. She thinks of Bird Dog, waiting at the flagpole, soaked through, but no—she'll be tucked away as well. Along with everything else. Wanda carefully puts her soap back in its box, slippery and graying and down to the nub. It's a precious resource, this sliver.

She clambers down to the platform shielded by the tin roof, still naked, and steps beneath its protection. It's hard to dry off and what's the point; everything is wet now. She skims the excess water from her skin and flicks it away. Nothing can escape the rich humidity of this weather. She sits on the bare wood as she is, her rear leaving wet heart shapes behind whenever she moves, and works at making traps to set among the mangrove roots. There are still some creatures to catch with them—squirrels, possums, sometimes an otter—but making them is more soothing than practical. She doesn't lay her traps anymore, not since she accidentally caught one of the feral cats she throws fish guts to. It was still alive when she found it, its leg snared in her wire so tightly bone was showing. It wouldn't have survived. She used her knife and made it quick, but it wasn't the same as silencing squealing possums or slicing open fish bellies. It was crossing a line she'd forgotten was there. She goes on making the traps because she needs something to do with her hands and because someday, she'll have to start setting them again. The fish are growing more temperamental lately. It's hard to tell which changes belong to the seasons and which are the way it will be from now on.

Phyllis would tell her to go back to the data, but the thing is, Wanda doesn't collect data anymore. It hurt too much after Phyllis passed. She's fallen out of the habit. Now she lives night to night. It's simpler this way. She can find things to love about this place in a night-size window, but the idea of looking ahead, marking the decline, year by year, is too much to bear. There is less and less to love the longer the timeline grows, so she doesn't project. She resides in the length of a thunderstorm, the overhead sweep of a constellation, the time between one sleep and the next.

As she works, the rain begins to thin. When the sky has closed and the flood has ceased, the only sounds are the water dripping down off the leaves and the fronds and the flower petals, a familiar melody ringing out all across the swamp. The sun manages to peek through the clouds, just the tiniest glow near the horizon, and Wanda realizes she hasn't missed dusk after all. If she wants to meet Bird Dog, she should go now.

And she does want to. The problem is, she shouldn't. She dresses, threading her arms through a damp, torn T-shirt and sliding into little spandex shorts that dry quickly. The elastic waistband is shot and she is constantly sewing up holes that appear in the seams, but everything she wears is falling apart in one way or another. It will do. Climbing into her boat, she tries to make peace with the foreboding sensation that creeps along the back of her neck by promising herself that she's only going to see if Bird Dog is waiting for her. She'll just take a peek from behind the ruins of the marina. That's all. A peek and then she'll leave. She wants to see the body attached to that voice. Surely this is an acceptable risk?

She can hear Phyllis chiding her as she unties the canoe, telling her to stay home, to stay safe. This idea of safety is something Phyllis drilled into her, as if it were the most important thing, the only thing. An idea synonymous with survival. But Wanda has begun to suspect that this isn't true. She coils the rope at her feet. What if survival and risk belong to one another?

The water is high and rough after the downpour, but the current is in her favor. The heavy clouds still drooping low over the horizon take on colors as the setting sun illuminates them from behind the waves: orange, blush, violet. Wanda lets the water carry her toward the marina, toward the ocean, occasionally dipping her paddle in to steer. Nearby, she sees a flit of striped fur among the vegetation, a spark in this luminous moment before the colors fade and the light dims. The tomcat. Whether he is following her or running from her, she couldn't say. It's usually a little of both, and that's why she and these feral creatures understand each other as well as they do. Yearning and fear, bound together as violently as the wire traps she doesn't want to set anymore.

Arriving at the marina, she slots her canoe in among the ruins and hangs on to an old beam to anchor herself. She finds an angle so she can see the flagpole but still remain hidden behind the rotting, caved-in roof. It occurs to her that the journey home will be difficult—the tide is rushing out, all that rainwater determined to meet the sea. She sees Bird Dog arriving from farther south, near where the causeway—mostly submerged rubble now—used to connect Beach-side to the mainland. Wanda watches her pilot the raft, taking stock of this strange woman's strength and agility. Her grace. Wanda decides then that Bird Dog is beautiful.

When Wanda was still a little girl, Phyllis warned her that as time progressed and the swamp encroached, as the temperatures rose, as the population of Rudder thinned…the people who remained would become more and more ruthless. "Count on it," Phyllis said, and she'd been right. More than once, she'd been right. Wanda watches Bird Dog bump up against the flagpole and tie off. She seems so vulnerable out there on the open water, so trusting. But maybe this is how she sets her victims at ease. Wanda wonders if some part of her wants Bird Dog to be one of the predators Phyllis warned her about. She thinks of the feral cat in her snare, the terrified, spitting, violent look in its eyes as she approached it. The frantic scrabble. But then, as she took out her knife, something unexpected: It stopped struggling. Perhaps it understood in that final moment that Wanda had come to set it free. Not free to limp back into the swamp with a mangled leg, but an actual freedom. An end.

She knew then, as she knows now, that there are worse things than giving up. What is this half life worth to her anymore? The lingering obligation she feels, to Phyllis, to Lucas, to her father and even her mother, to the pump of her own heart, could be over. Her duty to the breath in her lungs could cease. Her grip on survival could loosen. The Edge used to be a physical place, a line between the ocean and dry land, approximately nine feet below the hull of her canoe where she floats at this very moment. Now it is a state of mind, an undertow that tickles her feet no matter where she goes. She's felt it since she was a girl, and she feels it now.

Wanda releases the beam that has anchored her, and plunges her paddle into the water, skirting the larger chunks of debris that float, pressing on toward the flagpole. The closer she gets, the lighter she feels. The clouds fade from violet to indigo to midnight as she rows. Even if all of this is a mistake, it is her right to make it. Perhaps even her duty. Rounding the last stretch of the marina's ruins, she reaches Bird Dog's shadowy craft, slowly fading into the backdrop of settling darkness.

"You came," Bird Dog says. "I didn't think you would."

"I came," Wanda replies. She slides in beside the raft, her canoe brushing up against it with the raspy whisper of plexiglass against rough metal. Skin on skin.

Squinting into the darkness, she tries to make out Bird Dog's features in what little light is left. Something tickles at her memory.

"You still don't recognize me, do you?" Bird Dog says. A charge of electricity jumps inside Wanda's chest. Panic. She stares, her mind scrambling from one possibility to the next. Bird Dog's face is angular, sharp cheekbones and a high forehead, features that look as if they've been sculpted by an exacting hand. Her hair is cropped close to her head, bristling and blond. Her skin is scored, pinkish, pale.

"I don't..." Wanda tries to remember. Yes, there is something familiar. But it's been so long. She can't quite reach—

"I knew it was you the minute I saw the lagoon all lit up like that. I just knew. I've only ever seen that once before." And now Wanda does remember. She remembers it as if it's happening to her right now. The Edge. The sixth graders. The water, the burning in her lungs, the salt in her eyes, the hand pressing her head down into the depths. One twin holding her under, while the other hung back.

"Brie," Wanda says.

Bird Dog nods. "That name never fit right." The light is gone now; her nod is just the shadow of a movement. The sharpness of her face has blurred in the darkness, her features melting into one another. Surely the sun is laying its fingers on some other part of the world, but here the night's grasp is tight and sticky and feels as though it might never let go.

AFTER LUCAS LEFT, Phyllis watched, helpless, as the spark that used to flare in Wanda flickered yet again. The breadth and newfound height of her strong shoulders seemed to droop, her head to wilt like a spent flower. There wasn't much Phyllis could do for her young friend, but she tried anyway: special foods, day trips to their submerged permanent plots, art projects, board games, hard labor. None of it helped. How could it? A few months after Lucas said goodbye, Blackbeard disappeared as well. At first, Phyllis was relieved that they couldn't find her remains, but for Wanda, the uncertainty of the disappearance, the denial of finality, of a goodbye, was worse. Yet another missing piece. There and then gone, never found, just like Kirby. Her grief might have made more sense to Phyllis if it were loud and weepy, as it had been after her father died, but it was eerily quiet. When Phyllis looked into her eyes, it was like peeking into a darkened room.

Wanda started taking the canoe out alone, after their work was done, disappearing for hours at a time. She didn't ask if it was all right, she just went. Phyllis bit back her objections as best she could, telling herself it might do Wanda some good. She'd have to trust her to navigate the wild on her own someday—it might as well begin now. She was young but also capable, and that's what mattered. Phyllis leaned into the idea that Wanda had already learned more about survival than most adults. Even so. She worried.

On one of these afternoons, Phyllis stood in the driveway, shifting from one foot to the other as Wanda pulled the canoe out of the bramble where they hid it and down toward the water. Phyllis almost stepped forward to help, but then held herself back. Wanda had to be able to do these things alone. She struggled under the weight of it, but she kept it aloft, careful not to drag it across the rocks and scratch up the hull. It wasn't so long ago that she wouldn't have been able to manage it. Phyllis remembered the day they brought it home—how firm Wanda was in wanting it. The way the old fire chief just shrugged. Phyllis tried to pay him, but he wouldn't take her money. "There's people in this town freaked out by that kid," he said to her when Wanda was busy cramming the paddle into the back of Phyllis's car. "But I never been. You gotta be made of something extra, coming into this world like that. I don't know what she wants that old piece of shit for, but she can have it and good luck to her." Phyllis wondered where Arjun had ended up. If he was still alive.

At the water's edge, Wanda slid the canoe down off her shoulder and it landed with a smack in the stream.

"You're sure you don't want company?" Phyllis knew she didn't.

"No, thanks," Wanda said.

"But you'll be careful. Not too far?"

"Not too far."

Phyllis stared at her old mailbox, all but submerged beside the canoe, its little red flag valiantly lifted against the push of the current. Inside, the box would be full of water and algae and maybe a creature or two seeking refuge. She wondered what species had claimed it. In another time, she would already know the answer to that question. She would have been watching since the day they moved in. Wanda was not the only one struggling in the wake of Lucas's departure. "We should build a dock one of these days," she said, trying to keep Wanda here just a little longer. Reaching for something, anything, that might occupy her interest. Wanda only grunted in response. The truth was, such an addition would attract too much attention. Someone might see it and wander up toward the blue house, now completely hidden by the bramble she had been cultivating for more than a decade. And they would almost certainly steal the canoe if it was left in plain view. But Phyllis wanted to pretend such concerns didn't matter, if only for a moment. "That'd be a good project, wouldn't it? I've got that lumber set by, it would be fun, we could—"

Wanda hopped into the canoe without answering and pushed it out into the canal in the same fluid motion, leaving Phyllis there at the foot of the driveway, the water lapping at her feet. She trailed off, her sentence unfinished. Wanda's paddle began to flicker in and out of the water, and soon enough, between the pull of the current and the determined press of her arms, she was gone.

After Lucas left them for good, the constraints of their life revealed themselves. To Wanda and Phyllis both. Before, the dissolution of society had felt like a release from a structure that no longer made any sense. There was relief in that, and excitement. But once that final human tether to the outside civilization was cut, isolation crept close. The tides pressed in, rising higher and higher. The sun beat down, shining hotter and hotter. The monotony of their days took on a foreboding as the swamp spread and deepened.

Hurricane season arrived, stretching well beyond its usual confines. With it, spikes of uncertainty. Without the constant deluge of the weather service's predictions, they had to rely on their own observations. Every time the sky darkened and the needle of the old-fashioned barometer began to swing, they prepared. Sometimes Phyllis cranked the radio to try to glean what she could, but the forecasts were written for the north and the signal was barely there now that all the nearby repeaters were decommissioned. Officially, there was no one left here—no one to warn, no one to rescue. Their information came from what was left unsaid. Eventually, the two of them began to rely on the color of the sky and the smell of ozone that rolled in off the ocean instead. They stopped bothering with filling in the blanks of the weather service's broadcasts. Their own forecasts were more reliable. Wanda especially, Phyllis noticed, seemed to know when it was time to strap in. She knew even when the sky was still clear and the air pressure had yet to drop. Once Wanda made the call, their preparations were a well-oiled machine.

Bit by bit, the Wanda she remembered returned. As far as Phyllis could tell, it was the storms she had to thank. As the first hurricane season after Lucas left swept through, Wanda clicked into that rhythm of preparation, endurance, recovery. The work required a degree of innovation and each storm was its own surprise, washing away the monotony that had colored the preceding spring. It was as if the storms were filling her internal stores with that great, churning power they wrought, feeding her in some extraordinary capacity. Shocking those batteries back to life. Phyllis watched the smooth, almost effortless way Wanda navigated the storms, wondering, not for the first time, where the lines between what was explained, what had yet to be explained, and what was wholly inexplicable were drawn. There was data Wanda could hear that she couldn't. Which category did that belong in?

There were a great many storms that year, some harsher than others, but all demanding in their own way. In October, Wanda turned seventeen. During another time and in another place, she'd be a girl toying with the idea of adulthood, just beginning to shake off the vestiges of childishness. But here, now—she was grown. The luxury of that transition had gone the way of gasoline and beach bungalows.

As the season wound down, they decided to see what might be salvaged from some of the big box stores up north. It was a long way by boat, but now that the water had swallowed the old Highway 1, it was the only way. Paddling that far upriver took time and muscle, and in the past, Phyllis reasoned that whatever treasures they might find weren't worth the exposure of the trek. But she wanted to give her young friend a treat. And, if she was being honest, she needed one for herself as well. The relative calm of winter's skies after such a tumultuous summer beckoned them away from the haven of the blue house. She decided that the risk, just this once, was acceptable.

They struck out when it was still dark. The humidity of the summer months still hadn't broken. Most days, the temperature would creep into the nineties and maybe beyond by the time the sun gathered its strength above the horizon, but none of this was unusual anymore. They reasoned that if they got an early enough start, they could be back before the hottest part of the day. Taking turns rowing, they made good time. Phyllis began, then passed the paddle to Wanda when she was tired. Wanda leaned into it, sliding the blades in and out of the water so cleanly they barely made a sound, propelling their vessel faster and straighter than Phyllis ever could, a coordinated dance of muscle and tendon flickering underneath the skin of her bare arms. She thought about what Lucas had said to her before he left, that his little sister belonged here. Watching Wanda, she understood what he'd seen. And she understood that he was right. Loss was a part of life above the Floridian border and below it. Whether he'd taken her or not, she couldn't have escaped it. At least here, Wanda not only understood her ecosystem, she was a part of it. It was the water-bound light that flocked to her, but so much more—the storm predictions, her ease in the water, the way she adjusted to the changing environment almost effortlessly. *Leaps of adaptation are what's necessary now*, Phyllis thought. If humans desired a future, if they deserved one, it would have to come from a generation made like Wanda.

When they arrived at the abandoned strip mall, the sun had risen and the wet heat was intensifying by the minute. The white letters that hung on their destination were mostly missing. It read: WA M T. The parking lot was too shallow for the weighed-down canoe, so they got out and waded, pushing it alongside. Half-sunk shopping carts and abandoned cars dotted the expanse. Oil slicks swirled on the water's surface. Garbage floated. Phyllis had foreseen this; they both wore waders, not because they were squeamish about getting wet, but because the stagnant water was filled with trash and sewage and dead things. Evidence of previous looters was clear: plywood torn away from windows, broken glass, graffiti. The damage looked old and worn, which set Phyllis somewhat at ease. But not completely. They were exposed here—there was no getting around that. She felt for the gun she wore in a homemade shoulder holster and tried to remember why she'd thought this was a good idea. The hot metal was comforting. She'd strapped it on that morning feeling certain she wouldn't need it, but what-ifs governed her entire life. She had never not paid them heed. What if she did need it? She fingered the leather straps she'd scraped and tanned herself. This skin used to belong to a deer. Now it belonged to her. *How delicate life is*, she thought. *How unjust.*

They entered the building easily, stepping over splintered plywood and shattered windows. Inside, a foot of water rippled. They brought the canoe with them, nudging it down the flooded aisles, filling it with whatever useful scraps they could find. The store was dark and hot. Turning around, Phyllis saw that the hole they'd entered through was a blinding sunburst amid all of these shadows.

"Shoulda brought a flashlight," she said. "Stupid. Maybe we'll find one, though—wouldn't that be something."

"Or…" Wanda reached down and brushed the water with her fingertips. A glimmer spread across the surface so quickly it reminded Phyllis of lightning. For a brief moment it was bright enough to see everything. They stood in an aisle that used to be full of hair products but was now mostly empty shelves, the canoe floating between them, the illuminated water lapping at the thick rubber of their waders.

"Don't do that," Phyllis hissed.

Wanda looked surprised. Hurt. The light went out almost immediately. The aisle darkened. "Do what?"

"You know what. Not here. Not where anyone could see." Phyllis knew immediately that she should have said this differently. But she was scared. She hadn't been this exposed in a long time, and all she could think about was the gun pressing into the soft flesh of her side, the postman throwing rocks, the curious stares of the fishermen as they helped Lucas into the trawler. The roll of the deer's eyes as she crept forward to end its suffering. The fact that they were women was enough to mark them as prey—if anyone saw Wanda's light, they'd never forget it. How could they? They would hunt her; she was certain of it. Not because they'd understand it or know how to use it, but because humans are a peculiar sort of predator, cruel and curious. More interested in pinning specimens to a corkboard than watching them flutter.

Wanda waded on, tugging the canoe behind her, careful now not to touch the water. "Didn't know it was a crime," she mumbled. Phyllis opened her mouth to bring context to the moment, to remind Wanda that while the things she brought forth in the water were extraordinary—in the most literal sense of the word—that special-ness only made it more important to stay hidden. Just as they hid the house, the mouth of the driveway, the garden, so too they must hide Wanda and the things she could do. But she'd already disappeared down the next aisle. They would talk it through later, she promised herself, when they didn't have to whisper.

In that dim warehouse, a place that used to be overflowing with products and people, the only sounds were the soft ripples of water as Phyllis and Wanda moved down the aisles, surveying empty shelves, picking through trash, occasionally finding something of use. Wanda whistled to get Phyllis's attention and held up a coveted six-pack of soap. Phyllis flashed her a thumbs-up as Wanda nestled her treasure into the canoe. They spent hours in this way, squinting at the cavernous, mostly empty shelves, feeling around at the very back for anything that might have been missed by previous scavengers.

Eventually, the canoe could take no more. They waded out into the parking lot with their load and climbed aboard where the water was deepest, navigating back onto Highway 1. A lazy current caught hold and Wanda took advantage of it, the sun beating down on them, smudges of an afternoon thunderstorm lurking to the north. Phyllis heaved a sigh of relief and began to sort through their bounty. She was pleased with what they'd found. "Not bad," she said, picking up a box of casing nails, giving them a shake, then setting them back down. Wanda only grunted, leaning into her stroke.

Neither Phyllis nor Wanda saw the young man watching them from the roof of a nearby building as the current hurried them home. Shading his eyes against the bright noon light, Corey lay close to the hot shingles until they were almost out of view, then slithered back from the edge and down the fire escape, the metal burning his hands. Inside the decrepit fast-food restaurant below, behind the defunct fryers and darkened heat lamps, he found his sister, up to her thighs in polluted water, still looking for nonperishables among the wreckage.

"We gotta go," he said quietly, pulling her outside to their raft. Neither of them had waders. There was a lot they didn't have. The water caked their clothes and skin in a gray film. "Brie," he hissed. "Hurry." She clambered aboard as fast as she could, not wanting to upset him. It was never a good idea to upset him. He shoved the raft out into the parking lot, then hopped on and picked up the quant pole.

"Why?" she ventured.

"Like Dad always says: easy pickings." He smiled at her: cold, joyless. His sister didn't smile back. She pulled a cap down low over her face and said nothing.

ASSUMING BIRD DOG will give chase, Wanda paddles as fast as she can for the maze of the swamp. As long as she's caught out on the open water, she's vulnerable. But if she can just make it to the ruined buildings and the twisted mangroves and the tangled palms, she might be able to disappear. There is Phyllis's voice in her head, telling her to run and hide, run and hide, run and hide. So without pausing to hear the words Bird Dog is saying, without looking over her shoulder, Wanda churns toward cover with every shred of energy she has, every muscle engaged in propelling her toward the trees. The canoe darts across the water like a quick-finned fish, a metallic streak in the darkness. Her ears are roaring with her own breath, Phyllis's pleas to go faster, faster, faster drowning out her own thoughts. It isn't until she's among the tangled mangrove roots that she realizes Bird Dog hasn't followed her. Brie. Whatever she calls herself now. Wanda holds her breath and stays very still to listen, but there is nothing to hear except the usual night sounds. It doesn't make any sense. Why lure her here if she meant to let her get away so easily? Wanda tries to decide whether it's safe to go home—but that would involve trusting her own senses, and how could she trust anything her brain tells her after such obvious self-sabotage?

She glides deeper into the swamp instead, westward, where the water is fresher and the alligators like to cluster. Going in circles, keeping her eye on the stars through the web of mangrove branches so she doesn't lose her way, she pours herself into the thrust of her paddle and stays vigilant. Every sound is a threat, every creature an enemy. Every splash is Bird Dog, come to finish her off. Surely that is her plan. How could it not be?

Only when dawn nears does she head for home. By now, her thoughts have settled somewhat. It's next to impossible that someone has managed to follow her this far without her knowing. She is beginning to process, to dissect what happened at the flagpole. To discern how keen the threat is, how imminent. She must be invisible for a time—no more fishing, no more trips to the spring. She'll drink rainwater and make her food stores last. The real question is whether her home is still safe. Wanda glides toward the tree house on the warming water. The paddle grows heavy in her hands. A feverish dawn approaches. Sweat pools along the ridges of her collarbones and drips from the backs of her knees, landing softly on the bottom of the canoe. When she met Bird Dog at the spring, it felt like a kind of reward for all this time alone since Phyllis died, a new chapter, a way forward. But now it is just confirmation of everything Phyllis ingrained in her. All the suspicion, all the fear. She chastises herself for not recognizing Bird Dog sooner. It's been years since she last saw her, but even so. It's not the kind of thing one forgets.

At home, Wanda goes through the motions of getting ready for bed while the sun's tendrils creep up over the horizon and charge the air with the kind of heat that sends living things scurrying for cover. The tomcat is back, asking for food, but she has nothing to spare for him, especially not now that she must be wary of fishing on the open water. If she could be a little girl again, she would go hungry on his behalf in an instant. She would have starved for the kitten her father gave her just before he died. Blackbeard, who rode around on her shoulders, peeking out from under her curls. Blackbeard, who stalked the nature reserve with her when she was young, and later, the rooms of abandoned homes Phyllis told her never, ever to enter. Blackbeard, who walked into the swamp one day and didn't return.

She can't afford to coddle these feral cats that roam the mangroves, these creatures that stay for a while but always disappear eventually. Always leaving her. Everyone always leaving her, no matter what she does, vanishing into the dark and never coming back. She forces herself to eat some of the dried fish before bed. She doesn't want it, but her body gave everything it had to work all night. She must bolster her strength. Chances are, she'll need it soon enough. Before she lies down, she can't help but give the tomcat the tiniest sliver of fish. It disappears into the pink curl of his tongue and he looks at her, pupils so wide in the dark they've swallowed the green: two mirrors, pleading for more. He will leave, too, she knows. The only mystery is when. It's always just a matter of when. He butts his head against her palm. For now, though, he stays.

She doesn't sleep that day, just lies there, staring up at the ceiling, palm fronds woven together and lashed to the frame of salvaged wood that is notched among the branches of the mangroves. The blue house still stood when she found this place. It was a sort of hideout at first, just a cluster of trees she liked to sit in. The place she came when she wanted to be alone. A few months after Lucas left, she built the first platform using a patchwork of materials that she salvaged from the house where she grew up. She took the sheets of plywood her father used to cover the windows, the half-rotten porch railings, the paint-peeled siding. Nails from Kirby's flooded toolshed. His rusty hammer. It was just a distraction back then. Something to do with her hands. A shrine to the family she had lost. It was only later that it became her and Phyllis's home—but Wanda doesn't like thinking about the night they left the blue house.

What she thinks about instead, as she contemplates the knots in the rope and the layering of the fronds, is the fact that the thatch will need replacing soon. She remembers the last time she replaced it. It was hard enough to do on her own, but then her foot got caught in the crotch of the tree trunk and twisted on the way down. She spent two days on her back, hungry, thirsty, wondering if it was broken. If a snapped ankle would be the thing that killed her. By the third day, the swelling began to go down and her panic subsided. Life went on. And if it hadn't healed fast enough? If it had been her back instead of her ankle? The takeaway was that only one of a million things needs to go awry to upset this teetering balance of survival. Just one.

Lying here, thinking of all her other close calls now, it occurs to her that the entire structure she inhabits feels suddenly unsteady. The physicality of it, the wood and the nails, but also the intangible framework: the beliefs she holds, the rules Phyllis set out. She has begun to suspect that somewhere deep in the foundation of this life she is living, a mistake was made. She can't quite discern what it was, or how she knows this, or how to fix it, but that makes it all the more disquieting. Something doesn't add up, and Bird Dog is part of it somehow. Why didn't she give chase? If Wanda had glided into her trap, then why is she here, safe and sound? How did she escape so easily? There is something that she doesn't understand, and it nags at her.

The more Wanda thinks, the farther from sleep she gets. The tomcat has retreated to the edge of the platform, but he's still there—far enough that she can't reach out to touch him and close enough that she can hear him chuffing occasionally as he grooms. He licks his grizzled paws, and together they bear the hottest part of the day until it passes and a cool front arrives. The smell of rain floats in off the ocean. The tom stops his licking and looks at her, eyes glinting green in a single sliver of sunlight that punctures the thatch. He cocks his head. And she realizes she's already made the decision she spent the day circling. Hiding herself away here will achieve nothing; she needs to know more.

Didn't Phyllis teach her to adapt over everything else? Didn't she drill into Wanda again and again the importance of responding to her environment as it changes? As they both change? She tries to make peace with the knowledge that her plan may fly in the face of what

Phyllis would have said ten years ago. She would tell her to run. To hide. To start again, somewhere new. She would say, *Once you're found, you can never be unfound.* How could Wanda forget? But it isn't that night they left the blue house. And Phyllis isn't here to advise her. Dusk falls. Wanda rises, ready. She'll go after Bird Dog. Not because she trusts her. Not because she doesn't. But because there is more to discover. What was it Bird Dog called to her as she fled? It didn't register at the time, but somehow the words are still there in her memory: *It's not what you think.* Wanda doesn't know what she thinks anymore, but these years spent melting into the trees, gliding through the water unseen, eschewing risk of all kinds, must end. Adapt or die. It isn't clear to her yet what the former looks like, but the latter is vivid.

Wanda couldn't explain how she knows where to find Bird Dog; she just knows. The lights guide her, even when they're unlit. The path her canoe cuts through the water is crisp and silent. Her wake closes behind her, as if she were never there. In a way, the place she's headed no longer exists, either. The Edge once marked the line between water and shore. It was razor thin back then; now, it is everywhere. The landmarks are gone, too. Underwater, or washed away. It doesn't matter. Wanda knows where she's going—the swamp is whispering. Telling her what she needs to know. She's going back to where all of this began. Where this voice found her. Where Brie and Corey found her. That hot afternoon when the lights claimed her as one of their own.

The closer she gets to this place that no longer exists as it once did, the less she breathes. Every drop that falls from her paddle makes her cringe; every ripple that follows her movements is a siren. She is as close to invisible as a person could be, but if someone were waiting— still, quiet, sharp-eyed—she'd be seen. There's no way around it. It doesn't matter. She's come this far. She keeps going.

Sliding through the new growth that has flourished around the place where she sat so many years ago, she slows her craft and finds a place to wait among the rushes. Maybe she has miscalculated. Maybe the little whisper in the base of her skull has led her astray. But no, just as she's beginning to think that this is the wrong place, she hears Bird Dog's voice. The breath leaves her lungs. There's another voice. And another.

In the dim light of a waxing moon, Wanda sees Bird Dog's raft congregating with another vessel on the open water. A little rowboat, it looks like, riding low in the waves with two people in it. She hears a man and a woman.

"You catch anything?" the woman asks.

"Nope," Bird Dog replies.

"That's all right, we got two big guys," the man says. Wanda can hear the slap of a live fish trying to return itself to the sea. "Whoa there."

"That's real nice work, Freddy. Enough for everyone?"

"Enough for everyone."

The two boats begin to move away, in unison. Wanda dares to edge her way out of the rushes, and when there is enough distance between them, she follows. They keep to the open water, which she would never do. Such an unnecessary risk, being exposed like that. Wanda can't understand it. But then, maybe because there are three of them they don't worry about such things. Maybe they have guns with bullets in them. She keeps to the snarled growth of the swamp, but she can't move as quickly here. There are roots to navigate, weeds to slow her, branches that reach out and grab at her hair. The bottom of the canoe skims across the nose of what she guesses is a sleeping alligator. She can feel him buck, surprised, and then sink, leaving her to this pursuit.

In the end, it isn't far to go. Bird Dog and her companions cut inland, weaving in and out of the old bungalow ruins on Beachside. Wanda rode these water-filled streets on her bicycle once. Now they are unrecognizable. She follows the others easily, navigating by their low chatter about where to fish and what sort of bait they've had luck with. She's amazed by how much noise they're making, as if they don't even care who might hear them. They sound so relaxed. Almost—happy? Wanda isn't sure she knows what that means anymore. Or what it sounds like. She watches from the shadows as they stop at a two-story ruin, the ground floor completely underwater by now. They lash their boats to the building and climb inside the darkened second-story windows, and soft cries of welcome ring out. More voices. Delight over the fish.

Wanda waits in the nearby ruins, listening. She can't hear what they're saying anymore, just a low murmur, a word here and there. Inside the house, a spark. The glow of a small fire, the smell of cooking. She doesn't quite understand what she's seeing, what she's hearing—she has not dared light a fire in years. Her brain rushes to fill in the uncertainty, telling her this hive of remnants is bigger and therefore more dangerous than she could have imagined, but another voice is whispering to her, too.

It says, *Help them.* It says, *Let them help you back.*

THE INTRUDERS CAME at night. Back then, nights were still for sleeping. Phyllis was dreaming of her old job as a college professor. She was in the building where she used to work, teaching a class full of bedraggled climate refugees. From her place at the front, she could see rows and rows of shaggy heads and dirt-smudged faces receding into a misty distance. Kudzu vines uncurled across the walls, and delicate orchids threaded their way up the legs of the desks, propagating before her eyes. She noticed that her students were rapt, and Phyllis realized she'd already begun the lesson. She looked to the right and saw the two versions of Wanda she was presenting to the class: the little girl she'd taken in and the woman she'd grown into, as if they were specimens to be displayed. "Evolution," Phyllis said, "is always occurring." And on cue, both Wandas burst into light, a glow evident even beneath the fluorescent bulbs.

Phyllis opened her eyes and heard a scuffling sound coming from downstairs. The reason she was awake. Then a thump. It took her a few seconds to understand, and by then her instincts had already pried her aging body away from the sink of her mattress and propelled her to the handgun she kept in her bedside table. She opened the drawer, silent, and retrieved the weapon. Moving swiftly, quietly, she went to Wanda's room, pressed the gun into her hands, whispered, "Safety is on," and then went to fetch the rifle from the hallway closet.

She could hear the sound of the invaders moving past the front rooms of the house, which she and Wanda had made to look as dilapidated and worthless as they could, a facade to hide the price-lessness of what lay beyond: the food, the resources, the tools. There was a dull thud, the scraping of the furniture that barred the door leading to the rest of the house, then a murmur of delight. This had always been the weakest part of her preparations. She'd understood so much of what was to come before it arrived, but human beings— human beings she understood the least.

She stood at the top of the stairs and listened to a low, excited murmur of voices: two men, she thought, maybe more. They knew exactly what they'd found. Phyllis and Wanda's luck of staying hidden this long had run out. Was it chance that the intruders had chosen this house, a simple hunch that propelled them past the disguise of those front rooms? Or—she tried to think back, to pinpoint a mistake she or Wanda had made, some beacon of their thriving lifestyle. It didn't matter. They were here now. She heard the sound of them discovering the pantry: a whoop of joy, quickly shushed.

Well, it had been a good run, she thought. Whatever happened, their time in this haven had come to an end. They would never be safe here again. She could feel Wanda arriving on the top step behind her. Phyllis looked back and saw that she was dressed, the gun pointed at the floor, her arms taut, spring-loaded. *Good girl*, she thought. By now, Wanda was taller than her, stronger than her, quicker than her. Phyllis knew if it were just she alone, there would be little chance she'd last the night. These intruders would ransack her stores and either kill her quickly or kill her slowly. But with Wanda by her side, grown and fierce, there was still some hope they could defend what was theirs. At the very least, they would make it difficult for these scavengers. Or— they could run. Now. They could slip out the back door and melt away into the night. But what if the intruders gave chase? She could tell Wanda to go while she stayed and held them off...Possibilities flashed through her mind, none of them good. Each one with its own fatal flaw. If they ran, they left with nothing. And having nothing in a place like this was just a slower death sentence.

"Ready?" Wanda mouthed. Phyllis reluctantly nodded. It was too late to make a different plan. Every second they spent hesitating was wasted. They descended the stairs in tandem.

"Pantry," Phyllis whispered. She went first. Inching down the hall, she tightened her grip on the rifle, the butt nestled up against her shoulder, her trigger finger ready. There was the rumble of a man's voice, low, quiet, and then nothing. She took a deep breath, stepped into the doorway of the pantry, and loaded the rifle in one fluid motion.

She was fast, but not quite fast enough. Phyllis didn't know what was happening until it had already happened. The rifle was snatched from her hands and then jabbed into her gut. She couldn't breathe— a hollow ache vibrated in her solar plexus. *Broken ribs*, she thought, her mind cataloging the pain from a great distance. She felt a sharp crack to the side of her head and fell to her knees, the floor rushing up to meet her. *Concussion. Cracked skull?* Crumpling, her ears ringing, her sight smearing, she saw her attackers looming over her. The older man had her gun in his hands. The younger had an assault rifle slung over his shoulder that he hadn't even bothered to raise. He hadn't needed to. She glimpsed, for a moment, how pathetic she must look to them. How easy to snuff out. The older man raised her own gun. Pointed it at her.

And then the shots: three of them, sharp and even, one after another. The older man's head snapped back, pieces of it spraying backward, while the younger looked down at a dampness spreading across his chest, confused to find two holes in his torso. Phyllis could see his mind catching up with his body, the slow, horrible realization that his companion was dead, that he would die also, that he was already halfway there, the threads that kept him connected to his body quickly unraveling. The two figures fell in slow motion. Wanda walked into the room, gun still raised. Phyllis watched as she stepped over the corpse of the older man and looked down at the dying boy. She could see now how young he was: barely older than Wanda. Phyllis's head was still roaring where they'd hit her, but she swore she heard Wanda say something to him. She struggled to match the sounds to words as her brain shut down and consciousness slipped away from her.

Phyllis came to on the floor of the pantry. She wasn't sure how much time had passed. Her head felt like a shattered egg. Strong arms lifted her, propped her against the wall. Wanda knelt down in front of her and held a cold washcloth against her forehead. Phyllis tried to reach up to touch her temple, but Wanda caught her hand and laid it back down in her lap.

"Don't touch it," she said. "I've got you."

"What…" Phyllis tried to reassemble the jumble of moments that had led to this one. She looked past Wanda's concerned face and saw the bodies on the floor behind her. She saw the blood, sticky and bright, congealing in a wide, shining pool. She remembered enough, in pieces. It took a little time to make sense of it, but that would be the concussion slowing her down. Wanda cleaned the wound and stitched it as if she'd been practicing for years. And in a way she had been. No, in every way. What had Phyllis been preparing her for if not this?

After the wound was bandaged, Phyllis and Wanda sat in the kitchen and drank tea so honey-sweet it made Phyllis's teeth ache. Every few minutes, Phyllis would forget what had happened and everything seemed almost normal. But then she felt the pain in her head, the sharp stab in her ribs. She reached up to touch the bloodied gauze wrapped around her head and saw the dark stains on Wanda's nightshirt, and it all came rushing back. Phyllis focused her eyes on the tablecloth, trying to will her swollen brain to hold on to the moment. Wanda had carried them through the night. It was Phyllis's turn to carry them into the day. Her hand shook as she raised the mug to her lips.

"What do we do now?" Wanda asked. Phyllis could see the

exhaustion beginning to take hold of her young friend. She was in shock—they both were—but there was so much that needed to be done.

"We move," Phyllis said with a deep sigh. "It was always gonna happen someday. There's no way to know if someone will come looking for them. If there are more."

Wanda shook her head in disbelief. "There has to be something else. We could set traps. We could…we could be ready for them."

Phyllis was having a hard time not slurring her speech, and she didn't want Wanda to notice. She focused all her energy on forming the words she needed to get out. "We're not set up to fight. But we are set up to hide and hide good. If they found us, it's only a matter of time before someone else does, too. Fair chance there's more, someone to wonder why they didn't come back. And next time, who knows what happens. The water's rising anyway, honey. It's time." Phyllis watched Wanda's face as she resisted this, then accepted it; the shift happened so fast it was almost invisible, but Phyllis knew this girl, this woman, inside and out. She could see the understanding take root and begin to grow. One minute Wanda was prepared to defend this house to the death, and the next, she was cataloging what she would bring and what she would leave behind.

It wasn't just the intruders. The water was already taking the driveway, the lower garden beds, the citrus grove. In a year, it would be lapping at the house. They could wear their muck boots downstairs, wading to the kitchen instead of walking. They could keep mostly to the second floor. But even that was temporary. A waiting game, to see how fast the water would rise and how long the wooden frame of the house would stand against the tide. No, life had already changed in unimaginable ways, and now it would change again. This had always been the way it would go. Creating this off-the-grid sanctuary was a stopgap. A bridge to span the chasm between the old world and the new. But even the idea of the grid, of being on it or off it, was just another ruse of civilization. The grid was gone. In some ways, it had never existed at all. She hadn't ever imagined that she would live to see things progress this far, but here she was—living. She watched as Wanda came to terms with all of this.

"I know a place," Wanda finally said. "In the nature reserve. I...it's where I go when I want to think. The trees are sturdy enough to build in."

Phyllis nodded, suddenly aware that by now Wanda knew this land even better than she did. "All right. That's where we'll go."

"But what do we do with the..." Wanda trailed off, unable to choose the right word. "We can't just leave them. Can we?" Phyllis considered the corpses in the other room. If only she'd been faster, been stronger, if only she'd been the one to pull the trigger. But she hadn't. The days of wishing for things to be different were gone. Those men were dead because Wanda had killed them. Ruthlessness was not such a bad quality in this place.

"We burn them," Phyllis replied. "We burn everything."

In the pantry, Phyllis filled a plywood crate with glass canning jars containing the harvests of years past. These stores had diminished over time, but that only made them more precious. There would be no more harvests from the garden, no more days spent over a hot stove, sterilizing jars, boiling vegetables, slicing fruit, making jams and sauces and sides. This was all of it. Stepping around the drying blood, she tried not to look at the bodies as she gathered the last of the jars, but there they were. The smell of them was already blooming. The heat of the early-afternoon sun shining through the window grew more intense by the hour. She would have opened the window, but pieces of the older man's head had spattered against the latch and she couldn't bring herself to touch it.

She realized she had stopped packing up the jars without noticing, that her hand was grazing the bandaged wound on the side of her head while she stood, frozen, staring into the open eyes of the dead boy. He was so young. There was something almost familiar about him. The older man she couldn't bear to look at. The pink of his head, the crush of it, the pieces that were missing and the pieces that were still there—she recalled the shape of his mouth as he trained her own rifle on her, a smile, a laugh even, and was glad he was dead. And then it hit her. The day at Target. The father and his twins.

She was sick in the corner. As quietly as she could, so that Wanda wouldn't hear. Her head pounding, she retched until there was nothing left. She put her hand against the wall to steady herself and waited until the static intruding on her vision cleared. She filled the crate as quickly as she could and left these two bodies to their pyre. There was nothing more she could offer them. Not even her remorse. She told herself that if she were a better woman, she would say a few words. A prayer. A scrap of ceremony. She paused in the doorway, the crate heavy in her arms, and tried to locate some semblance of respect. But she couldn't.

Upstairs, she could hear Wanda packing. Drawers thudded against the bureau, plastic hangers clattered, the closet door smacked the wall. Phyllis understood the urgency, but she was having trouble convincing her body to meet it. She roamed the first floor, gathering items in what she hoped was a logical process. Later, she would look at her choices and shake her head, but for now, she did her best. Pots, pans, books, tools, batteries, a camping stove, and as many propane tanks as she could carry. Matches. First aid. Iodine. Needles and thread. Tarps. What else, what else? She chided herself: "Focus," she whispered.

There was so much they would have to leave behind. So much work she had done over the years that could help them no longer. They agreed that Wanda would take as much as she could to the new place in the canoe—mostly the lumber and tools they'd need to build, but also some of the food—while Phyllis hid the rest in the swamp, to be fetched later. It was a good plan. The only plan. There was too much to do and too much to transport for them to stay together. Still, it was hard to let Wanda out of her sight after everything that had happened. Phyllis tried to give her the handgun as she climbed into the canoe, fully loaded and riding low in the water.

Wanda shook her head. "No," she said.

"Please."

"I don't want it."

Phyllis watched Wanda row away without the gun and couldn't tell what worried her more: the violence of the night's murders, or the idea that Wanda might not be able to do such a thing again. *Give her time*, she thought. *Give her time.* She would become whatever this place needed her to be.

After Wanda had made three trips and Phyllis had hidden what she could in the swamp, they came together in the living room for the last time. A dim, murky light tossed up shadows on the walls and made the piles of rejected items strewn throughout the rooms look like monsters. The careful order of the blue house was unmade. In its place, panic. Was this finality really necessary? Was it just an ill-considered reaction to the violence that had found them here? She asked herself again, for the hundredth time, if leaving the house behind was the wrong thing to do, if the reward of making it through the night was that they got to stay…but then she remembered the rising water. The threat of more drifters lurking nearby. If they stayed, they would always be afraid. There would always be an invisible clock. Human or nature. Either, or both. No, they had to leave. It was time for the next phase. Phyllis's head throbbed so hard it was audible—a beating drum. She tried to concentrate.

"I think we have what we need," she said, surveying the chaos. Wanda was quiet. Phyllis looked over and saw the glimmer of unspilled tears accumulating in her eyes. Pulling Wanda in close, she smoothed back her curls. "I know," she said. "I know."

"You don't," Wanda snapped. The thrum inside Phyllis's skull beat harder, louder, faster. She struggled to stay upright, to hold not only herself but also this girl, this child, who had left something precious behind in the night. A thing she'd never get back. Innocence? Hope? Phyllis couldn't possibly know.

"You're right," Phyllis said, dismayed that this was true, that Wanda had gone somewhere she could not possibly follow. She tried to think of something she could say that might help, but there was nothing. They just stood, propped up against each other like a lean-to, and were quiet. Eventually, Wanda separated herself. She straightened her spine and rolled back her shoulders. She wiped her face. "It's time to go."

Watching Wanda pour the last of their gasoline down the hallway and out the front door, Phyllis understood that willingly destroying this house she had given so much of herself to, the structure that had kept them safe for all these years, was in many ways the final act of what it meant to teach Wanda about survival.

Homes could no longer be rigid, immovable things. That way of life was changing. Had already changed. She'd been languishing in being ahead of the times for too long. Now, she was behind. The blue house was a relic, as all the houses in Rudder were. Structures that belonged to an old paradigm. A series of rooms built upon a series of ideas, none of which had withstood the test of time: the idea that what was here would always be here; the idea that the limestone beneath their feet would go on holding them forever; the idea that the coast was a faithful, unmoving line in the sand. None of this was true anymore. The thing was, it never had been.

Wanda lit the match and ran to join her in the shadows. The flame raced across the ground and up the steps. It clawed up the porch, then engulfed the doorway. This house and the land it stood on had never been hers, not really. They watched the blue house burn from the bottom of the driveway, the canoe ready for them. The fire moved faster than she'd thought it would, from the tip of a match to a hungry, roaring blaze in just a few minutes: cremating their shabby comforts and this notion that being sealed inside was the best thing, the safe thing.

Wanda leaned into her as they watched. "Are you sure we had to burn it?" she asked, a tremble in her voice, the reflection of the flames in her pupils.

"It's better this way," Phyllis said. She wanted to explain that it was the ideas woven into the siding and the shingles and the door frames that needed to go, that sometimes humans need to see change, to literalize it, in order to know that it's arrived, but she couldn't manage to put the words together.

She could already glimpse what was to come: a new kind of life among the mangrove islands that were bursting forth, thriving in the ruins of this flooded town. Wanda would show her where, and this was correct because as much as she had taught Wanda, she had learned even more by raising her. There would be no walls and there would be no windows. They would endure the elements as the very first people had, with respect and curiosity and the interdependence Wanda was born into. This would be how Phyllis spent her remaining time on this earth. Hadn't humans lived this way for thousands of years? They must learn to live this way once more—she was certain of it. The structures they built would bend and break, and they would make new ones. There would be nothing so precious that they couldn't begin again. And again.

Watching her home of so many years beginning to collapse in on itself, the flames licking around the eaves, the window sashes glowing red hot, the skeleton of it revealed before her, beams and doorways and the staircase at its center, she mourned what had been. They watched in silence until the second floor fell into the first. The roof kissed the foundation, and finally, with a crack like bones breaking and a spray of sparks, all that remained was a pile of flaming rubble. She became aware of Wanda's hand in hers. "Ready?" Wanda asked.

"Ready," she said.

And in the center of the clock, inside the now—choices gather, waiting to be made. The swamp is alive with information. Dangers and saviors. Lovers and predators. The lie is in the separation. The truth is always growing.

WANDA RETURNS TO this carefree community again the next night, and the next. As the moon waxes, she watches these people leave and return, work and rest in its light. She listens to them talk. And the more she watches and listens, the more baffled she feels. They are kind to one another. Sometimes they argue, but mostly they discuss fishing and trapping, harvesting fruits and tubers from the swamp, repairing boats, sewing clothes, child-rearing, cleaning, building…they are engaged in the work of survival, not plunder. Just as Wanda is. But they do this work together.

Wanda counts six of them. There's an older man with very dark skin and a shock of silver hair—he's the one who Bird Dog called Freddy. He moves slowly getting in and out of the little rowboat, but he knows a great deal about fishing. Wanda can tell; he never comes back empty-handed. A pale woman with fiery red hair that spills out in a wave from beneath her ball cap has a son who is quiet and goes everywhere she goes. Her name is Gem, and his is Dade. The boy is young, Wanda guesses a few years younger than she was when Kirby died. It's good, she thinks, that his mother is with him in this place. He seems fragile, like he wouldn't last very long on his own. The mother is good with traps, always coming home with squirrels and possums hanging from her fist by their tails, and the boy is good with knots. Wanda sometimes watches him sit on the roof and toy with bits of rope: tying, untying, tying again.

There's a couple: a man and a woman. The woman's belly is as round as a melon. Wanda sees how everyone likes to touch her stomach, how much she enjoys the attention. Her name is Ouita, and she sings quietly when she's alone in the house, which is rare—songs that tickle Wanda's memory but that she doesn't know the words to anymore. Her man is loud and smiles often. They call him Skipper, and it's clear that these two belong to one another. Ouita comes to kiss him when she hears his boat brush up against the house, before he's even had a chance to disembark. She leans out the window while he leans in, and in these moments Wanda suddenly feels that she shouldn't be watching, but it's hard to look away. She's never seen love like this, nor has she ever seen a boat like his—wooden and hand-carved, the lines of it as smooth as the curve of a tree trunk, rippling through the water like living things do. Ouita made this for him, Wanda learns. It has never occurred to Wanda to make such a thing.

And then there is Bird Dog, who comes and goes. Sometimes she disappears for days, but she always comes back. When she does return, she brings all kinds of treasures—old fabric, hand tools, a spool of wire, wild mushrooms and herbs, sometimes even bright plastic toys for Ouita's baby. Wanda understands now why they call her Bird Dog. She is their seeker. The longer Wanda watches, the more she wishes to be found also. Her suspicions of this little clan gradually fade. Now she envies them. She goes on watching, night after night, neglecting her own chores so that she can be close to this strange family—unable to join them, unwilling to stay away.

When she's not spying from among the ruins, she wanders and thinks about the night Phyllis put a gun in her barely awake hands. The night she left any vestiges of childhood behind. It was either kill Corey and his father or watch them murder Phyllis. She would have been next. She knew this then, and she knows it now. Even so. It changed her. She's always wondered what happened to the other twin. The boy and the girl; the cruel one and the quiet one. When they were young, Wanda feared the first and was fascinated by the second. Little has changed. Corey may be gone, but the kick of the gun, the sound of the shots, the gore of bullets entering bodies—these things are not forgotten. In the years after, Phyllis tried to absolve her of these deaths, but taking a life, two lives, wasn't something she could just wash away.

And the sister. Brie. Bird Dog. The girl with the sunburn and the pale blue eyes. How different she looks now. For the first time in many years, Wanda wonders if she looks different also. Touching her own face, she can't tell. The two men must have left Bird Dog behind that night—but why? Wanda imagines her, somewhere half-way between the child she remembers and the woman she sees now, waiting for her father and brother to return. Just waiting and waiting. How long did it take her to realize they weren't coming back? And how did she survive all these years alone? Wanda catches herself. Not alone, that's how.

The next time Bird Dog leaves on one of her trips, Wanda follows. She can tell from the way they all say goodbye that Bird Dog will be gone for longer than one night, and without really thinking too hard about it, she lets her get a head start and then pushes off after her. Her ears are sharp and the moon is almost full; in this way she follows easily, at a distance. They paddle through the night, and it isn't until dawn nudges up against the horizon that Wanda worries about where she'll weather the daylight. It occurs to her that she isn't sure where they are. This is beyond her radius, a direction she rarely ventures in.

There's something familiar about the ruins they pass, but she can't remember what they used to be. When the sun is beginning to crest, Bird Dog heads for the only building still standing above the water line and disappears inside. Wanda looks for nearby shade, but there aren't many options: a young mangrove island growing up out of the middle of a parking lot, decrepit streetlights looming above it, or a more mature canopy back the way they came. The young mangroves aren't thick enough to shade her yet. It'll have to be the older grove—it doesn't have a clear line of sight to where Bird Dog is resting, but Wanda is out of options. She's about to circle back toward the mature trees when a voice rings out across the water.

"Wanda," Bird Dog calls. "You can sleep here."

Her thoughts whirl. How did she give herself away? She was so careful. So quiet. It's been a long time since anyone got the better of her in the swamp.

"I figure you been watching me long enough to know I ain't my brother." Wanda is still so shocked she can't move, but she gathers herself enough to assess this statement and find it logical. "Come on, if I was gonna hurt you, you'd be hurt by now. I'm the one should be scared."

Hesitant, Wanda paddles toward Bird Dog's voice. The sun is beginning to edge higher, the sky coming alive with soft lilac brushstrokes. She can just barely see Bird Dog's face, propped up on her hands in the second-story window, the first floor almost entirely full of water. "You knew I was watching?"

"Sure I knew, just didn't see any need to rush you. You got a right to make up your own mind about us. About me."

Wanda considers this. "Don't know what I think, really."

"So then stay," Bird Dog says. "Find out."

Here, the opening she yearned for, the invitation, being offered to her. It's impossible to say no, not after all that wanting. So she lets out a breath she didn't know she was holding and says yes.

They sit on opposite sides of a room that used to be someone's office. There are three windows, hung with rags cut in strips to let the breeze pass through. Two face north, one east. Good ventilation, not too much solar gain. Wanda realizes that Bird Dog has chosen this place carefully, has probably stayed here many times. Reading her mind, Bird Dog says, "This is my stopover when I go south."

"To Miami?"

"Sometimes."

"That's a long way. I only been to Miami twice, when I was little. Before. What's it like now?"

Bird Dog thinks for a minute. "Sunk," she says. "More to salvage. But more people, too."

There's a long desk, pushed up against the wall, and a nest of old sleeping bags and leaves on the floor. Arranged on the desk, a collection of items: framed photographs, the glass gone cloudy with mold and condensation; a stapler; an old telephone.

"This was the manager's office, I think," Bird Dog says, seeing her looking. "Used to be a bank downstairs."

"How can you tell?" She squints into the cloudy glass of one of the picture frames and can just barely make out a smiling face looking back at her. It startles her, that pair of crinkly eyes peering out.

Bird Dog crooks an eyebrow. "'Cause I remember. My daddy had an account, I guess. He took us here, me and Corey, when we was little. They gave us candy. You know, with the stick. Pops…something like that." The fact that Wanda has forgotten so much of this embarrasses her. She feels off-balance with this woman, still recovering from the shock of being seen when she thought she was so well hidden.

"What happened to them? Your people, I mean," Wanda asks. She hadn't planned on asking it so abruptly, but it's out of her mouth before she can stop herself.

"I should probably be asking you," Bird Dog says, settling into the sleeping bags. A rich, mildewed stink rises from them. She balls one up and throws it at Wanda, who catches it. A bolt of panic runs through her, but she wills herself to stay still, to learn what there is to learn. "It was hard when they didn't come back, but it was better in the long run. They weren't…" Bird Dog makes a show of patting her bedding into a comfortable shape, but she's just stalling to gather herself. Wanda can hear the barely there cracks in her voice. What they are revealing, she isn't sure. "They weren't good people," Bird Dog finally says. "I reckon you know that."

"I dunno what you mean." Wanda tries not to give herself away, but even she can hear that she sounds like a liar.

"Oh, come on. I knew where they was headed that night. Only thing I wasn't sure about was if you got out before it burned. If you lit that fire or they did. But I had a feeling. Me and Corey, we weren't like how twins are supposed to be, you know? Close and like-minded and all that. But even so, I could feel him go, I think. That night. Found the ruins later. And then I started seeing your traps. Don't know how I knew they were yours. Little hands, little traps, I guess. But you stopped setting 'em, didn't you?" Wanda nods slowly. She should be rigid with fear, but she's not. "I just about gave up on you."

It would be logical if Bird Dog wanted her dead, except that nothing about these past few weeks since they found each other at the freshwater spring has been logical. Or, Wanda silently corrects herself, since Bird Dog found her. "At the spring…" Wanda begins.

"I saw the light between the trees. You don't forget that kind of thing. I knew it was you."

"You could have told me then, who you were."

"Maybe should have, but didn't wanna scare you away, did I?"

"Don't see why you'd care." Outside, the sun has risen past the water-line, a yellow morning spreading across the water, thick and stifling. The rags over the windows flutter, letting shards of brightness in. She can see Bird Dog clear and up close for the first time in more years than she can account for: forehead high and worn, cheekbones too sharp to touch. The blue eyes, boring into her from across the room.

"I care because I'm sorry. For when we was kids. And I'm sorry for later on. It was me that tracked you from the old Walmart. Corey couldn't keep a trail to save his life, that was my job. That's how we did things, us three. I didn't like it, but I did it."

"We always wondered how they found us." They are quiet for a long while then. Nearby, a gull cries. Just one. A rare bird now. Wanda sneaks a look at Bird Dog. Her eyes are closed and her forehead is creased, as if she's in pain.

"I reckon I got a lot to make up for," Bird Dog says.

Wanda realizes that this is the moment to say that she was the one to pull the trigger. Bird Dog may know more than Wanda thought, but she doesn't know everything. And if this is real, this kindness she's offering, this absolution, this acknowledgment of harm done, then it means nothing without an exchange. Isn't this what it is to exist alongside another person? It's been so long, she isn't sure how. She tries to say it, but the enormity of what she's done is hard to articulate, and Wanda has never been good with words—especially not now, when it's been years since she had the opportunity to use them.

Then she remembers that day the twins must have followed them home. She remembers Phyllis resting across from her while she wielded the paddle, leaning into the wind, savoring the sun and the salt and the feeling of being on the open water. She remembers the two of them hauling the canoe into the bushes, unloading their spoils, and carrying them inside just as the afternoon thunderstorm landed. She remembers how safe it felt inside the house, rain beating against the windows, thunder pounding its palm flat against the sky. Then she remembers all of this being taken away a few nights later. And she doesn't feel sorry. She feels vengeful.

"It was me," she says. "I killed them."

Bird Dog is quiet, looking at her for a long time. Finally, she says, "Okay."

"Okay?" Wanda wants more than this. She wants, she realizes, a fight.

"Makes us even, don't you reckon? Was they gonna kill you if you didn't kill 'em first?"

Wanda nods.

"Then okay. It was a long time ago, Wanda. We both done things we had to. But it's done. Can't change none of it." And somehow, that is all there is to say.

Bird Dog eventually sleeps—or at least, she does a good job of pretending. Wanda doesn't. She listens to Bird Dog's slow, deep breath and lies still, sweating and reexamining every memory she has of the younger Brie, trying to reconcile the past with the present. Thinking back that far requires her to exhume an entire life in which she had a brother and a father, a friend and a pet, a bicycle with a basket, an abundance of solid ground to walk on, and a verdant, sunlit wilderness to explore and enjoy. The old conviction that these things she had would go on being hers, that she might grow up to accumulate even more—the ordinary pillars of lives children were so carelessly promised back then: jobs, houses, loves, families.

She has none of this. It doesn't occur to her to feel cheated very often, but she feels it now. Who is left to blame?

When Bird Dog finally wakes, the sun is going down. They wait for darkness and then board their vessels. Wanda is torn between trusting her and not, joining her and not, but in the end, she is too curious to turn back. There is more to know. This, at least, she is certain of.

In the remains of another town, a few miles south, Bird Dog shows Wanda how she scavenges: quietly moving from one ruin to the next, assessing what is visible in the moonlight, but also maybe sensing what isn't. What's left of this town is mostly beneath the surface of the water. It's a strange landscape of gentle waves and crumbling roofs and cockeyed streetlights. In one house, or what remains of it, Bird Dog dives and resurfaces with an old toolbox covered in algae. Inside, a treasure trove of hand tools. Wanda picks through the jumble, much of it worse for wear but still useful. Metal is always useful. She inspects with her fingers and the soft rays of a nearly full moon illuminating the bounty in front of them. She weighs a pair of needle-nose pliers, fused shut with rust, in her palm. "How do you know where to dive?"

"I just look till it feels right. Sometimes there's nothing. Sometimes there's something. Depends. Why don't you try?"

Wanda's head jerks up involuntarily. She puts the pliers back in the box, and the clatter of metal on metal is too loud for this quiet place. The echo is enormous. "I can't."

"Why not?"

"You know why."

"'Cause the lights? There's no one to see. I'd know if there was."

"No." Wanda doesn't intend it to sound so harsh, but the word is brittle and sharp in her mouth.

"It's special, what you got. Could be a big help. The water ain't dirty like it used to be. And I never seen gators this close to—"

"No," Wanda says again, and this time she means it just as harshly as it sounds.

"That's okay." Bird Dog shuts the toolbox and tucks it into her boat, unfazed. "Come on, there's a place a ways down I been wanting to look at under a good moon like this." She takes up her oar and Wanda watches her make long, languid strokes. She'd like to follow. She'd like to be as close to Bird Dog as she can possibly be for as long as a world like this might let her. This woman who says "okay" to both her darkest sin and her deepest secret, like it's nothing. And she'd also like to be miles away, tucked up in her nest, alone and unaware that Bird Dog even exists. Above all, she'd like to be safe and she'd like to be sure—but neither of these are possibilities, not here. Maybe not anywhere. She thinks of the two bodies in the pantry. The wild stare in their dead eyes. The undisturbed blood snaking down the grooves between the tiles, a strange sort of beauty in its glimmering surface. The weight of the gun. The crack, the kick. The mineral stench of gunpowder. And she thinks of the fear that gripped her windpipe when she saw Phyllis on the floor. The agony of waiting to see if she would ever wake up.

Wanda realizes she's paddling in the other direction, back the way they came. She has no idea how long she's been going, but she's covered a great distance by the time she understands that her body has made a choice without her mind. Bird Dog is behind her. The ruins, behind her. Ahead, just the rippling grave of a highway laid to rest. The shadows of young mangroves, rising to take back what is rightfully theirs. She leans into her stroke and goes faster. As fast as she can; not nearly fast enough.

What does Wanda imagine she is fleeing from: Grief or shame or danger? All three? Or is it the unbearable fragility of everything Bird Dog offers her, the tenderhearted possibility of a union bound to the jagged-edged certainty that nothing lasts? Perhaps it is these whispers that have followed her for a great many years now, that have been growing louder every night since she met the manatees under a dark sky, louder and clearer, until they are crashing into her like waves, whispering, shouting—these voices that say *we we we you you you us us us.*

It would be easier if it were one of these things. It would be easier if it were all of them. Wanda paddles as fast as she can and the truth is, she doesn't know what she's running from. Her body has made a decision of its own accord. There is no thought guiding it, no reason. Tendons pulled taut beneath her skin with a conviction that she didn't choose. This is survival. This is how the vessel protects the mind, how the mind protects the heart, how the heart goes on forgetting that its calling is to be undefended, that being broken is part of being whole.

Wanda sprints for so long the sun is near by the time she becomes aware of what her body is doing. Her consciousness slides back into her skin; where it went she isn't sure, but it fuses with her senses once more and she can suddenly feel the burn in her shoulders, the crackle in the back of her dry throat. She can hear the rush of hot blood pressing against her eardrums. She can smell the sweat that pours down from her forehead and taste it on her cracked lips.

The gradient of the sky brightens and brightens. Wanda stops to drink; she can't spare the pause but she also can't spare the moisture that is rushing out of her pores. She needs to rest, but there's nothing here except open water and mangroves too young to offer shade. Onward. The sun crests, a molten slice of fire that gets bigger and rounder by the second. There is extraordinary beauty occurring; all she has to do is turn her head to see it, but she doesn't. To admire is to slow and to slow is to succumb. She keeps going, letting the splendor unfold without witness. She cuts west, into the swamp. A heat shimmer begins to rise from the water, from her skin. She can't tell if it is the light refracting or her own vision blurring, but either way the space she occupies has begun to warp all around her, the shapes to distort, the colors to burn. The prow of her canoe glides across flame, through lava. She vaguely remembers a game she played when she was young—the floor was red hot and she had to build a pathway to the kitchen with couch cushions and table mats and even, to make it those last few perilous feet, Kirby's and Lucas's upside-down hard hats. She remembers gingerly placing her little foot inside the crown of her father's hard hat, the slipperiness of the plastic yellow dome against the laminate flooring, the ripe sweaty smell that all their work clothes had, and that final leap onto the cool, comforting tile: safe.

But there is no such thing as safety here. The flames lick all around her—no, the waves. She can't tell the difference. The paddle burns her hands and she grips it tighter. Her brain is hot inside her skull, her blood steaming inside her veins. The sun is free of the horizon now, climbing and climbing, growing stronger with each minute that passes. There—a mature mangrove thicket with a broad canopy and enough soil to lie down on looms up into her blurring vision. She beaches the canoe on a tangle of roots, then hauls it up and into the underbrush. She collapses. Drinks. Sweats. And waits to see if she has pushed her body beyond what it can recover from.

When the sun sets, Wanda wakes. Surprised that she was able to sleep at all, she takes stock of herself. Her brain whirs, sluggish but functioning. Her limbs do what she tells them to, albeit very slowly. She finishes the water because her body needs it, but seeing the empty bottles glittering in the fading light makes her uneasy. When she pushes the canoe back into the water, the roots scrape against the hull. She doesn't have the strength to lift it.

Going slowly through the dark canals and the moonlit rivers, she heads for home and tries to understand how she got here—exhausted, dehydrated, stinking of sweat, and weighed down with a mantle of emotions she's forgotten the words for. She goes slowly, her muscles barely able to do their work.

She gets home and ties off and hauls up the warm glass jugs she keeps suspended underwater so that their contents stay at least a little refreshing and drinks deeply—not too fast, her stomach can accept only so much. Then she lies down, lets loose a long, shaky exhale, and waits to feel relieved that she's made it. Instead, a crushing sadness washes over her. There are too many losses to grieve: Phyllis, Blackbeard, Lucas, Kirby, the Rudder she knew as a child, Frida and Flip, who she never even got a chance to meet. And now Bird Dog, this woman whom she is too broken to join. She understands that it isn't enough to have made it home. It isn't enough to be alive after all these years. There is a deficit here that she is unable to reconcile. Life costs more than it gives.

For the first time in a long time, she cries—big, choking sobs— the whole time worrying about her tears. She needs that moisture for other things, she tells herself, this is a waste, an extravagance, a careless use of precious resources. But even so, she cries, and even so, the price of these tears is tangible, exacting, steep.

THE PLACE WANDA chose for them was a good one. Phyllis recognized it as the lagoon where Wanda fell in back when they'd just begun to spend their afternoons together, but so much had changed in the years since she was last here. The land was gone, to start, replaced by ripples and a cloudy sheen. Many of the trees she'd tagged had succumbed to the brackish water, their rotting trunks still teetering among the living like pale ghosts. Others had flourished, crowding out their malnourished neighbors and sending down seedlings by the hundreds.

At first glance, Phyllis mourned all the delicate mosses and ferns that had been lost beneath the rising water, but she was soon distracted by a riotous new generation of aquatic plant life. Everywhere she turned she found something new to admire: sugarcane plume grass and duckweed, cattail and maidencane and bulrush; water hyacinth, water spinach, water lily, water shield. Little yellow lantana flowers that sprouted wherever they could. Wild coffee that grew in the cracks of tree trunks and staghorn ferns that hung from their branches. And others, plants she didn't even recognize. It was, in many ways, a hopeful place. A little platform, barely wide enough for the two of them to lie side by side, was already there, built into the trees. She remembered all the times Wanda had disappeared with the canoe. So this was where she'd come. Always a few inexplicable steps ahead.

"Yes," Phyllis said, taking in the clumsy platform, the verdant new growth, the strategically hidden entrance. Additions were already taking shape in her mind. "It's good. It's what we need."

For all its beauty, it was most importantly a practical place. A safe place. Many of the trees were sturdy enough to take on plywood and nails and human weight. The water was deep enough for them to come and go in the canoe. The canopy was thick and the underbrush rose up like an impenetrable, snarled screen to deflect unwelcome eyes. There was little chance of anyone happening upon them by accident. As much as any wild place could, it welcomed them and it held them. It became the refuge they needed.

The longer they spent in the swamp, the more Phyllis realized that she had no idea what she was doing. The certainty she had felt watching the house burn, then seeing this place for the first time, the clarity of what was to come, did not last. How could it? She was a woman accustomed to planning, to knowing what came next and being ready for it. This—this she was not ready for. This she had not planned. But here it was anyway.

They started by widening the platform Wanda had already built, and from there, Wanda began to expand into the trees, building more platforms as high as the boughs would allow, while Phyllis sat down below and worked on weaving thatch and cutting wood to size. She was frequently nauseous and dizzy, plagued by migraines that lasted for days on end, but she kept her pain to herself. She knew what a traumatic brain injury was, and she knew there was little she could do about it. There was no need to add to her young friend's burden, which, in the aftermath of the invasion, was visibly substantial.

The work was good for Wanda. Good for them both. The tree house took shape. In many ways, the trees were their architects, showing them where they could build and where they couldn't. How high. How heavy. And the ruined town gave them their materials. Their nest among the boughs made sense in a way the homes of Rudder never had. It belonged here. And on some days, they belonged here, too. On others, not so much. Their first week, a torrential rainstorm washed away a few of the lighter hand tools, a ball of twine, and an entire box of batteries. During their second, Wanda encountered a colony of fire ants living in one of the trees she'd planned to build in and fell at least fifteen feet into the water as she scrambled to escape them. The stings lingered for days, but the water caught her gently. More weeks went by. Then months. Then a year.

A great many creatures watched as these two humans settled in, their eyes wide and mirrored in the dark, hanging from tree branches or lurking among the exposed roots or peering up from the warm murk of the water: curious and wary. Even as Phyllis and Wanda grew more comfortable with the shape of their lives here, the wild continued to remind them that this place was not theirs: an alligator heaving itself up out of the water to snatch a string of fish Phyllis set down while she went to fetch her knife, Wanda waking up to find a snake slithering across her legs. They learned to share.

Phyllis stored a pile of blank notebooks she didn't remember packing in a plastic tub and began to record the daily happenings of the lagoon. It was an extravagant thing to have brought, but it felt good to return to this habit. She hadn't realized that she missed it. The years since Kirby died and Wanda came to live with her had edged out her careful documentation of local ecology—all that time spent exploring and noticing was time she'd suddenly no longer had. But now, without the careful cultivation of the garden, the chickens, the house, as Wanda grew more and more capable, as the demands of life in the swamp became ever simpler, she found that there was once again space for such things.

In her previous life, these observations had been carefully measured, recorded, compared, always with an eye toward the scientific method, an aim to collate her findings and perhaps one day to publish. In this life, her note-taking looked very different. She still collected some hard data, but in between the numbers were thoughts, feelings, sketches, little details that had no place in a research paper but that meant something to her. Details like a clumsy moth, drawn to the beam of her flashlight. The congregation of egrets that habitually descended in the very early mornings, standing in the shallow water and pecking at tiny fish that tried to dart past their spindly black legs. A thick carpet of pink water lilies blooming, making the water's surface blush with their flowers; the black aphids and grass carp that arrived soon after to munch on all those beautiful petals. There was so much to notice.

But of the lagoon's many inhabitants, Phyllis continued to observe Wanda most closely of all. It was miraculous, how much she had grown. How tall she was, how strong. How capable. How many years had it been since she'd made space in her life for a curious little girl in men's T-shirts? It felt like just a moment ago. But here was this woman—brave and ruthless and tender all at once. Wanda was doing the work of building the nest and then maintaining it, of fishing, trapping, fetching water, and foraging. Phyllis helped where she could, but her headaches got worse, not better. The nausea, too. And lately she couldn't seem to remember the smallest things: how long since she last ate, where they kept the sewing kit, what task Wanda had asked her to complete. Her memory was becoming a gap-toothed smile.

During their third summer there, a heat wave settled over the swamp like a thick blanket and never lifted. They didn't have the tools to measure heat in degrees anymore, but Phyllis wrote down her guesses anyway: 103? 105? They began to rise earlier and earlier, trying to capture the coolest hours for their work. In the middle of the day they rested, then resumed their chores in the darkness. Even as the seasons changed, the heat didn't ebb. If anything, it increased, thickening the air until just breathing was a task. Eventually they transitioned into an altogether nocturnal life. In the dark, Phyllis found a whole new world to observe—bats and insects, opossums and raccoons, night-scented orchids and evening primrose and moonflowers. Feral cats stalked the trees, growing ever wilder, drawn to this pair of humans but terrified of them at the same time. Once she was almost sure she saw a Florida panther loping through the underbrush, a species long thought to be extinct.

As much as she loved the nights, they disoriented her. The headaches continued to squeeze her brain so tight she thought it might burst from the pressure, and her memory was growing more and more porous. She couldn't tell if it was her age or her injury, but it didn't really matter which—there was nothing she could do but adapt. At night, she lost track of time in a way that unrooted her completely. Duration was impossible to discern; one night and the next bled together. She tried to hide her confusion, not wanting to weigh Wanda down any more with the slow decay of her mind, but there were some things she couldn't hide.

One evening, Phyllis took the canoe out to gather mushrooms. She often went on foraging trips as dusk settled, taking stock of what was growing in the fading light, seeing how many delicacies she could find before turning on the precious flashlight. Both she and Wanda knew that their little stockpile of batteries wouldn't last forever, but the longer they lived in the dark, the less they needed to use them.

The surface of the water parted for Phyllis like silk, the smoothness of it catching the fading dusk and holding it. She made her way slowly through the narrow streams, paddling between young mangrove islands and old cypress roots. A great horned owl looked down at her from a bough overhanging the water and she stopped to write down the sighting in her journal. She was sure she'd seen him before—there wasn't much in this swamp that could escape her attention. The owl cooed at her and cocked his tufted head as she wrote. It wasn't until she took up her paddle once again that Phyllis realized she'd lost her bearings. It seemed silly at first, a momentary lapse that would be easily corrected, but as the minutes slipped past and she turned this way and that, letting the canoe drift, she began to understand that she was lost. The swamp she knew so well had tricked her somehow. She didn't recognize it anymore. She saw the owl again, but as if for the first time, and suddenly it scared her—the severity of its face, the sharpness of its beak. Frightened, she chose a direction, but the farther she went, the more unfamiliar the landscape became.

Soon, night swallowed her. She turned on the flashlight, swinging it wildly across the trees, frightening the creatures with her bright light and ragged breath, sending them scampering back into the shadows. She called out for Wanda as loudly as she dared, worried about attracting the wrong kind of attention, remembering the twist of the intruder's mouth as he looked down at her and feeling suddenly like a lost child. A little girl, alone in a dark wood, more frightened than she'd ever been.

When Wanda finally found her, Phyllis was curled up in the bottom of the boat. The flashlight was dead, clutched against her chest, and her face was streaked with tears, white hair coming undone from its thick braid. Phyllis heard the ripple of something moving in the water nearby and shut her eyes tighter. It wasn't until she heard her companion's voice calling her name that she dared to look. She saw a distant brightness coming nearer and nearer, spreading across the water, birthed from darkness, Wanda at its center, swimming toward her.

"There you are," Wanda said.

Somehow in the glow of this living, ambient light, a glow that brushed the bottoms of the palm fronds gold and drew the night creatures close to see what was happening, the swamp once again revealed itself to Phyllis. She knew exactly where she was, and the shame of her lapse, of her childish panic, nearly crushed her. Even amid all this beauty, she felt sick. Wanda, still in the water, pushed the canoe over to a spit of mud so that she could climb in. "Are you all right?" she asked, sitting down on the bench seat, luminous and dripping. "What happened?"

"Nothing," Phyllis snapped. "It's not safe for you to be in the water. Anyone could see. No wonder they found us the first time." All around them, the light diminished. Wanda took up the paddle in silence and used it to push them away from the rushes. She was drenched, a puddle forming in the bottom of the boat that still shone ever so slightly. The water that dripped from her hair and her clothes shimmered in the darkness and then went out.

Wanda said nothing as she propelled them back to the tree house, but the wounded look on her face spoke for her. Phyllis's head was pounding, her thoughts smashing against the inside of her skull. She knew she needed to explain, to take back this horrifying insinuation that the intruders had been Wanda's fault, that all this time she'd held her young friend responsible for what had happened—but she couldn't find the words. Her brain pulsed. Her stomach churned. All she could do was put her head between her knees and wait for the spell to pass. And by the time it did, she had forgotten she'd said anything at all.

Years passed—or was it just a moment? Hard to say. Phyllis's cognitive mind slipped farther and farther away and a different kind of awareness bloomed. The swamp breathed and she breathed with it. She saw everything: the creatures, the flowers, the tender shoots of green and the towering trees, the depths of the water. All that was dead and dying. All that was bursting with life. Her notebooks, tucked away in their plastic container, were gradually forgotten. The urge to record, to quantify, left her. Instead, she returned to the inclination that had guided her through all the years when her mind was sharp. The root of her curiosity: a simple and enduring desire to notice. There were moments during this last stretch when she occupied herself so completely that she forgot there had been any other time than now, any other way to exist but this. And there were also moments when she fought against the ebbing of logic and analysis, feeling adrift and upset, as if something precious had been taken from her that she would never have again. All of this was true. All of it was right.

Memories of childhood dusted her skin like pollen. All it took was a brisk gust of wind to send it all scattering. She remembered learning—the crispness of a washed blackboard, a good mark on her paper, the perfect loneliness of a library; she remembered men she'd known and she remembered intimacy; she remembered her parents, having them and losing them; she remembered her sister, pretty and harsh and unwilling to imagine the future Phyllis had foreseen; she remembered teaching—the way her hands shook at the start of every term, her students and their litany of excuses; she remembered her research—working in the field, working at her desk, the minutiae of life glimpsed through a microscope; she remembered every forest she'd ever walked through; she remembered every city she'd ever visited; she remembered preparing, preparing, preparing. And then all of this was gone. Piece by piece, Phyllis said goodbye to each part of her life that had come before.

She held on to Wanda the longest. As long as she could. She replayed every moment they had spent together. She repeated Wanda's name to herself when Wanda left her alone in the tree house, reciting it like a chant, a prayer, so that when she came home, it would already be on her tongue. This didn't always work. Sometimes Phyllis arrived in a moment she hadn't been aware of—like time travel, hopping from one place to another with smooth, easy leaps. It was only when she saw the exhaustion on Wanda's face that she realized she had missed something in between.

"I'm sorry," Phyllis said. "I think I…was somewhere else."

"That's all right."

"What are we doing?"

"We're weaving nets. Do you want to help?"

"Yes. Yes, please."

They sat together and they weaved in a soft light that was either just beginning or just ending—Phyllis couldn't tell. Her net looked misshapen and full of too-big holes. How could she ever catch a fish with this? She looked at Wanda's—tight and controlled. *That's good,* she thought. *The girl knows things.*

But then, a leap, a landing—"I'm sorry."

"What for?"

"I think...I think I've forgotten what we're..."

"We're weaving."

Phyllis looked down at her lap. "So we are."

A moment later, Phyllis was alone. It was dark, but with a thick curve of moon above, casting a silvery glow on the water. She looked at her hands: empty. Across the lagoon, a white egret stood in the shallows, its feathers luminous, legs invisible, as if it were levitating. Phyllis decided she had been watching this bird, so she went on watching it. She thought to call out, to know if someone was nearby, but she didn't want to disturb the egret and couldn't seem to remember whose name she should call. The egret darted its head down into the water, a sharp, abrupt movement, and when it came back up, a silver fish had appeared in its beak. She felt proud of the egret: graceful and clever and quick.

"That's my girl," she whispered, and it all came rushing back. The day Wanda first came to her, not yet ten and already more curious and capable than any pupil she'd ever had. The squeak of rubber waders, slung across her shoulder. Wanda's curls with a fistful of wind in them, water rushing past, slippery roots and slimy rocks. The rumble of Kirby's truck in the driveway. Baggies full of alligator jerky she started keeping in her pocket in case Wanda was hungry. Petri dishes on the dining room table and a tousled head bent over the microscope. A glow spreading across a dark body of water. The moment she realized that it was her job to keep Wanda safe. The moment she realized how hard that would be in a place like this. The moment she failed. Three shots, four staring eyes, and the roar of flames crawling up the sides of her little blue house. She remembered all of it in an instant, and she felt it, too: the intensity of her love, the ferocity of her protection, a sense of wonder as she watched a little girl grow. And then, just as fast, she forgot it. Maybe for good this time.

Above her, the thud of footsteps on a wooden platform. Feet

coming down the ladder. Out of the dark, a woman she didn't recognize appeared.

"Who are you?" Phyllis asked, afraid and curious at the same time.

"It's okay, my name's Wanda," the woman said. "And you're Phyllis."

"Wanda," she repeated, but it didn't mean anything to her. "Phyllis…" she said, but this didn't mean anything, either. She could see that she was supposed to know these names and was upset that she didn't. Her mind was cloudy, grasping for something to hold on to. "Where…"

"You're in the field," the woman said.

Ah, she thought. *The field.* Even at the end, she knew this was where she wanted to be. There was so much to notice. So much to learn. She saw an egret standing in the water and pointed it out to the woman.

"Isn't it magnificent?" she said.

"It is."

WANDA RESTS FOR as long as she can, but after two nights spent tending to the damage that heatstroke has wrought on her body, her supply of water runs too low to ignore. She would like to ignore it. She'd like to go on lying here in the nest that she and Phyllis built, pretending she doesn't have a choice to make. But doing nothing is its own decision.

More than anything, she'd like to ignore the fact that she can't stop thinking about Bird Dog. When Bird Dog strides into her dreams with her shorn blond head and her snaggle-toothed smile and those long, elegant fingers and calloused palms, she'd like to pretend that this appearance is the work of a feverish brain. She's never touched anyone in the way that she'd like to touch Bird Dog, and it terrifies her.

What Wanda wants is to go back to her hiding place outside the sunken bungalow where the others gather, that place full of voices, bodies, endless activity. And concurrently, she wants to never go there again. She wants to wrap herself around Bird Dog like a starfish and to stay as far away from her as possible. She wants everything to change and she wants it all to remain the same. She wants and wants and wants. At least here, lying still underneath the thatch, she can go on wanting everything without the complication of having any of it.

But all things end, especially the moments in between. Her supplies dwindle and it's time to return to the endless work of survival. When the sky loses its pink on the third night, she ventures out for the freshwater spring—arms still weak, mind still cloudy. There's a strange scent in the air, a prickle at the nape of her neck, something she would immediately notice if she were well, but tonight she isn't well at all. Her attention is on the strain of wielding the paddle, the tug of the water against the hull of the canoe, the ragged inhalations that scrape up against the insides of her throat. She can't hear the lights whispering when the machinery of her body is so loud.

The pitch dark of an overcast sky settles, and beneath it, Wanda begins to feel more like herself. It isn't until she's filling her bottles in the freshwater pool that she realizes what has been nagging at her, trying to get her attention since she struck out. The smell is ozone. And the feeling is anticipation. A hurricane. She caps the bottle in her hand and reaches down to count how many empties she has yet to fill. *There's time*, she tells herself, *just fill them fast.* There are no manatees tonight, no swooping birds. The creatures are all tucked away in their homes. They know what's coming, and now, a little late, so does she.

The rain begins just as she's finishing filling her bottles. It doesn't arrive gently or gradually—one moment the surface of the lagoon is smooth and undisturbed; the next, Wanda is being pelted so hard it hurts. There will be bruises later. The torrential rain knocks the last jug out of her hands and she lets it go, frantically grabbing for her paddle lest the rain knock that into the water, too. She wields it blindly, only just able to make out the parting between the trees that will lead her back toward the river. In this leafy corridor, the canopy does its best to shield her from the sky, but even the trees are being beaten back by the onslaught. Leaves and fronds are stripped from their branches, flowers are crushed, young plants that are just beginning their journey upward are smashed back down.

The wind hasn't begun to scream yet, but when it does she'll have to seek shelter wherever she can find it. She hopes there's time to make it home before that happens. Usually, she doesn't need to hope, because she knows these things. Not tonight. Tonight, all of these little voices that have been guiding her since she was a child—the whispers that usually tell her where the fish are swimming, whether her traps are full, when the winds are coming, how long they'll last—have gotten lost. Or worse, were dismissed. She's been working so hard to silence her mind as it brims with thoughts of Bird Dog that she's silenced everything else, too. Now all she hears is the cacophony of the storm. Rain smashes into her knuckles and drills down on her scalp. The bottom of the canoe begins to fill with rainwater and the current catches hold of her, trying to pull her in the wrong direction. She refuses to be scared, not yet. Without the wind, this is only a storm. The hurricane isn't far—this much at least she knows. Her aching body, still healing, is reticent to provide the strength she needs to battle the waves, but this will not do. She pushes herself harder, to the brink, a torrent of adrenaline coursing through her veins to match the roaring canal on either side of her.

She pilots her craft by instinct and memory, the water slamming into her from every direction. All around her is darkness, the moon and the stars sewn shut. Water continues to accumulate at her feet, glimmering now, sloshing in over the sides and pounding down from above. She gives the paddle everything she has, and just as she feels the bow of her canoe break free of the current the paddle snaps in two. A sharp crack and then she's left holding one piece, the other washed away, the splintered end slicing into her palm. The canoe slips back into the current's grasp and there is nothing she can do but let it carry her wherever it wishes.

So she lets it. She huddles in the bottom of the boat, still holding the broken half, the glimmering water growing brighter as it swirls around her. Curled like a child in the womb of her canoe, the water cupping her like amniotic fluid, she squeezes her eyes shut and wonders if this is the end. The canoe is wrenched back and forth by the current— whitecaps break over the bow, rocks slam against the underbelly, and the water pulls her, faster and faster, toward the ocean maybe, or away from it. She's lost all sense of direction now. She could bail out and take her chances swimming, but even at her strongest she is no match for a current like this. She could try to grab hold of a branch or a rock as it rushes past, but she can't make anything out, it's all going by too quickly, and the part of her that wants to survive is too tired to fight. The wind comes to bear as she thinks all this, loud and jagged and riotous. It's here. While the storm churns all around her, trying to penetrate this little pocket of stillness she has created in the slim space between her face and her drawn-up knees, Wanda finally hears the voice she's been missing. But it isn't a whisper; it's a shout.

Wind snatches it away before she can make out the words. Nearby, the sound of a thick tree trunk cracking in half and an enormous slap as its weight falls into the water. The air is full not only of rain now, but of branches and leaves and whatever else the wind can pick up. And then—the canoe jerks and spins, caught on something strong. Wanda can feel the water rushing past, but the canoe isn't pulled along with it.

She uncurls, opens her eyes, and there is Bird Dog, her face lit by the glow of the water Wanda's vessel has taken on, holding the edge of the canoe, her mouth open. Shouting, Wanda realizes, shouting her name. Bird Dog reaches in and grabs a fistful of Wanda's shirt. She pulls her out and keeps hold of the boat at the same time, dragging them both up onto a narrow spit of land. Bird Dog pushes Wanda down on the ground and in one smooth, steady motion she flips the canoe over them both.

The change in sensations is so fast, it leaves Wanda breathless. Rain thrums against the hull but cannot reach them. The wind howls over-head but cannot touch them. The mud is slippery, the air dense. She can feel Bird Dog's body against her, warm and alive. It is shocking to be this close, but all she can think about is how much she'd like to be closer still. The darkness should be complete, but it isn't—the water coating Wanda's skin still glows ever so slightly, just enough to illuminate Bird Dog's face.

"How?" she asks, and her voice is louder than she intends. Her ears are still recovering from the roar of the storm. There is more to this question, but she can't find the words. Bird Dog exhales and she can feel it on her cheeks.

"You're your own goddamn spotlight, you know that? Storm come up outta nowhere. Smashed the raft to pieces. I haul myself up onto the bank and what do I see just about ready to pass me by? A god-damn spotlight." They're quiet then. The canoe shudders overhead, the wind trying to claw it from the ground, but Bird Dog holds it tight by the bench seat and the gust moves on, slipping over the smoothness of the hull. The glow that clings to Wanda's skin dims and goes out. She is braver in the dark.

They move toward each other in increments: an inch toward the other is an unspoken question, the next inch its answer. Above, the hurricane shrieks and wails through the trees, but below, here, inside this dark cocoon, two women say yes with these tiny movements, again and again. Crushed between them now, Wanda's fear has no space to protest. Her body tells her what to do and she does it, pulling Bird Dog toward her until there is nothing separating them but fabric and skin.

It's hard to say how long they spend huddled together beneath the overturned canoe, but eventually the wind quiets. The rain stops.

"I think it's over," Bird Dog whispers, and Wanda, not wanting it to be over, says nothing. Bird Dog pushes back the canoe to reveal a clear, starry sky. A subtle brightness has begun in the east. The water rushes beside their little island, so high its waves almost reach them where they lie. Thrust out of the safe, close darkness, Wanda feels suddenly exposed. The brutality of the past few days—the sun beating down on her, the rain beating down on her, the wind and the waves roaring on either side—comes to bear. Then she feels Bird Dog's warm, rough hand find hers.

"Don't run off again," Bird Dog says, helping her up out of the mud, each of them relying on the strength of the other. Bird Dog's hand travels up to brush the side of Wanda's face and then to cup the sloping base of her skull, fingers threaded in her hair, a place Wanda didn't know was made for this hand although it clearly was.

"I won't," she says, and when Bird Dog leans in and kisses her, it sends a jolt from her mouth, down her spine, through her groin, into the earth she's standing on. She is rooted and airborne at the same time, wanting and wanting and wanting, but also finally understanding that this is what having feels like. She fills her hands with Bird Dog's waist and her mouth with Bird Dog's mouth and her lungs with Bird Dog's breath, and for the first time in a very long time, she knows what it feels like to have more than enough.

Wanda and Bird Dog make their way to the sunken bungalow with sturdy branches as quant poles, slowly maneuvering through the overflowing canals of what was once Beachside. Bird Dog has promised Wanda a new paddle when they get there. Other promises float between them, not spoken aloud but understood. They move past broken trees, debris in the water, ruins in a state of even more ruin, but neither woman is fazed. They have seen all of this before. They understand this cycle.

And so when they arrive at the sunken bungalow and see that the roof has been torn off and the foundation is beginning to collapse, when they see that the community Bird Dog has bound together is busy trying to load what they can salvage onto the boats that remain, they don't bother with surprise. They help.

"Who's this?" Ouita asks.

"This is Wanda. I known her a long time," Bird Dog says.

There are a few raised eyebrows, but everyone here trusts Bird Dog. And so now they trust Wanda, too. There will be questions later, but for now, they all work side by side. Saving what they can, leaving what they can't to sink along with the house. Every second matters as the sun pulls itself up over the rim of the ocean and into the sky, as the structure of the house groans and slumps farther down into the water.

"Time to go," Freddy says. He helps Gem and her son, Dade, into his little rowboat. Skipper brings out a last armful of supplies to where Ouita waits in their dugout. Bird Dog appears in the window of the collapsing house with the promised spare paddle for Wanda. She hands it down and then hops lightly from the window into the canoe.

Wanda reaches out to steady her without thinking. Looking up, she sees Ouita smiling at them and almost snatches her hands away. But instead, she leaves them just a little longer than she needs to.

"Where'd you have in mind?" Skipper asks.

"Old marina maybe," Freddy replies.

"Roof's gone. Saw it just now," Bird Dog says. Freddy grunts, a sound of muted distress.

"Town hall?" Gem suggests.

"Could do." Freddy digs his fingers into the white tufts of his beard. He doesn't sound convinced. "Water might be too high, but we could try."

A thought begins to form in Wanda's mind as the others discuss where they'll weather the unforgiving sun. It surprises her. Unsettles her. But it's a stubborn thought. It has roots. Wanda can see it so clearly it's as if it's already happened. "I know a better place," she says. It's the first thing she's said to any of them. They all stare at her, and it reminds her of the last time this many eyes were on her. A classroom-ful, menacing and childish and confused—seeing everything that made her strange, all of her otherness and all of her power. Hating her for it. A spark of panic wells up in the back of her throat, but she swallows it. No. This is different. They are ready for her now.

Wanda starts paddling because there is no use explaining a thing they must discover for themselves. She doesn't wait to see if they are wary, if they hesitate, if they doubt her. They are, they do, but it doesn't matter. They'll follow eventually.

The new paddle is smooth and easy in her hands. After so much rain, the air tastes like minerals. A squirrel scampers along the ridge of an old ruin and stops to look at them. An unusually cool mist rises from the water. The trees lean in. Bird Dog grins as she watches Wanda row and Wanda discovers that she is beginning to like being looked at.

"Where are we going?" Bird Dog asks.

She searches for a word she hasn't used in a long time. Finds it. "Home."

TIME

The passage of years could be assigned a number, but in this place, time has a different measure. Its progression is marked by the smoothness of water where ruins once broke the surface. The thickening of a young grove's canopy. The collapse of an old utility pole. It is marked by the end of one species or the beginning of another. Here, time sprawls and curls. The land returns to the way it was; it becomes something brand new.

WANDA IS VERY old now. The number doesn't matter. Her skin is etched and loose. Her hair is pale gray, curling past her shoulders like vines. She can't move as quickly or as deftly anymore, but she doesn't need to. She has earned the right to rest.

The treetop home she built has grown. All around the lagoon, new dwellings are tucked in among the mangroves. Their community builds where the trees make room for them. Some of these nests are perched up high in the foliage, where they can wait out floods; some are low, nestled into the roots. There are no walls in this place. No doors. Where Wanda sits, she can see the flickering of bodies moving among mangroves, going about their work. It's dark, but also bright. In the center, the water is lit, by her own hand, as it is every night. There is a shared language that passes between the light and its keeper. A whisper; a thought. Without speaking, she asks it to glow brighter and it does. She asks it to shine until morning and it will. She no longer worries that someone might see. She hopes they will. There's room for newcomers.

Beside her, Bird Dog eats mayhaw berries that one of the foragers brought them. It is a simple gift to sit side by side with her beloved and watch the night unfold. She wordlessly offers Wanda a handful of these red jewels, cupping them from one gnarled palm to another. They eat, quiet, enjoying the sour flavor. The platform that holds them is old, Wanda's first, made of materials she salvaged from the house she was born in. When a surge comes, the platform disappears altogether. But tonight it's here for them to sit on, their backs propped up against a thick tree trunk, their legs intertwined. The luminous water laps at its edge. Wanda crushes the berries between the teeth she still has, savoring the tartness, enjoying the heat where Bird Dog's skin touches hers, losing herself in the playful movement of the lights skimming across the water.

She wonders what will happen to the lights when she dies. They are hers and she is theirs—but belonging slips in and out like a tide. Maybe they will find a new keeper. Maybe they will dim and darken. Either way, she trusts that this place will go on changing long after she is gone. The elderly die, and the old ways die with them. The young are born, and fresh traditions begin. One of the children here sees through the darkest nights as if it were day. Another can hold her breath underwater for a long, long time. Another has learned to hear the fish chattering beneath the waves. They do not call these gifts magic and they do not call them science. They call them what they are: change.

Wanda isn't scared of the ending she feels nearby, but she worries about how Bird Dog will cope when she's gone. Someone is always left behind; it gives her no peace knowing that this time it won't be her. Bird Dog finishes the berries and crawls forward to rinse her fruit-sticky hands in the water. Specks of light still cling to her skin as she sits back. They both watch them smolder and then go out. "I was just thinking—do you remember taps?" Bird Dog asks. Her voice has grown deeper in her old age. Raspier. But it's still the same voice Wanda heard calling out to her in the dark all those years ago.

"Taps?"

Bird Dog mimes the turning of a faucet. She opens an invisible channel of hot water and cups her hands to her face. "Taps. I think that's right." Wanda laughs at this pantomime. She does remember. She remembers how she and Lucas used to share the bathroom sink at night, brushing their teeth side by side. She can just make out the shape of him in the mirror—young and mountainous. And she remembers her father, on his knees, running a bath for her, making sure the temperature was right. How easy it used to be. But also— how excruciating. They fought so hard to keep a world that was not meant to stay the same.

"Strange, isn't it. How different it was."

"Strange," Bird Dog agrees. She slides her hand into Wanda's, their brittle fingers laced together. "You've been quiet the past few nights."

"Just…thinking." She can't bring herself to say the goodbye she feels coming out loud. They are so old now—maybe it doesn't need to be said. Maybe it's already woven into each moment they share. Someone will be left behind; this is what love costs. Wanda steals a glance at Bird Dog. Over the years, her angles have softened into slopes. Her skin hangs in luscious folds, a delicate necklace of wrinkles around her throat, an intricate crosshatch on her cheeks. Her lips are still stained red from the mayhaw berries. Wanda has memorized this face many times over the years, but it's always changing, so she memorizes it again.

Across the water, children have gathered to hear a story. A nursery rhyme. Wanda can't make out all the words, just fragments, but she thinks it's her story. Their story. *A lonely pirate and her light. A seeker and her sight.* There are other stories, too—the one about waking with the sun and sleeping with the moon, the one about miles and miles of something called sand, the one about how people used to live their entire lives in boxes. It won't be so long before these stories are all that's left of that time. She's passed on what she can remember. Bird Dog has, too. And there are Phyllis's notebooks—while the paper lasts. These women haven't shared their genes, but they have given freely of their memories. Their ideas. Their skills. There is more than one kind of legacy.

A little dinghy cuts through the lagoon, captained by a young woman Wanda remembers arriving a few seasons ago. It used to be that Wanda knew everyone's name, everyone's history, but she can't keep up anymore. That's someone else's work now. The fisherwoman whose name she can't quite reach has come home with a good catch—Wanda can tell from the hint of satisfaction flickering across her face. She rows with an easy mastery, extending the oars and pulling them in as if they are part of her, but Wanda can tell that not much else has been easy for her. There is a heaviness on her face. The kind of loss that seeps into the bone. It is a weight Wanda recognizes. The lights spin around the hull of her boat, thickening where the blades of her oars slip into the water, showing Wanda how much they like this woman. They don't usually pay attention to boats passing through.

Wanda leans into Bird Dog, and Bird Dog wraps an arm around her. They watch the fisherwoman tie off and disappear into the shadowy mangroves with her fish. "She reminds me of you," Bird Dog says. Wanda replies with a gentle pat on Bird Dog's thigh. Some things don't need to be spoken aloud when two bodies have become one shape.

Wanda closes her eyes, and maybe she dozes a little, her head tucked into Bird Dog's neck. It's hard to tell the difference between sleep and wakefulness lately. It feels like she's always in the process of drifting away—a tethered vessel wandering the waves until the line goes taut and tugs it back. One of these days, the line will slip its moor and she'll keep drifting.

Bird Dog feels it, too. "Are you sleeping?" she asks, hungry for more moments.

"No," Wanda replies, although maybe she was.

"Liar. Look." Bird Dog points and Wanda sees one meteor, then another, darting across the exposed sky overhead. There are murmurs as others come to the edges of their platforms to watch. She can hear the children getting excited by each new streak, can see the dim outlines of their little arms pointing. This meteor shower falls every summer; she'd forgotten to look for them this year, but here they are anyway.

"Phyllis woke me up in the middle of the night to see this, once. When I was a girl." Thinking of her old friend, Wanda feels tears prickling in the corners of her eyes. After all this time, the aches have grown softer but also deeper. They both know the looping shape of pain—it changes and quiets but never ends. There is a strange comfort in its constancy. Memories of what was lost are also reminders of what was held. She feels that tug again, a current asking her to follow it into new waters. She'd like to stay, but she isn't scared to go.

Across the lagoon, Wanda notices the young woman reappear. She sits cross-legged on one of the platforms close to the water and begins to clean her fish. She glances up at the meteor shower from time to time, but she is intent on her knife work. She doesn't notice Wanda watching her, and the beauty unfolding above does not distract her from her task. It's familiar, this focus. Wanda remembers when the labor of survival was all she had.

As the young woman works, the lights slowly begin to congregate at the edge of her platform, forming a deep band of brightness in front of her. Focusing on her cuts, she doesn't see them at first. They drift toward her from every edge of the lagoon, their luminosity gathering until finally she notices. She puts aside her knife and watches, uncertain at first, then curious. When their collected radiance is undeniable, she slowly kneels down to lay the palm of her hand against the water. An introduction is made. Wanda can't see her face, but she can feel the young fisherwoman's longing—to be part of this awareness that is deeper than she can imagine. And her fear—of what it might mean to join. The meteors fall, thicker, faster. The water-bound lights spin and brighten, asking the young woman if she is willing to do this work. To keep them, and to be kept by them. The whole swamp pauses, held between two palms of light, above and below, listening for her answer, but Wanda doesn't need to hear it. She already knows how this story ends.

GRATITUDE TO—

Jen Gates, my beloved agent and friend, who has been my champion since the beginning, and whose patience and insight and support have seen me through the last decade.

The entire team at Aevitas, but especially Allison Warren and Erin Files.

Karen Kosztolnyik for giving *The Light Pirate* a home. Also, Rachael Kelly, Ben Sevier, Luria Rittenberg, Laura Cherkas, Andy Dodds, Theresa DeLucci, Alexis Gilbert, Andrew Duncan, Joe Benincase, and everyone else at Grand Central who made this book what it is.

The Kerouac Project and The Studios of Key West for the time and space to work on an entirely different novel that was not meant to be, but which gave way to this one instead.

Chuck Peters, Jessy Van Horn, and Michael Jordan for advice on ecology/forestry, data collection, and ham radio emergency services, respectively. All the errors are mine.

Jeff Goodell's *The Water Will Come* and Elizabeth Kolbert's *The Sixth Extinction*.

P. C. Cast—I shudder to think how many years it took me to fulfill this promise, but I did not forget. Thank you.

Lauren Smith, with the impeccable taste and keen eye. Meredith Hall and Shane Abrams, for thoughtful reads and profound insights. Yana Tallon-Hicks, Malia Márquez, Sally Clegg, Amber Schaefer, Devin Conroy, and Nikita Gale, just because.

My mother, for help with plants and spreading serenity wherever you go. My father, for knowing how things work and always being prepared.

Ofurhe Igbinedion, for all of it.

The many climate activists, frontline communities, and environmental & economic justice organizations who are on the ground, doing the work of protecting our natural resources and imagining a sustainable future.

A different kind of acknowledgment, one that I feel is particularly important for a story that, at its core, is about land: This book is set in a fictional town but also in the actual locale of southeastern Florida, a place that was violently stolen from the Indigenous tribes who have lived there for thousands of years. The setting of this story is the unceded homeland of the Seminole and Miccosukee people, who live there to this day, and was also the ancestral home of the Tequesta, Calusa, and Jeaga Native nations. I want to honor these people and their communities—past, present, and future—for their work as stewards, activists, and visionaries. My profound gratitude, respect, and a portion of my proceeds from this book will go to the Indigenous Environmental Network. Visit www.ienearth.org to learn more about their work.

ABOUT THE AUTHOR

Lily Brooks-Dalton's first novel, *Good Morning, Midnight,* has been translated into seventeen languages and was the inspiration for the film adaptation *The Midnight Sky.* Her memoir, *Motorcycles I've Loved,* was a finalist for the Oregon Book Award. She currently lives in Los Angeles.